C000117865

CHOSEN MISTRESS

ELIZABETH CONTE

Chosen Mistress is published by:
Jane Writes Press, www.JaneWritesPress.com
Cover Design: Elizabeth Conte
Jacket Design: TannasCreative.com
Cover Art Provided by:
Metropolitan Museum of Art, New York, NY
Painting Credits:
Study of Female Nude (1840) by Henry Lehman
Editing and Publishing Services:
Michelle Morrow, M.S. Publishology, www.Publishology.net

CONTENTS

1. Business Affairs   1
2. Returning Home   14
3. Separation   23
4. Courtship   32
5. Pearls of Sadness   42
6. Introductions   60
7. Nathanial   72
8. Settling In   85
9. The Peacock   97
10. Laws of Attraction   110
11. Morning Reflections   123
12. Shame   125
13. Euphoria   130
14. Guilty Pleasures   138
15. The Talk   141
16. Lydia's Plan   146
17. Family Matters   152
18. The Favor   159
19. The Decision   168
20. Avoidance   172
21. Truth Be Known   183
22. Lydia's Deception   190
23. Awakenings   196
24. Distractions   202
25. Expectations   212
26. Confidants   221
27. Woman in the Mirror   229
28. Regents Park   241
29. Innocence Lost   254
30. Tessa's Question   266
31. Seduction Lesson   274
32. The Theatre   286

33. Drunk & Disorderly 299
34. Truths 309
35. Assessments 322
36. Lessons 328
37. Judgments 335
38. Interludes 345
39. Jealousy 354
40. Unexpected 364
41. My Father's Room 372
42. Options 385
43. Playful Competition 397
44. Possibilities 403
45. Rivalry 413
46. Poking the Beast 421
47. Secrets Uncovered 427
48. Exposed 437
49. Shadow of Doubt 446
50. Accidents 452
51. David's Goodbye 460
52. The Truth 467
53. Goodbye, My Love, Goodbye 477
54. Proposals 482
55. Surprises 490

Acknowledgments 503
About the Author 505

My father was my teacher of language, literature, and wisdom. As my mentor, he instilled in me the virtues of keen observations and contemplation—the cornerstone traits of a formidable writer. He kindled my passion for reading and sparked the fuels of my writing. I hope he is looking down from heaven with approval, knowing I am, creating beauty for the mind, a pursuit that binds us across realms.

CHOSEN MISTRESS

BUSINESS AFFAIRS

*C*harlotte stared at the letter in disbelief, the ink-stained paper crumpling between her fingers. She pressed her temples trying to halt the dizziness swirling in her head, questions flooding her thoughts as she read the words for the third time. The realization sank to the pits of her stomach causing her breathing to become shallow. Life as she knew it was about to be turned upside down–a life that had been so busy caring for her father, she had failed to create one for herself.

She pressed her back against the seat, and rubbed her neck, stiff and strained, as the carriage rattled across the cobblestone streets through Boston heading to the bustling ports where Charlotte's father's business resided. Her heart raced listening to the horses' every stride of their hooves clicking against the pavement. Prudently, uncrumpling the paper clenched in her gloved hand, she read the letter one more time. Holding back tears, she tried to make sense of the words written boldly across the paper:

You are to vacate the premises within a fortnight.

Unbeknownst to her, following her father's death, his business, bank accounts and assets, including the family home, had been bequeathed to his business partner, Giles Milford.

She ran her hand over the wrinkled papyrus, smelling the tannic acids of the freshly inked words, folded it, and shoved it into her pocket.

Charlotte could never have imagined her father would leave her penniless. Merrill Ashford claimed he was building his import/export business for her and future generations of Ashfords. Making a name for his family in America was important to him. For the last eight years, he had taken the greatest of risks, leaving England with his wife and daughter, and severing his ties to the prominent Ashford ancestral dynasty for dreams of greater prestige and wealth. Proving to his brother he could be a business success in his own right. There was no explanation that could account for losing the Ashford legacy he had been creating.

As Charlotte neared the waterfront, her hand pulled away the curtain, carefully unveiling the world outside her carriage window. The foremasts of the cargo ships soared above the rooftops indicating she was close to her destination. The streets clamored with patrons–ladies, maids, sailors, and gentlemen alike–making their way from shop to shop of the surrounding port streets. A bakery and a tailor shop filled the spaces below her father's office. *Merrill Ashford Trade* resided on the second floor, where her father could have an advantage of watching the ships arrive. Large floor to ceiling windows fronted the office space where Charlotte often spied on her father buried deep in thought at his desk. On rare occasions, while shopping, she would catch a glimpse of him from the streets below, where he would wave, inviting her upstairs.

Surprise visits were no longer an option.

Her father was dead, buried with her mother in a small cemetery overlooking the sea, underneath dirt covered mounds with squared marble headstones simply bearing the names and the dates of their short lives.

The horses slowed and eventually came to a stop in front of the tailor's shop.

Mr. Spidey, the manager, waved to Charlotte as she exited the carriage, but she ignored the gesture, not wanting any distractions.

Dumbfounded by the letter, but more scared of what was to become of her, it took all her willpower to push herself to confront her father's business partner. Her father's lawyer and friend left the letter for her in the early morning, leaving his carriage with instruction to meet him at his office after she arose. Charlotte's first allegiance was to obey. For surely, her father's lawyer would help clarify the situation. As she dressed, an anger began to crawl from her gut, forcing

3

her jaw to tighten and her fists to clench, suppressing the tears that should have overtaken her upon the news of being left destitute. She promptly instructed the carriage driver to proceed to the waterfront instead.

She halted at the street door leading to her father's office, allowing herself a glimpse of the windows above. How she ached to see her father's tall and lanky stature, a smile spread across his face at the sight of her. Instead, she spotted a short, bulbous man in a blue suit bending over her father's desk, a greasy, balding head distinguishing her father's business partner from the other full-haired men who worked in the office.

Charlotte shuddered; a cold tingling spread from her spine to her shoulders.

Giles Milford was a short man, but his gut made up for his lack of height. He waddled to the window and looked to the ports in the distance, eyeing his watch before putting it back in his pocket.

Eager to address her current situation, Charlotte hurried up to the office, her shoes pounding firmly against the stairs.

She found two of her father's employees hovered over papers on their desks. The swishing of her skirts dragging across the wooden floors alerted the well-groomed men she had entered, and they looked up simultaneously. They stood immediately and nodded at her presence.

"Good afternoon, Miss Ashford," the men said in unison.

Charlotte returned the greeting with a slight bow but did not allow for her usual smile.

Cameron Taylor, her father's secretary, suddenly appeared to greet her. "Miss Ashford, what a pleasure to see you."

She surmised by his speedy attentiveness that he was sent by Giles Milford to waylay her.

"Good afternoon, Mr. Cameron. I wish to see Mr. Milford."

"Mr. Milford is rather busy at the present. If you would like to discuss anything of importance, I would be happy to address the issue with him at his earliest convenience," he replied.

Charlotte's fear was palpable. Beads of sweat rolled down her spine, her underarms moist with perspiration. A ruthless man was swindling her of her father's legacy, and nothing was going to stand in her way to get to the truth, not even this well-dressed, well-mannered secretary. Charlotte moved towards Mr. Milford's office without invitation, as if her father's hand was pushing her forward.

Cameron Taylor's mouth gaped, but he moved aside, allowing her to enter with little resistance.

"My father trusted you," Charlotte stated through clenched teeth, announcing her presence to the man sitting in her father's office. "He is barely in the ground, and you are going to deny his legacy?"

Mr. Milford rose and walked around his desk to greet her, a lame left leg dragging his shoe across the wooden floor. "Please sit, Miss Ashford," he insisted, grabbing her elbow and leading her towards a chair.

She wrenched her arm away from him, refusing his invitation. She was not so naive to understand her advantage was towering two inches above his stance.

"You are obviously upset concerning matters out of your control, my dear," he muttered, flapping his long lashes over his deep-set, ice-blue eyes.

They were a shade of blue most would consider handsome in a man, but to Charlotte, his double chin distracted her from admiring his one and only handsome quality about his face.

"A young woman should not have to be burdened by such problems," he continued. "It is unfortunate one so lovely should come to these circumstances."

"You stole my father's business!" Charlotte declared.

"I see you are going to make this difficult," Mr. Milford replied under his breath, and summarily walked back to his chair and sat.

"Difficult?" Her voice pitched. Firmly gripping the edge of the desk, she leaned in. "You are taking possession of my home, leaving me with no inheritance, and you accuse me of being difficult?"

"It is such a shame your father did not anticipate *this*. He had hoped you would be married and taken care of before these matters would come to fruition. As you have been informed by your father's lawyer, Mr. Commons, the matter has been legally authenticated by the courts that I am the sole beneficiary of you father's business and his accounts."

His words did not shock her but confirmed the news in the letter she received that morning.

Her shoulders sank and her head fell. She swallowed hard to dispel the tears threatening to surface, suppressing the depths of despair pitted in her stomach.

With forced composure, she lifted her head, raised her chin in the air, and eyed him from across his desk. "How can this be? My father would never have given *you* his business. He built *Merrill Ashford Trade* with his own two hands. He made sacrifices. He would never have been so careless with his future, or mine."

"Ah, my dear, *you women* know so little about business. I am the one who helped finance your father's business. It is I who took the risk, and thus, he gave me his trust." A smirk slowly crossed his face, his blue eyes disappearing behind fat hooded lids.

"Trust? What do you know of the word? How can you do this to him? To me?"

Mr. Milford rose slowly from his chair. He walked to the door and closed it, causing Charlotte to turn at the click of the latch. Leaning into her, he moved his lips close to her ear.

Words slithered from his lips. "I did not do *this* to you. The blame is your father's burden. He was careless in his finances and thus it fell to me to be more diligent. The roof over your head and the clothes you are wearing are yours because of my business savvy.

7

Not your father's. You would be homeless and naked if it were not for me."

Charlotte wanted to flee, but he grabbed her and pulled her closer. She winced as his sweaty palm wetted her wrist and his sour breath blew across her face.

"I am not as heartless as you presume. I will allow you to stay in your home as your father would have wanted," he proposed.

Charlotte looked at him, comprehending the weight of his statement.

Sweat moistened his brow as his eyes met hers. His breathing became heavy. "I am but a simple man. I will not be demanding of you, only... *I will expect companionship.*" His gaze followed the lines of her neck, sliding over the pleats of the fabric tightly framing the curvature of her breasts and stopped at her cinched waist.

Charlotte raised her hand to slap him, but he was too quick and halted it from coming down on his face.

"You are no match for a man, my dear. You are a mere woman, barely twenty-four, with nothing but the clothes on your back. If you are smart, you will take my offer. For it is far better to be a mistress to one than a whore to countless others." His tongue flopped from his mouth and lingered at the corner before he swooped it back to add, "I can assure you; no one will please you the way I will."

Charlotte stood still, fighting to keep her legs from buckling underneath her. All the fight she had come with vanished. What he was offering was despicable, but his assessment of her situation unfortunately could become a reality. The city streets welcomed many desperate women who found themselves penniless and nowhere to go.

"You loathsome man!" Charlotte exclaimed. "I would choose the streets as my bed before accepting your appalling proposal."

She threw the door open and stalked into the outer office, finding her father's once loyal associates with their heads bowed towards their desks.

The men did not dare to risk eye contact.

"My father was a decent man who gave you a good life," she shouted at them, her voice crumbling as she continued. "He was generous and grateful for your service. He loved you like sons. You, too, are accountable for the deception that man is committing." Charlotte gulped down her tears. "Shame! Shame on you all."

No one spoke, their mouths apparently sealed by their adoration to their pocketbooks.

Charlotte understood she had no power. *Mr. Milford had stolen that, too.*

She bolted from the office, down the staircase, and into the waiting carriage. Charlotte did not sob. She would not give Giles Milford the satisfaction as he watched the carriage pull away.

It did not take the driver long before the carriage arrived at its destination–the office of her father's lawyer.

Mr. Commons promptly greeted Charlotte at the office front.

Her face paled and hands shaking, he put his arm around her and ushered her inside.

"Tea... quickly," he ordered his secretary, closing his office door for privacy. "There, there, my dear. It's not as bad as you imagine." He pulled a handkerchief from his pocket and offered it to her.

"Thank you," Charlotte said, accepting his offer and dabbed at the falling tears. "Tell me it is not true. Did my father truly give that loathsome man everything?"

"Your father never intended for Giles Milford to inherent his business. He and I discussed his financial affairs on numerous occasions. You were always to be cared for. I showed the courts proof of his intentions. But it seems Mr. Milford has provided the courts with signed financial documents to the contrary. And they have ruled in his favor."

"How is it possible? And why was I not informed?"

Mr. Commons tried to explain, "I did not want to concern you until I sorted through the evidence. The courts ruled on the issue yesterday. I had hoped for good news. But I fear I miscalculated." His hands shook as he pulled the spectacles from his face and placed them on the desk. "You see, Giles Milford has succeeded in swindling your father's legacy, and you of your inheritance. There is nothing more I can do."

Mr. Commons' words punched her in the gut. She

groaned. Thoughts twisted in her head. *What was to become of her?*

"My dear?" Mr. Commons said, seeing the last of the color leave her face.

Charlotte leaned back and stared at the thin man across the desk.

His lips pursed and his brow furrowed, the lines on his forehead exposing the worry he harbored.

"He has taken *everything*," she whispered.

"I am afraid so."

Charlotte fell silent as she contemplated the situation.

She finally asked, "What am I to do?"

"Well, I have done work to prepare for such an outcome," he replied. He walked back to his chair, sat, and pulled out papers from a folder. Placing his spectacles back on the bridge of his nose, he browsed through the documents. "You have relatives in England. But it is a Mr. Nathanial Hammond who has been corresponding with me."

"Yes, my cousin Lydia's husband." Charlotte nodded.

It had been a half a year–*longer really*– since she had received letters from Lydia. One was an announcement of the birth of their son, *Peter Sebastian Hammond*. Then came the news of the death of her parents, Charlotte's aunt and uncle–a tragic carriage accident. Their losses devastated Lydia, and the letters stopped. Charlotte understood why. She, too, knew the unbearable sadness of losing her mother, then her father.

"Mr. Hammond has requested you return to England to live with his family and share companionship with your cousin. He has made arrangements if you choose to accept his offer." Mr. Commons looked up from the document to gauge her response. He continued, "Your cousin, Mrs. Hammond, added a personal note, *'Without delay, send my dearest Charlotte to me at once. Please do not spare any expense for her care and comfort. My home is hers for as long as she will grant me the honor to care for her.'*"

"Lydia will take me in?" For the first time since her father's death, a glimmer of hope surfaced in Charlotte's thoughts. The possibility of returning home to England was more a dream than a reality. Her father had little intention of returning to his homeland. Hopes for a reunion with Lydia were merely a long-lost fantasy.

"Yes, she was quite adamant."

"But she has a family now, and her own life. She cannot assume the role of caretaker for me. There has to be another option."

"My dear Charlotte," Mr. Commons said, "I cannot take the place of your father, but you are as dear to me as if you were my own child. I have seen you change from a young girl to a beautiful woman. You have had more than your share of grief. Let me give some advice you may not want to hear. The waterfront is no place for a woman without money. You have been born of privilege, which I fear leaves you at a disadvantage. You have no one here to keep you safe. I could find you employment as a governess if you choose, and I have friends on the waterfront willing to employ a woman with your education. But those options are limiting for a young woman's future. I'm afraid it will be only a matter of time before you succumb to a life unworthy of you." He stood and walked to her, taking her hand in his. "Accept your cousin's generosity and be glad you have family to go to. What Mr. and Mrs. Hammond offer will be far better than a life here, I fear. Your cousin seems fond of you and has much more to offer. There is nothing left for you here."

RETURNING HOME

The brightness blurred Charlotte's view as she moved through the dark corridor of the ship and into the daylight of the deck preparing to disembark. With a firm grip on the railings, she descended the wood-planked ramp, releasing her hold only when she reached the solid ground of Liverpool.

"Excuse me, Miss," a porter said, forcing her to move aside.

"So sorry," she said, only to find two manservants asking her to move again to make way for a large trunk they held in their grip.

Charlotte pushed forward onto the quay, finding herself wedged in between the bustling crowds of porters and patrons trying to get somewhere, each in a different direction. Amidst the chaos, she stopped, closed her eyes, and allowed herself a moment's reprieve to steady her nerves. She had crossed the ocean as a girl with a family, and a fortune all planned for her. And now, six years later, she crossed it again but as a woman, alone, impoverished, and with no prospects. She was on the precipice of a life unknown, and she needed to conjure bravery to face what lay ahead.

A breeze blew across her face, and she coughed, gagged by the odor of the sea mixed with the unbathed bodies of men working the bustling sea-faring port. Hops wafted through windows of nearby pubs. Stews, simmering over fires, released enticing aromas out of chimney stacks of neighboring kitchens. Tobacco smoke drifted from the alleys, permeating the stagnate air of the overcrowded walkways. All, reminders of the life she left in England many years ago, stirred her to move onward.

The commotion of hollering sailors, the pandering of the fishmongers to the passing tradesmen, and shoes clapping against the ground recalled the days when her father brought her to the docks and planned their future across the ocean. As she scanned the crowded dock, a sense of belonging brought a tingle up her spine.

She was home again!

Once disembarked, it was no less an ordeal to find her way through the crowds who exited the ship. People pushed and shoved their way forward, eager to find loved ones waiting for them. Liverpool was a cesspool of filth, crowds, and vice. A condition with little change over the years, and where Charlotte did not want to find herself alone. It was a window to a life she might have faced if she stayed in America, as a penniless unmarried woman. Standing now alone on English land, she was never more grateful than when she heard her name called, taking her closer to Lydia and her new life.

Eyeing the crowds, she saw a man, a head above the throng of black-hatted men, walking towards her. He stopped in front of her.

"Mr. Hollister, I assume?" she asked.

The tall gentleman blinked and bowed, tipping his hat. "Just Hollister," he corrected.

"My father's lawyer, Mr. Commons, informed me of your escort," Charlotte said. "It seems a rather frenzied situation to navigate on my own."

"At your service, Miss," the tall man responded, little expression attached to his reply. "I will accompany you all the way to *Lottington Manor.*" He grabbed her bag and motioned to two men awaiting in the distance for his cue to collect her luggage. "This way," he instructed, making a way through the crammed aisle of people who were also collecting their trunks.

Charlotte said nothing further and followed his lead, trying to keep pace with his long-legged stride through the bustling streets to the train station.

Settling in the train carriage, Charlotte unpinned her hat and placed it on the seat next to her before she nuzzled herself into the cushion, adjusting to get comfortable. She let out an exhaustive sigh, relieved to be off her feet. "What a nice reprieve," she said to

Hollister as she looked around the well-appointed carriage with its tufted, fabric-padded walls and curtained windows. "I cannot believe I am almost home."

Hollister's face remained stoic. "We will have another half-day trip, taking us in the late hours of the night until we reach the Hammond Estate." He stowed away the smaller bags and seated himself across from Charlotte.

Although tired, wanting nothing more than a hot bath, fresh clothes, and a nice meal, Charlotte was undeterred by his pragmatism. "Well, that will allow me to take in the countryside that much more." She leaned back and allowed a smile to spread across her face.

Hollister folded his arms in front of his chest, stretched his legs across the small space separating them, and closed his eyes.

Charlotte watched his body sway to the hypnotic motion of the train. Her curiosity got the best of her, and she found herself staring at Hollister, trying to guess his age. His hair was a deep black with grey, invading the once rich dark color at the temple and sides. Engraved lines crossed his forehead, but she wasn't sure if that was from age or from his continual furrowing. A shade of red colored the tips of his cheeks, but not his lips, which were thin and color-less below a broad nose. She was trying to recall the color when suddenly his eyes opened. She startled.

They were grey.

"Is there something you need, Miss?" he questioned, lines on his forehead forming.

Charlotte shook her head.

"It's a long ride. Why don't you try to get some rest," he suggested.

Charlotte was too eager to settle down. Too many thoughts and too many worries lay ahead. Hoping her companion would indulge her curiosity, if not help dispel her anxiety, she asked, "What do you do in the Hammond household, Mr. Hollister?"

"I tend to the personal care of Mr. Hammond."

"Oh." It seemed to explain his very well-mannered behavior, as well as his refined attire. "Have you worked for Mr. Hammond very long?"

"Yes."

"I only had the pleasure of meeting my cousin's husband once. It was when they were married. It was quite a momentous event...unforgettable, really." She tugged at the pearls around her neck, remembering. It was a memory that lingered...and haunted her since.

Hollister blinked but added nothing to the conversation.

"Do you have a family, Hollister?"

"Yes."

Charlotte tried again, confident there was no way of answering her next question with less than four words. "If you had not found me leaving the ship, what would you have done?"

"Search for you."

She chuckled at his cunning.

He, on the other hand, unaffected by her gaiety, tilted his head back, indicating he preferred to end her interrogation.

"Just in case I am ever lost, I thank you for your diligence," Charlotte replied, allowing him a reprieve from further questioning.

As the train rattled onward, Charlotte stared out the window watching the passing countryside. She had not fathomed how much she missed the moss and lime green colors of England. It was the abundance of rain which gave her homeland its distinctive verdant terrain. Although Massachusetts received its fair share of rain, as well as frightfully snowy and cold winters, the virescent landscape was more olive and loden in hues. England's greens seemed brighter, more alive, even during the grey, rainy days only England offered. But England was *home* to her, no matter how gloomy the weather, and therefore more beautiful than anywhere.

When her father uprooted the family, he had taken Charlotte away from all she had known and loved about England, especially it's countryside. Just before her introduction into society as an eligible young woman, he took her away from her standing in society, her extended family, and friends with whom she had ties. And most importantly, from her cousin Lydia.

A mere pawn in her father's aspirations, she was heartbroken.

She supposed she would never know happiness

again, no matter how beautiful the house, how modern the city, or how pretty the dresses were. And her predictions were right. Once settled into their American home in the bustling sea town of Boston, her mother grew ill with influenza and Charlotte had to focus on her care. After her mother died, her father nearly succumbed to the same illness and Charlotte had to shift her focus to caring for him, anchoring her in a new life in America. England and its memories had fast faded.

After her mother's death, Charlotte had to fill in as the matriarch at the ripe age of seventeen, managing the household, entertaining her father's business acquaintances, and accompanying him during his social obligations. When not playing hostess, Charlotte tended to her father as a dutiful daughter, reading to him, playing the piano, and keeping him in good spirits. She found meaning and purpose learning the skills needed to be a lady of the house. But the older women she entertained were not her peers, and the younger women were preoccupied with other duties, mainly seeking eligible men with sufficient incomes and proper standings. Parties and dances were for the business of marriage, leaving Charlotte home many nights with her father, too tired to involve himself in frivolity. She became stuck somewhere between daughter and wife, and her social standing fell between the cracks. Charlotte grew more dependent upon her father's companionship, he for hers.

When he died, she was left truly alone.

Except there was Lydia, one of the few she had to call *family*–cousins by blood, sisters by bond. But as the train moved away from the sea and into the country, the scenery becoming more familiar, anxiety pulsated through her. Memories flooded her mind. Happy memories. Dead memories. Too many years passed. Charlotte questioned if she and Lydia would be the same together. They were now grown women, no longer silly girls who had childish dreams and who made foolish promises to each other. Intermittent letters were their only ties through the years. Their communications were mere summations of their lives, not substitutions for sharing their lives. Charlotte wanted to re-establish what they used to have–a friendship and love that no one could separate, but she worried Lydia wouldn't feel the same. She had an urge to jump out of her seat and demand Hollister turn the train around and go back.

But back to where? Tears slid down her face faster than she could wipe them away.

Mr. Hollister uncrossed his arms and reached in his jacket.

"You have been away a long time?" he said, handing Charlotte the linen from his pocket.

Charlotte dabbed her wetted cheeks. "Yes, eight years."

"I dare say it will be quite an adjustment. Being away for so many years changes things."

She peered out the window, fearing his words rang

true. "It all looks the same to me—as beautiful as the day I left. But…" Her voice trailed off.

"Aye, it's beautiful," he agreed. "But nothing is what it seems. You may have forgotten the dreariness and the gloom of your homeland. Prior to your arrival, we had days of rain. It seems the sun has come around just in time for you. Maybe that's a good omen," he said and winked at her.

Charlotte managed a smile. "Thank you, Hollister. You are very kind."

With surprise, his thin lips curled at the ends. It was enough to bring her comfort.

"Now, maybe you could get the rest I suggested earlier. We still have a long way to go. I promised to take good care of you, and that is what I shall do."

"You already have."

Charlotte settled in her seat, and to Hollister's surprise, her eyes closed.

SEPARATION

Charlotte recalled the day well when her father definitively decided to separate himself from the family and move to America. She had never heard him rise to anger so passionately, or so loudly.

It started as a pleasant enough afternoon. Her mother called to her from the bottom of the stairs for her to quickly gather her cloak and meet in the foyer. Her father was granting Charlotte a reprieve from her studies to visit her Uncle Edmond, Aunt Clara, and, most excitedly, her beloved cousin, Lydia. She had not seen her cousin in weeks.

A torment beyond proportion! Charlotte would cry to her mother in the privacy of her room. Her mother would not disagree with her father's decisions–the long intervals between visits to see her cousin–but she never dismissed Charlotte's feelings, whether good or bad, right or wrong. She encouraged the interactions of the two cousins as often as it was feasible to arrange.

The unexpected trip that morning was, no doubt, precipitated by her mother.

But soon after they arrived, before Charlotte had the chance to engage her cousin with their habitual exchange of girlish gossip or discuss plans for their fantasy future lives, her father's voice reverberated through the hallways.

It was not his usual heated temperament. He was enraged.

"What must our fathers be arguing about now?" Lydia questioned, rushing to the top of the stairs, Charlotte following.

Charlotte peered over the railing to see her father exit from her uncle's study, red faced, and his feet pounding across the floor to the entry. Her mother and Aunt Clara's footsteps in lockstep scurried to the foyer to find her father putting on his coat and reaching for his hat a groomsman had stealthily retrieved.

Charlotte started for the stairs, but Lydia stopped her.

"Merrill, what has happened?" her mother asked.

"Disown me? Who does he think he is?" her father bellowed, ignoring his wife's inquiry. "He may be the oldest and heir to my father's fortune, but our father never intended for my brother to control me into subservience to his will."

"Merrill, please try to calm yourself. You will upset Charlotte," her mother pleaded, spotting her daughter at the top of the stairs. "She has been burdened with your arguments too much lately. We all have…"

"Damn the walls if they come tumbling down. Let her know her father's power to fight for this family. Family is sacred and should be honored above power and money. Why can't my brother see that? Is his pride greater than his honor?"

"You are going to work yourself up. Let things settle, and I am sure your brother will be more forthcoming. After all, you have such a good plan. I am sure he will see it your way soon enough."

"Merrill." Aunt Clara tugged at his arm. "Let us take some tea and allow Edmond to explain himself. I have your favorite lemon tarts today…" She took his coat from his arms, handing it back to the waiting groomsman, and put her arm through his and led him to the drawing room. It was a skill she learned living with an Ashford man…addressing heated emotions with a soft voice and a request to partake in a more civil activity, like taking tea.

Charlotte heard the doors shut; their voices muffled by the walls. A familiar hand took hers and dragged her away from the top of the stairs.

Too many times of late, Charlotte and Lydia lingered at the top of the stairs, listening to the arguments between their two fathers, the brotherly niceties lost in egos and power struggles. When the yelling ceased, the two men would emerge with scowling faces. Charlotte's father would call out her name and obediently she would scurry down the stairs to be taken away. The two girls' time together became less and less, as Charlotte's father and uncle found more and more to argue about.

"Come," Lydia said. "Let them have their time."

"It's not right that they argue so," Charlotte bemoaned.

"No, but they are men and will do what they want." Lydia brought Charlotte to her bedroom and closed the door behind them. "Let us have the little time we have together. Although mama's lemon tarts are irresistible, I have a feeling tea will not soothe your father for very long, nor mine."

UNCLE EDMOND and Charlotte's father were barely on speaking terms, the girls' relationship became the collateral damage.

Charlotte's father prepared to embark on a new business venture without the consent of the Ashford family, namely his brother. Always considered more daring, and maybe even a rebel, Merrill Ashford was a risk taker. He saw opportunity in America and was planning to move his family and fortune overseas, even with the disapproval of his brother.

Edmond threatened to disown Merrill if he took the family's money overseas. He saw no advantages to leaving England. Edmond was against the whole idea and the battle over control of the family money became bigger than the both of them.

While Merrill plotted his family's financial future in America, Edmond worked on his own family's prospects in England. That included marrying his daughter to a stable and established family.

Lydia's eighteenth birthday arrived amid the family drama, and she was thrust into society, immersed in parties and entertainment. Lydia had become the center of attention, on top of everyone's list of invitees. After all, she was Edmond Ashford's beautiful and eligible daughter. A highly regarded prize. Her social schedule filled, while Charlotte remained isolated.

Charlotte was not completely cut off from Lydia's new life. Their mothers were still socially intertwined, and thus the young cousins managed social obligations outside of their fathers' control when possible. But Charlotte's personal time with Lydia was all but memories for both of them. Lydia was expected to sit with the older women and engage as an up and coming equal. Being interesting to those women was the gateway to their eligible sons. Charlotte, being still a few years younger, was relegated to the side, to sit and politely listen, as all the younger women were expected to do awaiting their turn to engage with eligible suitors.

On the rare occasions when their fathers put aside their differences, Charlotte and Lydia indulged in the private time granted by their fathers' reprieve from arguing–intervals of a few hours, separated by weeks. Charlotte soaked in Lydia's stories of how Mr. Daly and Mr. Cranston, two of the most handsomely dressed men in town, let alone blessed with family money, flipped a coin as to whom would dance with Lydia next. Or how Antoinette Berkley slid her sleeves off her shoulders to purposely attract the attention of the men on the dance floor. The stories were abundant depicting the bold and the beautiful, the privileged and the elite, and how they spent their evenings mixing, mumbling, and murmuring, all in the pursuit of matrimony. No longer did they have to imagine a world of dances and parties like they did when they were little girls. Lydia was now living among them. All the gowns they fantasized about wearing, Lydia was now choosing from her closet. The estates they passed on Sunday drives, decorated in extravagant interiors, Lydia was now invited inside as a guest. The men they used to fantasize about meeting, Lydia was now among them.

Many times, Lydia complained about her obligations and the demands placed upon her, but there was no dismissing her excitement for the nights ahead. *Who could blame her?* Men, dancing, and being noticed were new adventures for Lydia–adventures she assured Charlotte would someday soon experience but was unable to join her cousin all the same.

"But look at me, talking on and on about all my adventures, all the while uncle keeps you locked away."

"I adore your stories, dear cousin. How exciting it

all is...your life so full of possibilities..." Charlotte looked away, not wanting to own her disappointment about her own life.

"Oh, dear Charlotte, why so forlorn? It will be your life, too." Lydia turned Charlotte's face to hers. "You will be by my side in no time. Then, we Ashford women shall take on the world with fury."

"I do not begrudge your happiness," Charlotte replied, trying to brush away Lydia's concerns. But she was not far from the truth. Jealousy reared its ugly head. Her once skinny, jaunty, and gangly cousin blossomed into an elegant, noble, and beautiful woman. Her transformation surprised many, especially her male counterparts who had teased her in her youth. Her golden-wheat hair and blue eyes only made her a rare beauty. She could not be overlooked by anyone who was anyone. With a gentle demeanor taught by her mother, and a sharp wit inherited from her father, Lydia Ashford was a force to be reckoned with. Beautiful, well-educated, and wickedly charming, she was no match against the other young ladies seeking suitable husbands. And while Lydia was enjoying all that a young society woman dreams about, Charlotte's life was becoming more and more isolated, entangled in her father's decisions, that included avoiding society at large which he felt was judging him.

"Who are we to fool ourselves? Our lives are changing. I do not see my life as fanciful as yours, Lydia. Father has sealed my fate, even with mother's protests. It won't be long before a handsome suitor asks for your hand in marriage. How could he not? You are upon the precipice of a married life, a home to manage, and with children to care for. It is what you have always dreamed of."

"We both have dreamed of… Charlotte. Our situations may change, but our dreams never will. Soon we will be two married women in our own right."

"Living separate lives across the sea," Charlotte added.

"But we shan't ever be apart! I will not even think such a fate is possible," Lydia declared, her blue eyes narrowing on Charlotte. "We will find brothers who are close, to marry us and to keep our lives connected, and never be separated. We must insist we live near to one another. If they are to love one of us, they must love the other."

"I could not think of anything more perfect," Charlotte agreed, forcing a smile across her lips.

"For who would not love both of us?" Lydia lifted her well-groomed brow. Something she did when she was scheming. "We are a set. They cannot take one without the other."

Charlotte's smile faded. "But Lydia…"

Lydia's hand went up. "No! I will not hear of it. Your father cannot take you away yet. He mustn't!"

Charlotte reached for her cousin's hand, enwrapping hers around it, knowing her destiny was already planned.

Leaving for America was on the horizon sooner than anyone anticipated–within the next year. Before she could be introduced to society. Before she had a chance to dance with prospective suitors. Before she could meet someone, fall in love, and be married. No, the plans Lydia and she made of a life shared were not in their destiny.

"No matter how our lives may play out, I will always cherish you."

"I too, dear cousin," Lydia replied, touching Charlotte's cheek. "We are very lucky, you and I, to be so blessed to have one another. Nothing–not even our dreadfully behaved fathers–shall ever come between us. We shall always be together. Always and forever."

"Always and forever," Charlotte echoed.

The two squeezed each other's hand to solidify their pact.

"Charlotte!" Her father's voice reverberated through the halls.

Charlotte knew that nothing good lay ahead. She bolted to the door.

"Now!" he ordered.

Charlotte was not to see Lydia again until her wedding.

COURTSHIP

*A*t nearly eighty years old, Lady Bellingham, a strong-hold in society of important women, still had the gift of pairing women and men together, introducing many of the notable couples in town. She had a well-respected and long relationship with her own husband, with whom she was very happy until his death. Because she was so blessed, she felt it was her duty to bring people together who were well suited for each other. For she believed that youth had a way of dismissing critical factors that ensured a prolific and successful marriage. Men wanted pretty girls; girls wanted security. Both factors not to be overlooked, but pretty and rich wouldn't assure happiness, nor the stamina for commitment. They all had family heritages to secure, as well as social standing. It was her job to seek out what was best for those involved, despite their youth and eagerness.

Her latest target was Nathanial Hammond, a respectable man from a well-established banking family. He was an up-and-coming gentleman who was soon to finish his studies in law. There was no doubt a wife and family were needed to make him a respectable man in society. So, when Lydia Ashford entered the scene, Mrs. Bellingham was more than pleased. She discerned they would be well suited for each other. "Beauty and strength matched with honor and duty," she quipped. Her instincts told her Lydia would complement Nathanial's aspirations and Nathanial would match Lydia's will.

The opportunity to introduce the two had not presented itself at her previous parties. Nathanial did not attend the three events, leaving John Daly and Edward Cranston, both too arrogant and ignorant for the well-educated Lydia Ashford, behaving like children as they gambled between each other for her attention.

"Simply unacceptable," Lady Bellingham declared to her dead husband when she stared at herself in the mirror that evening. It was a usual habit before bed—summing up the evening with her deceased husband with whom she assumed was watching from the heavens above.

So, when she planned for her last party of the season, she made every attempt to assure Nathanial Hammond's acceptance by showing up at his estate, a personal invitation in hand. When he arrived the evening of the party, she did not hesitate to escort

Lydia straight to him as he came through the door, leaving no room for another mother cunningly sneaking their over-coiffed, desperate daughter in his path.

Nathanial was instantly taken by Lydia from the moment he saw her. So much so, he left little time for any other man to distract her, occupying Lydia's attention and dance card, for the whole of the evening.

"You are very beautiful," Nathanial said as they danced across the floor.

"Beauty goes only so far, Mr. Hammond," Lydia replied. "If *that* is all you are seeking, you will grow very weary of me in a short time."

Nathanial couldn't help but laugh. "I am sure, Miss Ashford, I seek more than you accuse me of. But I must admit, I have met many beautiful women, but few who have put me in my place."

"Is that what you believe I am doing?"

"Yes," he replied. "And I rather enjoy it."

"Now you are just being smug," Lydia accused, looking away.

"Are you upset because I am admiring your beauty, or that I find you intriguing?"

Lydia eyed him but did not react to his cleverness. "You will have to do much better, Mr. Hammond, if you are to capture my interest."

"And what must I do to capture your heart?" he asked, the dance ending, but her hand still in his grasp.

Had Lydia known, she might have told him. But she had never thought much about falling in love. Her father wanted her to marry well. Her mother wanted her to be cared for. The gentlemen she had been introduced to in the past few months wanted a dutiful wife, a prized possession, or a mother for their heirs. A combination of two or more was considered gold. Her heart was of little consequence.

Nathanial's eyes met hers. Surprising to Lydia, they did not reflect insincerity.

She finally replied, "You may call on me again."

NATHANIAL HAMMOND CALLED upon the Ashford house numerous times before summer's end, making his intentions clear. He did not disappoint the awaiting social circle. Before the holidays, he asked Lydia for her hand.

A COLD WINTER passed with little time shared between Charlotte and Lydia.

Their fathers constantly fought. *Money this. Disgrace that.* The words flew at each other like daggers. The divide between their fathers kept the two families as distant as if they were already on different continents, forbidding any interaction with each other.

It is pure selfishness, Lydia wrote to Charlotte.

Terribly cruel! Charlotte added.

During their separation, Lydia continued her courtship with Nathanial Hammond. By the change of the weather, green leaves sprouting from the dead branches, and yellow snowdrops peering through the cold soil, Charlotte received a letter.

I am to marry! Lydia announced. *This spring! I wanted to tell you in person; to introduce you to Nathanial. I know you will love him! Mother and father are making plans as I write. And mother is working on father...we shall be together soon.*

Soon did not come soon.

Two more months drew to a close, with Lydia's marriage only a few weeks away before Charlotte's father conceded to her mother's constant requests to allow Charlotte to spend quality time with her cousin.

"OH, DEAR COUSIN!" Lydia swirled around in the dress she was modeling for Charlotte, and exclaimed, "Is it possible to be so happy?"

"You beam. I do not believe I need to answer," Charlotte replied.

"Nathanial is quite a catch, so they say," Lydia exclaimed. "He is terribly attentive, and I shamefully admit, quite dashing."

"I overheard father speak highly of him."

"He is good and kind. His heart is as gracious as..." she paused. "Well, as yours!"

"Then he must be wonderful," Charlotte quipped.

"He is…"

Charlotte hesitated. "He loves you, doesn't he?"

Lydia tilted her head and didn't answer right away. "Yes, I believe he really does."

"Then I am happy for you. It seems you have all you ever wanted."

"Not everything, Charlotte." Her smile faded. "Life wouldn't be fair if we had all our dreams come true. Sometimes we must choose what is best…for everyone."

Charlotte wondered what Lydia meant but did not press her.

"Do you remember our plans?" Lydia's eyebrow arched. "About marrying?"

"You mean your plans that we are to marry brothers?"

"Yes! And I have the grandest news. Nathanial has a brother. I must admit, a charming one at that. Unfortunately, he is traveling for a year, and will not return before the wedding. But when he returns, I cannot foresee any reason you two should not be introduced."

"Lydia, that was our childish fantasy," Charlotte balked. "I can't marry a man just because he is your husband's brother."

"Why not? It would be all that we imagined. We would be sisters by marriage, and no one could keep us from each other." She grabbed Charlotte's hands and swung her around. "Think how fun it would be! You and me, our children growing up together, and our lives forever intertwined."

"Except your life is going to be here, and my life will be in America."

The words were spoken. The fate neither of them wanted to face.

Charlotte was leaving after the wedding, and the two would be forever separated by a sea.

Tears swelled in Lydia's eyes, but she willed them not to fall. "It is more than I can bear that you are leaving. What shall I do without you?"

Charlotte was not as brave. Tears rolled down her face.

Lydia pulled a hanky from a drawer and dabbed at Charlotte's cheeks, letting the linen absorb the wetness. "Please don't cry. Not today. We have so little time left together." Lydia brushed away some loose hairs fallen around Charlotte's face. "And we shan't be parted for very long. Uncle Merrill would never dream of leaving England forever."

"You don't know father..." Charlotte whispered, fearing the worse.

"Hmmm." Lydia rolled her eyes. "Unfortunately, my father is as stubborn as yours, I'm afraid. The two as bumbling fools can be. Do they not see how they are destroying our families? What do they gain by separating us all? Mother is beside herself, as I am sure your mother is. But we shan't ever abandon the bond between us. We are family, no matter what. Where there is love, there is hope. Let us always remember that."

Charlotte did hope, but it was impossible to imagine. Especially because it was she who was to be torn from the life she knew and loved. "I am going to miss you so very much," she cried.

"Miss what? I shall write and tell you everything, and you shall do the same. Nothing and no one shall come between us. Now come, I have something special for you." Tugging her arm, Lydia led Charlotte across the room and pointed to a box wrapped with a black ribbon. "Mother wanted me to wait until later, but now seems like the perfect time. Open it."

Charlotte untied the bow and slowly lifted the lid. Inside were layers of taffeta, the color of ripened plums. Pulling the dress from the box, she gasped. "It's stunning! And it is for me?"

Lydia nodded. "Mother had it sent from Paris. I personally chose the color to enhance the dark choco-late of your hair. Try it on," she ordered. "Mrs. Withers will have it fitted in no time."

Charlotte glanced at herself in the mirror. "It's exquisite, Lydia. I never imagined wearing a dress so fanciful." Charlotte eyed the intricate details, gliding her fingers across the satin ribbon and inlaid lace decorating the bodice.

"It is you who makes it stunning," Lydia quipped. "You are blossoming into quite a beautiful woman."

Charlotte shook her head. "I fear I am not half the woman you have become."

"Dearest cousin, you do yourself an injustice. Look at the young woman in the mirror." Lydia walked up behind her and the two stared into their reflections. "If

I am to admit, Charlotte, you will be the true beauty of the family."

Their family resemblance was clearly recognizable. They both had fair, creamy complexions, long lashes, and blue eyes. Most notable was a defined, pointed nose that was a legacy of the Ashford bloodline. Only Charlotte's hair was dark chocolate compared to Lydia's golden coloring–the distinguishable color of both their fathers. Her coloring softened the Ashford's rigid jawlines and high cheekbones, whereas Charlotte's coloring only made her look more austere. Maturity gave Lydia the advantage of femininity. Charlotte's figure was transforming. Her womanly curves had yet to be refined, but the design of the dress gave hints of the slim waist and full hips that were hallmarks of her mother.

Lydia wrapped her arms around Charlotte and clung to her. "I am the luckiest girl in the world. For I have you to love forever no matter where you go, whom I marry, or what our circumstances are. We are as one, except you are the better half of me. I don't know how my life will be if I don't have you to hold on to…rely on."

Charlotte grew concerned. Lydia's life seemed to be perfectly falling into place. Yet her voice had a hint of desperation. "I pledge my utmost loyalty. I will always be there for you, Lydia. Always." She squeezed her tighter. "But you are being dramatic. Is not everything as you planned? You have found a wealthy and established gentleman, will live in a grand house, and no doubt have children running around in no time. There is so much ahead of you. Dare I admit we should almost be grateful for our separation by our fathers?"

Lydia shook her head.

"I would only interfere with your happiness. No one needs a third person in a marriage."

"I will always need you," Lydia insisted.

Charlotte smiled. "You have so much love to give, Lydia. I am a lucky girl to have your devotion. As I am sure Mr. Hammond is. I am eager to meet the man who has stolen your heart. I hope he likes me." Charlotte uttered, for she had not considered otherwise until that moment.

"How could he not? If he loves me, he will love you. For that, I am certain."

PEARLS OF SADNESS

*C*harlotte's father was in no hurry to enter the house of his brother. With the same stubbornness, and no outreach to make amends by either of them, Merrill Ashford had not stepped foot in his brother's house for over half a year. He had been too busy making plans and settling his own affairs, if not punishing his brother. But Merrill humbled himself, for his wife's and daughter's sake, and accepted the invitation to attend the wedding between his niece Lydia Ashford and Nathanial Hammond. For in two days, he and his family would head towards a new homeland and a new life.

His brother could no longer stop the cogs of the wheel from turning.

The celebration before the wedding day promised to be a grand affair; almost as resplendent as the wedding, and the Ashford Estate's drive filled with carriages of eager guests. Upon arrival, the well-dressed staff lined the entry, where everyone who arrived were expeditiously relieved of coats, hats, and gloves before being directed to the ballroom.

Charlotte's father handed over his ensemble while grumbling something about being *over-the-top* as he glared at the harpist in the entry who plunked at her strings. On the other hand, Charlotte's mother praised the heavenly sound filling the house, all the while fawning over the spectacular display of blush roses, apricot China asters, and white Lilium spilling from a vase decorating the table centering the entry.

Charlotte's aunt was just descending the stairs, the beaded hems of her dress cascading behind her, when she rushed to greet them. "My dears!"

Her aunt hugged them all, but Charlotte's father remained stoic in her aunt's warm embrace.

"Charlotte, darling, hurry along to Lydia. You should find her in her bedroom," her aunt said, giving her permission to escape the adults. "And tell her that the guests are waiting."

With a wink of approval from her mother, Charlotte rushed past her aunt and up the stairs.

Charlotte was excited to get a moment with Lydia by herself. But when she burst into her room, Lydia was nowhere to be found. She scurried from room to room, calling out Lydia's name, but to no avail. Without a moment to waste, she headed downstairs, only to find the rooms were more than half full, dissipating her hopefulness of alone time with her cousin.

For she knew that everyone who was anyone, and there were many of *them* gathering by the minute, would want Lydia's attention for themselves, as she did.

In the banquet hall, tables cascaded from end to end, with flower arrangements mirroring the assortment in the entry. Down the center, polished candelabras stood between bouquets, their golden flames dancing atop the wicks. Platters of cakes and breads graced the white linens, trimmed in French lace, while servants drifted by with large platters of roasted veal and venison, encircled by vegetables, followed by salmon and chicken. The first of the season gooseberries and strawberries had been placed next to the meat, along with an assortment of nuts, undoubtedly imported for such an occasion.

A sidebar was set of varying bottles of golden elixirs, particularly suited for the men to consume. The older gentlemen lingered nearby, talking, all the while, plundering the collection. The servants swiftly exchanged empty carafes for full ones in a silent ballet of the staff.

Musicians gathered in the corner of the connecting room, plinking as they tuned their instrument. The promise of dancing filled the room. But Charlotte had little aspirations of dancing. The young men paid little attention to her as she darted from room to room looking for Lydia. Maybe it was because she was absent from all the parties that had taken place that season, and she was unfamiliar to the well-dressed and well-behaved men. Their attention was more firmly fixed on the familiar young women in pretty dresses, hair coiffed, and bosoms on display, who were awaiting to be swept up to the music.

However, when Mr. Hobbs and Mr. Plinkett, two bachelors at the ripe age of fifty, gave Charlotte smiles from across the room, she felt anticipation for the evening's music, ensuring they would ask her to dance.

Charlotte continued her search for Lydia, gracefully slipping through clusters of conversing guests who were fully taking in the collective excitement about the nuptials to come. Weddings had a way of bringing out the best in people, and it was hard not to be caught up in the euphoria. She nodded politely to acquaintances and extended her hand to those she knew well.

Once she made the rounds of the large ballroom, Charlotte found herself plucked by old Lady Forester whose hand had extended through the air, drawing Charlotte to the chaise where the old woman sat. With her frail voice she invited, "Come, sit with me."

Charlotte obeyed, putting on a brave face, and patiently listened to Lady Forester's on-going health issues. Meanwhile, the first strike of the music began, and the dancing commenced.

It was only until Mrs. Halloway, equally old and equally inflicted with ailments, interrupted their conversation, eager to commiserate with Lady

Forester, did Charlotte have the opportunity to excuse herself.

Rushing to the nearest doorway, she slipped back into the banquet hall.

In their younger days, she and Lydia would conspire to sneak into the dining hall to steal treats before the guests would plunder the tables. That way they would get their pick of their favorites. Turning her head, Charlotte spied over her shoulder before she wily plucked a fresh strawberry and bit into the luscious fruit, savoring the sweetness. She giggled as red juice trickled over her lips and summarily swiped it away with her tongue.

She contemplated taking another, only to find someone standing at the doorway, watching her relishing the sweet strawberry. There was no mistaking the well-dressed man Lydia had told her about, with dark brown eyes and head of luscious dark hair, heavily oiled back to subdue wayward curls. The white boutonniere was also a dead giveaway. It could be no other than the infamous groom to be, Nathanial Hammond.

Their eyes met, and for a moment she forgot to breathe.

Quickly, she darted her eyes away, wishing for him to move on to someone or something else more important, only to find he had not when she looked back to him.

Was it shame that made her shiver?

Caught at her mischievous theft, she felt of rush of

heat to her cheeks. She touched them, praying they had not turned the color of the strawberry she just ate.

His eyes still on Charlotte, he stepped toward her.

She offered him a smile, praying it was enough to vanquish his first impression of her; hoping he would not hold the pilfering against her. Fortunately for her, his attention was diverted when a small crowd of ladies surrounded him. A consequence of being the honored guest in a room full of people.

His head poked above the crowd, but Charlotte slipped out of his sight.

She didn't dash *too* far, just hiding herself behind a grouping of potted palms adorning the entrance of the ballroom. Far enough, where she could watch Nathanial, remembering him growing up.

He was a tall and awkward boy at most that she recalled. Still tall, maintaining his advantage over most of the other men, he had shed his lanky boyhood physique, attaining more desirable looks in adulthood. High cheekbones and a cleft chin secured distinguishment, to his otherwise common brown hair and dark eyes.

He was admittedly handsome. Charlotte would have to be blind not to think so. *Did not Lydia tell her as much?* Adding to the prestige was his pedigree—coming from a highly notable family, known for their wealth, political influence, and charitable works around the world. All were factors in the carefully calculated match for Lydia.

"Is he not the most handsome man in the room?"

Lydia's voice came from behind, catching Charlotte's purview in her sights.

"Lydia!" Charlotte startled. She then nodded in agreement with her answer, not daring to voice her opinion.

Lydia threw her arms around her cousin, "Oh darling, I am so happy to see you. I was certain Uncle had taken you away in the middle of the night. Come," she grabbed Charlotte's hand, "I want to introduce you to my husband to be. I cannot imagine why you two have not met until tonight. How could that possibly be?" Lydia skirted through the crowd looking around the room for her fiancée. She sighed, "It will be lucky if he and I meet at the altar, let alone have you two be introduced beforehand. We have been missing each other at every turn."

"Do not fret, Lydia, you will soon have a lifetime of him by your side. Besides, there he is." Charlotte pointed, spotting Nathanial, his hand on his chin, listening intently to a gentleman speaking to him. He must have said something funny, for Nathanial threw his head back and laughed.

She liked that quality–a man with expression.

Lydia dragged Charlotte through the crowd, determined not to be stopped by the many guests vying for her attention. "It does not seem right that the two people I hold most dear are strangers. It is just not acceptable."

Charlotte halted Lydia. "Promise me you will stop anguishing about our time together, or lack thereof.

Or at the fact I have not been formally introduced to your fiancé." She glanced out of the corner of her eye to assure he was still in their sights. "I am merely a few feet away from meeting him. No need to put a damper on your special day. Neither of us has the power to change the things that have transpired over the last few months. Yesterday is gone. Today is here. Let us enjoy the day, and not think about what could have been, should have been, or what shall come."

Lydia touched Charlotte's face. "You know me too well. I am a bundle of nerves with the wedding now here, and that has nothing to involve you. I am terribly anxious for all to go splendidly."

"Perfect it will be!" Charlotte declared. "You wouldn't have it any other way."

Lydia released a sigh. "Thank you for being here, sharing this with me. It would not be the same without you." She squeezed Charlotte's fingers; their hands still intertwined. "But you must give me your word, Charlotte, no matter how far we are separated, that one day we will be together again."

"I…" Charlotte looked deep into Lydia's eyes and had no other answer. "Yes, of course. God could never be so cruel as to keep us apart."

"Oh my, I have forgotten!" Lydia exclaimed.

"Forgotten what?" Charlotte asked.

"Stay put, I need to get something," Lydia ordered, freeing herself from Charlotte's arm and disappearing through the door.

Left alone, Charlotte stood in the middle of the

room. She saw her mother and aunt talking with a group of ladies, knowing they, too, sensed the moments were slipping away between them, as it was for Lydia and herself. Mrs. Forester and Mrs. Holloway, now supplanted on a nearby sofa, watched the young ladies across the room. Pursed lips and raised eyebrows accompanied their stares. She saw Nathanial had re-entered the ball room.

He was now preoccupied by Mr. and Mrs. Allen, a relation to both Charlotte and Lydia, twice removed. Their son, Algernon, was a beast of a boy from whom they tried to avoid most of their childhood. He grew up to be an even more dislikable gentleman, having tried to kiss Lydia unexpectedly during a family Christmas holiday. Lydia slapped him and sent him away. Neither of them had spoken to him since; he avoiding them as well.

Charlotte calculated her avoidance of Algernon, eyeing the men in attendance. With him nowhere in sight, she sighed in relief. This gave opportunity for her to walk up to her relations whom she had not seen since her childhood, but when pressed for reasons that she must do so, she could not glean the necessity. Instead, she turned her back slightly hoping she would remain unnoticed by them and waited for Lydia to return.

With the music in the distance, and the echoed voices around her, she closed her eyes to capture the celebration in her memory. Uncontrollably, sorrow flowed through her, knowing this was the last time she and Lydia would share. Tomorrow was the wedding–*the finale*! Charlotte and her family would leave soon after. Hearing footsteps behind her, she quickly hid her angst, putting on a smile for the sake of her cousin.

"You are still here..." Lydia remarked.

"You asked me to stay. Besides, where would I go? To whom would I run?" She lifted a brow as she glanced at Mrs. Forrester and Mrs. Holloway, before tilting her head askew in the direction of the Allens behind her. "There is no one but you I would seek out."

Lydia smiled when she caught sight of her aunt and uncle talking to her fiancé. "I am surprised Nathanial did not come and whisk you away. You are like a flower in the center of a garden ready to bloom...ripe for picking." She made Charlotte swirl around in her dress so she could view her from all angles. "You are lovely. Had I not found him first, I am afraid you might have stolen Nathanial for yourself."

Charlotte blushed. "Don't be silly." She smoothed her skirt and glanced around the room. "There are so many beautiful young women to whom I am merely a shadow."

"Look around, Charlotte. They are all silly girls, I, being one of them. We put on facades of prettiness and perfection, all to capture a man, never asking if a man can capture us. But you and I both know most of them are droll young girls who will become mundane women and will live with tiring men. It is our destiny."

"Our destiny?" Charlotte questioned.

Lydia smirked. "No. Not you, my dear Charlotte. You have a goodness, a heart that has no limits. There lies your true beauty. You will not capture a man; you will captivate and seize him. Do not eye these women as superior, for your beauty is an unfurling fire, soon to ignite the world. I am jealous of the man who wins your heart. For he will find no other love as true and worthy." Lydia pointed to a mirror across the room. "Truly, look at yourself. Never doubt your worthiness in a room full of young women...they have nothing against what you offer."

Charlotte glanced at herself in the plum-colored dress she was now constricted. The seamstress did an exquisite job, molding her into the young woman Lydia was now admiring. The contemporary style, with its chiffon puffed sleeves sliding down her shoulder, the swooped, low collar, the fitted bodice shaping her rounded breast, and the cinched waistline, revealed she was no longer a girl. Being in the shadow of Lydia most of her life, watching her become a sophisticated young woman, she had missed her own metamorphosis. Until then, Charlotte had not taken the time to fully appreciate that she, too, was on the verge of womanhood herself.

But capturing a man and fall in love? That seemed very far away.

"Put out your hands," Lydia instructed. When Charlotte complied, she placed a green silk brocade bag in the palm of her hands. "Charlotte, even with all these people in the room, for me there is only one whom I most adore. This gift is from me to you...a token of our bond as the dearest of family. May we never be tempted to destroy each other–like our fathers–and always stay devout to what we hold dear."

Nathanial swooped in before them. "I hope I am not interrupting."

The sound of his voice took Charlotte by surprise. It was deeper than she expected, with the baritone reverberating in her ears.

"Nathanial, at last!" Lydia squealed. She pulled him closer. "Darling, I want to introduce to you the most important person to me, Miss Charlotte Rose Ashford."

He bowed. "It is an honor to finally have the chance to be introduced. Of course, I knew who you were the moment you walked into the room. The Ashford women are exceptionally distinguishable."

"It is my honor, Mr. Hammond," Charlotte replied, grateful for his omission of her indiscretion at the food tables. She extended her hand. His own wrapped gently around hers.

He stepped closer, his hand lingering. "There is no one else who holds Lydia's heart, and for that, you will also be important to me."

"I am not sure your admiration is deserved, but I thank you for your kindness, Mr. Hammond," Charlotte said retrieving her hand from his.

"Please, call me Nathanial. I think we are destined

to become more intimate than your formality requires."

"She will be *that* I am certain," Lydia declared, adding, "You will come to love Charlotte as much as I."

Charlotte rolled her eyes at Lydia. "My cousin is over enthusiastic. I will not hold it against you, Mr. Hammond...I mean, Nathanial, if you do not share the same affection as my cousin."

Nathanial nodded with understanding. "In this circumstance, I have no doubt as to her prediction."

"I can already see the fondness between you two. It is meant to be," Lydia exclaimed. "Now, open my gift before I do it for you."

Charlotte untied the ribbon of the brocade bag and pulled out a strand of milky white pearls. She gasped. "These are for me? How exquisite. But I cannot accept such an extravagance."

"Yes, you must," Lydia insisted. "Do you recognize them? They are the ones we used to play with as little girls. My mother gave them to me to wear on my wedding day. But with her consent, I insisted that you be the one to have the honor. My wish is for you to think of me every time you put them around your neck. I know our lives are becoming very different, but know you are always a part of me. No matter how far you travel, or what our circumstances may be. We are family, forever."

Family. The word seemed to hit her in the pit of her stomach. Charlotte searched the room for her father.

He stood in the back, his shoulder against the wall, her uncle equally keeping his distance.

Not even an ocean was far enough to separate those two, she thought.

"Yes, dear cousin, always and forever," Charlotte vowed, unable to stop the first of tears collecting at the corner of her eyes.

"Dearest Charlotte," Lydia scolded, "Now you have made me cry!"

Nathanial pulled out a handkerchief and let the two women share it between them.

Swiping at her droplets, Charlotte sniffled her apology, "I shan't ruin your lovely evening. It is too wonderful for the both of you."

"For all of us," Nathanial corrected her. "You will always be a part of us, Charlotte."

"We wouldn't have it any other way," Lydia insisted. "Now, let's see if those pearls around your neck can bring back some joy into that lovely face of yours. You deserve so much, Charlotte. More than I could ever give you."

"May I put them on you?" Nathanial offered.

Charlotte nodded in approval. When he leaned in, swooping the pearls around her neck, his head dropped alongside hers, and she could feel his breath blow along her neck. The heat of his body enveloped her. His fingers slightly brushed against her skin as he fastened the clasp, immediately sending an uncontrollable tingling sensation through her shoulders and down her back.

His eyes met hers as his head lifted, the dark pools penetrating her delicate blue glance.

She noted a rash of red flushed his cheeks, mirroring the hotness rushing to her own.

She promptly pulled away.

He stepped back.

Charlotte twisted her head to look at the guests gathered in clusters around the room. Mrs. Forester and Mrs. Holloway were staring her way. *Did they notice it, too? She* pressed the beads against her neck, hoping the coolness of the pearls would douse the heated feeling usurping its way through her body.

"The pearls are beautiful on you," Lydia declared.

Charlotte swallowed, hoping to stop the rapid pounding in her chest. *Was it shame? Embarrassment?* She couldn't define the feeling, nor did she want to. "I will cherish them forever," she finally said, placing a kiss on Lydia's cheek.

"You are so dear to me," Lydia whispered. "Think of me often, as I will think of you."

"Yes, of course. Always…"

Nathanial touched Lydia's elbow. "Your father is summoning us."

"Duty. We both understand that don't we?" Lydia said to him, donning a frown.

"Go," Charlotte gave her permission. "We will have time later."

Lydia blew her a kiss and glided towards her father in obedience, who was rounding up the guests for a toast to the happy couple.

Nathanial turned to follow, but not before he looked back at Charlotte, clinging to her pearls. He reached out to her, taking her hand in his. "It was an honor to meet you, Charlotte. I hope we have the chance to get to know one another better someday."

Charlotte looked down at his hand encasing hers. Had she allowed herself, she would have indulged in the touch. Instead, she lifted her gaze to meet his, slipping away her hand and letting it fall to her side.

"Yes, I would like that very much," Charlotte replied with frankness that even surprised her, releasing a new wave of heat throughout her body.

He tipped his head, turned, and walked away, stopping himself halfway between where Lydia now stood and where he left Charlotte. He glanced back at her, holding his stare before he finally turned away, finding his way to Lydia's side.

As the couple disappeared into the crowd, Charlotte's soul whimpered with loss. Everything was about to change. Her childhood was disappearing. Her lifelong companion was to become someone else's, the wedding the final act, breaking their girlhood bond. Lydia was to become a woman in her own right, and Charlotte sensed her own journey into womanhood was not far behind Lydia's.

But with Nathanial's last glance, she realized change was already upon her when she found herself affected by a man.

A man she had no right to.

~

WHITE ROSES INTERSPERSED with the sweet fragrance of Stargazer lilies adorned every inch of the chapel. Guest, both the distinguished and beloved, arrived in their finest attire. The weather was perfect, gracing the occasion with sunshine and a pleasant temperature that kept everyone comfortable throughout the ceremony.

Lydia walked down the aisle is a stunning gown of creamy layers of chiffon and silk taffeta, with ruffled edges of lace along the sleeves, and satin bows down the bodice. The ladies all agreed that she would set the fashion for future weddings.

Nathanial, who was as handsomely dressed in a black coat, white pants, and a silk-linen waistcoat, stood equally distinguished by her side. Lydia's eyes sparkled and her cheeks flushed with pride when, after the rings were exchanged, and the blessing granted upon them, as she gazed upon her newly betrothed standing beside her.

They made a perfect couple, as was the sentiment repeated throughout the day.

Charlotte dressed in a similar cream color as Lydia, bringing harmony to the ensemble of the wedding party's appearance as they stood outside the church doors to greet the guests descending upon them. She managed a serene smile as she held Lydia's bouquet, allowing guests to pass her by with little notice of the girl in the background. Their only desire was to wish the newly married couple much happiness.

Unfortunately, as the party continued onto the Ashford estate for food, wine, and music, there was little time between the two cousins throughout the day to share their joy; their sadness. Charlotte found herself with barely a hug between them before Nathanial and Lydia were out the door, headed on their honeymoon, and on their way to starting their new lives together.

"Come, Charlotte," her father demanded, "We are done here."

It would be only a few days later that Charlotte would leave on her own trip, with her trunks packed, the family house sold, and all their belongings sailing toward America. Charlotte's father was leaving no legacy to return to. She had little hope that she was ever to see England again. Her despair was overwhelming. She could no longer contain her tears, and they drizzled down her cheeks as she waved goodbye.

INTRODUCTIONS

*C*harlotte awoke, sounds of yelping dogs jarring her from a deep sleep. Lifting her lids open, she slowly surveyed her surroundings with hazy alertness. She lay in bed, tucked under a canopy swathed in floral embroidered chintz draping from the four posts anchoring the bed. The same pattern spilled onto the papered walls surrounding her in a floral tomb.

She jolted up.

A heavy-scrolled wardrobe butted against the wall; the door was slightly ajar with the fabric of dresses peeking through. She recognized her largest trunk placed in front of it, with more clothing inside, waiting to be unpacked.

An assortment of furniture was scattered throughout the room—a settee covered in a pink foliate motif placed in front of the fireplace, a patterned Bergere chair, and a mahogany footstool covered in a floral needlepoint were pushed off to the side. Equally rich in mahogany as the wardrobe, a secretary sat between windows, rosy-pink silk fabric curtains puddling to the floor flanking them. A delicately carved chair was tucked under the writing desk, with a vase atop filled with yellow roses spilling from its neck. As if begging for her to smell them, a faint hint of honey and citrus scent filled her nostrils. It was all very elegant and well appointed–the notable touches of a woman.

With a few blinks and a yawn, Charlotte eased her shoulders back to the fluffy pillows that cocooned her head through the night, unable to release the grin across her face.

She was with Lydia. She was home.

Charlotte had arrived at the house very late the prior evening, so late, the only two people to greet her were Lydia and Ada, her appointed maid. They were waiting by the door with a lamp in hand, eager to rush her into her room and get her settled.

Once upstairs and her luggage delivered, Lydia couldn't stop hugging her. There was so much to say– so much to make up for. But Lydia insisted they talk in the morning, owing to the late hour, *for they had the rest of their lives to catch up,* she proclaimed.

A tray of food arrived, and Lydia excused herself, insisting Charlotte eat a little before she went to bed. It took little convincing, and Charlotte, with her hunger satiated, was soon fast asleep in layers of linens and blankets she now found a reprieve.

The dogs continued to bark.

Charlotte slipped out of bed to see what was causing them hysteria. When she pulled the curtains aside, sunlight burst through, blinding her. She shielded her eyes and peered out at the green expanse greeting her. A gasp usurped itself from her mouth. She had forgotten how lovely the English countryside was when the sunlight danced upon it, the abundance of blooms promising an early summer.

A rap on the bedroom door forced her to turn away.

It was Ada with a tray.

"Good morning, Miss."

"It really is a glorious morning," Charlotte rejoiced as she returned to her view outside. "Is that little Peter running around out there? My, he is so big. Look at him go."

Ada glanced over Charlotte's shoulder at the little boy running around the lawn, being chased by two small terriers and she chuckled. "He is quite the little devil, that one. He found his legs and has not stopped since. Has too much energy, so Nanny takes him outside to tire himself. Otherwise, he is restless and will not nap."

He has Lydia's spirit, Charlotte thought.

"That looks delicious," Charlotte said, noting the display of jam and biscuits alongside a pot of tea placed on a table next to the sofa. Her stomach growled.

"Mrs. Hammond wanted to send up a little something to start your day. I will let you refresh yourself and have a bite to eat. I'll be up in a bit with hot water for that bath I promised you last night. Mrs. Hammond is eager to have you downstairs," she informed. "But emphasized I was not to rush you."

Ada left Charlotte to her breakfast, but before she could put jam on her biscuit, Lydia burst through the door.

"Please forgive my intrusion, but I could not wait another minute." Lydia rushed over to Charlotte and pulled her into an embrace, placing a kiss on her cheek. "It feels so good to have you here. I do hope you are being attended to properly. I wanted everything to be perfect." Lydia eyed the room to make sure it was all she intended it to be.

"It is more than one could possibly imagine. You certainly did not have to make a fuss."

"Who else would be so deserving?"

Charlotte sighed. "Lydia, I know you think of me as your guest, but I do not want to intrude on your lives. I want to fit in, be useful...at least until we can establish how I am to proceed forward with my life."

"Forward? Dearest Charlotte, my home is open to you for as long as you want to be here. We shan't say another word about it. Besides, you have just arrived, barely unpacked, let alone settled in. Rest and pampering are needed to recover from your long journey...from all you have been through." Her voice faded. Turning, she moved across the room, fluffing the pillow on the Bergere chair before she ripped the curtains completely open to immerse the room fully in light. Eyeing the unpacked trunk, she continued, "We shall get your things in place so that you do not have a moment's doubt of where you belong. When you are ready, I am eager to take you around the house, the property, the town...show you everything!" Lydia's eyes sparkled, a familiar smile curling her lips.

Charlotte wondered what was in store for her. A fissure of excitement tickled her tummy, knowing Lydia never disappointed in seizing opportunities to bring happiness into her life. The separation between them had only brought her sadness...a sadness that lingered in Charlotte's life in America. She hungered to rid herself of that familiarity.

Charlotte reached out for Lydia's hand. "I am eager to start my new life here, with you."

"Is that what it is, a new life? Or is it continuing the one we were denied?" Lydia's brow went up; her lips pursed.

"Father had so much hope," Charlotte defended.

"Well, you are now here with me and that is all that matters. What more could I ask for?"

"You seem to have everything you ever wanted, Lydia."

Lydia's face grew solemn, her eyes dimmed. She fidgeted with her hands before she turned away and headed to the door. "We shall continue our conversation when you are dressed," she said as she grabbed the handle. "I shall let you have some privacy."

Sensing more, Charlotte called out, "Lydia?"

She turned.

"You are happy, are you not?"

Lydia feigned a smile and left, neglecting to answer.

CHARLOTTE WAS GIVEN a tour of *Lottington Manor*, the family estate of the Hammonds, and an imposing mansion. It was large and well appointed...far more than Lydia had hinted in her letters to Charlotte.

It was given to Nathanial and Lydia upon their marriage–a stipulation in the will of Sir Alexander Hammond, Nathanial's grandfather. It had not been lived in by anyone after his death, and Lydia was given full authority to make it her own–which she did. It was an expansive estate, grander than either of them had grown up in. The Hammond family's money was greater than the Ashford legacy, and Lydia's married life was exceedingly privileged. Although she seemed accustomed to her role as the mistress of *Lottington Manor*, Charlotte still could see the young girl she used to be underneath her coiffed hair, rosied cheeks, and suitable dress. Although her chin was held high, and her shoulders pulled back, her hands still danced around in the air when she spoke, and her lids fell half-mast when she smiled, her long lashes concealing the guileful thoughts brewing in her head.

Charlotte was sure if left alone to explore the estate, she would get lost for days. Lydia assured her a search would ensue if she was absent for more than a few hours.

"I will not lose you again," she declared.

"I was never lost, Lydia," Charlotte reminded her.

Lydia arched her brow but said nothing in reply. "Tea?" she asked.

Charlotte nodded and was led to Lydia's favorite room–the drawing room. It was a paneled room surrounded with books, paintings, porcelain figurines, and crystal vases filled with flowers. Floor-to-ceiling windows opened to an expansive lawn where Charlotte saw Peter playing earlier that morning. Tea was brought, and they both found a seat to finally rest their feet. A silence fell between them as they sipped from their cups. Words seemed unnecessary.

They were together.

"Your necklace is lovely" Charlotte pointed to the sapphire decorating Lydia's neck, breaking the silence.

"Ahh," Lydia tugged at the strand. "My father gave this necklace to my mother upon my birth–a token of gratitude for bearing his child." Her voice lowered. "*Gratitude.* She almost died giving him a child. I almost suffered the same fate bearing Peter," she mentioned with little significance. "Mother gave it to me the night before she died–a symbol of the bond between mother and child. It rarely leaves my neck. I miss her terribly."

"Yes, I know exactly how you feel. How many times I have thought of my mother? Life was never quite the same after she died."

"How is it we are all that is left, Charlotte? When the carriage turned over, they found Father dead. Mother was still alive, but terribly broken. When she awakened to learn of father's demise, she was devastated. I believe that only hastened her own passing. I had not realized how much they relied on each other. Little did she know she was leaving me so alone."

"But Lydia, you have your own family. Your mother knew you were in excellent care."

Lydia exhaled and got up to pour herself more tea, leaving the conversation altogether.

Charlotte wondered what the exhaustive sigh meant. Looking around the room, Charlotte could not help but be jealous. Lydia had almost everything a woman could desire. A loving husband, a healthy child, a magnificent home. Most of all, a secure place in society and respectable standing. Charlotte had nothing–nothing left from her past. She couldn't help but notice the many pieces of furniture and accessories that once belonged to Lydia's parents, memories of the happy and comfortable life they once shared, now surrounding her.

There was a French clock with rococo scrollwork-mounts that Lydia's father adored. He was obsessed with punctuality, and she remembered he often cursed the French for their lack of precision every time he had to adjust it. She recognized the purple wood commode with a porter marble top that once adorned Lydia's mother's sitting room and now sat by the door with a vase on top cascading with pink peonies, white roses, and purple hyacinth, the combination filling the room with its dramatic heady scent.

Charlotte smiled fondly at a footstool with wool work of a child and a dog, placed by the sofa. When she would visit her aunt's house, it was her favorite place to sit with the ladies, giving her a special seat among them.

How she took it all for granted and now it was gone. Charlotte only had her mother's emerald studded brooch, a gold bracelet, and her father's pocket watch, safely placed in a box, tucked away in a drawer upstairs. The rest–if not valued by Mr. Milford–she left behind, stored in the house's attic he now owned. A painting of her mother. A writing desk her grandfather gave to her father. A tea set her mother promised her for when she married. They were not valuable to Mr. Milford, and thus he offered to store them until she settled.

Settled *where* and *when* were all unknown.

Blinking back to the present, Charlotte noticed a gold-framed painting prominently hanging over the fireplace. "When did you have this painting done? It certainly was when you were younger...I remember that girl well. But I do not recall you ever sitting for a painting. It is lovely."

"How smart of you to notice. Father had it done soon after my honeymoon, so that he could always have 'his little girl near him.' Funny how urgently he married me off, but yet wanted to keep his little girl," Lydia smarted. Walking up alongside Charlotte, she reached out and slowly brushed her fingers across the signed name on the portrait. "The painter, *Piero...*" she whispered. She looked at Charlotte as if to tell her something but decided against it.

"Piero Giordano," Charlotte pronounced the name. "He is quite talented. How did your father come to have an Italian paint the portrait? If I recall, Uncle was *very* English, all English, all the time."

"I was the one who suggested him to my father. I met him at one of Lady Bellingham's parties. Piero had just finished her portrait and as she does best, she pranced him around the room to introduce him to everyone. I was entranced, to say the least. He was quite gifted with conversation, as well as being a talented painter. One could not help but admire his eye for portraying beauty with his brush...even when the subject was Lady Bellingham."

"Lydia!" Charlotte bellowed.

Lydia laughed. "Oh, dear Charlotte, you are so easily shocked. But there is no falseness in my statement. I am sure Lady Bellingham was once a beautiful woman, for how could she have found a love like she had with Sir Bellingham? But I dare say, Piero was brilliant with his painting talent. He captured the goodness in her heart thus he captured her beauty. I would have no one else paint me."

"Well, he captured the essence of how I remember you before I left. Young, possessing, cheery…"

"Hmmm," she guffawed. "That girl is long gone. I had to grow up, for I have a child to care for, who is every bit as vexing as I am sure I was to my mother. But the painting is a reminder of who I am inside, hidden beneath the pomp and circumstance of being a grown woman with so many responsibilities beyond myself. He seems to have captured the essence of my soul and preserved it in that painting. For that, I cherish him…and the painting. Most importantly, it brings me joy, well because, it reminds me of you."

"Of me?"

"Yes. Because it embodies the person I was before. Before you were gone…before my life forever changed."

"As did mine," Charlotte reminded her.

Lydia squeezed Charlotte's hand. "What do we have to mourn about? Nothing, I say. We are together again."

Charlotte nodded in agreement. "Now tell me, I have seen every room in your house, met every servant and staff member, but where is your infamous husband?"

"Oh, I apologize. He had promised me he would be back to greet you when you arrived, but I received a note yesterday morning that he was delayed. He assured me he would be back in time for dinner tonight. He works tirelessly. Unfortunately, he leaves me more alone than we are together. He sends his apologies and promises to make up for it. Now come along…" She stood and made her way to the door.

Charlotte followed her lead.

When they reached the stairs, Lydia turned to Charlotte. "Why don't you rest for a while? I cannot think you are still fully recovered from your long travels, and I am sure you will want to look your best when Nathanial returns."

"I have to admit, I could shut my eyes for a bit." A yawned surfaced. "Do not worry. I promise to present myself like an Ashford. I am looking forward to getting to know the man who won your heart all those years ago."

"Remember our pact. If he doesn't win your heart, he doesn't have mine."

"If you love him, I will love him equally," Charlotte remarked. She kissed Lydia on the cheek and darted off to her room.

NATHANIAL

*C*harlotte only meant to rest her eyes while her maid was settling her things. But she succumbed to the comforts of the bed the moment she laid her head down. It was a knock at the door that finally awakened her.

"Come in," she called out as she rose from the bed.

"Good evening, Miss. I was sent to check on you," her young maid announced. With a candle in hand, she made her way to the bedside and lit the lamp. "There, that must be better."

"Yes, thank you," Charlotte said, noting the darkened room contrasting the small candle in the maid's hand. "I did not intend to sleep so long. What time is it?"

"Half-past eight."

"Oh, my!" Charlotte shrieked, quickly seating herself at the dressing table. She looked in the mirror.

"I am a mess. I wish someone had woken me earlier. I hope my cousin is not waiting on my account."

"Don't worry. Mrs. Hammond said that you were not to be disturbed. She instructed me to dress you for dinner and bring you down when you are ready...not a moment sooner. She said the guests can wait."

"Guests? I did not know Lydia was entertaining this evening. I wish she would have warned me."

"She had little warning herself," the maid said, laying out a dress. "Mr. Hammond arrived late this afternoon with a few people he invited for the evening," Ada explained.

"Poor Lydia. A hostess needs more time to prepare. Does Mr. Hammond surprise her often?"

"More often these past few months," Ada replied, "But her lady handles the unexpected guests with grace."

"I am sure she has no other choice."

"Aye, Miss," Ada agreed, as she brushed through Charlotte's hair. With no time to curl it, the attentive maid pulled it back into a bun, swooping two plaits around it, and inserted two garnet-topped pins on each side. Plucking a few errant hairs from Charlotte's brows, she powdered her face, adding colored pomade over her lips. Tucking in a few strands of loose hairs, she looked at Charlotte in the mirror. "You look very much like the lady herself."

"Yes, the older I grow, the similarities are undeniable."

"Beauty is also a family trait..."

Charlotte smiled at Ada. "You are being kind. I never noticed our similar traits when we were young. Lydia did. She saw me before I saw myself. I always admired her for her beauty. Everyone did. She had the advantage being a few years older. I was merely in the shadow of her light." Charlotte looked at herself in the mirror once more, scrutinizing the woman she had become. "I just needed time to catch up."

"Do you want to wear your pearls?" Ada asked, seeing them laying on the dressing table. With a nod, she put them in Charlotte's hand.

Charlotte rarely went anywhere without them. The feel of the pearls laying against her skin was to bring her comfort, rather than the purpose of accessorizing. She draped them around her neck and hooked the clasp, fingering the cool beads with her fingertips.

"Lovely!" Ada declared.

"Thank you, Ada," Charlotte said before grabbing her gloves. "I shan't keep Lydia waiting any longer..." Hurriedly, she opened the door only to be halted. "Oh!" she shrieked.

A man stood outside, the darkness of the hall shadowing his face.

"I beg your pardon," the man apologized, stumbling over his words. "I was about to knock."

He stepped forward, into the light.

It was then she saw them–his dark, penetrating eyes.

"Nathanial?"

"Charlotte..." he whispered.

The two fell silent, assessing the changes life had brought upon them.

"But of course, it is you," Charlotte mused, offering him a smile.

Nathanial had changed over the years, but Charlotte would have recognized him promptly if they had run into each other on the street. His dark eyes hadn't changed. They held hers the moment he looked at her. It was an instant recognition. Had they been old and grey, their faces unrecognizable from years of battered lives, his eyes would still give him away.

His shoulders were still broad, his stature still straight, but his body transformed from a lanky, lean youth into a sturdy, solid grown man. His face was showing signs of age, with shadowed lines across his forehead and creases at the corner of his eyes. Sure, signs of the responsibility of becoming a husband and father.

She thought age suited him, made him more dignified...*more handsome.*

"It has been many years. I have changed, grown older..." he admitted, rubbing his chin. "We have all changed."

Her hand swept along the side of her hair. "I am all grown up..."

"Yes, most assuredly. An adult version of the girl I first met. Except..." he paused. His brow slightly furrowed. "You remind me of Lydia...becoming lovelier with age."

Charlotte blushed. She had wondered if he would remember her.

Did she remember him? Yes. Every detail. The look. The touch. The goosebumps along her neck. There are moments a girl remembers all her life. Moments of joy. Moments of longing. Moments of love. Meeting Nathanial was all of those, her secret she shared with no one.

Eight years later, and she was back to being the sixteen-year-old girl and feeling foolishly affected by him.

"Charlotte?"

Charlotte's eyes focused. She had been staring at Nathanial lost in her thoughts.

He continued, "Lydia asked me to call on you if I saw your light under the door." His eyes swept to the invisible line separating the dark hallway and her lighted room. "May I escort you to dinner?"

She nodded and stepped into the hallway. When he extended his arm, she hesitated.

Seeing her pause at his arm's invitation, he added, "I frightened you. But I feel as if I know you, the way Lydia speaks about you. I should not presume a familiarity until I earn it. I recognize I am a stranger to you. I apologize."

Charlotte shook her head. "No. You were just unexpected."

A smile crossed his face. "Aww, good. It is a large house. The surroundings are unknown, and it will take time to get familiar. Lydia will not admit it, but she found herself lost frequently. But now, lady of the household, she has mastered every nook and corner, as I am sure you soon will."

"Yes. She seems very comfortable here. It is hard not to be. It is a lovely home."

"I am glad you like it. I had hoped you would."

Charlotte caught his gaze upon her but avoided it, choosing to look at darkened halls enveloping her instead.

"I am terribly late for dinner. Lydia will think the worst of me. I fell asleep," she confessed. "That is my excuse. What is yours? I would have expected you to be downstairs already, entertaining the guests that you yourself brought home."

He smiled. "Oh, yes. I suppose I should not have taken my time to dress," he admitted. "But my wife is more than capable of being the adoring hostess. And I am sure they prefer her company to mine."

His candidness surprised Charlotte. "Lydia does not protest when you arrive at the doorstep with an entourage?"

"I did not say that. Her wrath will come later. And I will be forced to attend someone's boring dinner party," he said wistfully.

"Or worse, you may have to take a penniless cousin into your home who will intrude on your family," Charlotte reminded him.

Nathanial stopped suddenly. "Accepting you into my home is not a penance, Charlotte. It is my honor. I hope you remember that."

Charlotte looked at him, but her words failed her.

As if on cue, a burst of laughter echoed through the halls, interrupting their conversation. They followed the cacophony of voices to the dining room.

Lydia stood to greet them, taking Charlotte from her husband's escort.

"We had to start without you, or our guests would be served cold soup. I hope you do not mind," Lydia said, eyeing her husband. "But you are exonerated by bringing Charlotte. For that, I am grateful."

Nathanial nodded to his wife with recognition of her reprimand, and grateful for his reprieve.

As they walked to the table, the room full of men rose at once, silencing the banter.

"Please sit, everyone," Lydia ordered, bringing Charlotte to the head of the table. "Gentlemen, this is my cousin, Miss Charlotte Ashford. I promise you will all have the time to greet her properly after dinner. Now please, enjoy your soup."

The men nodded as Charlotte's eyes surveyed the admiring faces staring back at her.

Once she was seated, the rumble of conversation commenced, and the dinner continued to be served.

Charlotte was seated across from two men who were brothers, Mr. Thomas Kingsley and Mr. Ellison Kingsley. Both gentlemen were in their late fifties and claimed to be good friends of Nathanial's father when he was alive.

"We are practically like family," Mr. Thomas Kingsley said.

"Indeed," Mr. Peter Kingsley confirmed.

They were regular guests at *Lottington Manor* since they lived on the connecting properties to the Hammond Estate. Both were widowers who spent their days roaming the countryside, sporting, and visiting people along the way, filling their idle time. They bumped into Nathanial at the train station, where he invited them for dinner.

Sitting to the right of Mr. Thomas Kingsley was a much younger man, Mr. Henry. While the two older gentlemen carried on with a multitude of topics, Mr. Henry sat silent, seemingly with little fortitude to add to the conversation.

With some prodding, Charlotte learned he was also a neighbor, married, and his wife was expecting their first child at the end of the summer. Other than answering a few more questions, Charlotte did not know more about him than when she first entered the room.

The final guest, Mr. Tatum, was a business partner of Nathanial. He was the most distinguished of the guests. His clothes revealed a man of impeccable taste: a black, diagonal wool twill tailcoat with satin faced lapels, a black silk vest, and a starched white shirt with mother-of-pearl shirt links and cufflinks to match. Freshly shaven, and his hair neatly combed to the back, his baby blue eyes were on display underneath curled lashes, a manicured brow, and an impeccable complexion. He was beautiful among the gruff, elderly men, and far out dressed anyone at the table. His chin stood firm against a squared jawline, and his lips, although very full, remained flat across his face throughout dinner. A little haughty for Charlotte's preferences, she had no concern about Mr. Tatum, for he showed little interest in her. She did not lack for companionship, despite his aloofness. The two Mr. Kingsleys were immensely engrossed in her journey back to England and engaged her with many questions to fill the evening with conversation.

Charlotte appreciated their attentiveness, but was relieved when dinner ended and desserts served, Lydia excused them both and whisked her to the salon, finally giving her a break from the very affable, but conversational brothers.

Lydia said very little at first to Charlotte, her hostess duties throughout dinner apparently having consumed her energy. She invited Charlotte to sit but didn't do the same. Instead, she meandered the room, lifting a book and reading the title on the spine, straightening a figurine on the mantle turned askew, smelling a yellow rose from a vase filled with a dozen more adorning a side table by the sofa, before she opened the glass-windowed doors, allowing the evening breeze to penetrate the drawing room. She closed her eyes and inhaled the fresh air, letting it out with an exhaustive sigh.

"Is something the matter?" Charlotte asked, following her cousin's slow, aimless movements.

"Besides being exhausted?" She smirked. "I am relieved to have you here, safe in my protection. A great weight is lifted."

"I did not intend to distress you. Had I known you were entertaining a room full of hungry and boisterous men, I would have hurried. I apologize, again, for my delay."

Lydia flipped her hand in the air. "There is nothing unexpected around here, Charlotte. I have it all managed, despite my husband's spontaneity."

"Do you entertain many nights?"

"Yes. But now that you are here, Nathanial will have little reason to bring home the strays of society to keep him preoccupied."

Charlotte raised her brow.

She explained, "He likes the company."

"Now that I am here, let me help you. I said it before. There is nothing I will not do for you. Even if it is to endure the Kingsley brothers..."

They both laughed.

"But in all fairness, Lydia, I do not intend on overstaying my welcome. Not a day more."

"And where do you plan to go?" Lydia questioned. "We both know you have little means to support yourself. Your safety and security are of the utmost importance." She reached for Charlotte. "What I have is yours––everything. My home, my life, is for you to share with me. We are not our fathers; we don't abandon each other. Do you not understand my intentions? I don't want you to just stay here, but to live here."

Charlotte shook her head. "It is too much, Lydia. Too much to expect from anyone."

"But I am not just anyone, am I?"

"And Nathanial? He certainly does not wish to have another woman in his home."

"I promise, Nathanial will only be too happy that you have come into our lives. You see, Charlotte, you believe you need us. But it is we who need you. So, before you make plans to flee, promise me you will stay. Or at least, for as long as you can stand it."

Charlotte looked around the room at the luxuries surrounding them. "You hardly need anything. What could I possibly give you?"

Lydia turned towards the door, hearing voices coming down the corridor. "Ah, but here come the men."

As sure as she predicted, the doors opened, and the men entered. The smell of tobacco preceding them.

Mr. Ellison Kingsley, who was a taller, thinner version of his brother, moved his eyes to the chair besides Charlotte. "May I have the honor?"

"Please," Charlotte insisted.

"How extraordinary for you to reconnect with your cousin." He glanced at Lydia across the room and looked back at Charlotte. After a second glance, he declared, "You two are extraordinarily alike. You could be sisters," he added.

"Yes, so it seems," Charlotte admitted. "If there is anyone in the world that I would be proud to call my sister, it would be Lydia. It has been far too long since we were separated."

"Yes, yes…" He cleared his throat. "Your circumstances are a terrible shame. A woman with your upbringing should not have to be so humbled."

Charlotte feigned a smile but did not reply. Her situation had obviously been a topic of discussion before her arrival. The shame of it covering her like a summer shawl. There would always be whispers behind her back. *Did her father know the shame he has brought on her?* Mr. Kingsley was not being rude, but the truth of his words still stung.

The second Mr. Kingsley called to his brother from across the room. "Eli, we are old men. Too old for such a late night. The evening must end," he announced, apologizing to the group that he had to break up the party. But before their final goodbyes, more conversation ensued as they made their way to the foyer.

It was a half an hour later, with Mr. Henry joining them, before they finally left.

"It seems like I am the last man standing," Mr. Tatum said to Charlotte walking up to her. "I apologize if I seemed inattentive this evening. The evening got away from us and I am now at a loss for your acquaintance. I hope you do not find me ill-mannered."

"Not at all, Mr. Tatum. I pleasantly preoccupied my time with the other gentlemen. I am sure we will have an opportunity in the future to get better acquainted."

"I hope we do." He bowed his head. "Now, if you will excuse me, I shall allow Mrs. Hammond a reprieve from her unexpected guests."

"I'll walk you out," Nathanial offered.

"Good man," Tatum said, and bid the two ladies a good night.

"Shall we wait up for you," Lydia called after her husband.

Nathanial looked at Charlotte, then at his wife. "No, my love. I know better. You have Charlotte now. Go to bed. I put you through enough tonight."

"Come, dear cousin, I believe we have been relieved of our duties," Lydia said, taking Charlotte's arm.

When they reached Charlotte's bedroom door, the two women hugged.

"Thank you, Lydia...you brought me home. I will be forever indebted to you."

"Oh, how I have needed you so many times," Lydia said. "And here you are, by my side, once again. Forevermore, I hope."

"Yes, always and forever," Charlotte affirmed.

SETTLING IN

A fortnight and four days had passed, and Charlotte was finally settling into the harmony of the Hammond household. Her trunks were put in storage, and a routine established, she felt as if she was finally home.

"Good morning, dear Lydia," Charlotte greeted her cousin, who was already seated in the morning room, reading a letter.

"You slept well?" Lydia asked, placing her papers aside.

"Better than the night before and before that," Charlotte exclaimed.

"It shows. Your face is beaming and your eyes are sparkling. It is good to see you so happy."

"I have no reason to feel otherwise. My heart is overjoyed, all because of you."

Lydia patted Charlotte's hand and smiled at her in mutual satisfaction.

"Are we to breakfast without your husband?" Charlotte asked, observing his empty seat at the head of the table.

"He had business to attend to early this morning. He promised his full devotion at dinner this evening."

"Oh, what a shame. But I dare say I have distracted him long enough."

Breakfasts in the morning room, walks in the afternoon, dinners promptly at eight, many times with his associate, Mr. Tatum, joining them, and leisure evenings in the salon had become common in the Hammond household since Charlotte's arrival. Nathanial was more than gracious giving of his time.

"Don't be silly, Charlotte. Nathanial would not stay if he was not persuaded. Establishing notoriety in business law demands much of Nathanial's time. When business calls, he leaves. But with you..." Her brow lifted. "You have cast a magic spell, dear Charlotte, keeping him here."

"You jest, Lydia. Nathanial seems quite devoted to his family. I am just a benefactor of the circumstance."

Lydia scoffed with a delicate snort. "There used to be a time when I was Nathanial's constant companion–during the first years of marriage. I traveled to the city with him as his adoring wife. *And I did adore it!* It was exciting and new. It was all we had imagined it would be when we were girls, daydreaming of our adult lives. But I soon discovered, the days were endless, passed with women who bored me, and nights filled with men immersed in discussions about law and politics. Oh, it was exciting to be among the who's-who in the city. There is no one I do not know because of it. There were so many parties..." she recalled. "Coming from a banking family, Nathanial is determined to set his own path with interests in law. And behind the scenes, I hosted parties and planned events to secure his future in the political arena." Lydia sighed heavily, and admitted, "It all has become burdensome."

"Does he want to be in politics?" Charlotte asked.

"Whether or not he does, it is what he is destined for," Lydia answered indisputably. "I have done my job, as expected of me. He has been securely established, and my participation is no longer essential."

"But Lydia, he still needs you by his side. You are his wife."

"Do not worry, I am still fulfilling my role as the good wife. However, I am no longer needed in London as I once was. As I once wanted to be. After Peter was born, my role had to change. We settled at *Lottington Manor* permanently, where the air is filled with floral bouquets, the scenery is lush with greenery, and now with your arrival, the company is more satisfying." Lydia temporarily looked away, distracted by a bird landing on a branch of the tree outside the window. When it flew away, she continued, her voice lower; colder. "Nathanial accepts the way things are. As you are a witness, my role as the dutiful wife has not ceased, it is now just on different terms."

"I suppose it is what our mothers endured, what is expected of women."

"Love, honor, and duty, they call it." Lydia reached for Charlotte's hand. "And why I need you *here*. They had each other as we have each other."

"Certainly," Charlotte assured.

"Oh my!" Lydia's voice jumped an octave. "I forgot to inform you of our plans this afternoon. We have been asked to attend a gathering at *Penrose*, hosted by Lady Martha Knightly. She heard of your arrival and insisted on meeting you before the others send their invitations. It seems everyone wants to meet my beautiful cousin," she sniggered, crinkling her aristocratic nose. "And they shall, soon enough. But not before Lady Knightly. She will be the first to meet you."

"She sounds rather important."

"Her husband was prominent in politics. They lived in various countries through the years solving world problems. Good for them, really. Someone has to care. Their last adventure was living in China before they moved back to England five years ago. Sadly, Sir Knightly passed away not long after. Very tragic, for she was rather fond of him. They married quite young, almost fifty years, and she proclaims they had many years of happiness. Imagine!" Lydia shook her head. "She is full of stories of foreign lands and foreign adventures. Since her return, she has become quite the hostess and entertainer. I can only assume it is to keep her preoccupied in that empty house of hers. You remember *Penrose* as a child, don't you? A most exquisite estate...there's nothing like it."

"Did they have any children?" Charlotte inquired.

"Two children. Their first child was a girl. Laurel was her name. She died at an early age. They then had a son many, many years later. Unable to have more children after Laurel's death, she sought an Indian woman known to make women fertile. She was given some odd potion. It obviously worked, for she gave birth at nearly forty!"

Charlotte's eyes widened. "No! I cannot imagine..."

"It was all the talk in the day. His name is Andrew. In fact, he and Nathanial schooled together," Lydia disclosed.

"Andrew Knightly. I have no recollection of him. But I remember *Penrose*. Mother took me there as a child to view the gardens. Did we not picnic there on one occasion?"

"Yes, I believe so," Lydia recalled.

"I never imagined knowing someone who lives there. How exciting to be visiting as a guest."

"You are the guest of honor, Charlotte. Make no mistake, Lady Knightly is evaluating you."

"For what?"

"Her son, of course," Lydia declared.

"Is he not married?"

"That is the injustice of it all. Lady Knightly has coupled many single men and women over the years, but she has yet to find a match for her son."

"I am sure there is a good reason if he is not lacking looks or charm."

"No. He embodies the quintessential man. You will meet him today. He is quite entertaining, to say the least. A most charming man in his own right."

"It all sounds exciting."

"What is all the excitement about?" A male voice came from the corridor.

With great surprise to them both, it was Nathanial who interrupted their chatter.

"Are you two still having breakfast?" He pulled out his watch to confirm the hour for which he was referring. "It is half-past eleven," he declared.

"We were merely catching up. It is like old times," Lydia replied, her voice cheery and light. "We can chat for hours if we must."

Nathanial laughed. "You realize you are now bound together for as long as Charlotte grants us her company, if not before a young man steals her away?"

"That, I will not allow. At least not so soon. I have barely had her in my grasp. For you to suggest such a thing is only torment," Lydia pouted.

"We cannot contain this young woman forever, dear wife." He glanced at Charlotte. "Like you, her beauty and charm are too great to go unnoticed."

Charlotte didn't miss the statement was for her benefit as well. She looked down, hoping to conceal the undeniable rush of color in her cheeks.

"Well, I will have to try my hardest to hide my treasure," Lydia said sternly, swiftly taking Charlotte's hand in her possession.

"And how will that be possible without locking her away?" Nathanial questioned.

"One is not so easily stolen away if one's heart is preoccupied," Lydia schemed. "I will make sure she has no room for another."

He laughed at his wife's protectiveness. "I am a firm believer in your abilities, my dear," he stated. "Do you not have my utter devotion?"

Lydia lifted her chin and scoffed, "You charm no one with your insincerity. Now, if you will excuse me, I promised our son I would read to him before his nap." Lydia rose from her chair, bestowed a kiss on Charlotte's cheek, and walked past her husband with little more than a glance his way.

"I seemed to have ruffled a feather with my wife," Nathanial noted with a laugh.

Charlotte eyed the door from which Lydia left. "In all fairness, you were making fun at Lydia's expense."

"Fair enough," Nathanial conceded. "I will apologize to her at my earliest convenience. As I do so now, with you. I disrupted your lovely morning. Please forgive my intrusion."

"But of course, you did nothing of the sort," Charlotte offered, countering Lydia's rebuff. "Lydia implied we were not to see you until dinner this evening. Did your business conclude earlier than expected?"

"I needed to tend to some pertinent papers. The rest can wait."

"I hope you do not neglect your work for me. Lydia explained to me how generous you have been with your time."

"Neglecting you would be the greater evil," he offered. "Lydia has been a transformed woman since she got word of your return. You are of the utmost importance. I would be remiss if I did not give you equal concern."

"Nathanial, I am family, not the queen," Charlotte stated. "I am already humbled you are allowing me into your lives. I have told Lydia, and I say to you, please do not make a fuss over my presence."

"If I am, then so be it. I have never seen Lydia as happy as when she is with you. It was as if you took her joy with you when you left. Now it is returned, and you have given us something this house has been missing. You, Charlotte, are our savior."

"You give me too much credit," Charlotte said.

"I wish that were the case. But no. Long before your arrival, Lydia had become...well, I saw a light dim from her eyes. I fear I overplayed my hand, maybe. Life as an aspiring politician can be over-whelming. It seems no one is ever alone in London. Too many obligations. And with the loss of her parents, it all became too much. I thought a permanent move to *Lottington Manor* with our son, away from the crowds and social demands, would bring her back, ignite the woman she loved being."

"And did it?"

"Not right away." He paused, remembering. "Peter

was so small and demanding of her. But with news of your return, she changed for the better. The spark she once had was ignited, and a happiness returned to her spirit. You can see it all over the house–the prepped gardens, the new decor, the filled flower arrangements. Happiness exudes at *Lottington Manor,* now. So, you see, Charlotte, you are our spark."

He looked at Charlotte, and for a moment their eyes held–an opening of his inner soul for her to see. There was sadness. She wanted to reach out and touch his face and tell him everything would be alright. From what, she had no clue.

He cleared his throat. "I should not have been so forward. Please forgive me."

Charlotte touched his arm. "No. Do not apologize. I can see how much you care for her."

"Yes." He pulled away. "Well, my true purpose of intruding upon your morning is to discuss some business."

"Business. With me?"

"Yes. About your father's affairs. With your approval, I was hoping to contact his lawyer and investigate the matter."

"Do you really believe it could all be a misunderstanding?"

"I realize it is not my place to interfere, but I was uncomfortable with the outcome. I would like to make my own conclusions, if you would allow me."

"I have complete faith in Mr. Commons. He was undeniably loyal to my father. But he was only employed after the partnership was formed. There was much business conducted before he could know about the deal with Mr. Milford."

Charlotte recalled his deplorable offer.

Nathanial saw her face go white and her eyes dull. "Charlotte, is there something you are not telling me?"

"No. There is nothing more," she lied. She had never admitted to anyone what had happened in Mr. Milford's office. She was too ashamed. When she was told Lydia was sending for her, there seemed little reason to worry her about something that was never to happen. "I know my father would not have intentionally been so careless of his business. Maybe he thought he had time to change it...when the business was more profitable. But time ran out for him, and for me."

"I do not want to cause you false hope. My intention is to clarify the situation. Mr. Commons filled me in on the case as it was going to the courts. At the time, I saw no need to intercede for he seemed a capable man and he thought nothing would come of it. But with the outcome so unjust, I was hoping to get your permission to research further into the matter. Just in case something was overlooked."

"You realize I have no means to compensate you for your time."

"Dear Charlotte, I do this of my own volition. Let me look out for you."

"I would be forever grateful, but I see little hope."

"I cannot promise anything will come of it, but I would like to try," he appealed.

"Thank you, Nathanial. I trust you will do what is best."

"Good morning, Sir," Ada greeted, as she entered the room, before addressing Charlotte. "Mrs. Hammond would like to remind you of your afternoon obligations."

"Are you going somewhere?" Nathanial asked.

"Yes. We were invited to Lady Knightly's this afternoon," Charlotte replied, placing her napkin on the table, and rising.

"Ah yes, the Knightlys. Please, do not let me keep you from such an important invitation." Nathanial stepped aside, giving Charlotte permission to leave him.

"Then, I am to assume you will not be joining us?"

"It is yet another gathering of people I merely tolerate," he admitted with a sigh. "I am sure Lydia has many plans for you. But as I can see, the brightness in your eye and the color in your cheeks, you are eager to attend. Do not let my intolerance take away from your joy. Have a good time. It is good for you to meet new people."

Charlotte bowed, passing him to the door, but he stopped her with a touch of her arm.

"Enjoy your afternoon. I am afraid Lydia might be putting locks on your door as we speak, and you may never get a chance to meet another human being again."

Charlotte tried to conceal a laugh, but Nathanial only joined her.

"She does not deserve my betrayal."

He leaned in. "Well, it will be our little secret."

"Yes, I agree," Charlotte confirmed, composing herself and releasing her smile. "Nathanial, you say I am your savior, but it is I who was saved. You realize there is nothing I would not do for her, even if it meant being locked away. I cherish her that much."

He bowed in acknowledgement and allowed her to finally retreat.

THE PEACOCK

*L*ady Martha Knightly's afternoon gathering of friends was, in part, for the simple pleasure of entertaining. A task in which she was highly skilled, and found pleasure in. After all, *Penrose* was the idyllic country estate. It had history, gardens, art...all the quintessential elements of wealth she wanted to pass to heirs. Unfortunately, her only son was far from the task. Everyone knew if they were invited to her home, it was for the main purpose of presenting new prospects for marriage to her son. When she learned of Charlotte Ashford's arrival, she promptly sent invitations. She wanted to be the first to welcome Charlotte and give her son the first opportunity to make an impression before others had the chance.

Her son, Andrew Knightly, was well past the youthful stage of bachelorhood. His mother had indulged his desires to travel and *find himself* for too long. After roaming the world from Africa to America, he finally returned to England. Three years had passed, and much to his mother's dismay, he still had not settled on a wife. She was determined to not let another summer go by without at least an attempt at finding someone who would break through her son's disinterest. After much discussion with Lydia Hammond, a family connected to notability and prestige, she was excited to meet Charlotte.

When they arrived, Lydia and Charlotte were but two of the twenty guests who loitered about the estate, talking, and enjoying the sumptuous assortment of sweets set out for them to indulge. Some people stayed in the parlor, while a more spirited group found their way outdoors to partake in a game of croquet and to purvey the beautiful grounds.

Lady Knightly caught sight of the two and did not hesitate to stop her conversation with the small group surrounding her, eager to greet them. "It is a pleasure to finally meet you, Miss Ashford." She studied Charlotte. "Mrs. Hammond has spoken about you often. I feel as if I am already well acquainted."

"I am honored to be invited to your home," Charlotte replied, surprised by Lady Knightly's age. Noted for her wealth, education, and social standing, Charlotte expected a much older woman. Although a plump woman, her fair complexion showed few signs of her sixty-nine years, except a spattering of lines at the corner of her eyes and lips. Her hair smartly pulled to the top of her head, she wore a fashionable dress of silk shantung, and a layer of pearls decorated her neck. The pièce de résistance was a five-carat diamond adorning her ring finger, which Charlotte found mesmerizing. When Lady Knightly caught her staring at it, she offered, "It is lovely."

"Thank you, my dear. I had an adoring husband. Never settle for anything less." She winked. "Come, come, and meet my friends," she insisted, intertwining her arms with Charlotte's, and then proceeded to escort her to a gathering of women on the terrace.

All eyes fell upon her.

"Now tell me, my dear, are you finding life back in England pleasurable?"

"Yes, very much so. Lydia has made settling here extremely comfortable." Charlotte smiled at her cousin. "One can only be so lucky."

"How wonderful. Will you stay long?" Lady Knightly pried. "*Lottington Manor* is a lovely estate, and there is plenty of room for someone like yourself to find permanent residency."

Lydia interceded, gently squeezing Charlotte's hand. "I would have it no other way. Charlotte may stay as long as she desires. Our family is hers. I could not imagine her being anywhere else."

"Well, of course not. That is until someone captures her heart. I cannot imagine such a beautiful creature as she would go unnoticed too long," Lady Knightly said, never known for subtlety. "She will have many suitors calling upon your doorstep sooner than you expect."

"You and my husband are of the same mind. I intend to hold on to my dear cousin for as long as possible. We need time to reestablish our sister-like kinship, and I intend to hold on to her for as long as possible."

"You should not worry. I am confident we can keep you two in close proximity," Lady Knightly offered, before extolling the virtues of her son and his many accomplishments.

Charlotte listened, feigning interest, for she could never imagine herself as the mistress of *Penrose*. Surely, she would be last on the list of eligible women considered worthy of such a credentialed son. With the loss of her father's inheritance, she was merely a commoner to the Knightly wealth.

"Oh, here is my son now," Lady Knightly said, seeing him walk across the room. "Late as usual."

Charlotte followed Lady Knightly's gaze and spotted a peacock among peacocks. She had never seen a man so impeccably dressed. His finely tailored suit fitted his lean physique in exquisite detail. His coat squared his broad shoulders, which he wore unbuttoned, revealing a man of wealth by the silver threaded embroidery of his waistcoat. The long narrow pants, hemmed with precision, grazed the top of his shoes; his cravat notably aligned. A tall, slender framed man, he sauntered over to the small gathering of women. He leaned forward and brushed his lips against his mother's cheek.

"It seems I am late once again, Mother. You will forgive my delay?"

She spread an insincere smile across her face. "You are here now, let us not quarrel over punctuality." She suggested. "You know the ladies." He bowed, and she continued, "I would like to present, Miss Ashford. A refreshing new face added to our little community. She is staying with the Hammonds for what seems to be an open-ended time."

"Miss Ashford." He nodded her way, extending his hand.

"It is a pleasure to meet you, Mr. Knightly." Charlotte offered her gloved hand, for which he enveloped into his before releasing it. "Your mother was just talking about you," she added.

"Do not let a mother's prejudice sway you. I deserve no praise," he remarked. "She is trying to persuade you I may be good marriage material."

"Andrew, such impudence!" Lady Knightly scolded, but was not put off, accustomed to her son's flippant manner. "I am a mother who is proud of her son. No one can blame me for singing your praise."

"And I prove my point," he quipped before granting a smile to his mother. "As much as my mother adores me, she should know better than to represent me for something other than who I am."

"Be assured, Mr. Knightly, I am of no consequence to impress upon."

"Ah, Miss Ashford. It seems we need to discover truths." He extended his arm for her to accept. "Please do me the honor and walk with me. I will show you the gardens. It will give me the opportunity to prove my mother's good intentions, and to demonstrate that I am not the scoundrel I purport."

Charlotte exchanged glances with Lydia, then with Lady Knightly, who nodded her approval, before accepting Mr. Knightly's invitation.

"You hesitated…" he noted, as they slipped out the door into the gardens, and away from the ears of others.

"I…" Charlotte's body flushed with heat. "I did not want to be rude to your mother."

Mr. Knightly laughed. "My mother would have thrown you in my arms if she thought it proper."

"Mr. Knightly…" Charlotte's lids lowered, but she couldn't prevent her lips from curling upward.

Mr. Knightly caught her hidden smile. "You are very beautiful," he blurted, unflinching.

Charlotte eyed his audacity, wondering what he wanted. She saw nothing.

"You are being kind…"

"I was not being kind. Just observant," he clarified.

"You are quite direct," Charlotte declared.

"As are you," he countered.

Charlotte couldn't disagree, nor did she try.

She had heard about men like him–*arrogant*. She now damned herself for agreeing to join him. She searched for Lydia–anyone wondering about the gardens–praying for a rescue, but to no avail. Two gentlemen suddenly rounded the trees and walked across the lawn in their direction. She thanked the heavens in silent prayer and anticipated her escape, but Mr. Knightly did not allow her the opportunity. As the men approached, he kept her hand tightly under his arm, ensuring her company.

"Aw, gentlemen, may I introduce Miss Ashford, a guest of the Hammonds, cousin to Mrs. Hammond."

The two men tipped their hats, eyed Charlotte from head to toe, and proceeded their address to Mr. Knightly, affording little attention to her. It was obvious they purposefully sought Mr. Knightly's company to discuss pending business. With their purpose resolved, they once again eyed Charlotte from head to toe, this time offering her a smile, tipped their hats, and retreated.

"I apologize for my acquaintances. They are more concerned with their pocketbooks than interest in a beautiful young lady," he said.

"I was by no means insulted. They were of little interest to me as I was with them."

"Ha!" Mr. Knightly bellowed at Charlotte's wit. "My mother may have found my match."

Charlotte blushed with the indication but did not rush to defend or confirm. Instead, she stood silent, curious about the man who stood before her. He was blunt, on the verge of rudeness, and charming all the same. She had met no one so unaffected by those around him, and yet, very important to them.

She was intrigued.

"Shall we continue?" Mr. Knightly indicated to a walking path ahead. "You have had quite an introduction to my mother. I beg you to forgive her."

Charlotte crunched her brow at him. "Forgive her for what?"

"Her eagerness to find me a suitable partner," he said matter-of-fact. "She has not scared you away?"

"She is your mother. Mothers always have their children's best interests at heart. Especially unmarried ones. In truth, I found her quite entertaining."

"I do believe that is the nicest compliment anyone has ever said about my mother. And if I must confess, I adore her myself."

"You are blessed to have a parent still alive who cares for you so much."

His eyes softened. "Ah yes, I suppose I am grateful for having someone to watch over me." He pressed Charlotte's arm, "I heard about the recent loss of your father. I am sorry."

Charlotte cocked her head. "I am at a disadvantage, Mr. Knightly. You know about me, but I know so little about you..."

"It is a small community. My mother is well connected," he confessed. "We learned all about you before your arrival."

Charlotte clenched her teeth, feeling vulnerable and naked.

As if he read her mind, he continued, "I have spent some time in America, and I can assure you, gossip is also a common pastime as it is here, in England." He poked at her naivety. "You cannot be surprised you have been the topic of conversation for months?"

"You can assure them there is little about me to keep their rumor mills running," Charlotte snipped.

"Ah, how little you understand idle lives. You are an Ashford, after all. Your family's reputation precedes you. When your family did not return, it was assumed you had married a prominent American and lived in new-world wealth. Returning, unmarried...well, you were assured to have grown unattractive and dull," he shared, with a glint of devilishness in his eyes. "And, of course, there was the talk about your father leaving you penniless."

Charlotte huffed. "Do they have nothing more to talk about?" She pulled away from him and strode ahead, unable to tamper her anger. She suddenly turned. "Mr. Knightly, you may be a lovely man, but I find you more honest than I am accustomed to."

"Do not be offended." He hurried to catch up to her. "They cannot help themselves. Boredom, insecurities, justification for their own lives...it is only human."

Charlotte crossed her arms. She would have stomped her feet if she was not under observation by strangers who had now congregated outside, joining them in the gardens.

"I have upset you?" Mr. Knightly's voice softened. "I warned you. I am not as well behaved as my mother promotes." He bowed before her. "May I beg your forgiveness?"

"Please do not make a fool of yourself," she insisted, signaling him to straighten. "People are looking."

Mr. Knightly took Charlotte's hand, leading her away from prying eyes, through a thicket of trees, and to a distant pond. He offered her to sit on a near-by bench.

Grateful for the privacy, she sat and glanced at the surrounding landscape. It had been a long time since her visit to *Penrose*. Not much had changed. It was still an exquisitely designed garden housing marble statues, geese-filled ponds, manicured lawns, shading trees of cedar and plantain, and colorful blooms of pink phlox and purple campanula growing wildly amongst the more planned gardens of roses, digitalis, and foxglove. "It is quite impressive," she finally said. "You are fortunate to call this home."

"Not I. My mother would be more than happy to have me live here permanently. But I stay in the city more than not."

"You dislike living here?"

"Oh, it is more than lovely to visit. But if I stayed longer than a few days, my mother would have every eligible woman through her doors in a constant parade."

"And that would not please you...to be married?"

"I am not sure it is a desire of any woman to be attached to me." He laughed, and added, "It would be quite entertaining, though."

Charlotte found him quite contradictory. Sincere, yet flippant. Adoring, yet distracted. Charming yet intimidating. The man before her was, by all accounts, extremely desirable in looks. His fair complexion and autumn-blond hair only made his dark blue eyes, cradled by curled lashes, more prominent. High cheekbones and a strong jawline were softened by full lips. *Noticeably red,* she thought. When he laughed, they parted, spreading across his face, and his eyes lit up, multiple lines gathered at the corners. Charlotte found it rather intoxicating to be so careless of expression. There was no doubt he was targeted by many single women in the countryside, if not all of England.

"Mr. Knightly, fear not. You would not be discouraged if you directed your attention towards a woman," she admitted. "It would make your mother extremely happy."

"Hmmm, are you proposing interest?" he teased.

Charlotte blushed.

"I am going to like you, Miss Ashford. From the moment I saw you. I knew we were destined to be friends."

"But we have only met," she questioned. "How could you possibly know?"

"Ah, yes, we have just been introduced. But Mrs. Hammond spoke of you often, and something told me you were special. Now I can see why she was so eager."

"You flatter me, Mr. Knightly. Another charming skill women will find noteworthy."

"I have the feeling my mother has your ear."

"She seemed eager to sing your praises…"

"I believe we are victims of conspiracy. Shall we hide for a little longer to give her something to hope for?"

"You truly are mischievous," Charlotte declared.

"Oh, my dear, you do not know the truth you speak," he smirked.

"Should I be afraid of you?"

"Are you?"

"Surprisingly, no. Why should that be so when we have only just met?" she questioned.

"You have nothing to fear from me." He stood and looked around him. "Stay close to me. I promise to protect you."

His words were not sinister, but she felt it was a warning.

Mr. Knightly offered his arm once more. "Shall we return to mother?"

This time Charlotte took it without reservation, aware of the eyes on them as they walked across the lawns, headed back to the house.

When Lady Knightly saw Charlotte, still on the arm of her son, a broad smile crossed her face. She met her son's stare and nodded.

"You have made my mother happy," he whispered in Charlotte's ear. "For that, you will be rewarded."

He deposited Charlotte to Lydia's side, bid his farewell, and headed for the sideboard where whiskey was on display.

"It seems you have been busy entertaining Mr. Knightly," Lydia noted.

"It was I who was entertained. Mr. Knightly is more than he presents."

Lydia smirked, all too aware of Mr. Knightly's reputation–frequenting the whore houses, and gambling in back rooms. "He is quite more, yet at the same time, it is evident he is everything he presents."

"And what is that?"

Lydia hesitated to answer, unsure if Charlotte was ready for the rumors. Her innocence would be no match for a man with overindulgent tendencies. "He is still a man with little interest in responsibility. His bachelorhood is an accepted status in town. If there was no one who has captured his attention thus far, no one will on the horizon. I fear Lady Knightly will have to wait many years to depart this world if she wants to see her dear son married."

Charlotte scanned the room for Mr. Knightly, now more curious of the man she encountered. She spotted him among a group of young women. They were laughing, enjoying his company. She marveled about how long it would be before he committed to marriage, and with whom he would finally give his heart.

LAWS OF ATTRACTION

The weather turned. Possibly God was punishing the unjust.

Downpours of water fell from the skies, drowning the outside world. There were no surprise guests arriving for dinner, and no invitations to go out. No morning walks and no afternoon rides. A grey haze had set in inviting all to go into hiding.

Charlotte spent the rain-soaked days in quiet reverie or reading a book.

Nathanial retreated to his study and was barely seen. And when he was, his brow was heavy and his lips tight, preoccupied in his own thoughts.

Charlotte could barely capture his attention when they passed in the halls.

Lydia seemed the most affected by the bad weather. Her cheerfulness had faded, a somberness set in. She spent her time on duties concerning the house, giving orders, and overseeing to its management. And when not acting as lady of the house, she was with Peter in the isolated children's quarters of the house. The only time they were all together was when they dined. Even then, there was little talk that transpired.

Charlotte began to feel the pangs of being the outsider. *Where did she fit in?* Every household needed their privacy for days like this...when the people and their moods were disrupted. It is the position she feared the most...being the intruder in their personal lives. Everyone has their *behind closed doors* secrets, concerns, and fears, their intimate lives kept hidden from the outside.

The dreary weather brought melancholy, changing the disposition of the house and the people in it. It was uncovering the vulnerability of having an outsider in the house, and the cracks in the facade were revealing the hidden secrets to the intruder.

Charlotte hoped the tension would change when the rain lifted. However, even when the rain lightened to a drizzle, and the clouds thinned in the sky, the temperament of the house remained heavy.

They had all retreated to the salon after another quiet dinner. The room was cozy and warm, with a fire roaring.

Charlotte curled into the corner of the sofa, Lydia on the opposite end. Nathanial was restless and was roaming the room when he stopped behind Charlotte.

"What are you reading?" Nathanial peered over Charlotte's shoulder.

She turned the printed pages over to reveal the spine with the name on it. "It is *Jane Eyre,* by Currer Bell. I found it among the stack of books in my room. When the rains started, I began to read," she answered.

"I placed it there," Lydia confessed. "I found it quite enjoyable and wanted to share it with you. I hoped you had not already read it."

"No. The women at Lady Knightly's party were discussing it. I am glad I picked it up," Charlotte said. "I have not read a book so intriguing. Father was very indulgent with reading. And I was not denied a library of books. But I must admit, I have read more in the pursuit of science and philosophy than most women my age. His eyesight was not good in the evenings, and it was I who read out loud to him until he was tired. I fear my mind is filled with scholarly things many would consider dull."

"I am always one for conversation, dear Charlotte. Your father's interests will equally appeal to me," Nathanial said.

Charlotte tipped her head to him, he to her in surreptitious agreement.

"Good heavens, not I," Lydia interjected with a laugh. "I should care less about how the world works around me. Give me a novel and I will bask in its escape."

"And what must you escape from, my dear Lydia?" Nathanial remarked.

"Oh darling." She ignored his bitter tone. "We all need to escape our lives, sometimes, no matter how seemingly perfect things appear. In Jane Eyre's case, her life was not seemingly perfect at first. Quite the opposite...she was an orphan girl who had nothing. She was at the mercy of others. Much like our poor Charlotte. Until she meets a handsome man with whom she falls in love. But even she must escape her happiness. But the most interesting character is Rochester. He had everything a man could desire; his life seemingly perfect."

"And what must he escape?" Nathanial questioned.

Lydia's brow lifted. "A mad wife."

Nathanial scoffed, "And how does he propose to do that?"

"He falls in love with another woman..."

"It sounds rather sad for all involved," Charlotte commented.

"Sad for whom? The husband who finds a lover, Jane who finds love. Or the wife who falls into madness. I consider her the biggest winner of them all. She escapes forever..." Lydia mocked.

Nathanial and Lydia locked glances.

Nathanial broke his wife's stare, placing his glass on the table and turned to Charlotte. "I hope we did not spoil the story for you. I will let you get back to your book."

He left, with little more said.

If Charlotte did not know better, the subtle smile across Lydia's face told her everything. Lydia was pleased with herself.

~

SATURDAY BROUGHT with it clear blue skies and crisp air. Charlotte awoke to a pair of doves cooing outside her windows, signally the rain was gone. She jumped out of bed and pushed the windows open. She breathed in and exhaled, letting go of the gloom the rain had caused.

She called for Ada straightaway.

As if magic had been sprinkled over the rooftop, the mood among the servants was equally light.

Charlotte heard whistling coming from the stables and humming in the halls.

Curtains were pulled back, windows were opened, and petrichor permeated the air.

Still chilly and wet, she pulled her shawl tighter around her dress as she entered the breakfast room. Both Nathanial and Lydia were already at the table, Nathanial was reading papers and Lydia sipping her tea. They both greeted her in unison.

Charlotte walked around the table and gave Lydia a kiss, noting a smile upon her face. She looked well-rested, with rosy cheeks and a brightness in her eyes. She sported a cheery yellow dress, when against her golden hair, made her look like a celestial being. Her essence emanating into the room.

"You look bright and lovely," Charlotte offered.

"Thank you, darling. Nathanial was kind enough to offer the same…"

Charlotte raised a brow at Nathanial, but he didn't

look up, keeping his eyes focused on the papers in front of him.

Charlotte sensed the mood had shifted from yesterday, the tension eased.

Neither of them showed any signs of bitterness between them. All seemed *back to normal*. Charlotte blamed the dreadful weather as the cause of disharmony and was grateful the melancholy had finally lifted.

"How did you sleep last night, Charlotte?" Lydia asked.

"Very well," Charlotte lied. She didn't dare mention she stayed up late to finish the book.

"It is a beautiful morning. I had no choice but to rise early. That, and Peter sneaking into my room and climbing into bed with me." Lydia smiled. "What a nice way to begin the day."

Charlotte agreed.

"Nathanial," Lydia called for her husband's attention. "Can you not entice Charlotte for a walk? It is a rare day, and we should be indulgent to her after being cooped up."

"That sounds like a lovely idea," Charlotte said before tasting the first drops of her Ceylon tea. She purred with the delight of the flavor. "Nothing like a hot cup of tea on a fresh morning."

Lydia smiled. "You are like a child, Charlotte. Always noting the smallest of pleasures." She turned to her husband once more. "Can you not see her excitement, Nathanial? You cannot refuse to walk with her today. You can show her your favorite spot under the canopied trees."

Nathanial put his papers down and looked at his wife, mulling over her request. "It would be my delight, my dear," he agreed. "When would you like to walk?"

"Unfortunately, I am not available to join you," Lydia informed him.

Charlotte put down her teacup. "Do not be silly, Lydia. We can reschedule for another time. Besides, I am perfectly capable of walking by myself. I do not need a chaperone. I am twenty-four years old! I would not dream of taking Nathanial away from his obligations. It appears he is already deep in work."

"You have been shut up for days, as Nathanial has. He is in need of a distraction," Lydia explained. "Fresh air will clear his head and do him some good."

"My work can wait," Nathanial confirmed.

"But Lydia, you must join us," Charlotte insisted.

Lydia's hand went up. "No, do not entice me. I promised Mrs. Sotherby I would visit. I have already put her off because of the rain."

"Then, allow me to come with you..." Charlotte placed her napkin on the table and rose from her chair.

"No, Charlotte." Lydia placed her hand on her, inviting her to sit back down. "Mrs. Sotherby is a dreadfully dull neighbor, and a lonely one. I could not forgive myself if I subjected you to her woeful disposition. I prefer you to enjoy the afternoon. Finish your breakfast while I have the kitchen staff pack refreshments for a picnic." She kissed Charlotte on the cheek and excused herself.

It was within the hour, a basket in Charlotte's arms and a blanket in Nathanial's, the two were walking on a flattened path which meandered through tall grasses. Ignoring the dampness lining the bottom of her dress, and mud coating her hems, she kept pace with Nathanial, walking beside him.

"You are quiet this morning," she noted.

"If I appear rude, please excuse me."

"I did not take your behavior as such," she replied. "But…"

He stopped and looked at her with curiosity.

Charlotte hesitated. "We have never been alone together…without Lydia as our buffer."

"Do I make you uncomfortable?" Nathanial questioned.

"No…" Charlotte insisted. "Quite the contrary. I thank you for that." She smiled at him.

He did not reciprocate.

She cleared her throat afraid she was too candid. "What I am trying to say…I suppose that is why Lydia pushed us together this afternoon. She and I have a history. It is natural for us to be with one another. But as I have happened upon you, it will take us a little time to become natural with one another."

"My wife is very clever," he said.

"Yes…" Charlotte agreed, questioning if his comment was out of respect for Lydia, or scorn.

They continued to walk in silence, Nathanial taking the lead, Charlotte following. He guided her through a pillar of trees, along a narrow path, and up a small incline, and back down again, mulching leaves and sticks crackling with every step.

Charlotte looked overhead and saw nothing but leaves and limbs crowding around them. Had she been alone, she would have turned around long before invading the dense forest.

Nathanial pushed through the low-lying branches until an opening appeared into a den of moss and fallen limbs. Sunlight filtered through the treetops, allowing enough light and warmth to fill the space. Birds called to one another through the branches, and the trickling of water could be heard coming from a nearby stream.

"Here," Nathanial said as they came upon the clearing. "This is where we will picnic."

"It is perfect," Charlotte exclaimed, laying out the blanket and setting out their food.

Nathanial joined her on the blanket, laying out his long body opposite her.

"I did not realize all this existed outside my windows." She observed the dense and varied foliage. She closed her eyes and breathed in, filling her nose with the smells of nature—mulching leaves, decaying wood, and wet soil. "It's beautiful. A hidden gem."

"I think so. I came here often as a boy."

"And now?"

"Not so much... Peter is still too young, and Lydia

will not come out this way. She deplores the dampness." He added, "And the bugs."

"I do not blame her. Traipsing through the wild is not what most women consider pleasurable, by any means." She looked at the hems of her skirt. "Nor does it fare well for a woman's attire."

"But yet you are here."

"You must thank my father. He had an interest in entomology. I read to him quite often on the subject. And when he had time, we would explore the outdoors and all it had to offer. A little mud never stopped my curiosity." She lifted a thick piece of a tree branch laid on top a pile of leaves. "Look—worms, eating away at the rot and decay. Not a glorious life, but they restore the soil." Charlotte rose and walked over to a lime green creature with lacy wings sitting on a leaf. She pointed. "Isn't it fascinating? It's as green as the leaf it sits upon. How wonderful if humans could do the same; disappear into anonymity?" She bent down and touched it, causing the insect to jump away. She turned to Nathanial, who was watching her. "Shall we explore together?"

Nathanial set aside his plate and followed Charlotte as she searched and studied the area.

Charlotte came upon a tree with a large hole at its base. She bent over and looked inside. "This is the place fairies live..."

Nathanial walked up behind her and peered in. "Or a nice home for an animal at night."

"Are you always so logical?" she teased.

"Not always..." he defended.

A winged creature fluttered by, and Charlotte followed it until it landed. With precision, she cupped it in her hands, and brought it back to Nathanial, slowly parting her palms. "Isn't it lovely? Have you ever seen the color of orange so vivid?" She released the trapped specimen and continued to forage.

Stopping again., at a fallen tree trunk, Charlotte grabbed a stick and poked at a dark beetle uncovered from a pile of leaves.

Nathanial grumbled with disgust.

"Beetles are a curious insect. We humans have only flesh as our protective shell. Not very helpful in defending against harm. But beetles have a lovely hard shell, and its ugliness keeps it safe from predators."

"Aww, but its ugliness can scare away its supporter...namely a mate."

"Even an ugly beetle must reproduce."

"I fear our neighbors, the Hendersons, may find that argument hard to explain to prospects for their younger daughters."

A slow smile stretched across Charlotte's face. "You really can be a beast! Their daughters are certainly not *ugly?*"

"They are...beetles in the forest," Nathanial inserted. "Their beauty does not proceed them. It will be an appreciation of what they have to offer–which is to say they are well positioned–if they are to find a *supporter.*"

Charlotte pursed her lips. "I suppose everyone

finds someone with whom they are meant to be with." She arched her brow. "Even the Henderson girls."

"Well played, my dear Charlotte!" He grinned. "I will not deny, I prefer the beauty of the butterfly over the brawn of the beetle. It seems the beetle has much to defy to find its reputation among so much beauty."

"There is good and bad to achieve harmony, Nathanial. Do not mistake the balance of nature. The spiders eat insects. The worms till the soil. The beetles help in the decay. The butterfly carries pollen to plants. They are fulfilling roles, surviving, reproducing, and carrying on a legacy. All these creatures exist, come together, for something bigger beyond themselves. Each has a meaning and a purpose. Sometimes, something that may seem objectionable is not so horrible when you come to understand the beautiful purpose it serves."

Nathanial cupped his chin. "You may be as curious a creature as any of these specimens."

"Do you find me objectionable?"

"That is not what I said." He paused. "I am, in all sincerity, admiring your ability to appreciate the benefits rather than the harm. Seeing the natural balance is a beautiful gift."

"Hmm," she uttered. "Shall I take that as an apology, then?"

"If not, then a compliment at its finest. The more I know you, the more interesting you become. I merely wanted to express what a rare woman you are."

For a moment, Nathanial's eyes locked with hers.

Uncontrollably and unwittingly, she fell once again into the depths of his eyes, pulling her to him. She stopped herself, and looked away, breaking their connection. This time there was no excusing it. They were not innocent or young, nor unfamiliar. They understood their roles. He was Lydia's husband; she, her cousin.

Even if she wished it so, Charlotte couldn't stop the rash of heat to her cheeks.

He cleared his throat. "I have embarrassed you... and myself."

"No," Charlotte squeaked before turning away.

"Charlotte," Nathanial's voice breathed. "I should not have allowed...I lost myself for a moment."

She mustered her courage to face him. "We should gather our things. I am sure Lydia will scold us for being gone so long."

Nathanial agreed, saying nothing more. He followed Charlotte back to their picnic and helped pack their belongings.

"Shall we go?" he said, tucking the blanket under his arm.

Charlotte nodded and followed behind Nathanial as he led the way out of the trees.

They returned on the path from which they came, this time Nathanial slowed to keep pace beside her.

Neither spoke. There seemed to be little more to say. Charlotte deemed the silence as penance for discovering each other more compatible than they should be.

MORNING REFLECTIONS

*N*athanial rolled over in his bed and moaned. He rubbed his face, trying to wash away the many whiskeys he and the Kingsley brothers consumed the night before. If it wasn't for his manservant, Hollister, he would not be in his own house, or in his own bed. He cursed his neighbors' generosity. Eating well and getting drunk was a pastime of theirs, having no women to be accountable to.

He reached across his pillow, feeling for his wife. She wasn't there. She hadn't been beside him in months.

Forever, it felt.

"Damn!" he cursed out loud. But no one was there to hear it.

He sat up. The air was thick and cold. He let the fire go out.

The room was grey, the morning light struggling through the haphazardly closed curtains.

Noting his pile of clothes on the floor, he realized his nakedness. He hadn't even bothered to get dressed for bed.

Then, without willing it, Charlotte came into his thoughts. The enjoyable afternoon he spent with her, talking, laughing. He had forgotten what it was like to laugh; to enjoy himself without regard. Life had become so serious. Too disconnected. *The hustle for one's legacy*, he liked to call it. Hence his indulgence with his neighbors. The whiskey. For the times when he needed to escape.

*We all need to escape our lives...*Lydia's words flashed across his mind.

He had the urge to run away last night after his walk with Charlotte.

Damn! He thought, again. And cursed himself over. Not for the hangover pounding in his head. That he could solve. Avoiding the Kingsley brothers was the easy task.

Avoiding Charlotte was not.

SHAME

*C*harlotte couldn't face the new day.
She just couldn't!

Sleep eluded her, tossing and turning through the night. Her heart pitter-pattered against her chest, a thrust of warmth washed through her body from the inside out, and her toes curled as Nathanial penetrated her thoughts–the way his top lip created a Cupid's bow, how his hair curled away from his widow's peak, or how his brows were thick and straight against his dark brown eyes.

Was it possible to fall in love unwittingly?

There was no justification for the awakening of emotions for Nathanial. A touch? A glance? They were elements perpetuated by girlish naïveté and fantasy about love. She was well beyond her years to fall for such triviality. An attraction to a man, especially to one who was particularly unavailable, was unbearably humiliating.

If a person could shrink away to nothing, Charlotte wished for it, praying Lydia never discover her secret.

Her humiliation only heightened when she realized Nathanial was avoiding her.

The prior evening, he excused himself from dinner. He sent a note saying he was held up at the Kingsley brothers. He never resurfaced, leaving Lydia and Charlotte alone for the evening. Charlotte feared the worse—he knew of her fantastical thoughts. She cringed at the prospect. When Lydia had no concerns about his absence, Charlotte eased, thinking there was no reason to second guess his motives, nor his behavior.

Until she saw him at breakfast.

Upon entering the room, Charlotte found Nathanial alone, reading his mail. A sense of relief came over her, hoping her foolish thoughts of evading her were for naught.

He glanced her way but he avoided all eye contact. Clearing his throat, he set down the letter in his hand, gathering the paper collection in front of him, pulled out from the table, and immediately dismissed himself. *Obligations,* he mumbled, before heading out the door.

She sat down beside his empty chair and found that his teacup was full, and his plate of food was half eaten. Her fears were confirmed. He was avoiding her.

Her eyes still lingered at the door where Nathanial

rushed out just as Lydia bustled into the room soon after his departure.

"Good morning, my dear," she said, placing a kiss upon Charlotte's head. "My, you look forlorn. Whatever could be wrong?"

Did Lydia see her shame? Charlotte dared not explain.

"Now, do not tell me you are ill," Lydia questioned.

"I am tired, that is all," she explained.

"Oh my, I am sorry to hear that. But you must nap and gain your well-being before our evening ahead. You will want all the vibrance you can muster." She looked to Charlotte for recognition. "The Henderson party? We discussed it the other day."

Charlotte shook her head, not recalling the event.

"Nothing to concern yourself with," Lydia said, brushing away Charlotte's absentmindedness with a flip of her wrist. "Mr. and Mrs. Henderson are welcoming home their eldest daughter, Miriam. She was married last Christmas and her husband took her away to Scotland. They have not seen her since. Now expecting a child, she has returned to spend time with her family before she cannot travel anymore. Mrs. Henderson could not be more thrilled. She is going all out for this evening. This party is not only for her eldest, but for their two younger daughters, whom they hope to marry off. As everyone knows, young women love to dance, and young men love young women. The party is sure to be a success."

"It sounds like it will be an enjoyable evening, but I am not sure I am up to such entertainment…"

"Charlotte," Lydia cut her off. "This is an opportunity for you as well…to meet new people. The possibilities abound for you! As much as Nathanial teases me about being too possessive of you, I do long for your own happiness."

Charlotte understood exactly what Lydia was insinuating. She was unmarried and had no prospects at present. Nor did she expect any young gentleman to clamor for her hand in the future. She was penniless. Broke. Without monetary means to attract a man of substance. A healthy dowry was a key element for marriage within the elite society from which Lydia and Charlotte came. It was the unspoken truth Lydia couldn't avoid. If marriage was to find her, she would have to *seek and conquer* prospects to overcome her shortcomings.

"Lydia," Charlotte began, "I am not unaware of my circumstances. My father meant well, but he did not prepare for my future. Courtship did not happen when it should, and I have no expectations of what the future holds."

"Nonsense! You are a beautiful woman, Charlotte, with much to offer a man. You were never meant to be a spinster. You are an Ashford!"

"No man of means would be so foolish. There are too many other women with an inheritance whom they can fall in love with. I have no aspirations to think more about what is to come of my future."

Lydia frowned. "Not you, dear Charlotte. Do not lose sight of what is possible. You deserve happiness a thousand times over. I will find someone for you to love and be loved in return. Mark my words. I always get what I want."

EUPHORIA

There were few who missed the beautiful Ashford women who arrived at the Henderson party. Together, they were a force of beauty. Lydia with her slender figure, delicate features, and crystal blues eyes, set off by her golden hair, and Charlotte, fuller figured, creamy complexion, and equally blue eyes which sparkled against her dark hair. Both their dresses were crafted by the same dress-maker, featuring exquisite details of cording and tassels on Lydia's cream, silk-taffeta dress. Charlotte's pinky-peach dress, on the other hand, displayed rows of arranged bows made from sheeny-silk ribbon along the broad bertha collar. But more heads turned, and brows lifted, at Charlotte, however. She was the freshest and newest face in the room full of familiar women.

The brightly lit hall was already crowded with

people eager to see and be seen. The walls reverberated with the whispered voices of the women and the bellowed laughter of the men. When the music struck its first note, the clusters of chattering guests drifted in unison, as if in a trance, to the main room for dancing.

Lydia eyed the crowd, picking off the people to avoid, and targeting the ones she wanted to introduce to Charlotte.

Charlotte patiently stood by Lydia's side and longingly watched the dance floor, hoping the opportunity to participate would present itself.

But the men, giving side glances her way, made no attempt with an invitation to dance. No one wanted to be the first to cross Lydia Hammond's inspection. To fail her approval was detrimental to one's social acceptability. So, they waited, hoping some arrogant fool would take the chance.

Uninterrupted by dance requests, Lydia escorted her cousin around the room, eager to introduce her into the important social circle.

Many recalled Charlotte as a young girl with fondness and complimented her on how well she had progressed into womanhood.

"Lovely," a group of women agreed.

"Quite charming, indeed," another said.

"Continuing the Ashford beauty, I see," an older gentleman commented flirtatiously.

"Aww, Merrill's daughter," another man said. "An unfortunate circumstance."

Charlotte endured the small exchanges, required to subvert rudeness, as Lydia introduced her to the people eager to meet the "penniless" cousin. It was her duty, of course, but when she could, Charlotte would glance over her shoulder to the dance floor, envious of the young and old who were dancing.

From the distance, Nathanial watched his wife parade Charlotte around the room. He understood the importance of establishing Charlotte among the important people of the town, especially in her circumstances. Everyone loved gossip, and Charlotte was the topic at present. He knew it would fade, when some other unfortunate person fell upon hard times or fumbled into mishap. Only then would Charlotte be released from the burden of the spotlight. Although a distaste for busy-body chit-chat, the party and its circumstances were necessary for Charlotte to move forward.

But he could not help to observe the feigned smiles and polite handshakes to her introductions. Or the side glances to the room where the music was escaping. She was miserable. He felt sorry for her, prompting him to sidestep his obligatory appearance and get involved.

"Lydia." Nathanial bowed to his wife, "May I escort Charlotte to the dance floor?"

Charlotte took surprise at his request. She had not seen or heard from him until the carriage ride to the party. And even then, he chose to remain quiet.

With a nod from Lydia, she willingly extended her gloved hand into his.

Nathanial and Charlotte crossed the threshold of where the dancing was taking place. It was a room with the furniture moved to the walls, the rug lifted, and the windows open to allow the air to circulate.

Young women with flushed cheeks and men with sweaty brows circled the dance floor, awaiting the musicians to begin their next piece.

A cacophony of chatter and laughter filled the air.

A smile finally extended across Charlotte's face.

"That is the expression I wanted to see. You are lit up," Nathanial said as they waited for the music. "You seemed in need of rescuing."

"If you are assuming I was miserable…" She balked, dismissing the notion that he was watching her.

Nathanial smirked. "Charlotte, we have lived under the same roof for weeks now. If a man is to survive a woman in his household, let alone two, he must master reading innuendo. I did not miss the meaning of your ear to the music, or the yearning side glances. Besides, you are not unlike my wife in many ways."

"Well," she quipped, "I was very much intrigued by the introductions. Mr. and Mrs. Flattery were an engaging couple, with stories about their four children, ages two, five, seven and nine. Billy, the youngest who has biting issues, and Theresa, the eldest, has a fascination with astronomy."

His brow arched. "Does this prove your point or mine?"

"May I continue?"

He nodded, with a turn of his lips.

"Mrs. Quail is a lovely lady. I was sorry to hear her husband could not attend tonight's festivities because of his gout. Then there was Mr. Jameson, Mr. and Mrs. Henderson's daughter's uncle-in-law." She paused until Nathanial's smirk disappeared. "A rather interesting man who extolled the glories of Scotland, promising me a personal tour of his homeland–if I ever choose to travel there."

"Was that a proposal of marriage?" Nathanial teased.

Charlotte laughed, "I do not know."

"It all sounds riveting. Pease, go on." Nathanial insisted.

"Last, I met Mrs. Sotherby, your neighbor. She is everything Lydia described. Elderly, talkative, and dull. I dare say she convinced me to visit her next week."

"Then I am mistaken," Nathanial conceded. "I should not have assumed your plight. Shall I take you back?"

Hearing the music start up, Charlotte tugged on his arm, "No!" And then added, "You win. I was miserable. How could I not be? There is food, music, and dancing. Lots of dancing. And I was missing it all."

"Then let us not waste another moment," Nathanial said, and with her permission, swept her in his arms and glided her in a dance across the floor.

Within his arms, Nathanial could feel the heat of

her body penetrating him. She panted with exertion and her cheeks flushed pink. He couldn't help to react to her joy and enthusiasm.

It was not the first time Nathanial had noticed Charlotte's beauty.

No one could judge him...any man who had eyes could appreciate her obvious attractiveness. However, at that instance, with their hands entwined and bodies in close proximity, something stirred in him. Gazing upon her face, he felt an intense yearning to pull her nearer, and draw his breath to hers. While Charlotte's eyes were closed, swaying to the rhythm of the music, moving as if the entire world had faded away, the moment felt like it belonged solely for the two of him.

The music eventually faded, and their steps began to slow.

Charlotte's eyes slowly opened to discover Nathanial's dark eyes looking at her.

Intently, she pulled away.

"I...I...I should go." She looked around, desperate to find someone, anyone, who could take her away from him.

"Charlotte..." His voice breathed her name.

She turned to flee, but instead was halted by someone's hand upon her forearm, stopping her escape. "Mr. Jameson!" she shrieked.

"Miss Ashford," he said, tipping his head. "I apologize for the intrusion."

Nathanial quickly fell in-step at Charlotte's side.

"It is a pleasure, Mr. Jameson. May I introduce my

cousin's husband, Mr. Hammond?" She gestured to Nathanial, every inch of his stature overshadowing her.

Mr. Jameson extended his hand. "Nice to meet you, Mr. Hammond. I met your wife earlier. A beautiful woman, indeed."

"Yes, I am a lucky man," Nathanial agreed.

"If you would be so agreeable, Mr. Hammond, it is Miss Ashford I was seeking. I'd like the honor of the next dance."

"Of course. I release her into your good hands." Nathanial stepped aside. He bowed his head towards Charlotte and allowed the gentleman to take her onto the floor to wait for the next dance to begin. He walked away, but his eyes never left Charlotte, or her dance partner.

Mr. Jameson held Charlotte too close for his liking. He didn't care for the smile Mr. Jameson gave her, or the way he leaned closer to whisper in her ear. Nor the way he made her laugh.

Lydia walked up from behind, and finally pulled him away from his purview.

"Charlotte is captivating," she said.

"A family trait, indeed," he quipped.

Lydia smirked. "You have nothing to fear, my love. I am not a jealous woman. My cousin is dear to me. It is a great compliment that she captivates your attention," Lydia peered around the room. "Or bewitch any man in this room. It is my intention that she be alluring."

"There is no denying, she is an arresting woman. But if any man in this room has the most advantage, it is I who has the honor to escort the two most worthy women in the room."

"You are more than an attentive husband; you are very generous with your compliments. Unfortunately, your charade is useless with me," Lydia snapped. "You stopped looking at me long ago. Whether my fault or yours. We both know the state of our marriage."

"Ahhh, you are biting tonight, my dear. You could have warned me. I may have chosen differently about my evening."

"And miss dancing with Charlotte? I do believe that alone was worth your time...and hers." Her eyes scanned the room, past Nathanial. "Oh, there is Mrs. Cunningham, I must go and greet her. You will excuse me?"

Nathanial was unsure if he was being berated or commended. Either way, he was grateful for the opportunity to part from his wife. He joined the men in the other room where a game of billiards was being played, and where the whisky was being generously poured.

GUILTY PLEASURES

*N*athanial was drunk. Bloody, stinking, drunk.

He liked the feeling of numbness. He did not indulge often, but the host was generous, and Nathanial was in no mood to ride home sober in a carriage with Lydia, even if Charlotte was by her side. Indulging in whiskey was the only way he knew how to avoid his anger towards Lydia. She seemed to grow more weary of him with each passing day, displaying her disregard more and more.

As he entered the night air leaving the Henderson's, the coolness slapped him across the face, clearing the sedation of the whiskey, but not sobering.

Lydia and Charlotte sat across from him, swaying to the rhythm of the carriage, making it hard for him to focus on either of them.

Charlotte yawned from exhaustion, struggling to

keep her lids from closing. She leaned her head against the window and gazed out into nothing in particular, the crescent moon leaving everything in dark shadows. The corner of her mouth crept upward, and he wondered if she was recalling the events of the evening.

He smiled, too, happy she enjoyed herself.

Lydia noticed the smile spread across his face and followed his gaze to Charlotte. She knew he was drunk. She always knew when he had had too much to drink. To his surprise, Lydia didn't rebuff his behavior with a look or snide comment. Not this time. She just smirked at him, tilted her head against the cushion, and closed her eyes.

Nathanial stared back at her languid body and pondered what it meant. *Was she jealous?* He needed a clearer head to assess, but the whisky's effects lingered. He wished he had more. Sobriety would only remind him that his wife was only an arm's length, and he still couldn't touch her. Her swaying body was distracting him. The dress she was wearing was one of his favorites. He particularly admired the low bodice, which allowed the fullness of her breasts to peek out. He was all too familiar with the dark nipples hidden just beneath the thin layer of silk finely threaded and beaded. He wondered if she wore the dress for his benefit. He doubted it, but it was a nice thought. Even if she had no intention, he still desired her.

"Did you have a good time?" Charlotte interrupted him.

He moved his eyes to her. "Maybe more than I should have," he admitted.

"I must confess, maybe I did too. But maybe in a different way than you," she said with a twinkle in her eye.

"Am I that obvious?"

"No...not as much as the other men who faltered out of Mr. Henderson's study," she teased. "It was a joyous evening. There wasn't a person in the room who did not over-indulge in one way or another. No one is judging."

"Ah, you are a biblical woman," he proclaimed. "'He who hath no sin cast the first stone' or something like that?" he said, jumbling the verse.

"Yes, something to that effect," she giggled. "Or, to put it more simply, no one will remember your bad behavior over theirs."

"Ha!" he bellowed. "Righteousness with kindness. Charlotte, you should be sainted." His whiskey was talking. "And you, what was your guilty indulgence tonight?"

Charlotte did not answer.

The carriage came to a halt, as did their conversation.

The two women said good evening to Nathanial and parted his company. He watched them ascend the stairs before he headed to his study. He was not finished with his evening.

THE TALK

*B*eing with Lydia was on her terms. When she wanted him to visit her bed, she would signal him. Sometimes it was a touch on his leg, a lingering kiss on his lips, or when she would wear the perfume he bought her on their honeymoon, the smell sending him into a tailspin of desire. Most times she would leave her door slightly ajar with her lamp lighted, her way of letting him know she was allowing him to enter if he so chose to do so.

There was never a night when he chose not to.

That evening, her door was ajar, the lamp still lit. It was the first time he questioned whether to go in.

The whisky made the decision for him.

Lydia sat at her dressing table, braiding her hair, when he walked in. She was a vision of loveliness as he spotted her reflection in the mirror. Her lashes hovered over her sparkling blue eyes and her lips were full. She slowly lifted from the table, and through her gown he could see her slim waist and the curves of her hips.

He followed her naked form down to the tips of her stockings and all he wanted was to pull up the thin fabric and feel the silkiness between her legs. He approached her from behind and leaned over, placing his lips on the delicate skin of her neck.

He did not receive the reaction he was expecting.

She twisted her head and shrugged her shoulders, pushing his kisses away.

To be sure he did not misjudge her signal, he tried again. He wrapped his arms around her waist and caressed the curves of her body in anticipation that she would succumb to his desires. When his hand moved to her breast, she jerked away from his grasp.

"Please do not touch me like that," she demanded.

"Lydia," he growled. "I have not been with you in months!" He no longer counted the days. He only counted the times she allowed him to release his urges. There was no pen or paper needed to tally. The times they were together were too few to warrant the ink.

He knew he was drunk, but that was not the reason he was in her room. He missed being with his wife.

"I do not want to say it again, Nathanial..."

"Did you not ask me in?" He questioned.

"I did, but for a different reason. I want to speak with you." She walked towards the windows, leaving him standing across the room.

"Lydia, are you making conditions to make love to my wife? I am your husband, for God's sake!"

"And I am your wife!" she matched. "I have asked little of you over the years."

"No, you haven't asked much. So, what is it you are asking of me now?" His heart pounded.

"I want you to leave me alone." When he looked at her questioningly, she explained, "I do not want you in my bed."

"If you did not want my company, you should have had your door locked," he shouted, turning to walk away.

"I am not referring to *just* tonight. I mean I do not want you in my bed, *ever*," she said matter of fact.

He stopped and looked back.

"You must jest? Are you taking me for a fool?"

She shook her head without batting an eye.

"My dear woman, you do not know the burden you create by refusing my desires?" he warned her.

"That is where you underestimate me. I know exactly what may happen."

"Damn you, Lydia. I am a man!" He yelled. "I have needs like any blood-filled human man has. I have a beautiful wife whom I love. Is it not God's plan for us to be together? To share a bed as man and wife?"

"God's plan, yes. And I have fulfilled my role for over eight years. I have dutifully given you a son and an heir. But…" She paused and closed her eyes. "I have my reasons, Nathanial."

"Reasons?" His voice pounded.

"I have tried. Tried to be the woman you need. But I can't bear it. I no longer wish to submit to your impulses."

"Is that what you think my affections are, mere impulses?" he balked. "My dear wife, a man cannot adore a woman more than I you. I have given you my heart, my name, my loyalty as well as my body, all in the name of love."

"I have questioned none of that. You are a good man. It is not your honor I doubt."

"Then why?" he demanded. "Why do you feel the need to push me away?"

"It is not that I do not feel your love. You have been more than kind when I have shared my bed with you. But I feel violated when you lay with me…"

"You make it sound so vulgar." He turned away, as did she.

A silence fell in the room.

"Lydia," Nathanial called out to her. "What you are asking of me is preposterous. I have never forced myself upon you and have been nothing but patient with your capriciousness towards being with me. I have grown accustomed to the few intimate times we are together. But the prospect of no intimacy in this marriage is far beyond reasonable to ask of me."

Lydia crossed her arms. "Those are my demands, Nathanial."

"Demands?" he questioned. "I have been an honorable man. There has never been a moment of my dedication to you or this family." He paused when he saw her stone face.

He knew better than to pursue more from Lydia when she was in one of her moods. But this was going too far. She was pushing him to his limit. He could not even fathom his own wife completely denying him.

"You must realize the extremity of your request?"

"I do," she replied, affirming her position.

Nathanial stared at her. Her eyes were determined, her mouth hard. "There is nothing more to say. We can discuss this in the light of day."

"I have not finished with my demands, Nathanial," she called out to him.

With one hand on the door handle, he froze. He turned slowly and watched as she methodically started buttoning up her robe.

"I want this to be a civilized discussion. Please sit down."

LYDIA'S PLAN

*M*en were predictable. Lydia's husband even more so.

She had known Nathanial would be drunk by the time he made his way upstairs, giving her the opportunity she was looking for. But now she couldn't predict his response to what was to come next. She had to tread lightly, or she risked losing everything.

"We are not strangers, Nathanial," Lydia said. "We have nothing more to hide, do we?"

Nathanial didn't answer, nor did she want him to. Instead, he crossed the room and stood in front of her. His eyes targeted hers.

She braced herself.

"More demands? Have you not emasculated me enough, Lydia?"

"I am not a fool, Nathanial. Or unaware of a man's needs." She stepped back, breaking his stare, taking away his advantage of height and size hovering over her. "If you have not already been visiting the local street of whores, I am sure you have every intention."

"How dare you!" he retorted, arms flailing in anger. "I may have wished for such; on the many nights you rejected me...but I have never defiled the sanctity of our union."

"I cannot blame you," she said. "Even more so, now. It is inevitable. You are a handsome man who has a healthy appetite to be with a woman..."

"Not any woman, Lydia," he interrupted.

Her brow lifted. "Ahhh, Nathanial. Always honorable. Hence why I worry about you. I cannot bear to think of you visiting those places. It is shameful and humiliating, and below you to frequent such houses." She moved to the window and gazed into the darkness, needing a moment's reprieve to bolster courage. Turning back to Nathanial, watching him push his hands through his hair, his eyes half-mast from exhaustion, anger, drunkenness, she wondered how far she could push him. How far would he go for her?

"I have no intentions, Nathanial, of being talked about behind my back. There are too many rumors about husbands we know. Although, the secret lives of people and what is acceptable to them behind closed doors are of little concern to me, *your* secrets are my concern. More importantly, we have your political career to protect."

"To hell with my political career!"

"No darling. There are no negotiations about your

destiny. People rely on you. Good people. This family relies on you, as well as your son, whom you owe honorability. And that shall never be destroyed over your need to be satisfied."

The whiskey was churning in his stomach, the euphoria long dissipated. His stomach twisted with the need to retch. Nathanial wanted to walk away, but he needed more. He needed to understand.

"My need? *My need?* What I need is you!" He ran his hand through his hair trying to calm his urge to fight. "First, you deny my touch. Second, you restrict me from my rightful bed. And third, you dare to deny me of pleasure from anyone?" He sniggered at the absurdity of it all, his arms flailing. "And how do you plan to enforce all those demands?"

Lydia was hesitant to continue.

Nathanial's face raged red, his jaw clenched, and his lips tightened, the half-lit room defining his faint lines around his eyes and the shadow of his chin. He was still handsome in Lydia's eyes, marriage and fatherhood making him even more attractive to her. A wife should be so lucky to have such a strong and arousing man.

The truth was, she didn't love him. Not in the way she wanted to. Not anymore, and she no longer wanted to submit to his sexual desires, no matter how much he loved her.

Lydia was firm in her decision. Her plans were made, the steps were taken, and she was moving forward no matter how much he was affected. If she knew anything about men, Nathanial would obey her request. For no matter how angry he would get, she knew he loved her and would do anything to keep her happy.

She moved towards him and placed her hand on his.

His eyes lowered and his jaw softened.

"I am not so cruel of a wife to not understand your needs. Nor am I naïve to your ability to bed other women. I am fully aware of your requirements. But do not feel so distraught. I have a plan. I am offering you a mistress–the *perfect* mistress. Someone I approve of and will allow."

Nathanial yanked himself away from her touch. "My own wife has chosen me a mistress?" he scoffed. "Pray tell, my darling," he sneered, "who will be the unfortunate woman who must suffer through my contemptuous touch?"

"Why Nathanial, you must already know?"

He stared at her in disbelief. Her words may have been terribly unkind, but her intentions were even more wicked than he could imagine. "In heaven's name, what have you done?"

"The only solution I realized that would appeal to my husband," she replied.

"And sending me into another woman's bed is your idea of keeping me happy? Even if that woman is..." Her name got stuck in his throat. "...*your cousin?*"

"You scoff? Why Nathanial, *she* is a beautiful

woman. I am not blind to how you look at her. It is how you looked at me all those years ago."

"*You* are my wife," he harshly reminded her.

Lydia coldly defined the terms. "But she is the closest to me you will experience."

A chill went up Nathanial's spine. "This is preposterous! Charlotte cannot, would not, agree to this. She is a good woman," he shouted. "She is your cousin, for God's sake!"

"Tell me truthfully, Nathanial, would you not take a lover, or worse, find satisfaction in less reputable houses?" Lydia questioned. "Can you not see it? Charlotte is the perfect choice. Her circumstances are not uncommon for a woman in her position. Is not sex any woman's leverage? Charlotte is a realist and is all too aware of the desires of a man. But with you it can be different for her. In the end, this will please everyone." Lydia paused and watched Nathanial's questioning face. "It is no concern of yours of what Charlotte and I have agreed to. She has no illusions regarding the course of her life and the measures she must go to uphold it. She is true to me and for that, you should be grateful."

Nathanial's face drained of color.

Lydia wondered if she miscalculated his desires for Charlotte.

"I am offering you a beautiful gift; an opportunity to be honorable to me without burden."

"Honorable? Is that how you are justifying it? Is

there no boundary of your contempt for me?" he challenged.

They locked stares. Lydia's eyes filled with determination, his with anger.

Neither were sure what to expect from the other.

Lydia had not planned on Nathanial to be so apprehensive about the arrangement. He was no different than other men and their desires. Most men would gladly take a mistress. *Most men probably did.* It never occurred to her that her own husband would balk at taking a lover, especially one so purposely chosen. It would fulfill his desires and satisfy his needs. It offered him gratification without guilt.

It also offered Lydia a reprieve from her own guilt that she no longer desired him the way he needed. Or loved him how he deserved.

"The decision is made," she said with finality, determined not to falter from her courage. "Choose wisely, my dear. You have built a life and legacy for this family, only for it all to crumble for the sake of a few fleeting moments in bed."

Nathanial's eyes darkened. "You vile woman! Where did my beautiful wife go?" He thundered towards the door, swinging it open with force before pivoting to meet Lydia's cold stare. "Damn you!" he shouted, before slamming the door shut.

FAMILY MATTERS

*C*harlotte had a lovely time at the Henderson party. After her first dance with Nathanial, a line of men waited to fill in where the last gentleman had left off. She was charmed by many of them, but no one made her feel the way Nathanial did. She tried to erase the lingering effects of him by accepting every dance requested. The distractions worked. Her feet ached by the evening's end, but she had a lingering smile on her face.

Lydia commented on how much she enjoyed her evening as well, when they walked to their rooms. She kissed Charlotte on the cheek and headed to her quarters–the large two-bedroom suite at the north corner of the house, leaving Charlotte at her bedroom, four doors down the hall.

Nathanial did not follow them upstairs.

Charlotte's bed had already been turned down, her

night clothes out, and the lamps lit, filling her space with light. She threw off her shoes and donned her wrap over a chair, struggling to loosen the buttons along the back of her dress.

Ada had opened the windows and a cool breeze billowed the half-closed curtains. Charlotte pushed them aside and leaned out the windows to capture hints of honeysuckle that lifted through the air. She breathed in, filling her lungs, and let out a heavy sigh. All seemed at harmony in her world.

"Nice evening, Miss?" Ada asked, entering with a tray of warm milk.

Charlotte smiled. "I will need no help sleeping tonight. I am happily exhausted. I have never danced more in my life." Charlotte swirled around and dropped to the bed.

"Come." Ada tapped the chair at the vanity. "Let's take those pins out of your hair and get you ready for bed. You'll probably sleep like a baby this evening."

Charlotte rose and seated herself at the vanity, meeting Ada's eyes through the mirror. "It's happening."

"What miss?"

"My life is settling here. I finally feel *at home.* Happy."

Ada touched her shoulder, giving it a squeeze. "As you should, Miss…"

Before Ada could finish her thoughts, voices reverberated through the walls. They both turned towards the door as the rumblings grew louder down the hallway. Silence fell between them as they strained to listen.

Even though the walls were thick, hearing a door close, footsteps against the floor, or voices murmuring in another room was common. What was happening down the hall, penetrating the darkness, was something more.

The voices eventually simmered to a mumbling.

"Ada..." Charlotte said. "What is *that* we just heard?"

Ada stood frozen with the brush clenched in her hand.

"Ada?" Charlotte said again, firmly, demanding the maid's attention. "Does this happen often?"

Ada's eye widened. "I am sorry Miss. It's not for me to say."

"Has my cousin argued like this before?"

Ada's eyes lowered. "Yes, Miss."

"How long has this been happening?" Charlotte persisted.

Ada's lips tightened.

"Ada?"

"Oh, Miss, you're going to put me in a predicament." When Charlotte narrowed her stare and put her hands on her hips, Ada knew she had no choice but to answer. "There have been arguments in the past. Nothing like this, though," she admitted. "Upon the news of your arrival, the arguments ceased. We hadn't seen Mrs. Hammond this happy in a long time."

The two women snapped their heads towards the door once again as the angered voices returned.

Charlotte reached for Ada. "Is my cousin in any danger?"

"No, Miss. I don't believe so. Master Hammond is not an angry man by any means."

Charlotte paced the room before she pressured the maid to explain further. "Are Master and Mrs. Hammond unhappy?"

"He is very devoted to her," she carefully replied.

"Hmmm," Charlotte grumbled. "Is Mrs. Hammond unhappy with Master Hammond?"

Ada did not respond.

It was not surprising to Charlotte that a married couple would argue, but she had not witnessed many. Her father and mother were amiable with one another and there were very few arguments between them. Their anger was usually directed towards a third party. Her father would rage about some business that had gone awry, or her mother would be impassioned by some news she heard in the marketplace. Her overall knowledge of a married couple and what transpired between a husband and wife was very limited.

Charlotte pushed the girl again. "Do you know what they argue about?"

Ada bit her lip. "Oh, Miss..." she moaned. "'Tis nothing most houses must deal with. Master Hammond stays away for long periods of time...his work, you see. Mistress Hammond is left by herself to manage on her own. With a house this size, 'tis a wonder. It is only when he returns, there's a period of time they both need to acquaint themselves once again. Things settle down after that."

A door slammed and heavy footsteps pounded down the hallway. They came to a direct stop in front of Charlotte's door. The handle twisted but stopped.

Both held their breath.

They expected the door to swing open, but the footsteps continued onward, down the stairs, and another door slammed.

Silence.

"You should go," Charlotte said. "Goodnight Ada."

"Goodnight, Miss. Please try to get some rest. There's nothing any of us can do."

Charlotte walked Ada to the door and watched her disappear into the darkened hall. She saw a light from under Lydia's door. She grabbed her robe and headed to her room, not sure what she would find, or what she was going to say.

Charlotte rapped on the door.

"Come in," Lydia's voice called.

Her cousin was leaning against a chair by the window in a flowing gown of linen cascading to the floor. Her robe was layered in ruffles around the collar, and at the end of billowing sleeves, the abundance of layered fabric engulfing her petite frame. Underneath it all was a silhouette of her womanly form. Her golden braid, lying flat along her shoulder, drew attention to the cobalt blue of her eyes. Her cheeks, presently flushed, were prominent against her creamy complexion.

She is a vision of beauty, Charlotte thought. Had she not been witness to an argument, and hear her husband subsequently leave the room, she could have sworn the ethereal portrait of a woman in front of her was all for a man's seduction.

Lydia pursed her lips, when she saw Charlotte come through the door, and swiftly moved to hug her.

"You must think the worst of us?" Lydia said

"Of course not, Lydia. This is your home, and you should be able to have your private affairs without intrusion or judgement. I was just concerned about you. Was I wrong to come?"

"No. You are a dear. It is just..." Lydia collapsed on the edge of her bed. "Terrible. Terrible things are upon me..."

Charlotte went to her side. "Dear cousin, what could bring so much distress?"

"It is too much to discuss." Lydia turned away. "I am more than ashamed of what I must tell you."

Taking her cousin's hand in hers, Charlotte tried to console her. "We are family. There is no such greater bond. You have no fear of me. I assure you, there is no judgement on my part. What you say to me is strictly confident. But you must, tell me what distresses you to this point of agony. It does not suit you to be so unhappy, nor this household, to be a witness to such problems."

Lydia nodded. "Yes, I agree. That is why you are here. To better the situation...to better *us*." She paused.

"I do not understand..."

Lydia touched Charlotte's face. "Oh, my dearest, Charlotte, you are barely a woman. Your knowledge of a man cannot be more than as when you were a girl. Such innocence, yet I can see it your eyes you hold the passion of a woman. You cannot be prepared for what I am going to say. It may shock you. Maybe even scare you away."

Charlotte did not respond. She could not deny her innocence, or her naïveté. Nor could she expect to know what was to come next.

THE FAVOR

*L*ydia had not planned how to approach the topic with Charlotte, but Nathanial's outburst had provided the opportunity she needed. When he slammed the door behind him, she knew the impact it would have on Charlotte. That she came running to her room so soon was better than she could have hoped for. Having Charlotte catch her in a state of anxiousness was not by design, but the drama worked towards her benefit.

"Oh," Lydia moaned. "Nathanial is a good man, but he can be so forceful and demanding of me."

"Forceful?"

"No, no, not in the way you are thinking. After our son was born, my body underwent so much stress. It was a difficult delivery. Dr. Bellows warned another pregnancy could be fatal."

Charlotte gasped in horror. "You never told me…"

"It is not something one puts in a letter." She feigned a smile. "Nathanial has always dreamed of having more children, but with the circumstances as they are…" Lydia paused to let the innuendos settle with Charlotte. "When that accident happened with my parents…" Lydia's lids fell heavy, her lashes wetting with tears remembering the pain of that day. "There was so much to deal with. Father dead. Mother damaged beyond repair. The consequences of the doctor's words had not fully been scrutinized as I dealt with my dying mother; eventually burying them side by side. Following the anguish of losing one's parents, I could scarcely imagine a situation where I would not be alive to look after of my own son, let alone Nathanial." She whispered her last few words, "All for the sake of fulfilling my duties as a wife."

Charlotte remained quiet.

Lydia's eyes filled with tears. "You must not think the worst of me, dear cousin. I only confide because I know you love me without judgment, and I have no one else to turn to. If not for you, who should care for me and my family?"

"I am here for you Lydia. Please do not despair. I will help where I can. I give you my commitment."

"I know, and thus I bring you into my private circle. Let me try to explain." Lydia rose, delicately swiping away the tears that had wetted her cheeks.

"Nathanial has been patient with me. He only

comes to me when I give him permission. He has never demanded more. But I fear he has only so much patience, and is growing weary of the demands placed on him. No matter how understanding, or how patient, Nathanial is like any man with needs. Unfortunately, this puts me in a difficult position. I cannot continue risk inviting him into my bed, but I cannot risk rejecting him in perpetuity."

"Really, Lydia, you should have confided in me sooner."

"And tell you what? That I must play the guard of my body with my own husband? I am failing as his wife. And I fear I am losing him."

"No, I won't believe it," Charlotte questioned. "It cannot be so. He adores you! I have witnessed it with my own eyes. How foolish for you to even question him and loyalty to you."

"That is what I fear the most. There are too many opportunities in the city with him away from home. If I do not fulfill his needs, he will find other women who will be more than willing to do so. Just think, Charlotte, the shame of it all. The gossip behind my back and the pity of the town when they see our son and me...it is more than any woman should have to endure."

"Honestly, Lydia, have you discussed your concerns with Nathanial? He most certainly would take your well-being to heart."

"I tried, but as you witnessed tonight, he is growing

more impatient with me. Her lids lowered. "I cannot offer him what he needs or what he deserves." She paused, but before Charlotte could respond, she added, "He needs a woman, Charlotte!"

Charlotte's hand went to her chest. "I cannot sit here and watch your marriage be destroyed. There must be a compromise, lest he lose all he has achieved with his career and his family. He must think about you and Peter."

Lydia shook her head. "There are whore houses that might prove otherwise…"

"No!" Charlotte insisted. "You mustn't say that, or even think that a possibility."

"Oh, my dearest, you are the closest thing to me in my life. Thank you for not judging me harshly and offering your understanding. That is why I trust you with all that I have. You are the one person who would never hurt me or destroy my life."

Charlotte nodded. "Of course! I would give my life for you. Tell me, Lydia, what can I do to help you?

Lydia hesitated to answer. "It is you, Charlotte…" She paused and brought her eyes to Charlotte's. "It is you whom he must turn to in his need."

Charlotte froze in her midst, caught in Lydia's stare. Her lips parted to speak, but words couldn't usurp themselves from her mouth.

Lydia continued, "I am asking you something that may seem impossible, but with our love for each other, I believe it may be possible."

Charlotte shook her head. "I do not understand."

"Then allow me to explain…" Lydia took Charlotte by the hand and led her to a chair near the window instructing her to sit.

Lydia remained standing, taking solace in the night air breezing in from the opened window. Although the sky was dark, stars were abundant, twinkling against the blackness. Lydia lifted her chin towards menagerie exhaling a deep breath from within her chest. She wished upon the brightest twinkle to give her the courage she was now seeking.

"Oh Charlotte…" her voice crumbled. It had not been easy for Lydia to stare coldly at Nathanial and tell him she no longer wanted to be his lover, but it was necessary. Looking upon Charlotte, her innocence soon to be shattered, was much harder. Her shoulders slumped and her head fell into her hands. "What am I to do?"

Charlotte swiftly rose and embraced her cousin's whimpering body. "There, there, dear Lydia."

Lydia lifted her head and sniffled. "What you must think of me," she said, offering a perfunctory smile. "Would you mind grabbing me a hanky…there." She pointed, "In the drawer, next to my bed."

She watched as Charlotte obeyed her request. Never for a moment did she doubt Charlotte's loyalty or her ability to act in obedience when it was necessary. Her loyalty would never be in question, but her willingness to agree to her request was.

Wiping her tears away Lydia regained her composer. "Charlotte darling, let us not pretend what you must face. Your father took opportunities away from you. As much as I am trying to counter your circumstances, we are women bound by the rules of society placed upon us. Your present standing in society hinders prospects of marriage to a respectable suitor. At best, you will become the wife of a simple man, twice your age, who would be thrilled to have a young, beautiful wife, and who will bear him children. It's not the ideal of love, is it?" Her brow lifted. "Worse, is the thought of a man defiling you, treating you as nothing more than a place holder for his pleasure."

Charlotte shivered knowing all too well the truth of Lydia's words.

"I would never consider something if it were not the right thing for you. What I am proposing is far more dignified than most of the options granted you. You have a home here. You have a family. Above all else, you are cherished and loved in ways that surpass any future possibility. When I learned of your fate, I wanted nothing more than to save you. Little did I realize that it was I who needed saving. And here you are! It seems as if the gods have guided us to the right place at the right time for us to help each other. It's the perfect plan, don't you see?" Lydia took Charlotte's hands in hers and looked deep into her eyes. "Charlotte, there is no mistake you were sent here. It was a divine plan. The pieces all fit." Lydia's voice lowered to a whisper. "No one need know of our secret."

"Lydia?" Charlotte's voice wobbled. She quickly pulled away from Lydia's grasp. Her back stiffened and her eyes narrowed. "Maybe I am misunderstanding you, but what you are asking of me is to become..."

"To become my husband's mistress. But let us not call it that, Charlotte," Lydia interjected. "No, I am asking you to save my marriage."

"Is there a difference?" she questioned.

Lydia nodded. "Do you not see all the opportunity it offers? Nathanial cares about you. And, if I am not mistaken, I believe you care for him."

Charlotte's face went white.

Lydia was not unaware of Charlotte's attraction to her husband. After all, she understood Charlotte as if herself. Did Charlotte's face not lighten when Nathanial entered the room? Did she not study his face, as he spoke to her? Did her cheeks not shade when he lingered a stare upon her face. Lydia could not find fault with Charlotte. Or with Nathanial. They were souls of alike. *Had she not always known?* She knew that Nathanial would be a gentle and kind lover, never demanding or careless. It was more than most women were granted in marriage.

"Do not feel ashamed, Charlotte. I would not have asked this of you if I did not see with my own eyes. Nathanial is a handsome and charming man. Was it not inevitable? I do not blame you for how you feel. And this only proves my point. If not you, the one woman I can trust to never hurt me or my family, then who will it be?" Seeing Charlotte's lost expression, she put her arms around her. "Do what your heart tells you, Charlotte. I am entrusting you with mine."

Charlotte closed her eyes and took a deep breath. Her words came slowly. "I cannot, do you understand?" Her brow furrowed and her stare narrowed. Lydia's eyes were dark and calm, like an ocean before a storm. "I will not, with good conscience, do what you are asking of me. I am not capable of the task you put forth. I know nothing about men and relationships. What can I possibly offer?"

"You are a woman…that is all you need."

"Lydia," Charlotte pleaded. "This is about us! We have a sacred bond. What you are asking of me is to violate the most intimate part of your marriage. That is no place for me to be."

"Dear cousin, we promised to uphold each other… to be there for each other. I am drowning and I need your help. I do not ask anything that would destroy us. I believe you were sent back to us for a purpose." She lifted Charlotte's chin and held her questioning gaze. "I have watched him. I have watched you."

Charlotte looked away.

Lydia turned Charlotte's face demanding her attention. "I do not doubt my decision. I do not doubt my trust in you."

"Have you discussed this with Nathanial?" she questioned.

Lydia nodded. "It is not without his agreement I would come to you. Nathanial is an honorable man committed to me, but he is a man at the core. If I am to lose him to anyone, it is to you. I love you more than anyone. I trust you with my heart unquestionably." She lingered. "And I trust you with my marriage."

THE DECISION

*C*harlotte left Lydia's room not sure of what she had promised her cousin; only that she would do anything to protect her.

Was becoming her husband's mistress protecting Lydia?

Walking the half-lit corridor seemed a mile's retreat back to her room. She closed the door behind her and locked it. She wasn't expecting anything to happen that evening, but it made her feel safe.

When Charlotte was younger, she imagined her future with love and a family of her own. Although she found a few men compatible, she had to admit, love never presented itself. When her fortune was taken away, she knew her situation was irrefutably altered. She would either have to settle for anyone willing to take her with no money, or not marry at all. The latter brought about many distasteful options, one of which Guiles Milford was more than eager to provide, and the second, most likely in her destiny, was spinsterhood.

She never expected a third option such as Lydia's proposal.

Did she really agree?

The words repeated themselves in her head over and over again. Charlotte knew herself to be a virtuous woman. She believed in the sanctity of marriage and assumed everyone believed the way she did. Yet, it seemed to Charlotte that Lydia was more than willing to sacrifice that sanctity for the survival of her marriage.

Was that not a more noble purpose?

It was Lydia's job to hold her family together. *How far is one to go for the protection of family?* If Lydia was pushed to extremes, who was Charlotte to judge her desperation? Marriage was intricate, and the balance of a household was equally demanding. Albeit, it was unusual for a man to be denied by his wife. *But were not Lydia's circumstances demanding it?* Charlotte could not imagine Nathanial to behave with indecency. But when driven from his marital bed and denied by his wife, there had to be consequences. *He was a man!*

Charlotte could see Lydia's desperation. If she refused her cousin, it would cause injury to everyone she held dear. Everyone she had left in the world.

Hadn't Lydia and she promised each other–*forever and always.*

Charlotte's father, Merrill, believed that the love of family was more sacred than anything. It was more important than money, power, or prestige. To her father's dismay, he discovered his brother, Edmond did not hold the same sentiments. There were no two brothers closer the whole of their lives until the day Edmond refused to support Merrill's business aspirations. Edmond called Merrill a dreamer and a fool. Pride and arrogance got in the way. It began years of separation and heartache between them, their family unit broken. Each day the two brothers were apart, each year that went by, a little piece of her father's heart broke. He was saddened he could not share his successes, and his sorrows with the one person he felt the most connection to. They both died without ever reconnecting their family.

On the day they left England, Merrill Ashford pledged that his own family would not sacrifice the love of family over power and propriety. Looking out for one another was a moral value ingrained in Charlotte from that day forward.

If Lydia needed her, Charlotte had no other choice but to answer that call in the name of family and love.

"But how..." Charlotte had asked in confusion.

"I will leave it up to you and Nathanial to come to terms," Lydia had replied. *"My only request is to be discreet. I can count on you for that. I do not want rumors and gossip to come of this. And most of all, I do not want to disrupt Peter. Nothing should disrupt our lives. That is the beauty of it. We live as we have been doing. Nothing more."*

"But it is not nothing, is it Lydia?" Charlotte questioned. *"You of all people must realize the heartache it may*

cause. I do not want to come between you and Nathanial. Most importantly, I will not forgive myself if it was to cause a rift between us."

"Never!" Lydia declared. "You have always been, and will always remain, the dearest to me in my life, and nothing will destroy that bond."

The details of how a mistress arrangement was to be handled were not disclosed.

Charlotte now paced her room, nervously twisting her hands around and around. A guttural sigh released from somewhere in the depths of her despair with the realization that she was entering a deceptive world; more deceptive than Lydia could have planned for, and unsure of how to navigate it.

Was she not in love with Nathanial?

Her decision was convoluted, entangling her life from this night forward.

Andrew Knightly's words came flooding back to her, "*Stay close to me, for I will protect you.*"

She wondered if he knew something she did not.

AVOIDANCE

*T*he morning light burst through the windows too early.

Charlotte cursed herself for not closing the curtains before falling asleep. Lifting from her pillow, she rubbed her eyes, taking the sting out, and listened for anyone stirring as early as she was. There were no footsteps along the corridors, no doors squeaking shut, no calls from the workers outside. Just stillness. Eerily still, as if everyone knew something had changed.

The forward motion of time had halted and realigned itself for a new direction.

She called for Ada with hope of a hot cup of tea. If she was truthful, a glass of brandy, maybe two, would suit her better to calm her nerves. She placed her head in her hands, recalling the details of her conversation with Lydia. It all flooded back, and her stomach twisted. Facing Lydia about her decision in the light of the morning brought a slew of new fears. Nathanial being one of them.

Breakfast was out of the question. She wouldn't be able to keep anything down. Avoiding everyone and anyone in the house seemed like the best option.

"Good morning, Miss. You are up early this morning," Ada said when she walked through the door with a pot of tea. "I hope the happenings of last night did not cause you distress."

Knowing Ada was referring to the fight between Lydia and Nathanial, Charlotte only wished it was that simple.

"No. It is difficult to sleep with the morning light saturating the room. It is my fault. I forgot to close the curtains." She pushed her quilt down and dragged her body off the bed. She put on her robe and walked to the window. "On the positive side, it looks to be a splendid day."

"Aye, but in the distance, clouds are on their way. The birds are on the limbs, waiting. I fear a downpour is coming."

Charlotte stretched her neck to peer into the distance.

The clouds were lingering back. An omen of things to come.

"Shall I send up breakfast?"

"Not this morning. Thank you, Ada. I will dress quickly and head out before the others are up."

"Yes, Miss," Ada said, pulling out a dress from the

armoire. Once her hair was up, donned with a hat, Ada grabbed her a coat to put on. "You will need something to keep you warm, Miss. The air has an unexpected chill."

Once outside, Charlotte buttoned the front of her coat and pulled up the collar. Bad weather would not deter her. She needed to escape the walls of the house. They were closing in on her, or at least, the drama inside.

She strode through the worn pathway through the long grasses. Overwhelmed by her thoughts, she wanted to run through the field and get lost. Knowing it would only cause a party in search of her, she opted for a respite in the grass. She took off her coat and laid on top of it, the green of her dress blending with the blades of grass. Looking up to the sky, she let her mind wander–the how, the when, the where...

What has she done!

She sat up and peered at her surroundings. She was alone. Alone to allow her body to flush with heat, her cheeks to redden, and shame to wash through her. She did not want to think about what lay ahead. The thoughts were too...forbidden. She wanted to rest her mind and indulge in the harmony of the earth, the sky, and the air. She needed to breathe. For nothing had happened...yet. Nothing would if she didn't want it to.

Did she?

Birds called in the distance, the sunlight warmed her face, and for a moment she allowed her mind to relax. It was then she fell asleep.

"IT HAS BEEN difficult to find you," a man's voice said. "I worried we would need hounds to search for you."

Charlotte opened her eyes.

Andrew Knightly hovered over her.

"Mr. Knightly," she exclaimed, sitting up promptly. "What you must think of me, sleeping in the grass like a common girl."

Mr. Knightly extended his hand to help her stand. "Nothing is too inappropriate for me, Miss Ashford."

He retrieved her coat and helped her into it.

Charlotte brushed the loosened hairs away from her face and tucked them in the back of her bun. "I am rather embarrassed you found me this way. I must apologize."

"It is I who should apologize. I intruded on what seemed like a lovely nap."

"I am afraid I did not sleep well last night," she explained.

"A stolen slumber is not a crime. Quite necessary many times. Maybe I will join you next time."

Charlotte's eyes widened.

He laughed. "Really Miss Ashford, your naivety is charming." He gave her his forearm. "Come, let us continue your walk. I would hate to waste the afternoon. Now that I have found you, it will only be all the more pleasant."

Charlotte pointed to the dark clouds gathering

overhead. "We may lose the pleasantness. It looks like the rain is almost upon us."

"Then let us take advantage until it does…" he said, leading the way.

"And to what do I owe this pleasure, Mr. Knightly?"

"Curiosity," he stated in a matter-of-fact tone.

"Curiosity about what? Have not the rumors filled you in? I am no mystery."

"I doubt that. There is intrigue to everyone. You just need to find it."

Charlotte swallowed hard. His words rang more true than she was comfortable admitting. "Are you always so curious about strangers?"

"Come now, let us not call each other strangers. I would like to hope we will become good friends."

"You are ahead of yourself, Mr. Knightly. I have discovered little about you. And yet, you presume to know all about me." She added, "And where to find me."

"I will admit, a good woman is not hard to find. But a beautiful woman with a curious mind and a sharp wit? Now, that takes more pursuing. I must have luck on my side, for today I have found both."

Charlotte looked at him with curiosity. She should have feared a man like him—forward, bold, and mysterious, but there was something intriguing drawing her in.

"It is your misfortune you were not in attendance at the Henderson party. It was a lovely evening," Charlotte commented idly.

"Ah, but I was there!"

She could not help herself but ask, "Did you choose to be anonymous?"

"No, I was…entertained otherwise," he offered. A slow smile drew across his face.

She looked at him sideways, waiting for him to elaborate.

"You want more?" he answered her questioning pause. "I told you, my dear, everyone has intrigue. But do not fret, there was more than enough opportunity to watch you entertained by the many gentlemen in the room. You seem to captivate them all… even your dear cousin's husband. I, too, would have been disappointed to let you into another man's arms." He lifted his brow, "What is this power you have over men?"

Charlotte blushed at his implication. "I am only the freshest face. They will soon tire of me and find me as dull as the next woman."

"I find quite the opposite. The more I know, the more you become fascinating."

"You assume me to have more intrigue than I deserve, Mr. Knightly. I am but a simple woman with whom you, too, will tire."

"Then allow me the opportunity to explore the possibilities. May I call on you again?" he asked.

"If you so choose," Charlotte agreed. She watched that slow smile appear again and wondered if she was too quick to accept.

Mr. Knightly said nothing more as they walked back to the house, only stopping at a camelia bush where he snapped a stem and pulled off a pink-petalled flower from its branches.

"A beautiful flower for a beautiful lady," he said handing it to her.

Charlotte fanned out the petals, feeling the luxurious silkiness of the flower before she looked up at Mr. Knightly and thanked him. "What am I to make of you Mr. Knightly?"

"The bigger question is, what am I to make of you?"

Charlotte watched his pink lips purse at her, and she wondered why, of all the people, in all the world, or at least in their *little* world, why her? Why was the illustrious and hard to pin down, Mr. Knightly, seeking her out?

"There you two are!" Lydia's voice found them from across the lawn, waving her hand from the terrace.

Mr. Knightly took Charlotte's hand and hurried them to greet her.

"Mr. Knightly, I had heard you arrived at the house, but I could not find you anywhere, and now, I see the reason why." She noted Charlotte by his side, her hand encased by Mr. Knightly's, flushed and breathless from the jaunt across the lawn. "I do not blame you for disappearing."

"Ah, Mrs. Hammond." He bowed, releasing Charlotte from his grip. "I apologize for my lack of etiquette. I had not realized you were home."

"I was not, so you are excused. All is well." Lydia looked at Charlotte, "I was looking for you earlier. You disappeared. I was worried. Are you good…with *everything?*" Lydia questioned.

"All is…" Charlotte paused; her heart pounded. "…acceptable."

Lydia's face lit up. "I am so glad." Her voice lifted, and she looped her arm under Charlotte's. "And Mr. Knightly…you will join us for tea this afternoon?"

"With my pleasure, Mrs. Hammond," he agreed and followed the two ladies who took the lead into the house.

Nathanial abruptly turned at the collective clapping of the footsteps as the entourage entered the parlor. His eyes directly met Charlotte's, ignoring the other two.

His face was serious, his lips grim.

Charlotte halted, causing the others to do the same.

Lydia released her grasp of her cousin's arm, and walking ahead, presented Charlotte a reassuring smile. She went to her husband and brushed her cheek against his. "Hello darling, I had not expected you today. I was sure you would flee to the city. Mr. Knightly is joining us for tea this afternoon. It might be nice to have a male companion after days and nights with Charlotte and me. You must be weary of us."

Nathanial looked at his wife but said nothing in reply. Diverting eye contact, he extended his hand to Mr. Knightly. "It is good to see you again."

"Thank you, sir," Mr. Knightly greeted in reply.

Charlotte took off her coat and handed it to the servant. "Tea is here. Shall I serve?"

"If you will," Lydia agreed. "Come sit, Mr. Knightly, by the fire. I am afraid you have caught some of us..." She eyed her husband. "...pensive today. We will blame it on the coming rain. But do not abandon our moody household. You are just what we needed...a lively interruption for tea."

Mr. Knightly tipped his head to Lydia and obeyed her command, joining her, except choosing to stand, instead. He splayed himself against the mantle, giving himself the vantage of looking at his three companions: Lydia in a chair by the fire, legs crossed, her fingertips strumming the carved curve of the arm, Charlotte at a cart housing a tiered tray of cakes, plates, napkins, cups and saucers, preparing the tea, and Nathanial across the room, standing beside a writing desk, hand in one pocket, lips tightly pressed, his eyes following Charlotte's every move.

"Two sugars, Mr. Knightly?" Charlotte called to him.

He nodded.

"Aw, Mr. Knightly, you like your tea sweet. My husband enjoys more of the natural state. I cannot imagine not indulging when given the opportunity for something to make it more palatable. Can you?"

"Hmm. You are asking the wrong man, Mrs. Hammond. I never miss the opportunity to seek out the betterment of anything, whether it be sugar in my tea, refined worsted wool in my coat, or choosing the most charming of ladies with whom to spend my afternoon," Mr. Knightly replied.

Lydia smirked. "I wish my husband had your conviction of vitality."

As Charlotte poured the tea, her hands shook causing a momentary clanking of the cup against the saucer. All eyes were momentarily on her. She lifted her head and gave them an assuring smile, while Lydia seamlessly distracted Mr. Knightly in continued conversation.

Nathanial walked behind Charlotte and placed his hand over hers, making her set down the saucer. Whispering in her ear, he said, "You are not bound by her rules. Nor do you have to be afraid of me. Please do not allow her to change things, especially between us."

"I am not..." she whispered back, without looking at him. "...afraid of you."

Satisfied with her answer, Nathanial turned away, but was halted by her next few words.

"But you are bound to her," she added, meeting his stare. "For that reason, I plan to be honorable."

His eyes widened, while hers wetted.

To their surprise, Mr. Knightly stepped between them, causing Nathanial to step away.

"Please forgive my negligence, Mr. Knightly." Charlotte handed him his tea.

He took a sip, looked at Charlotte, then at Nathanial, and back to Charlotte. "Perfect." He eyed an assortment of cakes on the cart. "May I choose one?"

"Of course," Charlotte encouraged, pushing the plate in front of him.

Mr. Knightly eyed the assortment, choosing a vanilla cake with preserves between the layers. He placed it in his mouth and smiled. "Delightful!" He turned to Nathanial. "You are a fortunate man, Mr. Hammond, to be surrounded with such enticing pleasures. It is hard to pick just one."

Nathanial clenched his jaw. "Only if one is tempted. I try not to overindulge."

Mr. Knightly grabbed another cake and stuffed it in his mouth. "Sometimes they are too irresistible."

A thundering roar came from outside.

Lydia walked to the windows and looked at the darkening sky. "The rain will start soon. Mr. Knightly, you must stay for dinner. No formality required. It looks like the weather will not be your friend upon returning home."

"Unfortunately, I have committed to other plans. If I leave now, maybe I will escape the worst of it."

"Such a shame." Lydia called for his coat. "Promise me you will return soon and stay longer."

He looked at Charlotte. "I will, most definitely. Thank you for the afternoon. May we have many more." He bowed his goodbyes and left.

Thunder roared two more times before the skies opened.

"Aww, the storm is upon us," Lydia declared.

Charlotte looked at Nathanial.

Lydia's words were never truer.

TRUTH BE KNOWN

*T*he rain continued for days, keeping them in the house once again.

To pass the time, Lydia engaged Charlotte in simple pleasantries. Reading aloud, a game of cards, even lessons in needlepoint–a skill she had yet to perfect. All the while, Lydia behaved as usual toward Charlotte, as if she never made the request.

Charlotte almost wondered if she had dreamed the whole situation and was grateful for Lydia's pretense...but also burdened.

Nathanial used the solitude to his advantage as well. He hid away in his study for hours. It was only at meals when he appeared. Had Charlotte not been privy to their inner strife, no one would guess the secret in which she was now entangled. He played his role as devoted husband to Lydia, and Lydia played the dedicated wife.

But while Nathanial had maintained appearances toward Lydia, his relationship with Charlotte was different. His eyes rarely fell upon Charlotte, and he addressed her only when necessary. He was not unkind towards her, but he was not friendly either. If Charlotte had to put a name to it, she'd say he was *courteous.*

As the days passed, and the nights rolled into morning, his courteousness became politeness. Politeness became indifference. Indifference turned into straight-out disregard. In rooms where she was present, he walked out. And meals were skipped altogether.

Each night when Charlotte retreated to her room, she undressed, climbed into bed, and waited, ears perked, and listened for footsteps outside her door.

Nathanial never came.

A part of her wanted him to come and be over with it. It was the waiting that was unsettling; the unknown that frightened her. She was going to share her bed with a man who was not her husband. Nathanial was not making it any easier on her–making her wait. But the hallways always remained silent. She'd blow out her candle and close her eyes.

Sleep came slowly.

A week of dreariness left dread looming over everyone and on everything, but it felt as if it bore a hole in Charlotte and made its home in her heart.

"There have been too many days of constant rain. Peter is going crazy. Poor nanny has had to entertain him every waking moment," Lydia said, observing her restless son in Charlotte's lap, who was fiddling with his book as Charlotte tried to turn the pages.

"You can't blame him," Charlotte defended the small boy, who waited for her to continue. She ran her fingers through his soft brown curls. "I, too, am feeling eager to get outside again."

"More, Auntie," the young boy pleaded.

Charlotte smiled down at him, giving him a kiss on his head.

"More, Auntie!" Peter's little voice urged again.

Charlotte continued to read until the little boy was fast asleep on her lap.

"Shall I call for the nanny?" Charlotte asked.

"No." Lydia rose and pulled the boy in her arms. "I, too, am exhausted. I'll take him to bed. Will you come along?"

Charlotte eyed the fire still blazing. "No. I will stay and read a little longer. The room is too cozy to leave."

Lydia kissed Charlotte on the head. "Very well." Before she closed the door, she looked back at her cousin sitting by the fire.

Charlotte met her stare. It was the first time she saw her cousin look tired; her eyes forlorn. "Lydia, is there anything wrong?"

Lydia shook her head and feigned a smile. "Our family is truly blessed to have you returned to us," she commented before she turned away and closed the door behind her.

Charlotte's stomach sank. *Was she saving her cousin or destroying her?*

With the room empty, Charlotte indulged in the solitude. She found a comfortable spot on the sofa nearest the lamp, bringing a book to her lap. Two pages later her eyes drooped and her head sank into the cushioned back of the sofa.

When she opened her eyes, she found her book still in her hands, laying across her skirt. She closed it and put it on the table beside her. The embers popped, and she moved her eyes to the orange glow of the fire. It was only then did she realize she was not alone. She startled.

"I did not mean to scare you," Nathanial said from the corner of the room. He moved into the light.

She sat up. "No. I...I thought I was alone." She looked at the clock on the mantel.

"It is nearly midnight," he informed her.

"You should have awakened me..."

"You were so..." He searched for the words but faltered. He ran his hands through his hair and loose waves fell in front of his face. He pushed it back again, making sure the tendrils stayed in place. "I didn't want to disturb you."

His voice was tender, loving, and it washed over her like a warm bath.

She shivered from the effects.

His waistcoat was unbuttoned, his cravat loosened. She saw an empty glass by the chair where he sat. He had been watching her.

Then she knew.

There was no wall between them. It was a veil separating them, where they could see each other, but neither one wanted to lift it, for fear of what lay on the other side.

Charlotte did not know if that was better or worse.

"You did not have to wait for me. I am sure Ada would have come."

"She did," he admitted. "I sent her away."

Charlotte wondered what he wanted.

He walked to the sideboard and poured two brandies.

"Would you care for a glass?" he asked, turning to her with a half-filled glass in his hand.

Charlotte said yes but didn't move. She didn't think she could stand and breathe at the same time.

He brought the brandy to her and sat in the chair across from her.

Neither spoke.

She looked at the glass in her hand, and he looked at her.

"The rain has stopped," she finally said, looking out the windows.

"Yes, about an hour ago," he answered dryly.

Charlotte could tell by his tone he didn't want to talk about the weather. She took a sip of her brandy. Then another one. Then another, until it was almost empty. She privately wished it was full again.

Her fingers went numb, and her heart weighed heavy. Excitement and fear equally pulsated through her veins. The brandy finally giving her the courage she needed, she placed her glass down, pushed her shoulders back, and leaned forward.

"Nathanial…is there something you wanted to discuss with me?"

He didn't hesitate to start.

"Lydia's plan…" he began and halted. He gulped from his drink. "She means well."

"Yes," Charlotte agreed, waiting for more.

"Do you understand…" His hands went through his hair again. "What she has requested of you?"

She understood perfectly well!

It consumed her thoughts. Night and day. Day and night. When would it happen? How would it happen? What would it be like? And more importantly, was Lydia's request the source of her torment, or was it her willingness to agree?

"I did not misinterpret her intention," Charlotte said, not wanting to commit to her own feelings on the matter.

Nathanial took one more sip to empty his glass and placed it heavily on the table. "But what she has forced upon me is very difficult…"

It never occurred to Charlotte that he might not want to share her bed. Her lips quivered. "Nathanial, if you do not want me…"

"No, no, no," he said, and knelt before her. His eyes met hers. "No, you misunderstand. Or I am fumbling?" He shook his head. "Her request is not difficult. You are a beautiful woman, Charlotte…you have beguiled me from the moment I met you. I cannot claim to be innocent of desire for you, and I am finding it difficult *not* to stop at your door at night. *That* is my torment."

Charlotte touched his face. The prickly hairs poked against her palm as she brushed her hand across his cheek. A warm sensation spread from her fingertips to her toes as she gazed into the tender eyes that rested upon her. She coveted the man before her. He intoxicated her, and she wanted to inhale him with every part of her being.

Nathanial took her hands into his and brought them to his lips, tasting the saltiness of her skin. "May God forgive us," he whispered.

LYDIA'S DECEPTION

*A*da scurried to answer the door when a hard knock rapped against it.

"Oh," she gasped.

Nathanial crossed the threshold, making his presence known.

"Good evening." His voice bellowed.

Charlotte slowly rose from her vanity, steadying herself. Not that she wasn't expecting him–he made his intentions clear the night before. In fact, she had had all but given him permission. Still, both terrified and excited, she wasn't sure she would ever be ready for him to come to her.

"May I speak to you, privately?" he said to Charlotte.

Without answering him, Charlotte excused Ada. "Please hand me my wrapper, and that will be all, thank you."

Ada grabbed the robe and helped Charlotte cover her chemise-covered body. She whispered, "Are you sure, Miss?"

With a nod from Charlotte, Ada obeyed, shutting the door behind her.

Nathanial moved further into the room but kept his distance. He looked at the door, as if pondering his retreat. The fire crackled, and he turned his attention away from the door.

"Shall I put more wood on the fire?" he asked.

Charlotte nodded. She couldn't find her voice.

With the fire burning again, Nathanial slowly unbuttoned his coat, sliding it off his shoulders, and tossing it on the sofa.

Charlotte watched him as he loosened his collar and pulled the fabric from his neck. She should have turned her gaze and allowed him the dignity to disrobe, but she was mesmerized. Like her interests observing specimens in nature, she now watched him with fascination, intrigued by what was to come next.

The fire strengthened, revealing the fervor on Nathanial's face. His eyes were dark, his jaw was firm. He pried open the buttons of his waistcoat, pulling it off his body. His shirt fell loosely around him. He brought his wrist upward and unhinged his cufflink. He went to his other wrist and did the same, cupping the two cufflinks in his palm before placing them on the mantle. The buttons soon followed, and he again cupped them in his hand and rolled them next to the cufflinks. With his shirt unrestricted, Charlotte caught a glimpse of the man underneath, with dark hairs running down his chest.

All the while, his eyes never left her. They stared... watching her, the captor of his wanting.

Without hesitation, he took her in his arms and kissed her.

Charlotte melted in his embrace, folding inside his strong arms, allowing his body to wrap around her.

His hands pressed against her back, pulling her closer as if he wanted to absorb her very being. He was consuming her.

She followed, tasting his mouth, breathing his breath. The more she gave, the more he asked of her. With her desire aroused, she lost control of her body.

Pulling his lips away but keeping her captive with his gaze, he implored. "Tell me you want me, Charlotte. I shan't have you if you don't..."

She took off her wrapper and led him to her bed.

Her arms opened inviting him to her body, breathless in anticipation. He slid off his trousers and carefully laid down on top of her, letting his hand slide inside the fabric of her chemise, and caress her warm skin. His kisses moved from her lips to her neck. Her neck to her shoulder. Her shoulder to her breasts. Only when he placed his hot mouth over her nipple, did she realize she was holding her breath. She exhaled a long sigh, signaling him to continue. And he did, suckling harder.

She let out a muffled scream, delighting in Nathanial's ability to give her rapture.

Charlotte closed her eyes, savoring the pleasure of his hands caressing her body. His touch was hot against her skin, exploring every part of her. She writhed underneath his powerful male form, surprised by her lack of inhibition. Her hands made their way to the muscles of his back, and she pressed him closer. She trusted Nathanial and followed his lead, giving into her yearning, and let him spread her thighs. When he entered her, she whimpered, as he pushed deeper inside her. He panted in her ear continuing his motion until his final thrust.

Nathanial's head fell against her chest and his body stilled. Charlotte ran her fingers through his hair as she listened to his breath rising and falling.

"You have never been with a man," he said, his voice raspy and raw.

"No," her voice whispered into the night's air.

He rolled off her, the heat of his body instantly taken from her.

"Damn her," he uttered. He rose from Charlotte's bed and grabbed his trousers laying on the floor, hastily tucking in his shirt.

Charlotte sat up, pulling the quilt over her half-naked body. "Nathanial?"

He didn't look at her. Instead, he collected his waistcoat over the back of the chair, his coat splayed on the sofa, and his items from the mantle putting them in his pocket. Bending over to collect his collar and tie, he sat down and laid his head in his hands.

Tick. Tick. Tick. The clock hands clicked, the plink echoing through the silence of the room.

He brushed his hair away from his face and stared into the fire.

"Have I angered you? Have I done something wrong?"

"Charlotte…" He couldn't bring himself to look at her. "I would declare myself the victim if it were not I who was the perpetrator." He threw his remaining clothes over his arm, grabbed his shoes, shoving his stockings inside, and headed for the door. "What I have taken from you…" His head hung; his eyes still diverted from hers. "I am sorry for what I have done."

With those last words, he left.

Charlotte lay alone on her bed, the blankets twisting in her hands. Tears wetted her cheeks. With the slam of his bedroom door, dread filled her heart.

The fire crackled.

She lifted her head and saw the room had darkened except for the glow of the logs that had lost their flames. She rose, washed herself, and dressed for bed. She stared into the mirror to see if anything had changed. Beside her red eyes, she was still the same Charlotte.

A log crumpled in the fire, scattering orange embers at the bottom.

She turned away from the mirror. There was nothing more to see.

As if heavy chains encircled her ankles, Charlotte dragged herself into bed and pulled the quilt up around her. But when she closed her eyes, all she could see was Nathanial's face. A torment tugged at her heart, and she gripped her chest, wanting to rip out the pain.

She didn't understand.

Being with him seemed so natural. Her body moved uncontrollably with his. She couldn't stop if she had wanted to. *And she didn't.* She felt attached to Nathanial in a way she never imagined-- body to body. Even with the pain in their union, there was something more she had to admit, as a woman and as a lover. She liked his lips upon hers, melted with his touch, enjoyed his body crushed against hers. When he lay on top of her, she felt his heartbeat synchronize with her own. She couldn't imagine being with anyone else.

She wanted more of him.

He didn't.

The tears came again, only ceasing when she fell asleep.

AWAKENINGS

*I*t was late morning before Charlotte opened her eyes. She heard Ada come in at her usual time, but laid still, hoping she would not disturb her.

Ada tip-toed through the room, pushed aside the curtains, opened the window, and retreated, allowing Charlotte to continue to sleep.

A crisp breeze crossed Charlotte's face, finally stirring her awake. Rolling over, she saw the sunlight, pronouncing the night had ended, and a new day had begun. The storm had gone, the grey skies lifted. The treetops in the distance glistened as the light danced off the leaves; birds chirped to one another flittering from tree limb to tree limb. All seemed joyous outside the walls of her room.

With a wildly loud yawn, Charlotte sat up and stretched her arms over her head. She blinked a few times, rattling her head awake. It was then that the memories flooded her thoughts, bringing her back to Nathanial and their night together. She wanted to throw the sheets over her head and drown in shame.

A soft knock came at her door, and she froze.

She had barely faced the new morning; she was not ready to face her sins.

"Come in?" she called.

"Good day, Miss. You are finally up," Ada greeted. "I have checked on you three times this morning and not a movement from you."

"What time is it?"

"Nearly noon."

"Noon?" Charlotte shrieked. "Did Lydia question my absence this morning?"

"Mistress Hammond insisted I let you sleep," Ada informed.

Charlotte cringed. Accepting her role in the confines of her bedroom was one thing, but to face Lydia after her sinful deed was another thing.

"I might stay in today," Charlotte suggested.

"A young woman like you should not be sitting in her room on such a lovely day. Besides, a personal note arrived from Lady Knightly. She has requested you to join her for tea this afternoon."

"Lady Knightly requested me?"

Ada smiled, "Shall I pull out your yellow dress?"

A personal invitation from such a notable woman was more than an honor; to decline would be detrimental to her social standing.

"Please have a note of acceptance sent right away," Charlotte ordered, pushing her blankets to the side with one shove.

It was not until she stood, did she remember the discomfort between her legs, or the blood she washed away, reminding her that her duty was now done. Nathanial had come and gone. She cursed herself for expecting more. Wasn't it obvious, from his abrupt departure, his feelings were not equal to hers? As humiliating as it was to face, she was nothing more than his bed companion. If she were going to honor her promise, she needed to learn her role as a lover. She did not know exactly what that entailed...or even if Nathanial would come to her again.

A moan escaped her mouth as she tried to walk.

"Is there something wrong?" Ada asked.

"Nothing a warm bath cannot fix," she said.

Ada's eyes widened, but she said nothing.

AT THE DOOR of the sunroom, Charlotte stood frozen with her hand on the knob. She bit her lip, mustering the courage to face Lydia. More so, she did not know how she would react towards Nathanial. Angry? Hurt? Scared? She peered over her shoulder, calculating where to go.

Had the door not opened, pulling her with it, Charlotte may have succeeded in her escape.

"Nathanial!" Charlotte gasped.

Their eyes locked.

The memory of his naked body entangling her within his grip rushed back. Warmth surged through her.

A cold stare greeted her, and his lips remained tight.

"Charlotte," he said, and moved aside for her to enter, abandoning his own retreat.

The heated surge turned to cold shivers.

Lydia rose to greet Charlotte, giving her a kiss on the cheek. "You have joined me today. I was worried you were going to sleep the day away."

"I did not sleep very well," Charlotte apologized, looking away from her cousin. She felt like a fraud standing before her. Ten baths would not take away Nathanial's lingering touch...the smell of him against her skin.

"I am sorry to hear you had a restless night. Well, one would never surmise...you look quite cheery in that yellow dress." Lydia stepped back to assess her appearance. "Lady Knightly will be pleased. She is quite fond of you. Or more to the point, her son is. It is rare for a woman to capture his attention, so I am sure she is eager to find out more about you."

"Mr. Knightly? Fond of me?" Charlotte knitted her brow. "Lydia, he has yet to know me. His intentions are for no other than to get acquainted, I am sure."

"Oh, you underestimate the power of a woman, Charlotte. A woman's charm is hard to resist for any man...even for one like Mr. Knightly. Do not let it frighten you. His mother has her hopes. It would not harm you to indulge her. There is much she could provide if you appease her notions. Who knows what is possible in matrimony."

"Lydia!" Nathanial's voice boomed. "She is not a ware to be bartered for and sold."

Lydia smirked. "What do you believe marriage is, Nathanial?" Her chin lifted in the air. "Besides, why would a man, as notable and wealthy as Mr. Knightly, not find our Charlotte worthy of his admiration? He could offer her plenty."

"Charlotte is not interested..." he insisted.

Charlotte questioned if Nathanial was protecting her or admitting she was not suitable for Mr. Knightly.

Lydia turned her back, ignoring her husband's chastisement. "It will be a lovely ride to *Penrose* this afternoon. Maybe we will stop after tea and see Mrs. Sotherby. I am sure she would appreciate the gesture."

"Lydia!" Nathanial demanded of her.

"Nathanial, dear, I am not dismissing what you said. Only, the frivolity of what we women do and when we do it should be of no particular concern for you." With his glare still on her, Lydia added, "Besides, are you not leaving for London?"

Charlotte turned to Nathanial. "You are leaving?" A higher octave to her voice gave away her surprise.

Nathanial hesitated. "I...there is urgent business waiting for me." He held up letters in his hand to validate the need of his departure. "Mr. Tatum has written, and I must not keep him any longer."

Bravely, she asked, "Will you be gone long?"

His eyes did not meet hers, confirming her suspicion that he was running away from her.

"I am afraid his business affairs have suffered since your arrival," Lydia explained. "Mr. Tatum is at his wit's end, wondering when Nathanial is to return to the office. But do not fret, Charlotte. His needs eventually send him back home."

Charlotte pulled at the pearls around her neck as a feeling of shame washed over her. She couldn't help but noticing Nathanial's jaw clench at the same time.

Lydia was being purposeful with her words confirming Charlotte's suspicions–Lydia knew Nathanial had finally come to her.

Charlotte was not experienced in hiding secrets, and Lydia was too close to her to not be able to read her face. Was it shame for agreeing to Lydia's outlandish request, shame for failing to please Nathanial, or shame for indulging in their encounter?

"Come," she suggested. "Let us walk in the rose garden before we go. The fresh air will do you some good." She pulled Charlotte close to her, as if nothing had changed between them.

But for Charlotte, everything had changed.

DISTRACTIONS

*L*ady Knightly had invited a few of her neighbors and their daughters to enlarge the gathering of her *impromptu* garden party. But there was no mistake in the spontaneous invitation–no gathering at her home was extemporized. Her goal for this afternoon's party was to learn more about the woman whose company her son had been seeking. She was well aware of Charlotte's lack of fortune, but she also understood the Ashford name held integrity. Charlotte possessed good blood and proper upbringing, and although not ideal in terms of finances, she could not downplay the importance of someone who attracted her son's interests. A more personal assessment would allow for her to conclude that Charlotte was an acceptable partner for her son.

"I am honored you came today," Lady Knightly greeted the two Ashford woman as they entered the already filled sunroom. "I hope the last-minute invitation was not inconvenient. The day begged for a garden party."

"It is a lovely day to encourage a gathering," Lydia said. "We are delighted you wanted to share it with us."

"Miss Ashford." Lady Knightly swooped Charlotte's hands into hers. "You are making quite the stir around town. It seems you have captured many hearts at the Henderson party. I hear you are a charming dance partner."

Charlotte gave Lady Knightly a smile, offering no reply to the rumors.

Lady Knightly did not waste time parading her around the circles of woman for introductions. Some Charlotte had met upon her previous visit to *Penrose*, some at the Henderson party, while others were new acquaintances. All were equally curious to find out more about her, for there was no secret about Mr. Knightly's interest in her.

"Are you staying long with the Hammonds?" Mrs. Eckert, a close acquaintance to Lady Knightly, inquired. She had been given strict instructions to befriend Charlotte.

"Lydia would have it no other way," Charlotte replied in kind.

"That would be lovely for all of us," Mrs. Eckert declared. "Once you are settled, it would be my honor to have you come and call on us."

"I will arrange a visit soon," Lydia interjected.

"Then you will not be returning to America?" Mrs.

Stevens asked, a frail creature by the rest of the room's standards, with an equally frail voice.

Once again, Lydia answered, "I would be more than thrilled to have Charlotte by my side forever." She reached over and squeezed Charlotte's hand. "My heart nearly ceased to beat when her father took her away."

The ladies of the room all agreed in unison.

"I must say, how fortunate for Mr. Hammond to know that you are well cared for with such a close companionship while he is away," Mrs. Eckert inserted. "He does travel to the city often. I cannot imagine being left alone all the time. Your cousin can only bring you great comfort."

The frail voice wondered, "Does he visit the city for very long?"

Lydia carefully smiled at Charlotte, catching her gaze. "Unfortunately, my husband comes and goes at his own will, with little knowledge of when he will return. But I am confident that he is very comforted with Charlotte joining our little family."

Charlotte wondered if Lydia was torturing her. She rose and walked toward the open doors, the gardens expounding just beyond, wishing she could get lost among the trees. With the chatter of the women, she did not hear Lady Knightly come behind her.

"Are you familiar with Penrose?" she asked.

"Only from my last visit. Your son was kind enough to show me the gardens outside the ballroom. You have quite a passion for roses, I see."

"That I do. But there is far more to enjoy. May I be so kind as to invite you back and give you a proper tour?" Lady Knightly offered.

"I would like that very much," Charlotte accepted, knowing Lady Knightly's intentions had more to do with her son than her need to show off her gardens.

A sudden interruption came from across the room.

"Andrew!" Lady Knightly exclaimed as her son walked towards her. "I had not expected you today."

Andrew gave her his warm affection with a kiss on her cheek. "But I see my business is yours," he remarked, raising an eye at Charlotte. He bowed to her. "Miss Ashford, it is nice to have you visiting today."

"Mr. Knightly." Charlotte extended her hand, "It is good to see you again."

"The honor is all mine." His slow smile appeared.

Charlotte was not particularly impressed. She knew he was performing his charm for all the ladies in the room, whose obvious infatuation was less than subtle.

"And what do we owe the honor of your appearance," his mother asked.

"I heard there was a gathering of exceptional ladies and could think nowhere else to be," he smartly answered.

The ladies all feigned delight.

"Then you will join us?" Mrs. Stevens insisted. Her cheeks pinked with her own forwardness.

"Only if it is not an intrusion upon you ladies."

All the other ladies cooed, insisting he join them.

Mr. Knightly followed his mother and Charlotte back to the women, grouped in threes and fours, talking among themselves around the room. He circled the small clusters, offering a smile if someone caught his gaze, or answered a question if one so chose to engage him, eventually settling where Charlotte now stood.

She could feel the warmth of his body shadowing hers. His musky scent of ambergris filled her nostrils.

Just as Mrs. Stevens was commenting on her daughter's upcoming wedding, Mr. Knightly leaned forward and quietly whispered in Charlotte's ear, "I am sure she is more excited for the income her daughter gains than her endearment to her new son-in-law. He is by far the dullest man anyone would *want* to marry."

Charlotte tried to ignore his whisper, holding a steady smile towards Mrs. Stevens.

Miss Abigail, a young and pale creature who was no more than twenty, commented on Mrs. Steven's daughter's good fortune. "It is more than a blessing for your daughter to marry so well. I only hope for such an opportunity."

Mr. Knightly whispered again. "It is only by her own fortune that she will be of interest."

Charlotte tensed, throwing her shoulders back, wishing Mr. Knightly's whispers away. But when he leaned in one more time to impart his unkind thoughts about Mrs. Eckert's grandchild, a shriek escaped her.

All heads turned.

"Is something the matter, my dear?" Lady Knightly asked.

The other women stared at her, waiting for an answer.

"I do apologize," Charlotte uttered. A rash of red patterned her cheeks. "I feel a little faint. I think I need some air."

"You poor child," Lady Knightly sympathized. "Andrew, please escort Miss Ashford out to the path. She might enjoy the view as well as the afternoon breeze."

Charlotte shook her head. "But I cannot inconvenience your son..."

"Nonsense. Andrew?" Lady Knightly gestured to her son.

Before she could object, Mr. Knightly was escorting her out the door.

"HERE WE ARE AGAIN, Miss Ashford. It seems fate is to bring us together," Mr. Knightly said.

"I am afraid fate is ruled by your mother, Mr. Knightly," Charlotte quipped. She had no intention of encouraging his interpretation of destiny.

"Ah, my mother. She is a force to be dealt with. You remind me of her."

"Me?" Charlotte glared. "If you called me unappealing, it would be hurtful. But to liken a young woman to one's mother is insulting!" She quickened her pace, wanting to flee from him.

"Please wait, Miss Ashford." When she didn't slow her pace, he yelled, "I do not bite!"

She eased her pace, allowing him to catch up. "You are horrid!" she declared when he reached her side.

"And you are charming for allowing me to be so horrid. Come, Miss Ashford, those women were dreadfully boring. I just rescued you from an afternoon of doom."

Charlotte lowered her eyes, not wanting him to have the satisfaction of knowing he was right. She couldn't deny the walk and his company were far more desirable than sitting in the room with prying eyes on her. "I am not an equal participant in your wicked behavior. I am only benefiting from your escape plan," she admitted.

"Well, let us enjoy the fresh air together, and hopefully rejuvenate your faintly disposition."

Charlotte crinkled her nose at him, ashamed of her deception.

"You may be as wicked as I," he taunted.

"I have no such capability," Charlotte insisted. "Who could not feel faintly after your dreadful commentaries."

Mr. Knightly stopped, halting Charlotte as well. He met her eyes.

"What are you doing, Mr. Knightly?"

"I want to assess what exactly you are capable of. Wickedness is not there. But I am not quite sure. Something is different about you from last we met."

Charlotte blushed. She feared her face was exposing her secrets. She had no mask. The heat of embarrassment grew. She touched her cheeks.

"That is it!" he laughed. "You are in love. It always shows on a woman's face. Something beautiful comes to the surface, the flush of the cheeks, the sparkle in the eyes. There is no denying it." He smiled, pleased with himself.

"So now I am flushed. Which shall it be, faintly or flushed?"

"Hmph, now that is not as much as a mystery as you think," he stated. He rubbed his chin. "A woman grows faintly when she is ill, or ashamed. She flushes when she feels passion. When she does both...I can only assume she is in a torrid love affair."

"Mr. Knightly, you are contemptible!" Charlotte snapped and turned away.

He touched her arm. "Please do not turn away. I did not mean to offend. Had I thought it was truthful, I would not have been so careless with my comments."

"You do offend me. And how dare you insinuate indecency," Charlotte protested, tears tempting to surface.

"I apologize. If you had not learned from our first encounter, my behavior is contemptible. You have every right to claim me so. How can I make it up to you? Please, you name it and I shall be at your disposal."

"I am in no position to place demands on your behavior, Mr. Knightly. I can only choose to ignore it or escape it. I choose the latter." Charlotte turned around to follow the path from which they came.

"You are more spirited than I anticipated, Miss Ashford."

"Only when pushed, Mr. Knightly."

"I am not your enemy. I promise. Some may differ in their opinion, but I have much to offer you. If not friendship, then protection."

Charlotte suddenly halted. It was the second time Mr. Knightly had made such a suggestion. It seemed odd and ominous. "What is so demanding that I should need protection? I am in the greatest care with my cousin and her husband. You seem to think otherwise?"

"I just know more about life. It is not as simple as one might expect."

"And what makes you believe I am a naïve maiden unaware of the world and who needs protection? I may be young, but well educated and well-travelled. My father was not neglectful of my upbringing. I am no less or more simple than the next woman."

"That, I can observe. But you are new here. Secrets abound among the society you now are associated with. I do not want you to be caught up in them and lose your avidity for life. You have a unique narrative that would be a shame to lose."

"I am neither a newcomer, nor a stranger to the mysteries of life. As you recall, I grew up not very far from here. The people I am now associated with are not unfamiliar to me. I have only found the contrary, thus far, and no one has made me feel other than accepted."

"I have angered you. That was not my intention. I am merely being cautious for you."

"From what?" she demanded.

"I am not sure. Call it instinct? I exist walking between the two worlds: the secretive and the honest. There are few who can do that. You, my fair lady, are not one of them."

"Then I must thank you for your concern, but I think it unnecessary."

"Is it?" He questioned. He did not miss that she did not deny an affair. "May I take you back to the house?"

Charlotte hesitated to take his arm. He didn't scare her. He puzzled her. She knew she was either going to like him very much, or never want to see him again.

EXPECTATIONS

*L*ydia arrived for breakfast to find a letter at her setting. She sat and lifted it, running her fingers over the wax stamped with initials. "How lovely, a note has arrived from Nathanial."

Charlotte tried to smile, pleased he was not negligent in sending communication. To her dismay, he had not sent anything to her, as she had hoped.

"He writes all is well on his end. And hopes we are enjoying each other's company...sends Peter his love... and informs that business will delay him further," Lydia shared.

"Does he say when he will return?" she dared to ask.

Lydia read through the letter once again. "No. How extraordinary! Usually, he indicates when he *might* arrive. He knows I hate surprises."

"Lydia?" Charlotte questioned. "How can you

accept his carelessness? He leaves so unexpectedly, without the decency to inform you of his return."

"Hmph," Lydia scoffed. "You mean he disappears? For he never leaves us. Contrary to his action, Nathanial has the highest regard for his home and family. He will always return."

Leave, disappear, or run away? Charlotte wasn't sure it mattered. They all meant he was gone.

"And you do not feel abandoned? Disregarded? Lonely?"

"As big as this house is, the walls tend to close in on you," she wistfully said. "He escapes when it becomes too much. I find no harm in his actions."

She knew Nathanial's reason for escaping. Her heart sank.

"Charlotte, my dear." She lifted Charlotte's chin to meet her eyes. "Do not clutter your heart with sentiment, for you will always be disappointed. Marriage is like managing a household. It takes order, discipline, and acuity. An acquired perception of what is needed, and the disposition to govern it. It is only love that makes things become complicated. I do not mix the two. Nor do I allow my own temperament to be conflated with either."

She did not know if Lydia was referring to her own life, or a warning to Charlotte's. Either way, her words were haunting.

Lydia rose from the table. "Now, if you do not mind, my son needs his mother this morning. Nanny believes he is on the verge of a cold. I will be in his quarters for the rest of the morning. Join me later in the salon?"

Charlotte released her, hesitantly, feeling very alone. Not sure what she needed. *Companionship or a distraction?* Anything would suffice to keep her thoughts from Nathanial.

Since Nathanial's visit to her room–to her bed–her body had healed, but her desire had only begun to blossom. The warmth of his hands still lingered on her skin. If she closed her eyes, she could feel the heat of his breath on her neck. She yearned for the taste of his mouth upon hers. Charlotte was not sure what she was supposed to feel after being with a man. No one prepared her for the outcome, nor did she have anyone in which to confide. But the torment of his retreat and the agony of not knowing when he would return were far more agonizing to endure.

Finding sanctuary in the library, Charlotte sank to the sofa, fell upon her arms, and cried.

The door opened, and she heard footsteps enter.

"Excuse me, Miss, but there is a gentleman to see you," the soft voice of the maid informed.

Charlotte sniffled and wiped at her tears with the sleeve of her dress. "Whoever could it be? I am not expecting anyone. Please tell him I am not taking any callers," she ordered. "And I wish not to be disturbed..." she called after the maid as she retreated.

Charlotte heard the maid's footsteps along the corridor.

Once again silent, Charlotte lay her head down,

hoping sleep would soon find her, and take away her misery. But before her eyes could shut, she heard footsteps once again arrive at her door.

Without a knock, someone entered, shut the door, and proceeded further into the room.

She dared not look up for fear of showing her face blotted with tears.

"I have been turned away many times, but from you I expected more," Mr. Knightly's voice bellowed from across the room.

Charlotte squeezed her lids tight and turned away from him. "Please go away, Mr. Knightly. I am in no state to be seen or spoken to."

He walked nearer to the sofa. "That, I can see for myself. All the more reason I am not going anywhere. Not until you are back to your spirited self."

Charlotte rolled over and faced him. Her eyes were red, and strands of loose hair stuck to her tear-stained cheeks. She rose from the couch, pulled the wetted strands off her face, and addressed Mr. Knightly properly.

"You must think me to have no pride," she said.

"And you must think me a dishonorable gentleman barging in the way I did," he countered.

"Yes, I do." She pulled the hairs from her face and pushed them aside, tucking the ends into her chignon.

"Well, Miss Ashford, I must admit, with no pride or honor, we are quite a pair, indeed."

To Mr. Knightly's surprise, Charlotte attempted a smile.

Lifting her chin, he pulled out his handkerchief and wiped under her eyes, softly following the lines of her cheekbones to her hairline.

She batted her lashes, heavy with tears. "Thank you, Mr. Knightly…"

"There, that is what I want to see; the warmth coming back into those eyes. You are far too beautiful to be so sad." He studied the sadness in her eyes. "Love is such a treacherous thing. It can cause so much pleasure and so much pain. How strong are you to endure the battle between the two…"

"And why do you assume my tears are about love?"

"One's heart does not bleed tears like yours over superfluous things. No, this is love in the most hopeless way," Andrew surmised with resolve.

Charlotte's tears started again. Mr. Knightly dabbed a few more times at the streaks along her cheek and handed her his handkerchief to finish the job.

Searching the room, he asked, "Is there a bloody drink around this house?"

"I could ring for someone, or Nathanial has a room next door. I am sure he would not mind you helping yourself," Charlotte offered.

Andrew needed no more enticing. He swiftly left the room, returning a moment later with a crystal decanter in one hand and two glasses in the other. He raised them in the air to question her desire to drink with him.

Charlotte shook her head. "It is too early for me."

"It is never too early for me…" He filled his glass.

With the roar of thunder, rain began, and Charlotte moved to the window to watch the downpour.

It was a dreary day with a wind wildly blowing the leaves about on the trees. The grey clouds and wet mess outside seemed to mirror Charlotte's feelings. She watched as the storm swept across the landscape.

Mr. Knightly did not disturb her reflection, opting for the pleasure of the whiskey he poured himself. He took a sip, pursed his lips, and swallowed, awaiting Charlotte's next words.

When her tears eventually dried, Charlotte folded Mr. Knightly's linen and placed it in her sleeve but didn't move from her contemplation at the window.

"There is always something renewing about the rain," she said not turning around to her companion in the room. "The smell of the wet soil, the shine of the leaves, the cleansing of the landscape. It's as if life has a chance to be reborn; a fresh start."

"Ah, not only are you beautiful, but a poet as well. Will you cease to amaze me?"

"Now you are teasing me." She crossed her arms and looked over her shoulder at Mr. Knightly. She sighed, "I knew it could not last with you." She turned to face him directly. "You had me believing you were a man of feeling, Mr. Knightly."

"Maybe the rain will give me the chance to prove myself a decent man."

"Only time will tell, Mr. Knightly."

"That is enough," he declared. "When a woman

cries in one's presence, I believe he has a right to demand she address him by his Christian name. Are we to be so formal with one another after such intimacies?"

Charlotte smirked as she walked to him. "I suppose we are due some leniency...at least in each other's company."

Andrew lifted his glass to her and gulped to their agreement.

"It is still very early in the afternoon. You might want to slow down to compensate for the hours still ahead of you."

"And you are sensible! Charlotte, if I had any sense at all, I would fall in love with you."

"Are you mocking me? A man who doesn't believe in love should never claim the possibility to a woman who has hopes of such a noble pursuit."

"What naivety you still carry to believe in such nonsense. Love is a fairytale to entice lovers to be honorable. But honor is not always synonymous with love."

"You are quite cynical. Who has hurt you so to turn your heart cold?"

"Maybe I have not found someone to melt the glacial block that lives in my chest. Or maybe I was born without a heart at all."

"Andrew, everyone has a heart! It is how you wield its power that matters. You can love and be loved, or you can let it harden with bitterness and fear. It is your choice. The potential lies within you, not the ability of another to transform you. Why give or let someone take that gift from you?"

"Indeed, why would *you*?" Andrew threw the question back at her.

Charlotte pursed her lips, frustrated at being caught with her own words.

"Tell me, Charlotte," he said, twirling his empty glass between his hands. "Who is this man who has caused you such heartache?"

Charlotte turned away from him. There was so little she could reveal to him...to anyone. She, Lydia, and Nathanial were now entangled in a web of lies that could destroy all of them.

She did not answer.

Andrew walked closer to her, whispering in her ear, "What causes you more agony, the pleasure of loving, or the pain of not being loved?"

A coldness shimmied down her spine. Considering the memory of Nathanial abandoning her soon after they shared their desires, she would declare the latter.

"Is one better than the other in the end?" she pondered. "Maybe you are right, agony may ultimately be the outcome of love."

He rubbed his chin. "I misstated my assessment of you. I called you a poet earlier. I do suppose you are more a philosopher."

"I do not want to be like you, Andrew." Her brow grew stern. "You only see love as a sacrifice of oneself. Is not love about giving? I have to believe there is merit to opening your heart."

"Have to? Or want to?"

Charlotte scoffed. "Does it matter? If not to open our hearts, why do we continue to exist?"

For pleasure! Andrew wanted to answer, but he couldn't bring himself to expose himself completely to Charlotte. He liked her too much. "As I predicted, you are a rare woman, Miss Charlotte Ashford." He took her hand in his and kissed it. "Truly rare."

"No, I am nothing extraordinary. No woman is. And if you are waiting to find that creature, I am afraid no one will ever be able to live up to your expectations. Thus, you resign yourself to the impossible..." She paused. "When possibly, someone special may be right in front of you."

"What do I see? I see a woman who has earned her first battle wound from love, and for that it pains me. You have not lost your innocence, but I fear you are headed into the pits of Hell. Be careful, my dear. You have the heart of a lover, but not the strength of a warrior. There are demons out there waiting for fresh blood."

Charlotte wondered if the demons hadn't already found her.

CONFIDANTS

*O*ver the weeks, Andrew found himself a
regular guest at *Lottington Manor*. He made it
a habit to arrive at the stables and join Charlotte and
Lydia on their afternoon rides. By the first week's end,
confident in Mr. Knightly's good intentions for
companionship, Lydia excused herself as chaperone,
leaving the two in private company.

Charlotte found it difficult to not grow fond of
Andrew. He was funny, charming, and uninhibited. He
was a great distraction from thinking about Nathanial,
who remained absent. With Andrew's help, life
resumed to a sense of normalcy, and with it, a new
friendship blossomed.

"Do you not have other obligations?" Charlotte
asked, as they slowed the horses to rest under a tree.

"What better distraction than what I have right

here?" Andrew said. "Are you not enjoying our time together?"

"Surprisingly so," she admitted, taking off her hat.

"I am glad to see I have grown on you. My mother would be happy to see I have made some new, respectable friendships." Pulling a small blanket off the horse, he laid it down under the tree and invited Charlotte to sit.

She acquiesced, relieved to get out of the sun and rest.

"Respectable?" Charlotte questioned. "There you go again, Andrew. Expectations to live up to."

His eyebrow raised. "My dearest Miss Ashford, not you? Do you have something to hide? For you would be in good company."

"So, I have heard," she teased.

Lydia had told Charlotte about Andrew's propensities of gambling, drinking, and preference for visiting not-so-reputable places in the city. She didn't confide in Charlotte to discourage her affection for him, but rather to inform her to be cautious. Andrew came with a reputation that would be hard to leave behind.

Charlotte had to admit she was not shocked by Lydia's information. Andrew had made plenty of references to his past. But with the turn of events in her own life, Charlotte could not bring herself to judge his private behavior. He had never been less than a gentleman in her presence, and there seemed no reason to judge him by something that did not seem to affect her.

She watched the man who lay next to her on the blanket. He pulled at a long piece of grass and played with it between his fingers, before making a knot out of the end. He tossed it aside, only to pull another blade and do it again. She wondered why he spent so much time with her, was attentive with no apparent expectation in return. He made no advances, implying he wanted nothing more than the friendship budding between them. It was this sense of safety and genuine connection that filled her with gratitude for the relationship.

Her turned, catching her observation.

"Charlotte," he flicked the knotted blade back to the grass, "I hope I have proved myself worthy of your confidence. I have stated before, and I state it now, I am here to protect you."

"Why?"

"Why what?" he asked.

She need not explain. Her knitted brow pushed him to continue.

"Alright, I will let you in on a secret. I had a sister I never knew. She died long before I was born. But there always seemed to be a person missing from my family. I do not know why I felt that way, but if she were alive, I believe she would be very much like you." He paused to find the right words. "I find you comforting to be with."

That made Charlotte smile. She leaned against the tree and closed her eyes, relishing in the sweet moment.

Andrew, too, closed his eyes, and smiled to himself. He thought Charlotte very beautiful and deserving of the happiness she now exuded. The afternoon when he found her crying, she was burdened. Her sadness was tangible, pushing him to bring her back from such a dark place. Dark places were his area of expertise.

"Andrew..." She hesitated, "May I be so bold as to ask you a question? About being a man?"

Andrew's eye popped open.

"Do not look at me that way," Charlotte scolded. "I am relying on you to behave honorably."

With a rise in octave, he declared. "You do trust me!"

"Of course. Now, will you be serious and listen?" She pleaded.

Andrew nodded and sat up, giving her his attention.

"You are a gentleman with insight..." She hesitated to continue.

"Go on," he signaled.

"How does one capture a man's interest?"

Andrew was going to cough a laugh but controlled himself. "Well, beauty is always a top preference."

"So, I am to assume being a charming young lady is only appealing if she has acquired physical beauty?"

"That, and her inheritance," he added with much seriousness.

Charlotte's eyes lowered.

"I am sorry. That was insensitive." Andrew reached

for her hand. "But why are you to worry? You have both beauty and charm."

"I was foolish. I am sorry I even broached the subject." She pushed herself up, ending the conversation abruptly. She grabbed her hat and secured it to her head as she hurried to her horse. Taking the reins, she led the steed ahead.

Andrew called for her to wait, but she didn't concede. He grabbed the blanket from the ground, threw it over his shoulder, and grabbing his own horse, rushed after her.

"Charlotte," he begged from behind her, "It seems I am always chasing you. I implore you, please stop!"

She did not.

Andrew continued his pursuit.

"Is this about the gentleman who was the cause of your tears?" He huffed. "He does not deserve you if you feel you need to pursue him." He puffed. "You are better than that!" he yelled out, dragging his horse to follow faster.

She picked up her pace, kicking the hems of her skirts outward with every determined stride.

"Honestly, I have never known a woman who could walk so quickly," he grumbled, panting his way until she was a few steps ahead. "You realize you put me in a very difficult position to speak to a woman about such a topic? I did not mean to offend you."

She stopped and turned to him. "You did not offend me. I...I was the one who was inappropriate. I should be the one apologizing."

Andrew dropped the reins of his horse and walked over to Charlotte. He grabbed her hands in his and lifted them to his lips, placing a kiss on each. "Dearest Charlotte, it is this and so much more that endears me to you. Please never apologize to me again. Now, tell me, what is this really about?"

Charlotte pulled her hands away and resumed walking. This time, she paced her steps with Andrew's.

"I was asked to do something; to act upon something out of honor for someone I dearly love. But I fear I have failed, and I do not know how to fix it."

"I cannot imagine you disappointing anyone."

"Well, you seem to be blinded by your own prejudices."

Andrew could sense that she wanted to say more and waited for her to continue.

"But in the end, I am feeling rather foolish," she admitted.

"If we are talking about a man …you cannot hold yourself so accountable. It is he who has failed to see the lovely woman you are."

"You assume it is man," she challenged him. "You are very wrong."

"Then this isn't about a man?" Andrew's brow shifted upward.

"Not completely," she corrected.

"Ah, but there is a man! Who is it? Who has captured your heart? Or maybe has broken it?" His eyes squinted and pursed his lips. "I have seen no other possessing your time and attention, for I have made sure I have been preoccupying all of you," he declared.

"I am not at liberty to say."

"Well, if there is a gentleman in pursuit of you, and he is to ask for your hand in marriage, I want to be sure he is worthy."

Charlotte looked away.

"Charlotte, Charlotte, dearest Charlotte," Andrew blew his breath out. "What have you done?"

Her eyes darted to the ground. "What I have done is done. There is no turning back."

Andrew grew quiet. He was not sure he was shocked by Charlotte's admission, or proud of her ability to be so provocative. Either way, she was asking him for help.

"You do not need information about how to capture a man's attention. So, you are asking me for advice about…"

"I am tired. Can we please head home?" Charlotte obfuscated, quickening her pace once again.

"He is married!" he shouted.

Charlotte stopped in her tracks but did not give him the satisfaction of seeing the truth on her face.

"Charlotte, you become more fascinating, the more I learn. This man must be extremely important for you to walk on the other side of virtue."

"You are assuming I am deceiving someone. You must believe me when I say I am not."

"Then what causes your tears and agony, if not your guilt?"

Charlotte did not answer, giving Andrew more fodder to draw his own conclusions.

"This man, he is aware of your feelings? But how can he not be, you wear it all on your face."

"I was foolish enough to show him," she admitted. "But I fear my feelings are not reciprocated."

Andrew grew silent at her admission. The anguish flashed across her face, and his heart felt heavy for her.

"Charlotte, if anyone has the capacity to love, it is you. This gentleman, whoever has won your heart, is a fool."

"Please, Andrew, do not speak of him so harshly. He knows little of my torment; little of my shame. He has done nothing to deserve your scorn."

"He has hurt you. He brings tears to your eyes…is that not enough?"

Charlotte wiped away the corners of her eyes and sniffled.

"Do you love him?" Andrew asked but did not need her to answer. The truth of his words was apparent.

He requested nothing more from Charlotte, nor did she offer. He only knew he wanted to help her.

WOMAN IN THE MIRROR

*C*harlotte was the first to arrive for breakfast and sat down, anticipating Lydia's arrival was soon to follow. Nearly a half an hour had passed, she finally requested for her own meal to be served.

With apologies, Lydia's personal maid, Sadie, arrived to inform Charlotte that Lydia would be having breakfast in bed. She reported that Lydia had been up late with Peter, who was suffering from a running nose and a deep cough.

"Is he not getting better?" Charlotte asked. She had been told only yesterday, by Lydia herself, that he was on the mend.

"Nothing more than a small cough left, but it kept him up all night and Ms. Hammond was by his side until he fell asleep in the wee hours of the morning.

"Shall I go up and tend to him?"

"Oh, my dear, no!" Sadie explained. "He seems

much more spirited this morning. His nanny has him up and ready to get some fresh air. Mistress is relieved, but said she wanted to rest a little more before she tends to her daily activities."

"But of course. Let her know I am here if she needs anything."

Sadie agreed to pass along the message, and left Charlotte to herself to finish breakfast.

"Good morning, Sir," Sadie's voice echoed in the hallway.

"Good morning. Is Mrs. Hammond in the breakfast room?" a deep voice inquired.

"No Sir, it is only Miss Ashford who is dining. Mrs. Hammond is taking breakfast in bed this morning. Shall I tell the kitchen you are here?"

"No thank you," he replied.

Charlotte froze. Her heart pounded, the sound reverberating in her ears. She had not seen Nathanial in a fortnight. He sent no word nor informed the household of his return. And there he stood, only a few feet outside the door, his voice instantly affecting her. She did not know if she wanted to run, hide, or jump for joy to see him again.

He did not give her the chance to decide.

She heard his heavy footsteps come nearer, stop, and retreat, leaving an echoing of his heels clapping against the wood floors as he walked away.

Charlotte pushed away her plate and left. The walls of the morning room felt as if they were closing her in. *She needed air!* Finding the nearest opened door, she ran. No particular direction. Just anywhere to get away. Outside didn't help. The trees there felt taller; hedges closer. When she looked up, to the expansive blue skies above, puffy white clouds only seemed to swirl overhead, taunting delirium. She closed her eyes and clasped her belly. She teetered across the garden lawns before keeling over and gasping for air.

Fool! she yelled to herself. *Damn fool!*

"Miss?" A groomsman came from behind her. "Is everything all right?"

Charlotte quickly straightened, brushing her hand across her hair, tucking away loose hairs fallen from her bun. "Yes, quite." She feigned a smile and hoped it would suffice.

The groomsman didn't believe her and stood stoic waiting for more.

"It was a side ache," she explained, grabbing her waist. "I lost my breath for a moment. I am better now."

"Aye," he nodded and proceeded to continue on his way, eyeing her once more before he disappeared altogether.

The walls were everywhere!

She gathered herself, flattening the fabric of her dress, adjusting the belt at her waist, and lifting the fabric at her shoulder, before walking back to the house, realizing there was nowhere to run...away from *him.*

If Nathanial wanted to play the game of avoidance,

she could, too. The house was amply large enough for the two of them. He had made that perfectly clear.

Seeing the doors open to the salon, Charlotte scurried across the lawn, up the stairs. She slipped into the house with no one the wiser of her childish escape.

To her dismay, Nathanial stood directly ahead of her.

Their eyes met.

For a moment she thought about running. *Like he did*. Her anger swelled, a fierce surge of blood pulsated through her veins, giving her the courage to stay. She looked right at him.

His eyes were deep, dark as usual–and burdened.

Their effects did not sway her.

"Is this how it is to be between us? Strangers by day, lovers by night?"

Nathanial stiffened in his stance. "I prefer we do not have this conversation, Charlotte."

"Would you prefer that you never came to me?" The words flew out of her mouth before she realized she didn't want the answer. Her eyes narrowed; her hands fisted against the sides of her dress, not wanting to give into the tears threatening an appearance.

Nathanial didn't answer. His shoulders fell and he let out a heavy sigh instead.

Song Thrushes flew outside the window, and he looked towards them as if they had the answer he was seeking. When they were gone, he returned to the waiting Charlotte, who did not turn her gaze from him.

Her cheeks were flushed, and her eyes were cold, demanding him to speak.

"I was hoping with my absence..." he paused, struggling to find his words. "I was hoping the separation would help us see things more clearly."

"Nathanial, was I not clear when I invited you to my bed? I am sorry you felt it...I...was unsatisfactory."

"Charlotte," he interrupted. "Is that what I have led you to believe?"

"What else am I to assume?"

He leaned to her but offered nothing in response.

His lips were tight and colorless. Shadows hung dark under his eyes. The lines near his mouth were deep, and dark ridges crossed his forehead. Had she not seen the same in her own mirror?

She lowered her lids. "You left me with no other conclusion."

He stepped back at her words. Straightening his shoulders, he tugged at his collar and cleared his throat. "We are better off if we leave it be," he said. "Now, if you will excuse me..."

He abruptly turned and walked out the door, leaving her standing alone.

"How dare he!" she declared to the empty room. Stomping her feet across the parquet floor, she rushed after him. "I did not excuse you!" she yelled after him.

He halted at the sound of her voice but did not turn around.

Catching up to him, she tugged at his shoulder,

forcing him to turn to her. "Why do you run from me? Am I that much of a disappointment to you?"

He did not answer, his lips remaining tight across his face.

"Nathanial, *please!*" she pleaded. "You cannot avoid me forever."

He ran his hand through his hair. "I am not running away from you," he paused, looking at anywhere but her. "I am running away from me," he said with resolve.

She gripped her chest and jerked back. "I do not understand."

"You cannot know my torment," he said. He closed his eyes, shaking his head, mustering courage. "It is I who is the disappointment, Charlotte. I, who took you, selfishly. I...I had no right to you."

"Do you think I have not been equally affected?"

"Lydia is my wife!" he blurted. "And you...you were innocent."

Tears flooded her eyes. "If it were not for my love of Lydia, I would not be standing here in despair!"

"What I did...what I want..." his eyes darted away. "I have no right to you, Charlotte. No right at all." He turned and walked away from her, distancing the space between them, ripping away from the urge to pull her to him.

"Nathanial!" Charlotte shouted. "I willingly agreed to Lydia's plan. I wanted it so. Why do you punish me for my love of her...even if it means my wanting you?"

Nathanial stopped.

He turned his head and her brilliant blue eyes called to him with a magnetic force he could not resist. His body enclosed hers. He stroked her cheek, indulging in the touch.

Charlotte closed her eyes, tilted her head, and parted her lips, waiting for him to come down on her.

In the distance, twigs snapped, and Nathanial ripped himself away, putting much space between them, leaving her lingering.

"Ah, there you two are," Andrew's voice called out as he walked through the clearing.

They both turned at the intruder.

"Good afternoon, Mr. Hammond," Andrew said, extending a handshake. He bowed to Charlotte, noting the rush of color in her cheeks, as well as in Nathanial's. "I hope your day has been pleasant so far?"

"Very much. Thank you for asking," Charlotte replied. "And you, Mr. Knightly? What is your pleasure today?"

"You, of course."

Charlotte's face colored.

He was making a mockery of her, of them both.

"I was seeking your companionship," Andrew explained. "It is such a beautiful day I could not bear to indulge in it without an equally beautiful companion. But I see, Mr. Hammond has the same idea."

Nathanial swallowed hard. He glanced at Charlotte, whose face struggled to hold a smile.

"Aww, but who could blame one for such an indulgence," Andrew continued. "I should have arrived sooner to steal her away. Despite my own wishes to covet Charlotte, my visit is primarily at the request of my mother...she has grown quite fond of her." He slid a smile across his face. "As we all have."

Nathanial shifted in his stance, but his face gave no sign that Andrew's duplicity might be bothering him.

Charlotte took Andrew's arm. "Shall we continue to walk?" she suggested, hoping to distract him from the scene he happened upon. She could not know how much Andrew had seen through the trees. Her conversation with him the day before was innocent enough when the person of topic was a mere mystery. But now there could be no doubt Andrew was drawing his own conclusion after finding Nathanial and her together.

Andrew fell in-step with Charlotte, leaving Nathanial to walk alongside them.

Charlotte's voice lifted. "Will you stay for the afternoon, Mr. Knightly? Lydia will be so pleased; the day will not seem complete if you do not accept."

"Why certainly. I have already agreed to do so. Mrs. Hammond suggested as such before I headed out the door to find you. I was almost sure I had recently worn out my welcome. Come to find out, I have not."

Nathanial, "You have been visiting often, then?"

Charlotte caught his glower at Andrew and hastily added, "Peter has been ill, and Lydia has not been able to spend the afternoons with me." Facing Nathanial, she explained. "Not wanting me to be alone, Lydia encouraged Mr. Knightly to keep me company. He has been riding with me, joining me for walks. It has only seemed natural for him to dine with us after our adventures." She added, "Lydia and I have most certainly benefitted from his companionship."

Andrew chuckled. "I needed little persuading from your wife, Mr. Hammond. An invitation from her is coveted among these parts. And her cousin is a quite a delight. Who knew a woman could be so fascinating?"

Nathanial gave Andrew a nod. "We are in agreement, Mr. Knightly."

Andrew stopped, halting the three in-step, purposefully locking eyes with Nathanial. "Are we?"

Nathanial put his hand in his pocket and lingered with his thoughts before he replied. "I am sure the country, however, can become quite dull for someone of your interests, Mr. Knightly. Are you not eager to head back to the city?"

Andrew smirked. "Not as uneventful as one might seem." He glanced at Charlotte. "I never knew so much happiness could be experienced with so few distractions."

"But you will leave us…soon?" Nathanial pressed.

"I have no persuasion to depart. As Miss Ashford pointed out to me the other day, there are many indulgences here of which I have not taken advantage. Ah, but I am remiss in my duties." Andrew put his hand in his coat pocket and pulled out an invitation, handing it to Charlotte. "After all this talk of the glories of the country, my purpose is to take Charlotte away to the city. My mother is intent on having Charlotte as her companion for the theatre. She would be thrilled to have her join us in London."

Nathanial cleared his throat, looking at the note now gripped between Charlotte's fingers.

"I am honored," Charlotte said, opening the letter and reading it. "This is lovely. Tell her I would be happy to accompany her." She glanced at Nathanial. "It is just the escape I need."

Nathanial watched as she folded the letter and handed it back to Andrew, who returned it to his pocket from where it came.

"Mother will be so pleased. But you can tell her yourself. She has assuredly arrived by now to confirm your commitment, had I not secured it."

"Your mother is here? You should have said something sooner. We should hurry back."

Andrew took ownership of Charlotte's arm with presumption and led the way towards the house.

Nathanial did not join them. Not moving, he allowed the two to walk ahead, further distancing themselves from him.

"There you are," Lydia declared as Charlotte and Andrew came through the doors. "I was going to send out a search party for you. Look who has joined us?" Her hand fell to the sofa to where Lady Knightly sat.

Lady Knightly rose. "Now Mrs. Hammond, we should not scold the two. They are young and have much to discuss. Do you not remember what it is like to be unattached?"

"Mother!" Andrew reprimanded. "If you will not be

subtle, please be accurate. It was not I who delayed Miss Ashford. She was walking with Mr. Hammond. I only happened upon them. We returned as quickly as we could."

Lydia peered out the doors. "I wondered where that man was. He no sooner had arrived, and he disappeared again." She looked to Charlotte. "Did Nathanial follow you?"

Charlotte shook her head.

Andrew promptly answered, "Good man. He allowed me the honor of accompanying Miss Ashford back to the house."

"Oh…" Lady Knightly fluttered her hand over her heart. "How fortunate for you, my son."

Andrew rolled his eyes.

"If you will excuse me," Lydia hurried to the door. "I will notify the kitchen that we are now five." She pointed to a table topped with glass decanters. "Please, Mr. Knightly, fix yourself a drink. I shall return promptly," she said before scurrying out the door.

"Such a kind hostess," Lady Knightly commented.

Andrew, looking to Charlotte, uttered, "Yes, I am sure she does not miss a thing in this household."

Charlotte turned her back to Andrew, not allowing him the pleasure of seeing her reaction.

"Come, Miss Ashford," Lady Knightly invited Charlotte to sit next to her, "Did you receive my invitation?"

"Why yes, I did. Thank you for the invitation. I

accept wholeheartedly and look forward to joining you in London."

"I am so pleased. While in London, I want to introduce you to many people...of prestige and importance. I know they will adore you as much as I."

"Mother, Miss Ashford is not a pet. I declare, you will not shuffle her from house to house, putting her on display," Andrew growled.

"No, of course not, son. But if you do not want me to monopolize her, you must claim her for yourself."

"That, I assuredly will."

Charlotte sighed...heavily and loudly. The two turned their heads simultaneously towards her.

"Please forgive us, Miss Ashford. We are talking about you, and there you are, sitting before us." Lady Knightly acknowledged. "I beg your pardon. But of course, our little trip is for your benefit. My only hope is for you to enjoy yourself."

Andrew walked to Charlotte, placing himself in a chair by her side. "As is *my* hope as well."

REGENTS PARK

*C*harlotte left for the city a few days later with Lady Knightly, who was terribly excited to have Charlotte as her companion. Together they explored the newest museum exhibits, visited the finest dress shops, and introductions were made to Lady Knightly's dearest friends.

The matron was more than generous with her time, associations, and money. Charlotte was spoiled by her. *Undeservedly so,* thought Charlotte. It was well known in the rumor mills that Lady Knightly was not only chaperoning a new arrival in society, but also conspiring for a union between Charlotte and her son.

Charlotte knew better, though. Andrew was no more interested in her as she with him. She was there as a favor *to him*–to distract his mother. Not to win his favor. Thankfully, as days passed with endless invitations and outings, little time was left to contemplate her deception to Lady Knightly.

Andrew joined them on the trip into the city only to disappear for several days *to attend to his personal affairs*, he explained. He was not forthcoming as to what his *affairs* entailed but promised Charlotte his full attention upon his return.

On the fifth day of the trip, he finally appeared, dressed in a dapper light grey suit, crisp white shirt, and cravat of silvery grey. On his feet he modeled the latest Chelsea boots, and topped on his head was a new black hat, making him appear even more distinguished.

"You look impressive. Your spirits are quite gay. Is it for anyone in particular?" Charlotte inquired.

"I will take the compliment as sincere," he tipped his hat. "And to answer your question, *no*. No one is more deserving than you."

"Andrew, I have a hunch you are lying to me," Charlotte accused. "Lucky for you, I will ignore it because you are here with me now, after neglecting me for days."

"Ah, that is where you are wrong. You have been very much in my thoughts..."

Charlotte smirked, amazed at his quick wit and charm, but doubting his sincerity.

"It is obvious, Charlotte, by the brightness in your eyes, my absence has not hindered your contentedness. You look happy," Andrew noted.

"I cannot deny it. London is so exciting. *Your*

mother has made sure of that. I have not seen the city since I was a little girl. It is all so new again."

"Then let us not waste another moment of this splendid day..."

Andrew took Charlotte through the streets of London, leading her to Regents Park, notorious for the design and cultivated space, offering a blend of nature and artistry. The park's landscape featured meandering pathway, carefully curated flower beds filled with seasonal flowers, a focal-point lake, ornamental ponds, fountains, and sculptures of historical figures and mythical characters abound. Taking Charlotte's hand in his, Andrew paraded her down the gravel paths among the crowds gathered on blankets having picnics and sitting on benches under the tree lined walkways, taking advantage of the shade. Women in their finest dresses nodded their heads, and the men, equally dressed and coiffed, tipped their hats to them as they strolled by.

It was not by mistake Andrew was promenading with her. He knew people gossiped. Charlotte's reputation was growing with every step, and his own standing benefitted as well.

Word would assuredly get back to his mother.

Andrew squeezed her hand. "I am glad...thrilled to be the one with whom you experience it with. I want to share you with the world, and the world with you." Confirming he was showing her off, he added, "You are a beautiful woman. What man is not thinking he would rather be in my position, by your side? More endearing, you are authentic. I have yet to meet a woman so unpretentious and at the same time commanding an air of civility. I am confused to my own expectations as a gentleman. It is intoxicating. You inspire me, Charlotte. It renews a vitality in me to be a better man. And I am not sure if that draws me to you or scares me away. I was headed down a path of complete isolation…to rid myself of this dreadful place. And now, here I am, once again in the midst of it all."

Charlotte scowled, "Are you so terribly bored with the world, Andrew?"

"I cannot deny I have been less than thrilled. People are too predictable. Dull, really. They can't help themselves. The drama they create is far more fascinating. Then again, that, too, can grow mundane as well."

"Now you worry me. I must be careful not to make too many demands of your time. I fear you will grow tired of me as well."

Andrew lifted her gloved hand and lowered his lips to kiss it. "You are a refreshing drink of water on a summer's day every time I am with you. Fear not, I shall not abandon you."

Charlotte quickly withdrew her hand hoping to dissipate the stares of the people sauntering by.

"You are a woman of many faces." He grinned, happy to be caught. "Tsk, tsk, my dear, timidity is not in your nature. Your mere presence demands attention. Muster all the demureness and delicacy you can, but I am not the only one to have been the victim of your strong will. And may I add, your strong wit?" He teased. "If you are feigning reticent about your personal affairs, your face hides nothing. At least not from me."

Andrew's pointed observations made her cheeks flush. "Are you judging me?"

"No, quite the contrary. I am in awe of your ability to be so pure in spirit, yet seemingly involved in something indelicate. Maybe even sordid?"

Charlotte's mouth opened to reply–to defend her honor–but she halted her words. She proceeded cautiously. "You are very much misinformed, if at all, Mr. Knightly."

He chuckled. "Ah, we are back to formality...I must be onto something, *Miss Ashford.*"

"Why must you make everything seem lewd and licentious? It is nothing of the sort." Charlotte quickly defended.

He questioned, "What did I interrupt the other afternoon?"

Andrew Knightly was wicked, shameful, and downright rude at times, but he was no fool.

Charlotte was waiting for him to broach the subject. It would be only a matter of time with him. She could not deny what his own eyes had witnessed. She wasn't sure if he was asking out of concern or a thirst for gossip. Either way, she was cautious about revealing the details that caused her duplicity.

"You came upon nothing worth noting," she replied.

"It is your face, Charlotte; it exposes you," he noted.

Charlotte touched her cheeks. "Andrew, you know more than a respectable woman should allow," she scolded. "What more do you want to know? Do you really need to uncover my sins?"

"Sins," he cursed to the god of heaven. "Love is a funny thing. You cannot wish it away, no matter how hard you try, or how wrong it is." He looked at her, his face searching for an answer. "Do you believe it a sin to love a man, in spite of God?"

"Andrew, please!" She looked around to see if anyone was in earshot. A mother pushing a buggy was just beyond them, while another child, maybe four, tugged at the skirt of her dress. "It is more complicated than it appears," she finally declared when she saw them turn onto another walking path.

"Oh, I see." He rubbed his chin, pleased he had his answer.

She had shared Nathanial's marital bed.

"I do not *think* you do…it is not what you think," Charlotte protested.

"Does it really matter what I think? Are you safe? That is all I ask."

"I am in no danger." Her lids fell half-mast. "I promise. There is nothing more with which to concern yourself with."

Andrew wanted to believe her, but he knew better. A woman's heart is a formidable mechanism. She had practically confessed her feelings. He knew Charlotte would never give up on love. If he had to choose,

Nathanial was not the person he wanted for her object of affection. Andrew was not fond of Nathanial Hammond, for reasons beyond Charlotte. They had their own secrets between them. Charlotte's feelings for Nathanial only furthered his disliking of the man.

"Come with me..." He took Charlotte's arm and wrapped it under his, leading her farther into the park. "Look around you, Charlotte," he said, referencing the people walking by, families lounging on blankets with picnic baskets splayed before them, and ladies sitting on nearby benches with their men grouped together talking among themselves. He specifically pointed to a well-dressed couple a few paces in front of them. "See that man?"

Charlotte noticed an older man with graying hair dressed in a finely appointed blue suit. On his arm was a slim figured woman divinely covered in a garnet silk gown, with a large-brimmed hat decorated with black satin ribbon and a delicate netting covering her eyes, but not her crimson lips. She complimented the graying gentleman in all his refinement, although it was apparent, the woman was not equal in his age.

"He is Sir Malcolm Barton. The lady with him is not his wife. Her name is Mrs. Patricia Harrington. They met on a trip to India. Her husband, some sort of baron, lives there, allowing her to visit London half the year."

Charlotte gasped.

"Do not give it another thought," Andrew said, flicking his wrist. "His wife is fully aware of his companion. As long as she has his title and money, she is happy. He is satisfied because Mrs. Harrington is twice as handsome as his wife and gives him all the attention he desires. Mrs. Harrington is content to have a place in London to escape from her drunken husband, for which Mr. Barton endows. It works for all of them."

He then pointed to a man on a bench across the way, "That is Mr. Theodore Bowers. He is an American. His wife died several years ago from a long and debilitating disease. The woman in green, with the two little boys? She is his new wife."

"And what sin have they committed?"

"She was his wife's nurse. Many ostracized them when they married. It was not long after his wife's funeral they exchanged vows in a private ceremony. You see, his wife had all the money."

Charlotte watched the woman in green take the two boys by their hands and walk them back to their father. Mr. Bowers smiled as they approached, opening his arms for the boys to run into.

"They seem happy together," Charlotte noted.

"They are!" Andrew proclaimed. "Despite the gossip."

Two ladies with big hats walked by and Andrew tipped his own in their direction. They both smiled, but not before they assessed Charlotte from head to toe.

"You know them, I assume," Charlotte asked.

"I do," was all Andrew replied, giving her nothing further about their identities.

"Ah, there is Mother." He guided Charlotte across the path, onto the grass, and headed towards a large oak tree where his mother had congregated with a group of people.

Lady Knightly, dressed in a sunny yellow muslin, was surrounded by two older ladies, one in stripes, the other in a small-scale print. A third woman, apparently younger, in a dress layered with ruffles and a collar of white lace, stood silently beside them with her chin hung low, eyes down, and hands clasped, laying against her skirt.

A fourth person was a young man of maybe eighteen, hands in pockets, longingly looking at the passersby. He was attractive, Charlotte noted, with a head full of darling curls cascading over his brow. A cleft in his chin stood harsh against his baby blue eyes partially covered with long, golden lashes, and round baby cheeks.

As Charlotte and Andrew arrived at the small gathering, the young man recognized Andrew and smiled, giving way to dimples, only adding to his boyish looks.

"Ladies," Andrew greeted, tipping his black hat as he approached. "And Thomas, you are growing quite tall." Andrew extended his hand to the young man, who eagerly accepted it. "Would you care to join me for a walk? I am sure my mother would enjoy the intimacy of just the ladies."

The young man turned to his mother, who nodded her approval.

They both left with a promise to return in due time.

Charlotte watched Andrew walk away only to see him turn and give her a wink.

Lady Knightly patted Charlotte's arm, "Boys will be boys..." she said, before turning to the ladies among her. "Let me introduce Mrs. Wilton, an old acquaintance. She, too, has recently returned from the States with her daughter, Amelia. I was telling them how you are newly arrived from America as well. Come to find out, you were practically neighbors in Boston!"

"Well, I am afraid not completely," Mrs. Wilton quickly added. "We meant to get to Massachusetts... my husband has a cousin there. But we never made it out of New York."

Charlotte exchanged small talk with details describing her home in Boston, living close to the waterfront, and the trials and tribulation of traveling overseas, waiting for Mrs. Wilton to share similar stories of her travels to America. They never came. Mrs. Wilton, along with her daughter, who stood mute by her side, shared nothing in return. This suited the second lady standing among them, Mrs. Gilmore. She wasted no time filling the conversation concerning her grandchildren–*five little angels God had blessed her with.* Her youngest daughter's upcoming wedding–*grateful someone finally came along and asked for her hand in marriage,* and her husband's propensity to drink too much whiskey–*but never too inappropriate for a man of his size.*

Charlotte shifted from one foot to the other, holding her attention, even feigning a smile of interest once in a while, as Mrs. Gilmore droned on. All the while, her eyes strayed towards the pathways in and out of the park in search of her lost companion, wishing for his return.

As if God heard her prayers, and with a little time's passing, Andrew and the young man appeared, offering little explanation concerning their whereabouts.

Mrs. Gilmore invited them all back to her town-house, promising scrumptious cakes and tea. Andrew, eyeing Charlotte, politely declined for the both of them, explaining they promised their time elsewhere. *Elsewhere* was never specifically named, the excuse seemingly accepted, encouraging the small group to depart off to tea.

"Where did you wander to?" Charlotte finally asked, when they were a far distance from the park, Andrew's silence getting the best of her.

"A local pub," he evaded. "Poor Thomas was practically begging to be rescued. Did you not see his face?"

"I did..." Charlotte said, leaving out the many things she wanted to say.

"Did you enjoy your time with the ladies?"

"I am always delighted to meet new people," she replied, noting a hint of sarcasm. "They were lovely."

"They are. Or so it may seem," Andrew hinted.

When he saw Charlotte's questioning look, he explained, "Mrs. Wilton is not back from New York, as my mother proclaimed."

"Really, why does she claim to be?" Charlotte was now shamelessly intrigued.

"She was visiting a convent in France...where her daughter gave birth to a healthy young boy."

Charlotte's eyes widened.

"She is soon to be married off to a foreign diplomat and move away."

"And the child is not his?"

"Good God, no! He knows nothing of the child... the old codger."

If Andrew was expecting Charlotte to be shocked, she did not appease him. "There is nothing about that story worthy of gossip. It is very sad for all involved."

"Do you not understand, Charlotte? These beautiful people in their fine clothes, living in expensive houses, titled in nobility...they all have their secrets. What you see on the outside is a mere facade of the messes we all make of our lives."

"Why do you have to tell me this? Do they not have the right to privacy?" Charlotte chastised.

"I am not one to gossip, nor to judge. Understand, you are a mere grain of sand on the beach. You imagine you are a transgressor; but open your eyes." He threw out his hands to the crowds who walked about them. "We are all hiding something. The goal is to keep it hidden."

Andrew extended his arm for Charlotte. With her

white-gloved hand she gripped his arm to finish their afternoon stroll, which they did in quiet solitude between them—Andrew with no more to say, and Charlotte pondering how he was privy to the secrets revealed. She dared not ask, not wanting to know where or how he got his information.

Maybe that was *his* secret.

INNOCENCE LOST

*R*ise and shine! The day awaits us. Be ready in an hour!

Andrew's note, written in his own hand, arrived amid two dozen peonies.

Pink—the color of your cheeks, he wrote. *I look forward to seeing you. - Andrew*

Charlotte carefully chose her wardrobe for the day, knowing Andrew's discerning eye and propensity for style. She dressed in the latest floral-patterned silk in cornflower blue, of which the color highlighted her eyes, and the fitted bodice accentuated her small waist and full bosom. She was cheerful, having no reason to doubt the day would be pleasant. Being with Andrew guaranteed it. He spared no gentleman hospitality, taking her to gardens and galleries of the finest homes in London. It seemed Andrew Knightly had a standing invitation from everyone. A curiosity Charlotte was sure to learn more about at a later time.

It was only after spending the latter part of the morning leisurely strolling through the park, did concern arise. Instead of an afternoon at the arboretum, as promised earlier, Andrew turned down a street leading to a less desirable location. Her instinct gave cause for concern.

"Where are you taking me?" Charlotte questioned, as they passed aged buildings and darkened alleyways, the sunlight dimmed by the narrow streets. "It has been rumored this part of town is less than…"

"Respectable?" Andrew noted her concern.

"I would not be so unkind in my assessment, but yes, if you must put a name to it."

At first glance, it seemed ordinary: couples walking side by side, a mother pushing her two children along, two gentlemen strolling the pavement, talking.

They tipped their hats as they walked by.

Still, something made her feel uncomfortable. Maybe it was the young women lurking in the doorways, their dresses tattered and threadbare, eyeing them. Or the children left to play in dirty streets, running up to strangers begging for spare change. Charlotte brushed her hand along the crisp silken fabric of her dress, which far exceeded refinement, making her all too aware she was out of place.

A young girl came up beside them with a basket full of nosegays and presented a bouquet of campanula to Charlotte.

"Thank you, Penny," Andrew said, handing her a coin.

"Aye, Mr. Knightly. Always a pleasure doing business with a gentleman like yourself," she said, exposing a mouth of crooked teeth. She then skipped ahead to a cluster of women gathered at a vegetable cart.

Charlotte brought the flowers to her nose when a craggy voice called to her.

"Have yer palm read," an old woman said, sitting outside a tobacco shop.

Charlotte shook her head.

The old woman's eyes widened, the whites stark against black pupils. "Are ye sure? A man's heart is yearnin' for ya. A woman's scorn is coming."

Charlotte shook her head again.

Andrew tugged at Charlotte to continue walking, but she pulled back. She walked up to the woman. "Is his heart truly mine?"

The wrinkled face looked at Charlotte; her eyes falling into an empty stare. "Ah, I see this man," she cooed. "He is not in your possession...but he is possessed by you. Love from another time; two souls disconnected. *She* knows that. She has always known. It is her penance...for her sins."

Charlotte knitted her brow. "I...I don't understand."

"We never do until it is too late."

Andrew tugged at Charlotte again, "We need to go," he said.

Charlotte pulled a few coins from her purse and

handed it to the lady, along with the bouquet. "Thank you."

Andrew led her down two streets, away from the old woman with white hair and pruned face, but her cryptic message still lingered in Charlotte's thoughts.

"Andrew?" She asked, biting her lower lip. "What do you suppose it means?"

He smirked. "What it always is supposed to mean... Nothing and everything. Life is planned, is it not? We are who and what we are. God's plan, or maybe Satan's. Either way, our lives are written in stone. She sees nothing more than you and me when we look in the mirror, if we dare to look. There is no mystery. Think nothing more of her."

Charlotte nodded, in seeming agreement, knowing he was right. But still...the old woman's words were haunting.

Andrew halted abruptly. "Here we are."

He grabbed Charlotte's hand and pulled her across the road, a carriage barely swiping them. He stopped before a large wooden door, once painted red, with a heavy metal knocker near the top. Andrew lifted it and pounded twice.

A young girl, no more than fifteen, answered the door. Her face lit up at the sight of Andrew, inviting them both in. She popped her head out the door, eyeing both sides of the street before closing the door behind them.

"Aye, Mr. Knightly, you're back once again," the young girl greeted them.

Andrew removed his hat and gloves, handing them to her. "Phillipa, you are getting prettier every time I see you."

The girl gushed from the compliment, not hindering the smile it caused. "Go on then, sir. Always a kind word."

Andrew was not being disingenuous. Charlotte could not help but admire the beauty standing before them.

The young girl had a head full of burnt orange hair, uncontrollable curls cascading down her shoulders, unsuccessfully contained with a blue satin ribbon tied behind her neck. Baby-ringlets crowned her forehead, creating a halo around her heart-shape faced. She had fierce green eyes with orange lashes, which only made them more striking. Freckles blotted her nose and followed along her cheekbones. She had a rouge of red on her lips that Charlotte deemed the color too bold for such a young girl but couldn't deny it was appealing on her.

The girl curtsied and waited. Charlotte assumed she was to remove her coat, hat, and gloves as Andrew did. She looked to him and he nodded.

"This is Miss Ashford," Andrew said.

"It is nice to meet you, Miss."

Charlotte met her eyes, and the girl curtsied.

The entry was small, floored in stone, with a wooden staircase in front of them. A hallway to the left had two closed doors, and another was partially ajar.

Charlotte strained to peer inside.

A shadow passed, and the door closed.

Andrew looked up the stairs. "Is your aunt available?"

"Aye. She has been expecting you. She has every-thing prepared as requested," Phillipa replied, eyeing Charlotte. "Shall I take you up, Mr. Knightly?"

"Not necessary. Phillipa. I know the way, thank you," Andrew said, not hiding his familiarity with the house.

Phillipa fluttered her lashes and bowed.

Andrew handed her a few coins and she scurried down the corridor. He then started for the stairs.

"Where are we going?" Charlotte demanded.

"Is it not obvious?" Andrew answered, pointing to the second floor.

"You are incorrigible!"

He took a few more steps, then stopped, turned, offering Charlotte his hand.

She shook her head and took two steps up.

Andrew moved aside, allowing Charlotte to lead the way upward.

Charlotte took the steps slowly. One by one, she rose higher to the second floor, unsure of where she was being taken. The treads creaked with her every step, alerting anyone inhabiting the second-floor that company was afoot. A high round window at the top of the stairs allowed light from the sunny afternoon to brighten what would be otherwise be a dark and damp hallway.

When they reached the top, Charlotte felt Andrew's hand against her back, nudging her to continue down the hallway. Two women passed them, dismissing Charlotte altogether, vying for Andrew's attention.

"If it ain't Mr. Knightly!" one said to the other.

"Look who's honoring us today. And where might your gentlemen friends be?"

The taller of the two leaned into Andrew, pressed her hand against his chest, and moved it downward.

Andrew quickly grabbed the lady's hand, halting any pretense. With his hand still encircling the woman's wrist, she noted Charlotte beside him and backed away. Andrew released her.

A subtle, crooked smile tugged at the corner of her mouth as she studied Charlotte.

"Not like you to bring a lady of your own," she sniggered. "Is she to join you?"

"Come on Sarah," the second lady pushed her friend forward, "Let's get into the salon before the others pick all the good gents." She gave Andrew a smirk and furthered her friend along.

Andrew nodded to the two women as they passed.

"Shall we," he said, pressing Charlotte onward to the end of the corridor.

Charlotte, doe-eyed, did as she was directed, and continued along the hallway, where it ended at an alcove with a private door.

Andrew knocked with two successive raps, halted, followed with two more quick raps.

Before Charlotte could give into the urge to flee, the door opened. A silhouette of a woman, the darkness shadowing her face, invited them in. As they moved into the room, Charlotte saw she was not a young woman, the dimmed light accentuating the lines around her mouth. But redeeming qualities had not left her; her chestnut eyes sparkled, and her skin had a peachy glow. Her dark hair was down, pulled to the side, bound with a ribbon intertwined in a loose braid. Dressed for bed rather than to greet guests, her figure was covered in a pink, rose-printed challis wrapper edged in black lace at the edges of the sleeves and collar. With a loosely tied knot at the waist, it did not limit the view of her lace corset underneath.

Charlotte turned away her gaze.

"Mrs. Ryland," Andrew addressed the woman and bowed. "May I introduce to you, Miss Ashford?" He stepped aside to present Charlotte.

Charlotte bowed her head and gestured with a slight smile, coyly eyeing the ruby pendant hanging from her neck, the size noteworthy even for the wealthiest of women. The pastel cabochon opal on her right hand did not go unnoticed, either.

"Come in, my dear, and let me take a good look at you." She reached for Charlotte's hands and swung her outward, to assess the whole of her. "Lovely. Simply Lovely," she purred. "Andrew has told me much about you. I had to see for myself who captured Andrew's attention."

She released Charlotte from her grasp, and assessment, and led them further into her *parlor*, as she called it.

The main room, in which they were invited into, had a large fireplace with an elaborate marble mantle. Mrs. Ryland confirmed it was Italian, 'extracted' from a sixteenth century palace. A carved wedding armoire prominently sat against the wall. Four paintings, two on each side, hung next to the oversized closet, each still-life depicting various bouquets of flowers. Charlotte noted the same painter signed them all.

A settee and two upholstered chairs were placed around the fireplace with an inlaid walnut coffee table in between; a large flower arrangement was resting in the middle, fragrant lilacs burst out from an assortment of white roses. A chaise covered in a golden damask brought attention to a large bay window. A needlepoint pillow with bouillotte fringe depicting a white cat adorned the seat, while a pair of women's stocking lay strewn across the cushion. A bronze lamp sat atop a round table, along with a tray set for tea with an assortment of biscuits awaiting their visit.

"I have been blessed with fine gifts over the years," Mrs. Ryland explained, noting Charlotte's perusal of her luxurious surroundings. "Needless to say, I have many admirers."

"They are quite lovely," Charlotte's meek voice offered.

"Please," Mrs. Ryland fanned her hand towards the settee. "Have a seat. I will poor us tea and we will talk.

An interior door opened, and a girl appeared.

"Yes, Annie?" Mrs. Ryland eyed the girl.

"The bath has been prepared," the young girl notified her.

Mrs. Ryland clasped her hands. "It appears we need to begin sooner than expected. I hope you do not mind postponing tea."

"I...I" Charlotte paused, not understanding why she was there or what was going to happen.

"Forgive me," Andrew interrupted. "But I have not confided to Miss Ashford as to why she is here. She is due for an explanation. Will you give us a moment alone before I release her into your care?"

Mrs. Ryland agreed and excused herself, retreating to the connecting room.

Charlotte stood before Andrew, her mouth agape. She knew better than to be afraid with him there, but the situation warranted questions.

He put his hands up. "Before you think the worst, this is not what it appears."

"No? What am I to think? You have brought me to a house of ill repute, taken me into a room, and prepared a bath for..."

"You, and you alone," Andrew interrupted.

"I wish I could say that relieves me, but it does not." Charlotte walked to the window to assess exactly where she was, looking for a route to escape.

Andrew drew close to her and placed his hands on her shoulders, slowly sliding them down her arms. His eyes met hers.

To Charlotte's surprise, Andrew seemed to possess

a depth of wisdom she had never seen from him. She did not fear him, nor did she recoil from his touch.

"Andrew, what am I doing here?" she asked again.

"My dearest, Charlotte. I cannot claim to know your heart, but I can see the torment it has caused. I want to help you. Prepare you."

"Prepare me for what?" she questioned.

"I sense you are not ready for what you have been entangled. I have told you before, the world is not what it seems. People have secrets. You seem to have yours. But if you choose to be a lover, then a lover I will make you!"

She closed her eyes. *Lover.* The word was a dagger to her heart.

He laughed out loud. "You silly woman. No, I do not mean to seduce you, although you are tempting. I know your heart is not mine to have. It belongs to someone whom you will not easily let go. If I am right, your situation is or will be...what is the word you used...*complicated*? Mrs. Ryland means to give you the guidance necessary to control your *situation*." He paused and cleared his throat. "I mean to protect you, Charlotte. If you choose to enter into the world of deception, you need to wield power over it."

SHE DIDN'T MOVE. Andrew's words felt too fateful to ignore.

"My dearest, I am leaving you in good hands. Most

men will attest to Mrs. Ryland's skill." He gave her a smile. "You have trusted me, so far. Trust me now."

The interior door opened once again.

The maid poked her head out.

Andrew turned to the maid and nodded, signaling Charlotte was ready.

TESSA'S QUESTION

*C*harlotte heard the click of the handle as the door closed behind her, confirming her imprisonment.

She was now in what she could only assume was Mrs. Ryland's bedroom.

Paneled walls encased the space, with a large head-board-framed bed against the wall. Heavily carved, it was uniquely Renaissance. An assortment of pillows adorned the top of the bed, but the mattress was covered in the simplicity of white linen, taut across the mattress. A round table next to it housed a lamp which matched the one in the outer room; a few books splayed atop, as well as a painting of a Japanese Spaniel with a green ribbon around its neck, leaned against the wall. The same white linen fabric of the bed quilt decorated the windows. The curtains were sheer–not blocking the light, only limiting the brightness allowed in the room, as well as filtering privacy. The floor was covered with an oriental rug under the bed, however, in front of the fire, a bearskin, auburn in color, was on full display.

Charlotte gasped at the sight of it.

"It'll not bite ya," the maid giggled as she threw another log onto the fire. She signaled to a chair, "You may take a seat, if you like, Miss. Mrs. Ryland will join ya in a moment."

Charlotte moved to the chair and sat.

The maid left through a panel in the wall–a secret door–leaving Charlotte alone.

Eyeing the door the maid entered, Charlotte pondered if she should flee or stay.

The fire snapped, and she startled, jumping from her seat.

The panel opened again, and the maid returned. A few minutes later a knock came at the door and she opened it, allowing a young man to enter carrying two pitchers of water heaved in his brawny arms. He followed the maid to the secret door, not setting eyes on Charlotte, only to reappear empty handed, before retreating the way he came.

Charlotte, now intrigued, walked to the door-like panel, pulled it open, and entered. Her hand went to her mouth.

Contrary to Mrs. Ryland's bedroom, this hidden space was paneled in all white, with brass candelabras on each wall, and the entirety of the floor was tiled in colorful mosaics. Windows banked one wall, with blue silk curtains cascading to the floor. A brass tub, half-filled with water, lay in the center of the room. A sideboard was against another wall, topped with a concoction of toiletries, fragrances, and creams haphazardly displayed. A chaise, with room for two, was angled towards a fireplace, the fire ablaze, with three folded towels placed on top.

"I see you have made it into the inner chamber," Mrs. Ryland said when she entered. She walked to the windows, nodded to someone on the street below, and then pulled the curtains over them. The room darkened into a cozy cocoon of warmth from the fire and the glow of the candles.

"I…I am not sure…" Charlotte stumbled with her words. "Andrew did not explain to me exactly what was to happen."

"Come here, my dear." Mrs. Ryland extended her hand to Charlotte, inviting her to sit on the chaise. She dismissed the maid with her other hand and waited for her to retreat before continuing. "Miss Ashford… may we be less formal? Shall I call you Charlotte and you call me Tessa?"

Charlotte nodded.

"Let me reiterate, you are free to leave. You are not a prisoner here," she touched Charlotte's forearm. "You are safe. No one is in danger under my roof. Do you understand?"

Charlotte nodded again.

"Good. Now let me explain. Andrew informed me you need guidance. He believes that I may be of help.

He meant no harm or disrespect. So please do not reprimand him for disclosing your personal affairs. This is a private place, as you can gather. Who comes here and what they do is no one else's business. I hope you will honor my privacy."

"Yes, of course," Charlotte assured.

"In my world, it is my job to please men. Oh, do not look so shocked," she scolded, seeing Charlotte's eyes widen. "I have learned quite a lot over the years. As you can surmise, I am not a young woman anymore. But..." she raised her finger, "I am very much desired among some of the most important men in the city, if not all over the world. And do you know why that is?"

Charlotte did not answer. She couldn't. Her heart was beating too fast, and her voice was caught in her throat.

"Because I love what I do. I not only give men plea-sure, but I also receive pleasure from them. They could have any of my younger girls in the house, but it is me they seek." Tessa's lids lowered and she let a smile curl her lips. "Needless to say," she continued, "it is no secret a man seeks pleasure–*pleasure* he can find anywhere and from anyone. But what he *desires* is being wanted. Yes, there are the obvious reasons. He desires to be wanted for looks, power, money, love. But what he desires most, is to be wanted for the plea-sure he gives. When a man is able to please you, the stakes are raised. They want no other. I can see with my own eyes you have no issue enticing a man to want you. You are beautiful, and if I am correct, you have a figure worth coveting. If you want a man to desire you and only you, he must please you in ways no others can. For that to happen, you need to learn how to be pleased. Once he discovers your enjoyment of his lovemaking, he will want to seek it only from you. You will have him forever."

Charlotte stilled, shocked by Tessa's words. No respectable woman would speak openly concerning men and their intimate affairs. She dare not imagine such things, let alone talk about them. Fear of discussing the forbidden gripped her, nevertheless her questions begged for answers.

"What is it you are going to do to me?"

Tessa smiled. "I am not doing anything *to you*. You are going to do something for yourself–discover the sensual woman inside. I want to help you become a lover. It takes knowledge and a willingness to explore." Tessa smiled at her, waiting for Charlotte to comprehend what she was offering. "Do you still want to leave?"

"I am not sure," Charlotte answered truthfully.

"Well, your answer is more than I expected. Before we begin, may I be so bold as to ask, have you been with a man?"

Charlotte gulped, "Once. He has not sought me since."

"Oh," Tessa sighed. "Did you enjoy the experience?"

"I…yes, if I am to admit. With his touch, my body was not mine. I cannot explain it myself. I wanted him so much. It frightened me and excited me all at the same time. Being with him–the joy–was nothing like I had ever experienced. But…" Charlotte searched for the words, and the courage, to tell Tessa the truth. "As he lay with me, it caused discomfort. I was not prepared for my body's response to him, both pleasure and pain."

Tessa placed her hands over Charlotte's and explained, "My dear, it is very natural, and one of the many nuances of being with a man, especially if it is the first time." Her brow lifted. "But it can be pleasurable. Not all women learn this. That is the reason you are here."

"But…" Charlotte couldn't finish. She couldn't admit her failure as a woman.

"Charlotte…" Tessa squeezed Charlotte's hand. "Remember, you are safe here. You can tell me anything."

"He left me–fled, really," she cried. Charlotte told Tessa everything. The joy and the humiliation, the desire and despair. "And he has not returned to my bed. He barely can be in the same room with me."

"Oh, my dear, your experience is not unusual for many women…" Tessa shook her head, for she had known the dark side of sex. It was her life, and her life's work to counter.

"You do not understand," Charlotte protested. "I failed. I have a duty to fulfill, and the one man I must appeal to wants nothing from me."

"Duty?" Tessa questioned. "My dear, what have you gotten yourself into?"

Charlotte's eyes filled with tears; no words followed.

Tessa put her arms around her. "Come now. It cannot be all that bad. What causes you such torment?"

"I cannot explain," Charlotte insisted. "It would break a sacred trust."

"Charlotte, I have other women's husbands in my bed...there is nothing more private than that. I hold secrets I will take to my grave. If you need anyone as a confidant, I am the one to rely on."

"What you must think of me," Charlotte exclaimed. "I never planned to become someone's lover. It seems destiny has chosen this path, one way or the other. And here I am...I cannot change it."

"Do you want to change it?" Tessa asked.

Charlotte had not considered the possibility of ending the situation. *Had she not been given the opportunity by Nathanial's rejection?* Her head wanted to proclaim the more noble answer, but her heart wouldn't allow her to.

"I have an obligation and intend to honor it," she answered.

"Dear me! You are a complicated one. I will not pry. If you have committed to someone your loyalty, then who am I to say? That is your business. I can only help you with performing your duty. Are you willing to let me help? Because you are free to go." Tessa pointed in the open door's direction, waiting for Charlotte's response.

Charlotte walked to the door. She stood lingering at the threshold. Andrew claimed she was one for intrigue, but she wasn't sure she had the fortitude. She not only needed to leave, but she also needed to release herself from her promise to Lydia. She needed to run away from Nathanial. She needed to walk out the door.

"Can you really teach me to become a lover?"

Tessa walked to the door and called for her maid, closing it after her. "Let's begin."

SEDUCTION LESSON

The bulk of the afternoon consisted of Charlotte standing naked in the bath, Tessa and the maid staring at her.

"How can a man find pleasure in all *that* hair!" Tessa exclaimed pointing to Charlotte's most private of parts.

"It is a personal choice, Ma'am," her maid replied, easing the harsh criticism.

"Take it off!" She yelled to the maid. "And, Charlotte, make sure you continue to do so," Tessa directed.

Upon Tessa's command, Charlotte's body was rubbed with fowl smelling creams, only to be scraped with a pumice. The physical scouring was not as harsh as the mental anguish of having the maid snipping tirelessly between her legs. Although Charlotte was attentive to her hygiene, she was never instructed to remove *personal* bodily hair. She had viewed the paintings of naked women in the museum exhibit halls, much to her surprise, without hair covering their bodies. They were beautiful and godly–not reality. Little did she know of the torment involved.

"There, Miss, you are as beautiful as a painting," the young maid exclaimed, eyeing the bare woman in front of her.

Tessa walked around Charlotte to approve the work. Not until a smile crossed Tessa's face, could Charlotte finally hide her nakedness in the dark water of the bath.

The maid handed her a bar of soap smelling of rose oil and lavender. It filled Charlotte's nose with fragrance, wiping away the harsh smells of the depilatory cream. Tessa excused the young maid, locked the door behind her, and pulled a chair to the bath.

Placing her hand on top of Charlotte's shoulders, she ran her fingers down her arms, feeling the wet skin against her palms. "Your skin is like silk." Tessa noted. "Do you appreciate that? Not all women have such a velvet feeling."

"Yes, I suppose," Charlotte answered hesitantly.

"Well, cherish it," Tessa said. "You have much to learn."

"I do," Charlotte agreed. Her experience thus far was not frightening her; it merely felt unusual.

"Good," Tessa exclaimed. "You now know what it is like to stand in a room naked. It should not frighten you. Your body is beautiful, Charlotte. You have curves in the right places and you have lovely breasts. I have seen many women to judge you by. Do not doubt this about yourself. Your body is a temple, but it is also a source of pleasure as well. Do not overlook the joy a man feels when he gazes upon you."

The temperature of the room seemed to rise. Charlotte's cheeks warmed.

"I am going to ask you to do something you may be uncomfortable with, but I need you to trust me." She paused for Charlotte's sake.

Charlotte hesitated but then nodded to signal her compliance. She swallowed hard.

"Close your eyes," Tessa ordered, checking twice to confirm they were closed. "I want you to touch your arms. Glide your hands over your skin. Feel the texture."

Charlotte lifted one lid open, questioning Tessa's instruction. When Tessa gave her a stare, she obeyed. Shutting her eyes tight, she crossed her arms and slid her hands against her skin.

"Tell me how your skin feels."

Charlotte slid down her arms again, but this time slowly. "Soft, like what running water feels like. Or when a breeze blows across my face."

"Good. Now, slide your hands across your chest, moving to your breasts."

Charlotte's eyes jolted open.

"Do it," Tessa ordered. "Close your eyes again. Tell me how it feels compared to the skin of your arms."

Charlotte obeyed, but not without hesitation. As she slid her touch from her chest to her breast, she was surprised at the sensation. "They feel softer than my arms...silkier, like a silk stocking feels when pulled along the leg. It is light... creamy, except..." She tilted her head as she played with the protrusion, analyzing the sensation. Her nipple grew plump and hard between her fingertips. She quickly pulled her hand away.

"What did you feel?" Mrs. Ryland pushed her.

"It...it has a different feel. It is smooth like leather." She then added, "It tingled something inside of me."

"Yes, as it should. Remember the feeling; the texture of your body all over. Let a man get to know the difference. It is your job to show him how to touch you. They can only have this silkiness from a woman...don't let him miss out on the different sensations."

"Now, move your hand down and slide your hands across your belly and hips. I want you to know your curves," she suggested.

Tessa waited for her to acknowledge the touch. "Take your time..."

"Does a man want to touch a woman like this?" Charlotte questioned.

"Make him. Tell him what you like and don't like by the way you moan and move. He will want to rush, but you are in control. You show him by guiding his hands where you want to be touched. It will be pleasurable to him as well; he just doesn't realize it. But when he sees and hears your own satisfaction, his curiosity will give into exploration. You have the map.

Show him the pathway to you." She paused, trying to continue without frightening Charlotte. "Now...glide your hands to your legs, slowly down to your knee."

Charlotte couldn't help but enjoy the skin without hair. "The skin is different," Charlotte offered. "It is soft, not silky. Thicker and not as delicate."

Tessa smiled, pleased with her attentiveness.

"Charlotte, you know where I want you to go next. It is a sacred part of you, not a place of sanctity. Many beautiful things happen between your legs. A girl becomes a woman. A marriage is united. A child is born. Love is shared. It is a place of great pleasure if you know yourself. Explore yourself by releasing your thoughts to the touch. You should be aware of what sensations a man feels when he touches you, and how your body responds. You can derive great pleasure from his hands, his mouth, his tongue..."

Charlotte's eyes jolted open, but she could not look at Tessa. She stared into the blackness of the water. Goosebumps crawled over her.

Tessa touched her chin and lifted it upward. "You are a beautiful, wanting woman. I can see it in your eyes the willingness to listen and explore. Do not be afraid of your own desires. They are as God given as the desire to breathe. I want you to know your body and the pleasures it can receive. If you are going to enter a world of physical desire, you need to learn what it holds."

"I do not believe I can...it seems too forbidden," Charlotte objected.

"Has not a man already touched you? He had dominion over you without you knowing yourself. Shame! No man should know your body better than you. No man should control you because of it. Do you understand?"

Was it anger she saw in Tessa's eyes?

Charlotte closed her eyes again. She inhaled and exhaled several times before her hand slid between her legs. Slowly, she slid her touch over the newly groomed area between her thighs. It was nothing she had thought it would feel like. Soft, but textured...not smooth and silky like the rest of her body.

Tessa laid her hands against her shoulders. "Let your mind wander. Experience the way your body reacts. You are safe here, Charlotte. Your body is yours alone."

Charlotte allowed her fingers to continue to explore. The more she probed the more her body reacted. Her heart began to race and her cheeks grew warm. A breathless excitement overcame her causing an uncontrollable moan to escape from somewhere deep inside her. A wave of warmth enveloped her causing her body to go limp. Gradually, numbness set in and she descended deeper beneath the water.

Pulling herself up, she pooled water into her hands and splashed it across her face. When she opened her eyes, daylight was no longer penetrating through the curtains. Night had approached, and the glow of the fire was casting shadows on the walls. The stillness of the room frightened her.

She finally turned to face Tessa who had moved away from the tub, and now sat silently on the chaise awaiting Charlotte's discovery.

Charlotte's voice cracked, and tears pooled in her eyes. "Have I done something wrong?"

"No, no, my dear. You are discovering the nuances of sexual pleasure. It is a power so few women under-stand...*so few men allow*. Your body holds more plea-sures than you are aware. The skin on your arm differs from the skin between your legs. An arm should be caressed, a breast cupped, a thigh clenched. Do not allow a man to rush between your legs. Make him explore all of you. Allow him to explore the varying sensations. This will not only give him a new level of pleasure, but it will allow for your own wanting."

Charlotte sighed. "Do women have choices? Are we not at the will of the men and their own desires?"

Tessa smiled. "A man can demand and even be forceful, but only if you allow it. You may not have strength, but you have a woman's power. It dominates over brawn. Your hands are your tools. If he comes down upon you too fast, slow him down and guide him. Do not be afraid to touch him in the ways I taught you to touch yourself. He will enjoy all the same pleasures you enjoy. I will not lie; he is most pleased when you touch him between the legs. Hold his hardness and stroke him. Let him feel your finger-tips caressing him and embracing his manhood. Explore him and your own pleasure of touching him *and* tasting him. Allow yourself to indulge in the sensation it creates in you. Do not be afraid of how your body reacts. Allow yourself to respond. A male body is very exciting and pleasurable if you learn to wield it."

Charlotte wanted to cover her ears, for the words seemed too immoral to hear. Yet, she didn't. Silently, she cursed Lydia for putting her in this situation, cursed Nathanial for leaving her to doubt, and cursed herself for wanting more.

Tessa continued, "Men want their way, but they also have pride. A man likes to view a naked woman, to touch a naked woman, and even taste a woman's body. But he is most satisfied when he can please a woman. Show him how and he will desire to please you."

"Tessa?" Charlotte's voice softened. "Where is love in all this?"

Tessa's eyes lowered. "Love and desire. In my world, they are far apart. I am not one to come to for relationship advice. Husbands, come to me for their desires; their love stays with their wives. Do not fool yourself. You are walking a dangerous line to be respected or to be shunned. I have seen many women come through my doors who have fallen from grace. They, too, thought it was love until they found themselves with child, or were found out by the wife. Then, these naïve young women, some merely girls, were cast off with no more thought than changing a coat. You must be careful."

Charlotte thought about Tessa's surroundings,

filled with luxuries–gifts from her lovers. She seemed well taken care of, if not respected, in her world. Far from what Charlotte assumed upon entering a house of *irreputable woman.*

"Tessa?" Charlotte said, avoiding eye contact. "How did you end up here?"

Tessa sighed, turning her gaze to the fire, allowing her memories to flood her thoughts. It had been long ago since she had to think about her role as a courtesan of men.

"My father was a drunk," Tessa proclaimed. "A bastardly drunk!" She scowled, and a low growl followed. "When my mother died, I took her place in taking care of my brothers. Gradually, he decided I should replace her in *all* ways. It was not *too* bad. He never took long before he passed out. But he drank up his income and the wee ones starved. So, I took to the city and found I could make a living doing what I had done so many times with my father–lay there and let a man do his business. My father shunned me, but my brothers were fed."

"Oh Tessa," Charlotte winced.

She held up her hand. Shame had long left her conscience. "As a businesswoman–or maybe it was pure determination to be independent of anyone to be beholden to no one–I saved my money, as well as made a few investments. I was managed by one of the top financial men in London, a long-time client of mine. I made enough money to buy this building, and plenty more to live comfortably–which I do. I could have left long ago, for a better life...but there were the girls who needed me. Girls who were tossed into the streets with nowhere to go. I cannot save them all, but many I have, and continue to do so. I am discriminating in my choice of clients, guaranteeing my girls' safety. Dangerous behaviors are left to the girls who refuse help, and line the alleyways begging for sex. My business keeps the girls clean, safe, and happy, for which I pride myself. I even make a home for their children, many born within my walls. I provide a safe space, work, and an education that allows opportunities for a different way of life. Many have moved into important homes as nannies and caretakers. Most find good jobs as cooks and maids to sustain a comfortable life. The young women need me here. I need them. And there always seemed to be one more who needs help, showing up at my door. My path may have been chosen for me, but I chose to make it an adventure, not to be a victim of fate."

"But Tessa...the others...looking down on you." Charlotte lowered her lids, knowing she was one of those who judged people like Tessa. "I am sorry..."

"No, do not feel sorry for me. I am happy. I made a life of my own, where no man can ever control me. I rule in my world. The men I keep company are very loyal, and as you can see by my comforts, I am cared for. But on my terms. My father cannot hurt me anymore, and my brothers have a good life—hard, but a worthwhile one. I have quite the collection of nieces and nephews," she proudly added. "For that, I am grateful."

A knock came at the door and Phillipa entered.

"Excuse me, Madam, Mr. Knightly has arrived with Mrs. Ashford's attire for the evening. They are due at the theatre tonight. He would like to send word to his mother if they are going to be delayed. What shall I tell him?"

"Oh my, I had forgotten about our plans tonight." Charlotte looked at her naked body submerged in the water, thinking about all she had experienced in the last few hours. "I…I cannot imagine facing Lady Knightly, let alone Andrew."

"Charlotte." Tessa placed a hand on her shoulder. "You are still the same woman you were when you entered. Your sensuality is hidden beneath the surface. It is not painted on your face. No one need know what is between you and your body…except your lover, as it should be. I pray I have given you guidance. Most of all, I wish for your protection."

"Thank you…" Charlotte reached for a towel. "I do not know the choices I will make. My head says one thing, and my heart says another."

"Ah, the heart," Tessa moaned. "You seem like a sweet young woman. Be careful."

Charlotte nodded, not sure what the warning meant. She shivered as the warm water rolled off her body, wrapping the towel tightly across her body.

"Send up her clothes at once, Tessa ordered

Phillipa. "And tell my maid to assist us. We have a lady to prepare."

"Tessa," Charlotte's teeth chattered. "Thank you."

Tessa nodded, heading to the door.

"And Tessa…" Charlotte called after her. "Do not let anyone ever deny you the respect you deserve. Not even your father."

Tessa lifted her chin. "You remember that as well. You have more choices than I ever did. Do not lose yourself for the sake of others. You have the power to choose the course of your life. It may not always be easy, but it is your decision and not for anyone else to decide."

THE THEATRE

ndrew tapped his hat against his knee, waiting for Charlotte to come out of Tessa's door. He had the carriage park in the front, obscuring the view from passersby, giving her the privacy to retreat without being recognized.

Charlotte arrived at the awaiting carriage, swooping the dragging hem of her dress in one arm, and clutching her purse with the other.

Andrew promptly pulled open the door for her. "You look lovely tonight."

Charlotte nodded, accepting his compliment, knowing by his tone that he was trying to be gentle. When he extended his hand to assist her into the carriage, she did not meet his eyes, too embarrassed by what she presumed he knew. Although he did not know exactly what transpired behind Tessa's door, he was the person who precipitated their meeting.

Charlotte sat in the seat across from Andrew feeling his eyes on her–assessing her. *Did she look different to him?* She felt different. Changed. She was not sure if she was grateful for the experience, but there was no turning back. Her innocence was now stripped away...in ways she could not have imagined. She felt heat rush to her face, bringing her gloved hand to her cheeks to tamper down the effects before Andrew noticed.

Andrew reached for her hand. "Charlotte...do not hide yourself from me. It would be no use, anyway."

His comment only made her blush more.

"You do look lovely," he reiterated, squeezing her hand. "Mother will be pleased."

"I hope so," Charlotte said, her voice so whispered Andrew had to lean into her to hear her fragile words.

"You know mother...her joy to take you to the theatre *runneth over*."

Charlotte smiled with Andrew's tenderness and attempt at humor.

This was Charlotte's first play since returning to England, and Lady Knightly could not contain her excitement to be the one taking her. So much so, she took Charlotte to her favorite dressmaker, *The Dowinger Dress Shop*, in anticipation of the occasion. Anna Dowinger and her two daughters were dressmakers extraordinaire among the London shop, known to work miracles on impossible bodies, and to finish masterpieces in unthinkable time frames. Hence why Lady Knightly took Charlotte there as soon as they arrived in London. She was determined to have an extraordinary dress finished on time for the Theatre.

Mrs. Dowinger, in her expertise, had suggested a gown of silvery blue, which Lady Knightly proclaimed would be stunning against Charlotte's eyes, the metallic threads sparkling in the light. Charlotte insisted it was *too much* and Lady Knightly declared, "It is what mothers do!"

Alterations happened within days, and the shop owner's eldest daughter personally delivered the gown, along with a cape, hat, and purse to accessorize, on time, the morning of the play.

When Charlotte looked in the mirror before leaving Tessa's room she was pleased with her appearance, with her cheeks rosy, her skin glowing, and her eyes bright. Mrs. Dowinger's fashion-savvy color choice was all she promised it would be–*stunning!*

Upon their arrival at the theatre, patrons gathered at the front, greeting one another, while carriages queued up in a long line, waiting to deliver more elites dressed in their finery and adorned in their jewels.

Charlotte noted the stark differences just a few blocks away. As they rode away, through the darkened streets of Tessa's establishment, she saw the young women hiding in the corners. *How had she so disregarded them before?* She knew all too well the line of decency was only a circumstance away. Her hand went to her heart, aching at their plight to be so invisible. She wondered how many of the finely suited gentlemen were visitors to Tessa. And how many of the women were privy to their husband's visits?

As if a wind had swept across the crowd, the refined gentlemen and women became stripped naked, their silk top-hats blown away, and their jewels dulled. She saw the exquisitely dressed crowd for what they were...people shrouded in secrets.

"Charlotte," Andrew called, interrupting her thoughts. "Are you ready to go in?"

Charlotte blinked, erasing her thoughts. "Yes, of course," she answered.

Andrew led Charlotte through the crowded lobby, pushing their way through the talking and the talked about.

Passing every few people in the crowd, Andrew either tipped his hat to a lady or shook a hand of a gentleman, eventually working through the crowds to make their way upstairs.

"Andrew...Miss Ashford..." Lady Knightly called out.

She excused herself from the circle of friends she was chatting and reached for Charlotte's hand. "My dear, Miss Ashford, you are possibly the most stunning woman in the room," she declared. "Do you not agree Andrew?"

"That does not even deserve a response, Mother," he replied.

"Of course, she is," Lady Knightly confirmed, swatting away his sardonic tone. "Come, we are not far. I have a lovely balcony that will fit all of us."

"All? Are we to have people join us?" Charlotte inquired.

"Didn't Andrew tell you? I ran into Mr. Hammond and Mr. Tatum. They were coming to the theatre as well. I insisted they join us. Is that not a lovely gathering? It is a shame your cousin, Mrs. Hammond, could not be with us. It would have made the evening more special."

Charlotte agreed with Lady Knightly, all the while eyeing Andrew with a death stare.

He smirked–his way of acknowledging he had not been forthcoming with the information.

Dutifully, Andrew and Charlotte followed Lady Knightly to the balcony. When she pulled aside the red velvet, tassel-fringed curtains, the two men were found already seated. They rose simultaneously to greet the incoming guests.

"Oh, Mr. Hammond and Mr. Tatum, you have arrived. I apologize for our tardiness. I was worried Miss Ashford and my son were going to miss the curtain call. The crowds are dreadful! But here they are. I found them just in time," Lady Knightly explained.

Nathanial greeted Lady Knightly and moved aside for her to be seated, and glanced briefly at Charlotte, adding a slight bow of his head.

Charlotte moved past him, dismissing his nod, and followed Lady Knightly's lead to the seats at the front of the balcony.

Mr. Tatum bowed to the two ladies as they passed.

The lamps dimmed, giving no more time for further formalities.

Andrew offered the only other seat at the front to Mr. Tatum, who accepted the offer, while Nathanial and he took the seats directly behind the three.

Charlotte tried to concentrate on the play. It seemed enjoyable to the rest of the theatre patrons, but the presence of Nathanial was distracting her. She didn't know if she was angry or pleased to see him. In either case, an uncontrollable tingle slithered up her spine. She lifted her gloved hand and brushed the back of her neck, trying to halt the assault of goosebumps making an appearance along her shoulders, winding their way upward.

Nathanial whispered, "Are you chilled?"

His breath was a warm breeze sweeping against her skin.

More tingling replaced the fading sensations. Turning her head slightly she met his eyes briefly before she answered.

"A little," she lied. "It is nothing to concern yourself about."

He leaned closer. "Would you like me to get your cape?"

Her body quivered, the mere closeness of him reminding her of the intimacy they once had shared. Refusing to succumb to the pang in her heart, she turned away, leaving him to awkwardly stare at the back of her head once again, goosebumps and all.

NATHANIAL SAT BACK in his chair. He checked his watch a dozen times, hoping the evening would end quickly. He had not wanted to accept Lady Knightly's proposal, but Tatum was insistent on appeasing the woman. He was cursing the man until he saw Charlotte come around the curtains. Now, all he wanted was to flee from the theatre–*and her*–as soon as the opportunity allowed. Intermission could not come soon enough.

He had tried to see Charlotte sooner when he arrived in London, learning she had travelled as Lady Knightly's companion. There was so much he wanted to say. But he couldn't bring himself to face her. At the least, he should have written her to explain his feelings and his actions. But every time he picked up his pen, the words fell empty. *How did one explain his shame?* He believed his absence would make it all go away. He had hoped his distancing would make her realize he was unworthy of her. He had not meant to be a scoundrel, but knew his actions warranted her scorn, then and now. He vowed to himself he would never go to her again.

Now, as he sat behind Charlotte, an urge to pull her to him was maddening. She was like the nectar of a flower to a bee. *They were destined for each other.* It was hard not to brush his fingertips against the silken skin of her neck. A touch whose intimacy he remembered from the first time he brought his lips to hers and wrapped his hands around the nape of her neck, pulling her to him. He could not forget the way she folded in his embrace, or the way she willingly succumbed to his desires, releasing her own passion.

Watching the smooth curve of her shoulders rise and fall with every breath only reminded him of the night they were together, his head upon her chest, breathing as one. As he noticed the tiny bumps appear across her bare shoulders, his desire was newly aroused, and he no longer wished to run away from her.

He leaned in again, now with purpose, "You are very beautiful this evening."

Charlotte ignored him.

Undeterred, his lips brushed against her earlobe, "I am sorry, Charlotte. I have wanted to say that to you a thousand times, but the words always seemed so meaningless."

She turned, "Please, Nathanial..."

"Shush!" Mr. Tatum reprimanded them both.

Simultaneously, they both turned towards the reprimand to find not only Mr. Tatum's eyes on them, but Lady Knightly's and Andrew's as well.

"If you must discuss something, then by all means, please excuse yourselves," Andrew chastised, giving them permission to leave.

Nathanial rose, giving Charlotte a cue to join him. She hesitated even when Andrew gave a firm nod to the door.

Lady Knightly, who eyed Mr. Hammond standing

at the door, insisted Charlotte join him. "Go, my dear...It seems your cousin's husband would like to speak to you. No use disturbing the rest of us."

As the door shut behind them, they both walked down the dimly lit corridor in silence.

Charlotte's mouth started to open, but she shut it without saying anything.

Nathanial wanted to force her to say something, anything to him. *He needed to know.* But he didn't. It was enough she was alone with him. So, he walked content to have her by his side, even if she was the cause of the heat beneath his collar that grew hotter with every stride.

He halted at an alcove and grabbed her wrist, pulling her inside.

"Nathanial," she scowled.

"I must talk to you."

"It can wait, can it not?" Charlotte's eyes darted down the deserted corridor, knowing every hush of a voice, no matter how whispered, echoed, reminding her the walls had ears. "I hardly think this is the time or the place..."

He silenced her with a long, hard kiss.

Charlotte stepped back and touched her lips. She looked at him, her eyes wide and questioning. Just when she was going to speak, clapping began in the distance.

They both knew they were to be confronted by the people behind the door of the alcove they had retreated into.

Sprightly, Charlotte slipped into the hallway as the doors opened and the people piled out, before he could stop her. She soon was lost in the crowd.

He did not pursue her, but instead, leaned against the wall letting the people pass, eventually losing sight of the woman in silvery blue.

Lady Knightly appeared, eyeing him alone in the alcove as she passed, and looked into the crowd ahead.

It didn't take long for her to catch up with Charlotte, who was at the top of the stairs, her hands clinging to the railing. "There you are, my dear," she said, noting but ignoring Charlotte's flushed face now exposed under the lights. She interlinked Charlotte's arm with hers. "Come, let's get some fresh air."

Making their way downstairs, a young aristocratic couple waved them over.

"My dear, Lord Percles; Lady Percles." Lady Knightly leaned into the woman and gave the young lady a light kiss on the cheek. "May I introduce Miss Ashford?"

Both smiled at Charlotte.

Charlotte remained quiet, allowing Mrs. Percles to share stories about her three children, of whom she seemed very fond.

Mr. Percles stayed silent as well, allowing his wife to do all the talking. He seemed very fond of her, for his eyes beamed as she spoke, and his touch never lifted from her arm.

Charlotte had no doubt of his pride for his wife, for her beauty and congenial personality outweighed his own merits of attraction...a man's reward for wealth and title.

They invited Charlotte to visit them on her next visit to London, offering a tour of their estate, notable for its art collection of Lord Percles' family.

Charlotte agreed to the visit before they were interrupted by an older gentleman, giving the Percles an excuse to move on to other notables in the room.

The tall and bulky older gentleman seemed familiar to Charlotte when introduced. He was a previous lawyer of her father's many years ago. She did not recognize him at first, nor did he recognize her, for she was so young when he and her father worked together. But after a few moments of speaking with him, Charlotte remembered him. *Mr. Quigley!* He used to visit the house occasionally, bearing a box of chocolates or a bag of caramels for her. A child never forgets kindness expressed with sweets. She remembered his slight lisp when he spoke, having a particularly difficult time with pronouncing the "r" in her name. He had grown more grey since she last saw him, and a few more lines around his eyes, but his ruddy complexion and hairy brows were exactly how she recalled.

"I was saddened to hear of your father's passing. He was a good man...a good man indeed. It is inexcusable someone would take advantage of him. And you, of course." He briefly made eye contact with Charlotte before continuing, "Mr. Hammond is hoping my connections in America might help your case. Without those connections, I am afraid it is difficult to get anyone to talk. I hope you know we are doing everything we can."

"I am sure you are," was all Charlotte could answer. She was unaware Nathanial had been conversing with Mr. Quigley, nor had he informed her of the current status of her father's affairs. *Why was he keeping her in the dark?* She did not know if she was hoping to be forever tied to Lydia or wishing for her freedom. She wondered if he felt the same.

The bell chimed, and the crowds were instructed to head back to their seats.

Mr. Quigley bid his farewell, saying they would soon speak again. "With good news," he added.

Charlotte spotted Andrew across the room. He was cloistered in the corner, speaking with Mr. Tatum. She instructed Lady Knightly to proceed upstairs and informed her that Andrew would escort her back. Lady Knightly, giddy with the prospect, allowed Charlotte to find her son.

As Charlotte walked towards Andrew, he turned. His face was flushed, his brow heavy, and his lips were tightly pressed causing her to halt in her pursuit. With Mr. Tatum's similar demeanor, crossed arms around his chest and an angry scowl, it appeared the two were arguing.

Over what, she could only guess. She had not known they were intimate enough to warrant such a passionate display towards each other. Nor had she witnessed Andrew angry, worrying her that it was important.

Mr. Tatum spotted Charlotte first and stepped away from Andrew, as if to retreat. Andrew turned her way and his scowl disappeared; a smile appeared. He hurried to her, offered his arm, and asked if he may escort her back to the balcony.

Mr. Tatum did not follow but left the theatre altogether.

Not wanting to explain herself or what happened with Nathanial, Charlotte asked nothing of Andrew, and to her surprise, he obliged asking nothing of her.

The orchestra began to play and Lady Knightly noted the empty seats behind her.

"It seems as if we have been deserted."

Neither Charlotte nor Andrew looked back. They already knew their fellow companions were not coming back.

DRUNK & DISORDERLY

A week had gone by since the theatre evening, and Charlotte heard nothing from Nathanial, which sent a message all the same. She assumed he returned home–*where he belonged.*

Unbeknownst to the drama taking place under her chaperone, Lady Knightly insisted they extend their stay in London for another two weeks. "So many things to do, places to go, and people to see," she declared.

Charlotte agreed, grateful for the distraction of the numerous social engagements planned by Lady Knightly: tea with Mrs. Henderson and her daughters, dinner with the Percles, a concert at the music hall–all were welcome diversions.

Charlotte was not eager to return to *Lottington Manor.* Once a place of reprieve, it was now the den of deception. She hoped distancing herself from the estate would help clear her head, bringing sanity to a seemingly insane situation. She did not know if Nathanial's kiss, and subsequent return home, was another rejection of her. *Was there a difference?* Either way, Lydia was still at the heart of this issue; the pact between them a sacred bond. Charlotte wasn't sure what was worse, loving Lydia too much, or loving Nathanial more? Words of her father haunted her:

Deception leads to lies. Lies beget lies. And because of it, truth will leave nothing in its wake. Nothing.

Andrew stayed in London as well, but only appeared in the evenings for a quick drink before he would make his apologies, escaping to *other* engagements. Lady Knightly never seemed concerned about her son's whereabouts, and it was apparent she was very familiar with his disappearing habits. Charlotte, on the other hand, felt abandoned. She wondered if Andrew purposely left her to her ruminate about *her moral dilemma,* as he liked to refer to her entanglements.

"Oh, my dear, your face does not hide you. Please do not worry yourself about my son. He is very loyal to those he loves if I may be so bold to acknowledge."

Charlotte blushed at her assumption.

"I dare say he is an independent soul, but with the right woman, he will learn to be better. His father was very much distracted when he was younger, as well. But he was more than attentive to me through the years. I do not doubt Andrew will be of the same mindset."

"I am not concerned for Andrew," she assured. "And if he is anything like your dear husband, a woman should be so blessed. Andrew, in his own unique way, takes good care of me...in spite of himself."

"Aw, you know him too well," Lady Knightly agreed. "I have a feeling my husband would have liked you very much. He, like Andrew, was very fond of beautiful, younger women," Lady Knightly admitted openly. Seeing Charlotte's eyes widen, she laughed and explained, "My husband was very attached to our daughter. She was a beautiful little creature. Stole his heart the moment he held her in his arms. Every young woman was a possibility of what our daughter could have been. He hoped Andrew would settle down with a pleasant young woman, like yourself, and we would have a daughter once again in our family."

"I am very sorry you had to lose your precious daughter at such a young age." She could see the pain was still very apparent. "It would be a great loss to anyone."

"Oh, thank you, my dear. Losing a child is something you never seem to let go of. We tried. We traveled the world trying to forget what it felt like to have her in our midst. But you cannot run from such pain. Ultimately, coming home gave us the comfort we needed. It was like her spirit remained here, waiting for us to return." She smiled to herself. "I feel..."

"Please go on," Charlotte insisted.

"Well, you will consider I am a silly old woman.

But I feel she is with me every day…guiding me. In fact, I believe she guided me to you."

Charlotte's eyebrow shot up. "Really, how so?"

"Recently, I was going through an old trunk of her things I stored in the attic. I opened it and there was her favorite doll just staring up at me. As I lifted it in my arms, it was as if I could see her little face smiling right in front of me. *'I will call her Charlotte'* her little voice shouted up at me. *'Why Charlotte?'* I asked her. *'Because Charlotte is a beautiful name and she is the most beautiful doll I have ever seen,'* she replied."

Lady Knightly grew quiet and stared off into the far corner of the room lost in her memories.

Charlotte waited for her to continue.

"It was the very next day I heard the news; *Mrs. Hammond's cousin has returned.* When I heard your name, I knew it was a sign."

Charlotte's lips curled upward. "Or maybe a coincidence."

"Call it what you may. But you are here, sharing time with me, and that is satisfaction enough."

Charlotte was warmed by Lady Knightly's sentiments. If she were to admit, Lady Knightly filled a need for her as well. Traveling, shopping, dining, and passing along motherly wisdom were things she would have done with her own mother. If it seemed Charlotte was taking advantage of her, it was intentional only in that she missed her mother so terribly much. Sharing Lady Knightly's companionship was comforting if not fulfilling a role her mother left vacant too early in Charlotte's life. Hence the reason why she continued the charade.

Lady Knightly had hopes for more–she not only desired a daughter-like protégé, but she also wanted Charlotte to fill the role as her daughter-in-law, with the ultimate goal of bearing her grandchildren to propagate the Knightly bloodline.

Charlotte knew she could not do that. Andrew had no more intentions on her heart than she had on his.

With guilt overwhelming her, Charlotte felt the need to explain. "Lady Knightly," Charlotte's voice began. "About Andrew…and his intentions…"

"There, there," she interjected. "You will say nothing I do not already know. Give him time, my dear. He will give up his foolish ways one of these days." She smiled assuredly. "I will turn in. I need all the rest God will allow." She gathered the needlework from her lap and placed it on the table next to her. "Are you ready for bed?"

Charlotte shook her head. "I am not quite ready to rest," she said. "Have a good night."

Charlotte eased back into the cushion of the couch upon Lady Knightly's departure, finally left alone in the quiet hours of the evening. Most times she enjoyed the solitude, left to her own thoughts. But tonight, was different. Her mind filled with distraction about Nathanial…and the kiss still lingering on her lips. Desire rose in her, quickening the beat of her heart. The need to be with him surged, frightening her.

"Damn you!" she whispered into the empty room.

But Nathanial was not there for the condemnation. No one was there to hear her. "Damn you!" she cursed again.

She wanted him to explain himself. She needed for him to tell her what he wanted from her. His eyes were intense and meaningful when he pulled her into the alcove. His kiss was purposeful. *Was he expressing his love for her, or his desire?* She wasn't sure it mattered.

"Damn you..." she said one more time, except this time her voice was exhaustive and futile, a plea to God to make the passion subside.

She didn't want to *want* Nathanial. But she did, from the moment her eyes met his; his touch sparking the knowing between them. It was the secret she kept from Lydia when she agreed to become Nathanial's mistress. It was the truth she hid from Nathanial the night she allowed him into her bed. It was the torment she now felt when alone with her thoughts.

Her head fell into her hands.

"What are you thinking about?" A man's voice carried across the quieted room.

Charlotte slowly lifted her head to the voice familiar to her.

Andrew lingered at the door.

"How long have you been there?" she asked, her tone harsher than she intended.

"Long enough," he replied. "I have interrupted your *reverie.*"

He teetered over to the sideboard and poured himself a drink.

"You are very drunk," she duly noted.

"I am," he proudly declared. "And so is your Mr. Hammond."

Her heart jumped. "Nathanial is still in London?"

"It appears so. Ran into the old chap along with Mr. Tatum. We have been having a grand evening." He lifted his glass to Charlotte. "He seems to be in quite a spot."

"What do you mean?"

"Got himself drunker than I. Told quite a tale to me and Mr. Tatum," he taunted.

Charlotte stiffened, afraid at what was to come.

"It seems his dear wife kicked him out of her bed. Terrible thing for a wife to do. Don't you think?" Andrew directed his eyes to Charlotte.

Charlotte looked away, purposely avoiding his eyes and questions.

"But the story gets better. It would seem that his wife has chosen a mistress for him. Can you imagine? Choosing the woman your husband will bed?" He gulped down another sip of his drink.

Charlotte saw he was enjoying himself. Her eyes narrowed. "Why do you toy with me, Andrew?"

A slow but steady smile appeared on his face. He walked to where Charlotte was sitting and lifted his glass to her. "It seems I have truly misjudged you. You are more deceptive than I thought possible. Tell me, Charlotte, was it the love for your dear cousin that led you to behave so nobly? Or was it desire for her husband that helped you agree to such an arrangement?"

Charlotte lunged towards him. If she had the courage, she would have slapped him. Instead, she twisted her hands together, keeping them in tight control of lashing out. "Why would Nathanial confide such things to you?"

"Oh, forgive him. His words only came out of pain…induced by a bottle or two. He probably does not even know what he said. I will be surprised if he remembers how he cut his lip, or if he will be able to explain his bruised eye."

Charlotte's eyes hardened; her stare aimed at him. "What have you done?"

"Nothing more than men do on an average night when they want to forget about life," he coyly remarked, giving her few details.

"Is he harmed?" she demanded.

"He will survive." Andrew took another swig of his drink. "But it was not of my doing, as I believe you are assuming. He had a disagreement with a man we were gambling with. It seems the man was cheating us all. Nathanial thought he needed a lesson of honor. Unfortunately, the other man came out better, I dare say. And a few notes richer. Your man got a little bloody. But he gave it a good try! Tessa is cleaning him up and I am to retrieve a fresh shirt for him. She is having his jacket mended as we speak," he finally confided.

"Andrew! You did not take him there...of all the places. How could you?" Charlotte shouted at him.

"Calm yourself. He is in good hands, I assure you," he quipped, but Andrew had more meaning in his words.

Charlotte's hands continued to twist around each other. "Why did you come here to tell me this?"

"Because I wanted to see your own reaction. I wanted to know what really was behind all the deception. I suspected. But I wanted to know exactly what it was all about. I can see it now." Downing the last of his golden elixir, emptying his glass, he walked over to the sideboard, once again, and poured himself another drink. With his back towards Charlotte, he continued, "A man like Nathanial does not get blithering drunk for nothing. He was pushed into it. Now I know the cause and who pushed him there."

Charlotte crossed her arms, waiting for him to answer. He took his time.

He smiled right at her. "You!"

"Me?" Her eyes narrowed. "How dare you..."

He moved into her, closer, not breaking her stare, but matching it with intensity. His breath, laden from whiskey, blew across her face. "He's in love with you!"

Charlotte's shoulders stiffened, her neck straightened, not wanting Andrew to see his words were causing her legs to weaken or to know her heart was pounding in her ears.

"You have nothing to say to this? I would think you would be filled with joy," he smirked.

"You are being cruel," Charlotte reprimanded. "If you cared about me at all, you would not have come here and thrown this in my face."

"The truth is, I do care. I care terribly. That is why I am telling you. You should know his feelings run very deep... even if he is too much of a fool not to tell you himself. Maybe it is honor, or maybe it is his pride. Whatever the reason, you should know."

Charlotte paced the room. She wasn't sure she was pleased with the news. It was a betrayal to Lydia. She should ignore everything Andrew told her but couldn't dismiss Nathanial's confession–even if alcohol-induced.

He reached for her nervous hands. "You are a foolish woman," he said. But when he saw the anguish in her eyes, he added, "A very, wonderfully, foolish, woman."

Surprised by her own voice, she ordered, "Take me to him."

"I cannot take you *there*, at this time of night. It would not be appropriate."

"Please, Andrew, he needs me," she begged.

"Or maybe you need him," he sagely noted.

TRUTHS

*A*ndrew halted Charlotte from exiting the carriage when it stopped in front of Nathanial's London townhouse. "No need to get out," he said. "I had sent word to Hollister..."

Charlotte leaned back, her face falling into the shadow of the night, and waited, as did Andrew. Five minutes passed before the door opened and the tall silhouette of a man appeared.

If Hollister recognized Charlotte sitting in the carriage, he did not acknowledge it. He handed Andrew the items he requested, discreetly wrapped in paper, and retreated, climbing the stairs to the front door, and closing it behind him, not waiting for the horses to pull away.

Charlotte took the package from Andrew and clenched it tightly between her hands as the carriage rattled through the late-night streets.

It was eerily quiet except for the horses' hooves clopping against the pavement, the sound echoing against the walls of the buildings.

Charlotte eyed the streets they were traveling down, now familiar with where the driver was taking them. The horses finally stopped, the abruptness causing the carriage to jerk, almost unseating them both.

Instead of jumping out, Andrew adjusted himself onto the bench seat and slid back, indicating Charlotte to do the same.

The two waited in silence across the street from Tessa's establishment.

Two well-dressed men came down the street, their mumbled voices breaking the silence. Charlotte recognized Phillipa's red hair when the door opened for them. The two removed their hats before she allowed them inside.

Andrew and she waited an additional ten minutes before Andrew finally pulled the carriage door opened and took Charlotte's hand, allowing her to exit. He spied the darkened corridors, both ways, before he tugged at her to cross the street.

"Good evening Mr. Knightly, and to you, Miss Ashford," Phillipa greeted them.

The entrance was empty, and all doors were closed, but men's laughter seeped through the walls. Andrew placed his hand on the small of Charlotte's back and pushed her forward, up the stairs, making no waste of their privacy. The hallway was dark, but Charlotte knew where she was going. When she reached Tessa's door, Andrew pulled her hand away before she could knock.

Charlotte looked at him in questioning, "Is there something wrong?"

He shook his head, "Are you sure you want to go in there?"

"Andrew, is there something you are not telling me?" Charlotte questioned, her voice spiking, unable to hide her panic.

"No," he reassured her. "Just the truth."

"The truth about what?" She now wondered if Andrew had an ulterior purpose in bringing her there. "What am I going to discover behind this door?"

"I am not sure. But you need to find out." He kissed her hand and walked away, leaving her standing in the darkness.

Charlotte watched as he disappeared down the corridor, losing sight of him halfway, her heart thumping with the distancing sound of his footsteps. She waited until she heard them hit the landing at the bottom of the stairs before she knocked at the door in front of her. Taking a deep breath, she held it, waiting for someone to answer.

It was only when she saw Tessa's familiar face did she release her breath.

"My dear, what are you doing here...and at such a late hour?"

With a moment's hesitation, Charlotte debated the wisdom of running after Andrew, but with an invitation from Tessa to step inside, the door was shut before she could do so.

"Let me take that." Tessa offered to take her coat. "Have a seat."

Charlotte looked around the softly lit room, expecting to see Nathanial, but there was no one but Tessa.

There was no denying Charlotte caught Tessa unexpectedly. A bare leg peaked through the opening of her robe, hinting at her nakedness underneath. Charlotte could only assume Tessa wasn't alone.

Tessa caught Charlotte's stare and quickly cinched her gown, the red-silken fabric, with a majestic bird and cherry blossom branches woven in metallic threads, with a matching band of red silk, tucking away any nakedness.

Charlotte's heart sank with the realization that Nathanial was not in the main room because he was mostly likely in the connecting bedroom.

Horrified, Charlotte jolted for the door. "I might have been wrong for coming..."

"Charlotte," Tessa's voice commanded, "Where are you running off to?"

Charlotte turned her flushed-cheeked face towards Tessa. "I apologize. I was looking for someone, but I might have been mistaken. I did not intend to interrupt you."

"Sit," Tessa insisted, and poured her a glass of sherry. "Now, what is this all about?"

Charlotte sipped the sherry, trying to master her

thoughts. She did not know how to explain her own presence in a whorehouse late in the evening, searching for a married man that didn't even belong to her.

Tessa did not push her and waited for the warming of the sherry to affect her.

A shuffled sound came from the other room, jolting Charlotte from her seat.

Tessa placed her hand on Charlotte's shoulder. "Sit, my dear. Now tell to me, why are you here?" Tessa asked again, pushing Charlotte to explain.

"I brought Mr. Hammond a clean shirt," she said, referring to the package she had brought with her. "Mr. Knightly informed me of the situation he encountered this evening."

Tessa smiled with ease and took the package from Charlotte. "Is he the man you came to me about?"

Charlotte's eyes widened.

"You have much to learn, my dear. I have made a career based upon my instincts." She lifted Charlotte's chin to study her face. "Love is hard to hide." Her eyes moved to the doors of her private room. "Even on a man's face."

She walked to the large armoire, opened the doors again, and searched through the many gowns hanging inside. She pulled out a long blue robe, similar in style to the one she was wearing, with its metallic threads and bell sleeves. Handing it to Charlotte, she said, "Are you ready to master the fine art of lovemaking I have taught you?"

Charlotte's cheeks grew hot. Nathanial lay on the other side of the doors. Tessa was giving her the opportunity to seduce him. *What if she failed? Would she have the heart to handle his rejection again? Did she really have the ability to live in the world of deception?* Charlotte stared at the floral design of the robe that slung over Tessa's forearm.

Tessa had helped her out of her clothes and into the silky kimono style robe. She had never felt so exposed, knowing there was only a small tie around her waist that, if untied, would expose her naked body. Letting down her hair, and with a few sprays of perfume, Tessa pushed her towards the door where Nathanial was.

Charlotte did not knock but turned the handle on the door slowly.

The lamp was dimmed and there was a low-lit fire filling the room with warmth.

Nathanial was laying back on the chaise with one arm over his head, and the other falling off to the side. His eyes were shut and chest was rising and falling in slow rhythm.

Charlotte could see a large gash above his eye that had been cleaned, but dried blood lingered at the edges. A purple-blue ring was surfacing around his right eye as well on the corner of his lip. A bloodied towel lay in a bowl of water on the table, and his ripped shirt was on the floor, covered in dark red splatters. Charlotte did not know whether to chastise him for the getting into a fight or feel sorry for the bloodied and bruised figure who lay sleeping.

Nathanial was within steps, but her feet could not move. She stayed in the shadows and quietly observed his languid body.

It was a falling log on the fire that startled the sleeping figure.

As it crashed to the bottom of the fireplace, Nathanial jolted up. His eyes adjusted to the dim light of the room. His hand went to his forehead as pain surged the opened wound on his brow. It bled, and he pulled his fingers away to look at the fresh blood. He grabbed his torn shirt and blotted the cut until the bleeding stopped. He stood up and walked over to a basin filled with water. He splashed his face several times and gently wiped away the water trying to avoid his cut. He pushed back his hair with his hands and Charlotte could see his face on full display from the light of the fire.

The late hour revealed the dark patches of his unshaven face and tired eyes. But the golden light of the fire exposed the sinewy lines of his half naked body.

Charlotte came out of the shadows, the light in the room illuminating the metallic threads of her robe. As she moved, the red and yellow poppies meticulously stitched in the fabric danced across the satin like butterflies. The blue of the robe drew out her eyes and they seemed to glow in the room's darkness.

Nathanial blinked at the dream-like figure

appearing before him. His eyes widened when he saw it was Charlotte. He could barely get her name out, stuttering over his words, until he finally asked, "Why are you here?" his groggy voice grumbled.

"Andrew told me…"

"Of course, he went running to you," he growled.

"No, Nathanial, it is not like that. I came for *you*… to be with *you*," Charlotte whispered.

"Don't do that, Charlotte," he demanded. "I don't want you that way." He turned his back to her.

"Nathanial," she called out. "I am standing in front of you, offering myself freely. Are you going to push me away again?"

"I don't want you on the command of my wife," he scowled.

Charlotte walked to him, falling under the shadow of his stature. "I am not here because of Lydia. I am here because of you."

Closer to him, she saw his jaw heavily clenched. She ignored the signal and brushed her hand across his cheek, tracing his face with the tips of her fingers. Succumbing to her touch, he closed his eyes. She slid her hands around his shoulders, discovering the hard lines of his arms. He was strong and masculine, signaling to her body what Tessa had described–an arousal. It was as if heat was flowing from her fingertips to her inner thighs and she exhaled with the sensation.

NATHANIAL OPENED his eyes to see the seductress in front of him. He tried to resist the enjoyment of her touch, but his body was beyond his control.

She wanted him, and that aroused everything. He pulled her to him and placed his lips on hers. Charlotte did not resist, and her mouth opened for his tongue to indulge him. Hunger for her burst through him and he couldn't stop himself from demanding more, not wanting her lips to part from his. But suddenly, she pulled away, and the heat of her body parted from his.

He stepped back and looked at her.

How many times was he cast off for his hunger? He knew not to demand more from a woman who did not want him. Lydia had trained him well.

"What is it, Charlotte? Do you want to be with me?" he questioned.

Charlotte stood still, her chest lifting and falling with every breath. Her eyes locked with his, but she didn't answer. Instead, she untied her sash, and let the robe fall to the floor.

Charlotte's nakedness stood before him. The firelight danced across her creamy skin. Her breasts were large and round, her nipples hard, alerting him to her own physical desire. Her eyes were calling him to her.

His breath caught for a moment. He had seen nothing in his life—no thing, no object, no *one* more beautiful.

God, he needed her!

He swiftly moved, and with urgency, embraced the

whole of her body, absorbing her in his being, bringing his lips to hers again, this time, more demanding. He needed her more than ever. His lips consumed her, his tongue indulging in the saltiness of her skin, as he explored her body.

Charlotte's head fell back, and she moaned as the warmth of his mouth encircled her nipple where he played with the darkened skin until he felt it go hard against his tongue. She pulled him against her, urging him to indulge in the pleasure of her body.

He dropped to his knees and moved his kisses downward, tasting the suppleness of every inch of her nakedness, his hands taking in the contour of her body. The more he tasted her, the more she writhed, driving him to explore the beauty of the bareness between her legs.

She moaned again, only this time it was slower, longer, exhaustive, her breath releasing into the darkened room. Her legs buckled, and he caught her in his arms.

He led her to the bed where she laid down. As he cast aside the rest of his clothes, she gasped at his complete nakedness, gazing from his shoulders to his bare chest, following the trail of hair down to where it thickened in a curly mass between his legs.

He let out an uncomfortable laugh. He could not remember a time when he was this naked in front of a woman, bearing himself so completely. "I feel you are analyzing me like one of those creatures in the forest…"

She smiled. "Maybe I am," she admitted. "A man's nakedness is new to me." She glanced him up and down once again. "You are beautiful...truly a beautiful specimen. I never imagined it to be so."

He laughed again, joining her on the bed, laying his nakedness against her own.

"Charlotte," he whispered, pulling her into his embrace, "I am giving you everything of me. No holding back. I cannot hide from you anymore, nor do I want to. I give to you my body willingly, but know you have my heart and my soul, as well, if you will accept them."

Charlotte reached out for him and cupped his face in her hands, bringing her lips to his.

At first her kiss was gentle and her touch warm. But the more she kissed him, the more her tongue demanded of him. He returned her kisses with a fury, his mouth consuming her; his hands enwrapping his body with hers. To his surprise, her kisses moved from his mouth to his neck. Her breath panted against his face; her hands became fire-hot against his flesh. When her mouth encircled his nipple, her tongue exploring the hardness, he moaned. Too deep in his desire, he resisted the urge to pull away from the unexpected electricity it caused. But shock overcame him when her exploratory touch found its way between his legs.

He lifted himself from her, pulling away from her touch.

"Did I do something wrong?" she questioned, her voice hushed and uncertain.

Her face was flushed from passion. Her eyes were dark and mysterious, equally reflecting the desire that was flowing through her. She was not holding back feelings, or her body's reaction to his. He now wondered how a woman could be so transformed into the seductress he was experiencing.

"No," he assured her, not sure of the reason.

Her brow furrowed; her voice now steady. "Then what is it?" she asked.

"It's you," he said. "You surprise me. I have never been with a woman who could demand such passion and yet make me succumb to such tenderness all at once. You have bewitched me, Charlotte."

"I am neither a witch nor a seductress, I assure you. I am merely a woman following her heart. If it is passion that stirs inside you, I am equally guilty." Taking his hand into hers, she brought it to her lips and kissed the palm, before placing it upon her heart. "Should I be asking God to forgive me for the way I feel? I do not know if I am cursed or blessed. But at this moment, there is nothing between us. I freely give of my myself to you, under no one's asking but for my own desires."

He kissed her hard, the effects stiffening her nipples against his chest. Wrapping his mouth around one, he fondled it with his tongue, causing her to squirm beneath him. As his hips pressed against hers, her hands slid down his back, positioning him between her legs. As he moved inside, her pelvis moved with his in a rhythmic motion. He let out a loud sigh as her warm body enveloped him, inviting him further inside her.

Charlotte's breathing grew faster and faster as their bodies writhed in motion.

He moved to encapsulate her heated breath with his own mouth, but he halted as her body pulsated around him in a spasm. He could not hold his own pleasure and he released himself with one last jerk.

When his breathing has slowed, and the tremors in his body subsided, he rolled to the side, wanting to see the woman who had just given herself completely to him.

Charlotte's eyes were closed, but a smile was strewn across her face, her cheeks still flushed with passion.

If there was joy in the world, it was all in that room, laying at his side.

He swung his arm around her, bringing her closer into his embrace, his hand surrounding her warm, naked body. The last thing he remembers before sleep overcame him is Charlotte's breath slowing, her breath blowing against his chest, and her heart syncing to the rhythm of his own.

ASSESSMENTS

*L*ady Knightly had given Andrew strict instructions to keep Charlotte entertained while she was away. Her departure was due to the unfortunate circumstance of an elderly aunt nearly on her deathbed, leaving Lady Knightly no other choice but to rush to her side. To her dismay, Charlotte was to be left without a hostess for a few days.

"Please make sure our dear Charlotte is pleasantly entertained," his mother ordered as she kissed him gently on the cheek.

"You do not hide your intentions, Mother," Andrew wistfully answered, letting out an exhaustive sigh.

His mother ignored the flippant response and continued, "A young woman like Charlotte is not likely to remain available for too long, Andrew. You have charm, my son, but its effectiveness has its limits."

"Have a lovely visit, mother," Andrew said as he helped his mother into the carriage. "Tell Aunt Emily, I wish her a quick recovery."

"Such a kind boy, you are," she said, patting her son's hand as he closed the carriage door. Popping her head out the window, she added, "Promise me, dear, that you won't let another opportunity go by. I would so love to have a grandchild of my own someday soon."

Andrew tried to laugh off the suggestions as frivolous, but he knew his mother's request was not said lightly. She wanted grandchildren, but she also wanted to leave a legacy for future generations. Andrew recognized he was not the most helpful in securing that dream. A twinge of guilt stabbed at his heart. Although tormented by his mother's wishes, he knew she wanted for him to find the happiness with someone like she had found with his father. He gave his mother a smile, hoping it would assuage her anxiety about continuing the Knightly heritage. When she sat back in the carriage, he saw she was pleased with him. He waved to her as the horses pulled away, wondering if he could ever live up to her expectations.

Seeing Charlotte was all he had on his mind after his mother left. Entering the library, finding her immersed in a book by the window, joy replaced his anxiety.

"You are simply stunning today, my dearest," he

rejoiced. "That yellow dress brightens your whole complexion. I am a lucky man to witness."

Charlotte granted him a smile. "You are rather cheerful...and so early in the day. Why do I deserve this honor?"

"Why should I not be cheerful? You are a beautiful woman with whom I have the pleasure to be with." He poured himself a drink and sat down near her. "It is quite a lovely afternoon, and you are hiding inside. Would you rather not be out? I have a few invitations I can, and should, accept. Mother would have the best of me if I didn't."

Charlotte closed her book, tossing her gaze to the windows. "Not really. I am content with the quiet. Your mother has kept me very busy. It might be selfish to admit, but I am almost grateful for the break from her."

"Ha!" Andrew laughed. "My mother has that effect on people. Are you sure I cannot tempt you in a night of dancing? A terribly boring dinner party? Or maybe you would prefer another night at Tessa's?"

Charlotte blushed. "Andrew, you promised to be discreet."

He smirked nudging his shoulder against her. Discreet he was; subtle, he was not.

"Charlotte, you know if I adore anyone, it is you. But you put me in a terrible position with mother the other morning. If it was not for my discreetness, you would have had to explain why you were arriving home so early the other morning," he reminded her. "Do not begrudge me a little badgering."

"I should know better with you," she said, rolling her eyes.

He cocked his head, raised a brow, and nodded to her accurate assessment of him.

A smirk crossed Charlotte's face.

"You are exhausting." She reached over and placed her hand on his. "But if I did not say it, thank you for what you did for me."

"Oh, my dearest," he sighed, "I do not deserve your sincerity. It is I who should be grateful. You have given me some freedom! Accompanying my mother has brought her much pleasure. You have saved me her scrutiny of my time. If my aunt were not my mother's only surviving relative, she would have declined to leave you in London to yourself. You realize that she simply adores you."

Charlotte nodded. "Yes, and the feeling is mutual. I had not appreciated how much I have missed having a motherly figure in my life."

"Ah, she would be honored with the comparison."

Charlotte knitted her brow.

Noticing her affect, Andrew pleaded, "Speak truthfully Charlotte. Did I say something of concern?"

"Andrew, do you think this charade is wise? Your mother has hopes about us."

"Why, do you think there is none?" Andrew gulped down the last of his drink and placed the crystal on the table beside him. He leaned into Charlotte and took her hands into his, placing a kiss on her fingers. "My dearest, if you believe a married man is the least bit of a threat to me, then you know very little about me," he smirked. "You will grow tired of him," adding, "Or he of you."

"Andrew!" Charlotte scowled. "Why are you so unnecessarily cruel? It is not like that with Nathanial. You, of all people, to throw that in my face when you are the one who encouraged us."

He laughed at her.

"Please don't do that," she demanded. "I am not your entertainment."

He grabbed his glass and carried it over to the sideboard. He filled it up half-way and gulped it quickly. He wasn't ready to *really* tell her what he thought. He kept his back to her, knowing she wanted to pounce on him once he turned around. With one more sip of his whisky, he faced her, but not before he set up his defense.

"How you can remain so childlike in such an affair is beyond me. But it is very charming, I will say. I have done well with my protégé. It only makes you all the more desirable," he quipped.

Charlotte stood up and threw her book at him.

He dodged the blow but cowered as he heard the glass decanter shatter behind him.

"Well," he exhaled. "That is a waste of good whisky!"

A door opened, and the maid came in to clear the damage.

With the interruption, Charlotte took the opportunity to bolt to the door, but not before Andrew grabbed her by the arm and brought her close to him.

"I don't mean to hurt you, Charlotte," he said in a whispered voice. "Quite the opposite. I want to make you happy. You deserve to be happy."

"I am happy," she refuted.

"But for how long?" he asked, looking for the answer in her eyes.

She turned her face from his, he released his hold, allowing her to flee from his grasp.

She paused abruptly and leaned her head against the door. She finally said, "I am happy, Andrew. And it is because of you. Please do not ruin that. At least, not for now."

Andrew bowed his head to confirm his compliance. He watched her walk away, wondering if he was ready to give her up to Nathanial Hammond.

LESSONS

$\mathcal{H}$aving retreated to the morning room after breakfast to find a quiet reprieve, Charlotte was interrupted by a servant, bearing a bouquet of mignonette, heliotrope, and red carnations. To describe it as *large* was an understatement. It was over the top–enough to fill two vases, and then some. It was accompanied by a handwritten note with three words: *Please forgive me.*

Charlotte knew immediately who they were from.

She could not deny that she was angry with Andrew. His behavior was wicked. But she knew it came along with the territory of being his companion. She often pondered what was the driving force of his evil streaks. But she loved him in spite of it. There was too much good that made up for his turpitude. The flowers were unnecessary in her mind.

Moments later, the door rang again. A man's voice echoed from the corridor.

"Nathanial?" she questioned, surprised by his voice.

The servant showed him in.

Charlotte held herself back from wanting to rush towards him. Instead, she rose from her seat at the desk, interrupting a note to Andrew, and gave the servant permission to allow Nathanial to enter. "It is nice to see you again," she said as he stepped toward her.

She extended her hand and Nathanial enveloped it, letting it linger in his before he pulled it away.

Nathanial eyed the large bouquet, its abundance still wrapped and placed on the desk next to her. "Need I concern myself with an admirer?"

"Andrew being Andrew," she said, explaining it away.

Nathanial was not so easily amused.

"Would you care for some refreshments?" she asked, ignoring his concern. "Please, join me."

She handed the servant the flowers with instruction to place them by her bedside, and to bring a tray of lemonade and cakes.

Once they were alone behind closed doors, Nathanial reached for Charlotte's hand and brought it to his lips. "You look lovely this morning," he said.

"Nathanial," Charlotte scolded, pulling her hand away.

"How can you expect me to stay away? My heart melts at the mere thought of you."

Charlotte felt the same. It had been a few days since they were together, but there was no denying the passion ignited when in his presence. She was damned and yet redeemed in the euphoria of love all the same.

She knew, however, that what they were feeling was to be between them, and for them alone.

"Nathanial, you have no right to be so bold..." Charlotte paused as the servant arrived with a tray. "Thank you, Anna. I will serve the lemonade."

The servant cast a glance at Nathanial, and then to Charlotte, before she left the room.

"The walls have eyes and ears," she reminded him.

"Damn them!"

"Damn them in silence, Nathanial. We must be careful if we are to continue. I promised Lydia."

Nathanial scowled.

Charlotte leaned into him and brushed her hand against his cheek. "Please, my love. For me?"

He closed his eyes with her touch. "It is much to ask. But for you, I will grant you anything."

Charlotte rose and walked to the window. She had thought a lot about being with Nathanial. Her heart jumped and her skin tingled with the memory of his touch against her naked body. She could not deny the happiness he brought to her. But in the light of morning, after sharing a night of lovemaking, she awoke alone in her bed with the reality that they could never openly express their love for each other. Her feelings of happiness blended with dread, making the whole affair confusing, but something she neither wanted to give up nor rush into.

"You have me when you want, Nathanial. That has to be enough. I should not expect more from you, nor you from me. We are obligated by our roles. You are Lydia's husband. I am her cousin. We will have to be content with what we are granted."

"What are you saying, Charlotte? That you do not want me?"

"You are not mine to have...do you not see?"

"No!" Lines crushed across his forehead. "I am not some fiend, in spite of what Lydia may have told you. I will not come to you unless it is your will."

"Nathanial, I am not granted to make demands of you. That is how it must be."

Nathanial walked over to Charlotte and lifted her face to gaze upon. He smiled, absorbing the warmth it offered. Despite the pretense, he pulled her close and held her in his arms.

Charlotte didn't doubt the depths of his feelings. She understood the limitations. To want more from Nathanial would be an ultimate betrayal to Lydia. She trusted Charlotte to keep her marriage together, not be the one to destroy it.

"Right or wrong. I came to you because I wanted to. Never doubt the depth of my feelings, Nathanial. But do not ask more of me than I may give."

Nathanial nodded in understanding. "As long as you will have me, I am yours...on your terms," he agreed. His lips hovered over hers, but he didn't get the chance to bring them down.

Charlotte abruptly pulled away upon hearing Andrew's voice echoing in the hallway.

"Andrew," Charlotte called out as he entered. "What a nice surprise. I was told you were going to be gone all afternoon."

Andrew peered at Nathanial. "I see," was all he replied, noting the flush of color in Charlotte's face. He extended his greeting to Nathanial. "I see you are healing," noting the cut on his head from the other night was healing; his purple eye now hinting a shade of yellow.

"Yes," Nathanial coldly replied, rejecting Andrew's hand by turning away.

"Ah, good," Andrew smiled coyly. "I would hate for you to have to return to your wife in a battered state."

Nathanial's jaw clenched.

Andrew's eyes narrowed on him.

The room grew cold.

Charlotte recognized Andrew's wickedness, making it clear he held power over Nathanial–over them both. Stepping in between them, she broke their stare. "We must leave in a few days. Why not have dinner this evening? I am sure the Percles will be available, as well as Mr. Tatum," she suggested.

"That sounds like a wonderful idea," Andrew agreed. "The time we have together will soon end. Let us not waste a moment of our indulgence while in the city. Don't you agree Mr. Hammond?"

Nathanial ignored Andrew's comment and directed his response to Charlotte. "I will extend your offer to Mr. Tatum, with whom I am late for a meeting. I only intended to quickly stop by and inquire about you. If you will excuse me..." He bowed to Charlotte and turned to Andrew, and added, "I will see you this evening."

Charlotte excused herself from Andrew and escorted Nathanial out. "You do not have to leave on Andrew's account," she said as they reached the front door.

"This is his mother's house, and you are her guest. The room was too small for the three of us. And I did not lie, I do have business affairs to attend to." Nathanial looked around to make sure no one was in earshot. "But I needed to see you. To make sure it was not a dream."

She reached for his hand and gave it a squeeze. "It was real," she admitted. "But a dream all the same."

Nathanial brought her hand to his lips and placed a kiss upon her knuckles. "Even if I must dine with Mr. Knightly, it is *only* for you." He released her hand.

Charlotte lingered at the door, watching Nathanial retreat down the front steps and disappear among the passersby.

"He is a romantic man, isn't he?" Andrew commented as he walked up behind her.

"Of course, you were listening."

"With no intention on my part. These halls echo everything," he noted as he stepped back and pointed out the high ceilings and tall walls of the room. "It really is uncanny what you can hear."

"Andrew," Charlotte chastised. "Is nothing sacred to you?"

"Making love in broad daylight is not what a lady does," he scolded.

"That is not what was happening," she defended.

"Had I not walked in when I had, what would have happened?"

Charlotte was furious. Not because Andrew was wrong but pointing out the obvious.

"There is a time and a place for everything, my dear. If you are to keep your secrets, you must be better with your behavior and your feelings," he warned. "Otherwise, it is you who will lose everything."

"And what is your secret that keeps you on your toes?" Charlotte asked, sure there was more to his ability to know so much about deception and intrigue.

"Now you are thinking like me," he remarked, avoiding the question.

JUDGMENTS

The evening was unseasonably warm, leaving Charlotte with only a shawl needed to cover her shoulders when Andrew picked her up for dinner. The streetlights were being lit as the horses trotted along the road through town, the darkness descending around them. Charlotte was looking forward to dinner with the Percles, who kindly offered their home for the affair, insisting *it was the least they could do.*

It was a surprise then when the carriage suddenly halted in front of the Nathanial's townhouse across town.

"Why are we here?" Charlotte asked.

Andrew reached over and opened the door. "Out you go," he ordered.

Charlotte looked at him in questioning.

"You do not have to thank me," he said, retreating

back into the carriage by himself. "I sent word to Nathanial that dinner was cancelled. He shall be home soon enough."

"But I don't understand. Are not the Percles expecting us?"

Andrew smirked. "You could not be more beautiful than you are right now. Your face is beaming, and your eyes are sparkling after your secret interlude. You truly are a transformed woman! Who am I to deny you the opportunity to experience all that seemingly makes you happy?" He ignored her questioning face. "Everything is taken care of..."

"But I still don't understand."

"My dear, no one is better than I to make the indiscreet happen. You must grasp at all the opportunities you have," he tried to explain. "My mother is not due until tomorrow evening. I will not expect you back until then." He winked. "I sent Hollister to summon Nathanial. If you are clever, you will discreetly find your way to Nathanial's bedroom." He shut the door of the carriage and signaled the groomsman to ride on.

Charlotte did not get the chance to rebuke.

Andrew was halfway down the street before she could comprehend the opportunity she was given.

She looked up at Nathanial's door, a mere half dozen steps away. She wanted to rush, like a thief in the night, before anyone saw her. Instead, she took each step slowly and precisely, like any dignified woman would, the ruched edges of her hems dusting the cold cement behind her. She glanced over her shoulder as she reached the landing. The streets were quiet with no passersby who could start a rumor about why she was there, alone, standing at a married man's door.

When she reached for the knocker, she froze, unable to let it drop from her grasp. She knew the choice to be with Nathanial was in her hands.

Was this how it was to always be? She wondered, *sneaking in and out of places under the dark of night?*

Gripping the brass knob, she softly hammered it against the door.

No one answered.

She peered inside the window to her left, the curtains partially drawn. The room was dark. Nothing stirred.

She knocked again, her heart quickening its beat.

Nothing.

She slid her gloved hand over the brass handle and squeezed, pushing the door ajar.

"Hello?" her voice wavered against the walls of the small quarters of the entry–stairs to the right, drawing room to the left, and hallway straight ahead.

Nothing again.

Pushing the door open, she stepped over the threshold and quickly closed the door behind her.

The house was eerily still. A series of lamps, dimly lit, lined the entry and down the hall. Taking a few more steps inside, she called out again, for someone, anyone, to answer. And again, no one answered.

Andrew said Hollister was out, explaining his

absence, but she did not believe Nathanial would have so few servants who tended to his stay in London. She wondered if Andrew was conniving enough to secure privacy for them.

She peered up the stairs, contemplating her next move. Wait in the darkened drawing room, or find her way by herself?

She chose the latter.

Her shoes echoed as she tapped her way to the second floor, each foot taking her closer to the private spaces upstairs. A single lamp was lit on a table at the top of the stairs, the light stretching down the corridor. Three doors greeted her, all closed.

She opened the first door and found a small bed covered in a red quilt against the wall, and a child-sized table and chairs on the opposite wall. A kaleido-scope laid on top of it along with three books, and a teddy bear with a blue satin ribbon tied around its neck sat in the chair. Underneath the window there was a dresser with six small-sized drawers, three on the left and three on the right. A wooden model of Noah's Ark decorated the top and various animals surrounded it, the largest being the elephant and the tallest being the giraffe. A smile crossed her lips as she imagined Peter playing inside the childish room, the beloved toys awaiting his return.

She passed two more doors, overriding her curiosity of what lay inside. Instead, she continued to the end of the hallway, guessing they were the more important rooms of the house, and most assuredly, one being Nathanial's.

She opened the door to the right, noting it would be the room at the front of the house. Immediately she realized it was not Nathanial's bedroom, for it was obvious the room was decorated for a woman's tastes. Surrounded by yellow-floral papered walls, the bed was swathed in a curtained canopy of a golden silk fabric, fringed with tassels of the same color. The linens were white, meticulously ironed, and a mono-grammed satin pillow, adorning her cousin's initials, was laid at the head of the bed.

Charlotte should have quickly left, knowing the private space was Lydia's, but she heard horses' hooves on the street outside and rushed to the windows. She tore open the curtains hoping to see Nathanial exiting the carriage.

The horses did not stop, and the room grew quiet, now in full view as the moon's light came through the unveiled windows.

Charlotte eyed the private space.

It was not large, with enough room for an armoire between the two windows, a dresser across from the bed, a dressing table underneath a window, and a small writing desk next to the door.

The fireplace was cold, not having been used in the recent past.

She peered in the armoire, only to see it was completely empty; as if abandoned long ago and awaiting another to fill the cavernous space. The desk was cleared of any remnants of use, with an inkwell atop and a dried quill next to it. Curious, Charlotte opened its drawer to find sheets of paper awaiting someone to write upon them. She lifted the stack in her hands, knowing she was the recipient of the many letters written upon the papers, when a letter fell out.

Charlotte picked it up from the floor and noted the address: *Signore Piero Giordano, Villa Nuova, Umbria*. The name turned over in her head until she recalled it was the name of the painter of Lydia's portrait that now hung in her drawing room. She turned it over to see it was sealed...never sent, its contents unknown, left behind in the abandoned room. Placing it back between the sheets of paper from where it came, she put the stack in the drawer and shut it.

If Lydia was coming back, she left no sign of ever inhabiting the space, besides an unsent letter.

Entering the hallway, she halted and listened again for any life force within the walls of the house. The air remained still, and the quite lingered, pushing her to move on.

She crossed the hall and opened the door to what could only be Nathanial's bedroom, for it was dark and masculine. Quite the opposite of the room across the hall. Striped paper of forest green covered the walls that were not otherwise paneled in golden mahogany wainscoting. A heavy, ornate bed stood prominent against papered walls behind it. A series of landscape paintings adorned the walls, and a large mirror hung over the fireplace. Books were strewn about the room in stacks lying on the floor, near the sofa, on the table next to his bed. It was a small library unto itself. She walked over to a stack and noted his interests varied from Greek law to the poems of Coleridge–a familiar poet to her father to whom she read often.

A lamp was lit on a table, and a fire was burning, filling the room with warmth, awaiting its inhabitant. One finger at a time, she plucked off her gloves and removed her shawl, placing it over the chair by a desk strewn with papers. The papers splayed atop caught her attention when she saw her father's name standing out among the words. But before she could scrutinize them, she heard footsteps coming up the stairs.

"Nathanial," she called out as the door opened.

Much to her surprise, it was Hollister.

"No," he said simply.

"Oh!" Charlotte's eyes grew big.

Hollister moved through the room with routine. He lit another lamp on the table next to the bed, added logs to the fire, and brought out night clothes, placing them on the bed.

All the meanwhile, Charlotte stood frozen.

As he finished his tasks, he looked at her and asked, "Is there anything I may get for you?"

Charlotte shook her head, her eyes still wide.

"Mr. Hammond is out. He and Mr. Tatum are dining together," Hollister informed her. "But I can send word, if you like."

"No!" Charlotte blurted, a little too eager to stop him.

Hollister bowed his head. He waited for further instruction, but when he received none, he said, "The cook is out for the evening, but I am very good at tea."

Charlotte realized there was no surprise to Hollister about her waiting in his master's room.

"There are no secrets between you and Mr. Hammond, are there?"

"Very few," he replied.

"Then you know…"

"What I need to know," he answered without further explanation.

"Thank you, Hollister." She smiled, hoping he would return the gesture. He did not. "Tea would be lovely," she conceded.

"Yes, Miss," he responded, and left the room.

He returned a few minutes later with a tray in hands, placing it on the table near the fire.

"I took the liberty to bring you something to eat." He averted his eyes to the plate filled with sliced fruit, bread, cheese, and a slice of ham.

"Hollister, you should not have troubled."

"I believe it is my fault as to the reason you are waiting," he confessed. "When I received Mr. Knightly's note, I quickly went to Mr. Hammond's office to deliver the message. But Mr. Tatum had already been informed of the cancelled dinner, and convinced Mr. Hammond to join him in alternate plans."

"But I don't understand. How is that your fault?"

Charlotte asked.

"Mr. Knightly gave me the explicit direction to summon Mr. Hammond straight away. I seemed to have failed in my duties."

Charlotte now understood Hollister's lack of surprise at finding her in Nathanial's private quarters.

A flush of heat rushed to her cheeks. Nausea overcame her. She wasn't sure she was ever going to be comfortable with sneaking around and hiding secrets. She swiftly snatched her shawl, grabbed her gloves, and plucked her purse before rushing for the door.

Hollister tugged at her arm, halting her.

"This was a mistake," she said, meeting his gaze. "What must you think about me?"

"I hold no judgments," he said, releasing his hand from her arm.

She sighed, aborting her retreat.

Hollister grabbed her things out of her hands and put them aside. "Mr. Hammond is a good man," he said, not looking at her. "Loyal and honorable. But his family comes first. I do not take pride in telling any woman who comes between that. You should know where you stand with him."

Charlotte's head dropped, not disagreeing with him in the least.

He continued, "A man of means is resigned to duty, his individualism a family affair. At what cost of one's heart? Freedom is a poor man's wealth. I have been blessed to love the woman who moved my soul. Who am I to deny the same for him? Right or wrong, he is my priority. Do not let me be the one who stops what has allowed him to explore the part of himself that no one owns, demands, or dictates–his heart. What I think should have no bearing on you or your actions. But if it matters, your secret is sacred to me."

Tears fell from the corner of Charlotte's eyes. "If you were my father, I fear you wouldn't be so understanding," Charlotte cried.

"If I were your father, *no*," he said, granting Charlotte a half smile. "It is a good thing I am not your father."

That only made Charlotte cry more.

"Come," he guided her to a chair. He opened the door of the closet, reached up to the top shelf and pulled out a small Afghan, and brought it over to her. "This was a gift from my wife to Mr. Hammond. She loved him as if he were her own son. Before she died, she knitted this for him so that he would have a small memory of her. Mr. Hammond keeps it put away because it is so special to him." Hollister paused, unwrapped the Afghan, and laid it over her shoulders. "Sometimes the things that are special need to be enjoyed, lest they may be forgotten, or worse, gone forever."

Charlotte's tears slowed, and she wiped away the lingering droplets from her cheeks. "It is beautiful, Hollister," Charlotte pulled the small blanket around her arms. "I am honored you brought it out for me."

"What is important to Mr. Hammond is important to me," he said, handing her a linen from his pocket.

INTERLUDES

*J*t never occurred to Nathanial to decline
Tatum's invitation when he suggested
drinks and dinner. He had no one to return to in
London. When Hollister informed him upon his
return that Charlotte had been waiting for him, he
cursed himself under his breath. He ran upstairs,
taking two steps at a time.

Throwing open his door, the room was quiet; only
the flickering firelight was shadowing the walls. As his
eyes adjusted to the dimly lit room, he found Charlotte lay asleep on his bed, curled up with a small
blanket over her–the care of Hollister, no doubt.
Seeing her, atop his bed, in the privacy of his room,
brought a slew of thoughts, not the least of which was
arousal. But he didn't rush to her. He didn't want to
wake her. Not after making her wait for so long. She

looked too peaceful with her head on the pillow and her hands tucked underneath.

He pulled off her shoes and carefully put them down, next to the bed. He put another log on the fire and turned down the lamp, allowing the fire to be the only light he undressed by. He placed his coat and vest slung over a chair, and his cufflinks strewn on the dressing table.

He then poured himself a drink and sat by the flickering fire. He watched Charlotte from his chair, observing her quiet reprieve in a stolen slumber.

Here, he thought, *they could be happy–if it were just the two of them.*

If he was a good man, an honorable man, he should never have gone to Charlotte's room that first time. Lydia had pushed him away so many times that no one would have faulted him for straying. The opportunities abounded. The women numerous. But it was easy to pass up the many beautiful woman who had offered themselves to him. Lydia was twice as beautiful. The little she allowed seemed to be enough for him. He wasn't sure when enough turned into nothing. *Was it early in their marriage? After Peter was born?* When he got frustrated, even angry, he punished her by staying away. *Didn't the heart grow fonder when away?* Not for Lydia. It only seemed to make her happier.

They both became characters in the play called *family*. He played the devoted husband and father; Lydia played the adoring wife and mother. It seemed to work. They both kept busy in their perspective roles, never questioning how low the bar could go. His feelings dried up; his heart turned off. It was easier that way. If he couldn't have Lydia, he didn't want anyone. It would hurt too much to turn on his heart again. No woman was worth *that* pain.

Until Charlotte.

He hadn't counted on her re-igniting the passion he had left for dead.

It wasn't reasonable. It wasn't logical. How does one explain a spark of a soul, God-created, bound by something beyond the physical?

He hadn't meant for it to exist...until he saw Charlotte for the first time, standing across from him, relishing a strawberry, unaware of the power she possessed. For him, she was the only women in the room. She stood out like a jewel in a chest of gold; a sparkle that was blinding. Like a moth is drawn to the light, in those few seconds his eyes met hers, all he wanted was to watch her, and know everything about her. The fact that he was already betrothed to the most eligible, beautiful woman of all society, was not overlooked. Even as he was drawn to Charlotte across the crowded room, he was all too aware that he and Lydia were bound by commitment.

The perfect coupling, everyone called it.

And it was, had Charlotte not crossed his path.

Then he had touched *her.* It was swift, but magnetic, like a spark of lightning to his heart. It was a jolt he had never since felt. Until Charlotte returned to *Lottington,* when she opened the door in the hallway and their eyes met once again. So many years had passed, and yet...

There was no touch, no instigation, however, he was immediately drawn to her...a magnet force pulling him to her.

The dormant part of himself began to awaken. And as each day passed with her playing a more significant part in his daily life, her essence bathed his heart in a warm bath, melting the cold, hard shell that had once overtaken him. He started to feel again, Charlotte the undeniable object of those feelings, and he was unable to control the onslaught of emotions now consuming him.

After Lydia's final blow, he found no reason to deny himself any longer.

Did he first go to Charlotte out of anger at Lydia? Or did he run to her out of freedom to let go? Did it matter?

Charlotte was now here with him—the gods had spoken—and they were bound by body and soul.

NATHANIAL WAS AWAKENED from a deep sleep by fingertips outlining the contours of his face. Not wanting to break from his dream, he begrudgingly opened his eyes, one at a time. To his delight, he found Charlotte on the other end of that touch. Her lips came down on his, securing his reality. He didn't think twice to pull her into his arms and return her kiss, only now he did with twice the wanting, twice the needing.

Charlotte slowly pulled her lips away. "I didn't mean to wake you, but I had to find out if I was dreaming."

Nathanial looked at her, wanting more, but didn't push for it. "I am sorry you were left alone, my darling. I would never have kept you had I known you were waiting for me." He touched her face. "You are a lovely surprise."

Charlotte hushed him with a soft kiss to his lips.

A log crashed in the fireplace, causing them both to turn and stare at the darkened cavern, the embers emanating an orange glow.

Nathanial pulled himself away from Charlotte and threw more logs on the fire. "It is late, I should get you back," he suggested, confirming the time on the clock on the mantel.

Charlotte shook her head. "There is no need."

"Charlotte?" His brow raised, "Are you not the one who insists on decorum?"

"Only if it warrants necessity. For you see, no one is expecting me until tomorrow." Her smile widened.

Nathanial swooped her in his arms. "Charlotte Ashford, if it be true…" When he saw her nod, he came down on her lips taking full advantage of her own wanting.

"Nathanial," Charlotte said, when Nathanial's kisses slowed. "First things first. I need to undress. And a man should never be privy to that circumstance. You must excuse yourself, if only to give me the courtesy to present myself properly to you."

"Charlotte, there is no telling you that I have undressed a woman before. A circumstance you may not be fond of." He moved closer to her and took her hands into his. "And if you recall, we...you and I... really have moved passed *proprieties,* have we not? Now turn around," he said, "And let us not waste another minute of the precious time we have been given."

Charlotte hesitated, but when he kissed her once more, sealing her desire for him, she did as she was told.

Nathanial slowly unbuttoned her dress, planting kisses along her neck as he worked his way down the nine mother of pearl buttons, damning them. Hungry for the naked body underneath, he would have rather ripped them off. Instead, he was gentle and precise, preserving her beautiful dress. His hands wondered at times, but a swift slap from Charlotte kept him focused on the task at hand.

When he loosened the fabric from her body, Charlotte slipped out of the frock, untied her crinoline petticoat, and left the layers of fabric piled at her feet. Carefully she removed her stockings, gently laying them over the arm of a nearby chair, not to ruin them.

"You are very beautiful..." he said, watching her undressing ritual.

"Words from a man who wants to seduce a woman..." she quipped, removing her earrings and placing them on a table, along with her bracelet.

"No," he insisted, pulling her to him. "I do not want to seduce you, Charlotte. Any fool of man can do that. I want to make love to you...as long as the time allows us."

Running his fingers through her hair, he pulled the pins from her bun releasing her darkened waves to fall over her shoulders. He stroked her neckline, bringing his tongue to the soft flesh below her ear.

Charlotte tilted her head allowing his indulgent kisses to sweep across her skin.

Nathanial took little time to loosen the lacings of Charlotte's corset. With a little fumbling between his fingers, he managed to unhinged the busk, giving him opportunity to glide his hands over the soft curvatures hidden just below the thin fabric of her chemise. His body pulsated with desire for her, and he quickly removed the layer of fabric that lay between his mouth and her breast. Cupping her one of her breasts he brought his mouth over her hardened nipple and softly suckled as her final piece of clothing fell to the floor.

Charlotte moaned, and he moved to suckle the other nipple before he brought his mouth to hers once again.

Charlotte accepted his passion and doubled it with

her own need. She tugged at his shirt and pulled it over his head, her hands hungrily exploring the bare chest now uncovered. Her lips moved down and found the warmth along his neck, while her hands continued to discover the hard lines of his body.

Nathanial swiftly rid himself of his remaining clothes, now in a pile next to Charlotte's, and pulled her to his bed, the curves of her waist between his firm grip. She looked down at him, her hair falling over her breast, hiding her dark nipples. He pushed aside the tendrils, wanting to see her beautiful nakedness atop him. She laid her flesh upon his own naked body, and brought her mouth to his. As their tongues inter-twined, so did their bodies. Nathanial's hands slid down Charlotte's back, his touch caressing even the most sacred parts of her. She released breathless sighs as he guided her hips to move with his, until they found a rhythm together. Charlotte's eyes closed as a wave of warmth consumed her, before she fell into his arms, his own body equally erupting in pleasure.

It was late morning when Nathanial finally opened his eyes to find Charlotte already awake, reading one of his books. Her body was still naked and warm against his. Neither rushed out of bed, except to go to the toilet, and eat breakfast, quietly set outside the bedroom door. They repeated their lovemaking once more before Hollister discreetly notified them that Charlotte's carriage was waiting for her.

It would not be the last time for them to be together, but Nathanial knew Charlotte and he would have to be careful, more discreet. When they returned to *Lottington Manor*, they would have to resume a *normal* life with Lydia.

God help them!

Nothing any of them was doing was normal.

JEALOUSY

$\mathcal{N}$athanial used to eagerly glance at Lydia's bedroom, after returning home from his long stays away, hoping to find the door ajar. In the early years, he would race upstairs to find her waiting for him, her bed turned down, and his night clothes set aside.

Those days had long passed, and he only glanced her way out of habit. His returns only found Lydia's doors shut off to him.

The anticipation died long ago.

He wasn't sure if he hated her for that or was grateful for the new opportunity. Either way, he was neither expecting for the door to her bath to be open, nor for her to call out his name when he passed her room that morning.

"Nathanial is that you?" a spirited voice called out.

He had not heard that tone in many months.

He walked to the door, cracked it, and peered in, finding Lydia in the bath, her nakedness slightly blurred from soapy water floating atop.

"Come in," she suggested when she saw his resistance. "That will be all, Sadie. My husband can manage from here," Lydia said, flashing a look towards Nathanial.

Sadie passed Nathanial on her way out, exchanging glances with him, before closing the door behind her.

Charlotte and he were very discreet, but he bumped into Sadie earlier that morning coming out of Charlotte's room. With barely his shirt on, there was no explaining the circumstance. Being Lydia's personal maid, he had no illusions that she wasn't privy to the situation, nor that she probably informed Lydia of all she observed in the house.

He walked around the tub where Lydia lay naked, her breast peeking at the surface, and her knees breaking the water. He sat on the edge of the chaise near the window. He gazed out at the view, little interests for engaging his wife.

"I was searching for you last evening. You were not in your room," she casually stated, continuing to bathe, cupping water in her hands and pouring it over her shoulders.

Nathanial watched the sensual motion of the water trickle down her bare shoulder. He did not comment, but he did not turn away.

"Do you remember how you used to help me?" she commented. "You gave bathing a whole new purpose."

He *did* remember. He would slip into the bath behind her and she would lie against his chest, allowing him to fondle her small but rounded breasts. If she was in a generous mood, she would allow him to explore between her legs, his fingers the only thing to penetrate her.

Sexual intercourse was only permitted in the confines of her darkened bedroom.

It had been a long time since she had been alluring. Now she was distracting him. She lifted her leg and slowly ran a cloth from her ankle to her inner thigh.

He couldn't see through the darkened water, but he knew what lay just below.

"Where were you?"

"Excuse me?" he replied, not following the conversation.

"Where were you last evening?" Lydia asked again.

He stood, avoiding her gaze. The truth was that he was not in his room. Since his return from London, he had made regular visits to Charlotte in the late hours of the night, only to return before the sun came up. His wanting was insatiable, and she was eager to accept him. The lovemaking was becoming harmonious as they were discovering each other's bodies, exploring what pleased each of them. Charlotte was curious and open to his advances, never retreating from their nakedness or the sensations that followed. She enjoyed his skin against hers, softy brushing her hand to the forms of his entire body. He never knew a caress down his arm could stimulate the entirety of his being. They did not make love all the time. Many nights he would sit with her by the fire, his head in her lap as she would read to him. The act was as intimate as his lips upon hers. He loved just being with her.

"What is it you are seeking, Lydia?"

"You are still angry…" she mused. She got what she was looking for. His passion for her–love, anger or wanting–still existed. "Hand me my towel, would you?" She threw her arm out to the direction of the where it lay.

"Shall I call your maid?"

"No. There is no need."

Grabbing the towel, he opened it for her to fall into. She stood up, facing him directly, allowing the water to fall from her nakedness. Nathanial was not unaffected by her beautiful body. Her skin was pink from the heat of the water, her breast hardened by the cool air that touched them, and the hair at the back of her neck was curling due to the dampness. He could not deny she was a vision of loveliness.

She noted his excitement. "I see I have not lost your admiration."

He moved swiftly to wrap the towel around her.

"Mornings used to be an enjoyable time for us," she purred.

Nathanial turned and headed toward the door.

"I am to assume you prefer only whores now! Do not forget it was I who allowed you to have her."

Nathanial turned back. His eyes hardened on hers.

"Be careful, Lydia. You are treading a fine line with my temper."

"Very protective of you, Nathanial. I am glad to see you are so honorable towards Charlotte. After all, it is her honor she gave to me, and I promised I would watch out for it. I am glad you are beholden to my word. Do not get too comfortable with her. She may move on sooner than I did, for she has no lifelong commitment to you. That, my dear, is *my* fate."

Nathanial turned and pounded his feet against the wooden floor towards the door, indicating his urgency.

Lydia called after him, "Tell Charlotte I will be down soon."

Nathanial body shuddered. He prayed his anger would dissipate before he faced Charlotte.

"Good morning, Nathanial," Charlotte greeted, with a smile across her face.

Nathanial brushed his hand against her back as he passed her. "How could anyone think otherwise with you to greet at the breakfast table?"

She reached over and laid her hand upon his. "You make me feel happy…"

He did the same, covering her hand with his–a stolen, momentary touch. "And you do the same for me."

A servant walked in with a platter, and they quickly pulled their hands from each other.

"We really need to be careful," Charlotte berated more to herself, than to Nathanial. "The walls have ears and eyes."

"Charlotte, there is nothing they do not know or hear. You must know that by now."

"But Lydia…" she continued. "I made a promise."

Nathanial shrugged off the reprimand. "Lydia said she will be down after her bath." he said carelessly, reaching for his paper.

"You saw her this morning?" Charlotte asked.

He replied in a short, but firm, "Yes."

"Is there something she wanted?"

Nathanial deliberated how much Charlotte needed to know.

"She called me in to discuss a few things. It was nothing important," he answered, deciding to be as discreet as possible. He wasn't sure why he didn't trust her with the truth. *Did he have a right to be afraid of losing her?* He sighed. Fear was taking over his thoughts.

"Nathanial, is something wrong?"

"No," he quickly answered, and gently squeezed her hand.

Suddenly the door opened, Lydia surprising them both, prompting Charlotte to pull away.

Nathanial stood and pulled out the chair. "Lydia," his voice beckoned. He watched his wife kiss Charlotte on the cheek, circle around the table, and with a long-lost touch of tenderness, she brushed her hand across his back, before accepting his offer to sit.

"Good morning, Lydia," Charlotte greeted, not missing the way Nathanial's eyes followed his wife. It was hard for even her to ignore Lydia's radiance in her form-fitted, lavender muslin dress, the color brightening her blue eyes and bringing a rosiness to her complexion.

Lydia sat and unfurled her napkin, placing it on her lap, before she finally looked up at the both of them.

"You look lovely today, Charlotte..." she said from across the table, her voice almost lyrical with the compliment. "Simply radiant if I must put a word to it. Do you not agree, Nathanial?"

Nathanial looked at Charlotte, then to his wife, narrowing his eyes on her, choosing not to answer.

Lydia flippantly turned, scoffing his judgement. "I see you are almost finished," she continued, noting their half-eaten breakfasts. "But it is my dear husband's fault for interrupting my bath. I should have sent him away instead of postponing my morning. Now I am to eat alone." She reached for Nathanial, sliding along his sleeved arm before resting upon his hand, leaving the innuendo in the air.

Nathanial's hand did not move from Lydia's show of affection; his body remained stoic.

Charlotte didn't want to feel it, but her heart squeezed tight in her chest. If she could, she would have reached in and ripped it out to make the pain stop. It never occurred to her Nathanial's need for Lydia was still alive.

She forced a smile on her face. "You are being silly. Of course, I will keep you company. I can never do without another cup of tea."

"You are too good to me, Charlotte." Lydia removed her hand from Nathanial and reached for Charlotte's instead, giving it a pat.

Nathanial pushed out his chair from the table and placed his napkin across his plate. "I am sure you two do not need my company to distract you. If you will excuse me..."

"Always so attentive, my dear. But you are the distraction a woman likes. I am a lucky woman to be your wife."

Wife. The word bellowed inside Charlotte's head. Punched her gut.

She could feel Nathanial looking at her. She did not lift her eyes to him, pouring tea instead and placing a cup before Lydia.

"Good day, ladies," Nathanial's voice bellowed.

It was only when she heard his footsteps across the floor did Charlotte dare to look, her eyes lingering at the door where Nathanial exited.

"Charlotte?"

Lydia's voice snapped Charlotte out of her vacant gaze fixed on the empty doorframe.

"You do understand you are not my intended target," she gently spoke.

Charlotte brought her cup of tea to her lips and sipped, feeling a direct hit all the same.

"Now, now." Lydia lifted her napkin to her mouth. "Let us discuss happier things, shall we? Like Lady Knightly upcoming dinner party. Assuredly arranged for you." She gave Charlotte a wink. "She is very happy these days. Mr. Knightly's companionship with you has been the topic of conversation everywhere. You two were the gossip around London, seen almost everywhere together, so I was told."

Charlotte scowled. "What is it anyone's concern?"

"My dear, anyone who can distract Andrew Knightly for a series of a few days is of interest. A woman who monopolizes his time for as long as you have...well, that is something to talk about!"

"You realize he has no romantic fantasies about me. We are merely enjoying each other's company," Charlotte explained.

"Keeping a man interested is more than a reason for matrimony. But it is not I to whom you have to convince of your harmless companionship. His mother is most likely planning a wedding as we speak," Lydia tittered. "It would not be a bad arrangement, Charlotte. You might want to rethink your own feelings. He is a charming man who can give you a comfortable life. With or without feelings of love. Most women have less."

"You make it all seem so futile," Charlotte rebuked. "Is not love a component of marriage?"

"Love comes in many ways. Sometimes, the best

way is through companionship. The other compo-
nents are merely negotiable as you grow through the
relationship. As you are one to attest," Lydia openly
admitted and lifted her brow. "All I am advising to you
is to keep your options open. You might find this a
suitable situation in the end...for all of us."

Charlotte did not fully understand her final words,
but she knew they held meaning. She would be sure to
remember the conversation.

UNEXPECTED

Charlotte appeared at the top of the stairs dressed in a shade of blue, the color of a clear, unclouded sky. Nathanial found it hard not to be transfixed by the color against her creamy complexion and dark hair. In her tresses, she wore a blue ribbon, which matched her dress, interlacing the plaits woven around her head, ending in streamers down her neck. Wearing white gloves pulled past the elbows, she held a purse in one hand and carried a shawl over her forearm.

When she looked down at him, his heart jumped.

This only encouraged him to run up the stairs, as a schoolboy in unadulterated, eager youth, and meet her halfway. She smiled at him, and he had to gather his resolve to not press his lip to hers, which were enticingly adorned with a rosy rouge.

When they reached the bottom of the stairs, he pulled out his watch. He sighed. "Pray tell, where is my dear wife?" he grumbled. With the minutes ticking by, waiting for Lydia, he grew more eager to touch and taste the beautiful woman by his side. "She *does* realize she is now fashionably late?"

"I believe she does," Charlotte assured him, side-glancing the top of the stairs. "I am sure she will not keep us waiting much longer."

Nathanial put the watch back in his pocket, and not wasting the opportunity, leaned in and placed his lips to Charlotte's ear.

"You take my breath away," he lovingly whispered.

As if he willed it, her head tilted, her eyes closed, and her lips lifted to meet his. But he halted coming down on them.

They both heard the sound of Lydia's footsteps reach the top of the stairs.

Charlotte quickly stepped away from him and retreated in the shadows of the entry,

Nathanial wanted to pull her back, her blue eyes beacons in the darkness. She was a mere touch away. However, Lydia's approaching clapping heals kept him from moving. By the time Lydia reached his side, he appeared every bit the devoted husband at the foot of the stairs—stoically poised to escort his beautiful wife with Charlotte relegated to a mere accompaniment for the evening.

His hands reached for Lydia as she approached.

"Look what I found?" Lydia said. She opened her palm to reveal a gold bracelet topped with a garnet cabochon. "It was in the hallway. You must have dropped it on your way down, Charlotte."

"Oh Lydia!" Charlotte moved into the light. "You are a dear to have found it."

"But of course, darling. What is precious to you is precious to me. We look out for each other, do we not?"

Charlotte bowed her head, reminded of their life-long promise.

"Allow me," Nathanial offered, taking the delicate chain from Lydia.

"It was my mother's—one of the few items I have in memory of her. One of the few personal items Mr. Milford did not take from me." She shivered as his name rolled form her tongue. "I would certainly have lost it forever had you not found it, Lydia."

Charlotte extended her arm, and Nathanial grasped it, as if it was the most natural thing to take her arm, turn it over, and place jewelry around her wrist.

How many times had he touched her the same way, place his lips upon her wrist, his mouth reaching the nape of her neck, and indulge in the taste of her?

Placing the bracelet around Charlotte's wrist, he allowed her hand to linger in his own…perhaps a little longer than he should have. When he looked up, it was not Charlotte's flushed face but Lydia's stare that caught his eye.

Nathanial awaited some snide comment, an attack of the heart she was so good at. Unfortunately, it was not he to whom Lydia directed her contempt. She chose a better target to hurt him.

"That dress is *truly becoming* on you, Charlotte," she sneered, circling Charlotte as if she were on display. "It is generous of your curves. Your skin's radiance contrasts beautifully with the blue backdrop of your dress, enhancing the allure of your creamy complexion and making your rosy lips all the more enticing."

Charlotte brushed her hands against the blue brocade fabric. "Thank you," she replied. "Andrew's mother had it made for me while we were in London. She was quite generous during our trip."

"She will be pleased you are wearing it, as will the men who will be sure to keep you preoccupied this evening. I am sure my husband will be one of them..." Lydia's eyes darted to her husband. "Most importantly, it should please Mr. Knightly. That is the ultimate goal, of course."

Nathanial eyed his wife. Sinewy lines hardened across his face.

Lydia curled her mouth upward in wicked satisfaction. "Shall we head to the carriage?" she suggested, averting her husband's anger. "We do not want to be too late."

~

SITTING across from Charlotte was one of Nathanial's secret pleasures. Whether at the dining table, sitting in the salon, riding in a carriage, or even in the intimacy of her bedroom, he enjoyed looking at her.

No man was ever faulted for the admiration of an Ashford woman. Beauty was inherited in their bloodline. Charlotte's mother and Lydia's mother were the beauties of their day, as were their grandmothers before them. The Ashford men knew how to choose wisely.

But it wasn't Charlotte's family traits which endeared him to her; she had stolen his heart. Her eyes exuded love towards him and made him feel worthy. Important. Wanted. In his field of politics and law, taking down a man was fair game. The battle for worthiness was a constant struggle. In a loveless marriage, it was the ground he walked on. Charlotte compensated for that. *Was it selfish to revel in it?* He didn't know and didn't care.

The carriage straddled the uneven roads and rattled him back to reality of the two women with whom he was now entangled. Charlotte, who sat quietly and stared out the window, her fingers rubbing the stone atop her bracelet, and Lydia, whose eyes were watching him like a cat watches a mouse hole...waiting.

Lydia wanted something from him. *What?* He wasn't sure.

It did not go unnoticed she went to great lengths to

attract him this evening. If Charlotte was lovely, Lydia was alluring tonight. She wore a dress he had admired on many occasions that ended with him in her bed.

Like Charlotte, she chose to wear blue, only hers was cobalt, darkening her eyes, changing them into sapphire gems. When light penetrated them, they were sure to sparkle, dazzling anyone who was the recipient of the effect. The fabric was embroidered with roses of pink and white, as if a garden of flowers floated around her. It was an illusion of the eye giving her an ethereal presence. His fingers had traced the embroidered design while his hands searched for her body underneath the layers of silk, during those rare times, in her darkened chambers, when Lydia allowed him to undress her. The cream-colored lace edging the bodice now teased his eyes to glance at the small, but firm breast that lay just below. Sapphire earrings, he had given to her for her twenty-first birthday, dangled from her ears, the gems, a stark contrast against the creaminess of her naked shoulders.

Any man would be a fool not to be tempted.

Lydia smirked when she caught his roaming eyes.

"If you praise Charlotte's beauty this evening," he said, meeting her eye to eye, "You underestimate your own. You are a vision tonight, my dear. I will be the envy of all to be escorting such an enchanting wife."

Lydia reached for Nathanial's hand and smiled in a way she used to signal him of her need for lovemaking.

The lovemaking wasn't for love. It was purely about her need to feel wanted.

That he could offer.

Most of the time, after the chase, he was left to his own devices, frustrated and in an empty bed.

He knew she was teasing him that very morning, and now. He instinctively wanted to reject her touch, her hand that offered nothing more than an obligatory expression of affection. But he did not. If she wanted to play a game of devoted wife, he could play along as devoted husband. Unfortunately for her, that is all she would get from him; he had no desire to return to his wife's bed.

Charlotte glanced at them both, noting Lydia's hand now intertwined with Nathanial's, but said nothing. Instead, she directed her stare out the window once again.

Nathanial feared the worse. *Did she believe Lydia still had a hold on his heart?*

Lydia held their marriage with fierce reigns, but he felt she let go of his heart long ago. *It* was now in Charlotte's hands.

Nathanial grew impatient with his wife's touch. It was heavy and hot in his hand.

He dared not pull away; nor did Lydia seem to want to.

And Charlotte remained distant.

To his great relief, Lydia finally released him as they arrived at *Penrose*. Stepping outside the carriage, Nathanial helped his wife out, but quickly let her go to reach for Charlotte, wanting nothing more than to take *her* hand–not Lydia's–into his.

To his surprise, the pleasure was to be stopped by footsteps from behind him. Andrew Knightly was waiting in the darkness.

MY FATHER'S ROOM

*C*harlotte stood at the edge of the carriage, scanning the crowd gathering at Penrose. Andrew stood against a pillar by the door, his blonde hair luminescent against the night sky. Charlotte smiled at him, and he hurried towards her, taking two steps at a time.

Nathanial had already extended his hand, yet Charlotte hesitated. She anticipated Andrew reaching her before she had to accept Nathanial's chivalrous gesture. She wanted nothing more than to run from Nathanial. Not willingly, but out of the need to get away from him, from Lydia…from both of them.

How had she not noticed it before? The hostility. The anger. The disconnection destroying their marriage.

And she found herself in the middle of it all…*jealous.* She couldn't help it. Only moments before, Nathanial was all hers; a glance away. Until Lydia joined them and then he was drawn away.

She saw in the carriage how Nathanial watched Lydia; admired her. *She was stunning!* He didn't falter when Lydia reached for his hand. Nor did he rescind her touch. His gaze toward his wife was transfixed, as if she had held a spell over him.

Charlotte's heart winced at the reality of her situation. He was Lydia's husband, and Charlotte was Nathanial's mistress, reminding her that she was in no position to feel jealous towards her cousin.

But she was.

"Miss Ashford?" Andrew called to her, reaching for her. "Would you allow me to escort you this evening?"

"Mr. Knightly," Charlotte reciprocated in kind, side-stepping Nathanial, and interlocking arms with Andrew's. "Your timing is perfect."

"And you are late!" Andrew noted. "I have been waiting for you to arrive. Mother seems to have invited the whole of England and I have been playing host to them all." He shook his head in disgust.

"Andrew!" Charlotte scolded.

"Very well then." He rolled his eyes. "I had not realized I was in the company of my nanny this evening."

"Then behave better, especially when it comes to your mother. You know you are very fond of her. You do not need to pretend with me." She pressed her shoulder to him. "She deserves more from you. And as I am very fond of her, I do not want you treating her with disrespect in my presence."

"Yes, dear..." he teased. He pulled at his cuffs and straightened his shoulders. "Now come. Let us have a delightful evening, despite it all," he said wistfully. "And speaking of the devil in the midst..."

Lady Knightly waved the two of them down.

"There you are Andrew...and Miss Ashford, it is such a pleasure you are here this evening." Lady Knightly placed a kiss on Charlotte's cheek, taking a sweep of her presentation. "The dress does all I had hoped for. My son is a lucky man." She smiled at them both. "Now be off, you two, and enjoy yourselves."

With a flick of her wrist, she released them, not delaying her son's courtship.

"My mother is right..." Andrew said, guiding Charlotte away from his mother's side glances.

"About what?"

"You are stunning tonight, Charlotte. Look around you."

Charlotte looked over one shoulder, then the other.

"Women and men alike are glancing your way." He looked at her with one eye closed, the other assessing her from her head down to her toes. "It is more than the dress my mother chose for you, or the way you have done up your hair. It is not your rosy, poutful lips, or the way your skin glistens in the light of the room. It is..." He put his fingers to his chin and rubbed. "There is a fire lit inside, burning brightly."

Charlotte braced herself. Rarely did Andrew's

compliments come without purpose. Something sinister was about to come from his next words.

Touching Charlotte's arm, he drew her closer to him, tipping his head towards Nathanial and Lydia.

Charlotte followed his glance to her cousin.

"If I am to admit, Charlotte, my admiration is not for you alone. Your dear cousin is quite fetching this evening. She has outdone herself. It is as if a light is coming from the heavens and shining upon her."

Charlotte's chin lowered, as did her spirits. It was no secret. Everything Andrew said was true.

Andrew continued, "Look at how *he* stands by her side. So stoic. How admirable he is. Every man must envy him." He paused for effect, but not long enough for Charlotte to respond. "Even more so if they knew your secret."

Charlotte's hands twisted. The urge to slap him was animalistic. The urge to run was instinctual. The need to show decorum was far more bred in her, halting her from doing either, or both. She looked around the room, praying eyes were on Lydia, on Nathanial, on anyone but her, for the flash of red was surely showing on her face.

"You should be pleased, though," Andrew smirked. "He has not taken his eyes off you. What do you have to fear? He is yours in heart."

"Please, Andrew," Charlotte begged, turning away, hoping to halt his heinous behavior. But mostly, to prevent a surge of tears ready to fall.

She wiped away the water filling her eyes with a

delicate touch to the corners, the fabric of her glove soaking in the wetness. Averting a tearful display, it was Nathanial's eyes she met when she finally looked up.

He started to walk her way.

She had no other choice but to reach for Andrew once again. "Take me away from here without making a scene...quickly."

With finesse, Andrew slipped Charlotte out of the ballroom, down a long corridor, and through a set of paneled doors, closing them behind him.

A few steps in, he lit a lamp on the table. A dark paneled room illuminated under the dim light. Charlotte's eyes widened with the expanse of the libraries lining the walls, needing tall ladders to reach their heights. Large paintings of prominent men hung in salute, all dressed in elegant attire. Over the fireplace was the most prominent of the paintings. It was of a young woman with golden hair set up high with a crown of diamonds, dressed in a gown of white, and red slippers peeking from the hemline. Her blue eyes sparkled against red cheeks, setting off the porcelain of her skin.

Charlotte moved to admire it. "That is a lovely painting. Who is it of?"

"It is my mother in her youth. This..." he stretched out his arms, "...was my father's room. My father was very much in love with her–*my mother*. How could he not? She was the beauty of her time. The size of the painting signifies her importance to him. This space–

in the monstrosity of this house–is where he came to read and think. He entertained many important men here. Noblemen and royalty alike have stood where you stand now.

Charlotte looked down to the floor where she stood.

"I rarely had access to it when I was younger," Andrew explained as he walked over to a large side bar and filled a glass with whisky. "Now, it is rightfully mine." He waved an empty glass in the air. "Would you like a drink? Some port, maybe?"

Charlotte nodded a little too eagerly.

Andrew filled the glasses.

"Please have a seat," he said, motioning with a jut of his chin to the empty sofa near the fireplace. With two glasses in his hand, he seated himself next to her.

Andrew's proximity was such that Charlotte could feel his breath on her cheek, and the heat of his body. She attempted to shift away, but Andrew's gentle tug on her wrist drew her back to his side.

"Please do not pull away, Charlotte," Andrew pleaded. "I told you before, I am not the one you need to fear. I will do you no harm."

"Naturally, Andrew. I am well aware," Charlotte said, her voice laced with a hint of contrition. She settled back into her seat.

Andrew was the closest confidant she had. Other than his wicked wit, she had no fear of him. But sitting in a half-lit room, the slow-burning fire, and the lack of other people made her uncomfortable to be with him for the first time.

Men were men, regardless of what they proclaimed.

"Take a sip of your drink," Andrew instructed, handing her the glass containing a rich, tawny port. He already held his own glass, containing the golden elixir of Scotch. "It will help ease those nerves of yours," he added.

Charlotte twirled the crystal glass in her hands, contemplating his instruction.

Andrew laughed, downing his drink. He lifted his chin, indicating that she do the same. "Go on, it will not kill you!"

"Andrew, I am not one of your gentlemen companions," she scolded.

"No, you most certainly are not," he agreed. "Forgive me if I offended you."

"No," she sighed, lowering her head. "Please forgive me. I have been short with you. You are not the one I am angry with."

"That I have surmised. Might you be having a lover's argument?" Andrew questioned. "The fact that your cousin is quite enticing tonight can be… distracting for any man. Especially if she is his wife."

"Andrew!" Charlotte yelled. "I should throw this port in your face for that comment, and for all the others."

"And what? Run into the arms of your protector?

And who might that be? Lydia? Nathanial?" He leaned to her, tempting her to slap him.

Even in the dimness of the room, she could see his eyes glimmered with excitement. He had an agenda with his cruelty.

Charlotte met his eyes. "I have declared it before and say it once again, you are a fiend!"

"And yet you still remain," he chuckled, unaffected by her words. Taking her glass slowly out of her grip, he returned to the server, filling it.

Charlotte spied the door, listening to the voices and music rumbling through the halls. She debated her escape but had no desire to return to the party. Andrew brought her a refill of port, and she downed it, handing back the empty glass with a request for more.

"Ah, good girl..." he said, complying with her request.

"Andrew..." His name wobbled from her lips. "I believed you to be fond of me. Why do you feel the need to taunt me? What have I done to you?"

"I am not trying to hurt you. I am trying to protect you."

"What is this great concern for my protection? From what? I am not in harm's way. Nor am I unaware that my situation with my cousin and her husband is unusual."

Andrew's brow arched, and he laughed. "My dear, let us not fool ourselves. Your *relationship* is highly unorthodox...unconventional...radical, even."

Charlotte rolled her eyes. "You have made your point, Andrew. May I move on?" When he nodded, she continued. "You are under the notion that I am unhappy. Quite the contrary."

"Is that what I saw on your face when you arrived here this evening? Is that why you are here now, sitting in a dimmed room with me, hiding from *him?*"

"You may never understand a woman's heart, or the sacrifices one makes for love."

"Even if you have to sacrifice yourself?"

Charlotte gazed into the dark corner of the room. *What ghosts hid there?*

Andrew continued, "I am not sure of this word you throw about as if it has meaning. *Love.* Are you sure you know what it means, or the cost one must pay to have it?"

"You cannot understand!" she shouted. But shame got the best of her, and she lowered her voice before she continued. "I am safe, Andrew. I am with family. And, most importantly, I am being well cared for. You will never understand the value of those things as a man, and one who is entitled. You have autonomy and independence. A woman is not granted the same."

Charlotte wasn't sure who she was trying to convince, despite the u*northodoxy* of her position.

"I do not doubt the benefits," he jeered.

Charlotte jumped from her seat, and clenched her teethed, "Mr. Knightly!" she seethed.

He rolled his eyes. "Are we back here again, *Miss Ashford?*"

"Please do not dismiss my feelings as salacious. You know how I feel. I did not ask for this situation. If I am to have anything come from it, why not love?"

"Why not indeed," he snickered.

Charlotte abruptly turned from him and headed for the door.

"Wait!" Andrew yelled. "Please Charlotte, do not leave. I promise to be better."

Not sure why, she stopped, and returned to the couch, only this time she made sure Andrew was at an arm's length away.

"I am not judging you. I worry about you. You are too pure a spirit to be caught up in such intrigue. I sometimes wonder why you settled for so little." He paused. "Maybe...maybe, if you expected more for yourself, someone would be worthy of you. You deserve someone who can openly express his love to you, you to him. Do not disregard the opportunity if it should arise."

Charlotte laughed at the absurdity. "Are you a dreamer or a realist? Which is it, Andrew? For you are well aware of my financial situation and the limitation placed on my prospective future. I do not need to be reminded, especially by you." She let out an exhausted sigh. "We have been gone a long time, Andrew. People will talk if we do not return to the party."

"Let them talk. No, damn them!" He laughed. It was hard and guttural; maniacal. "Fools, all of them. What gives them the right to watch us, judge us, demand of us? Why are our lives run by everyone but ourselves?"

His threw his drink against the fireplace.

Charlotte jumped. Andrew was becoming reckless in front of her.

"Andrew, something is wrong. Or you are foolishly drunk. Which is it?"

He stumbled across the room, grabbed a new glass, and poured another drink.

Turning to her, he shouted, "It's you! Bloody you, Charlotte! Since you came into my life, I have been torn as to my feelings. You have vexed me with your thoughts about love. I used to question its significance, but you are showing me the power of it right before my eyes."

"Are you mocking me? Because I am in no mood to be tormented. I have had quite enough of you this evening."

He stared at her curiously. "Let us drink to that!" He swirled the liquid in the glass, took a gulp, and swiveled the liquid around his cheeks before swallowing.

"You are drunk!"

"Yes, a little. Maybe not enough," he replied.

"Oh Andrew…" Charlotte whispered, tired of his moods. "What am I to do with you?" She closed her eyes and rubbed her temples, dropping her head against the back cushion of the sofa. If she were to admit, she, too, had drank too much, and was now lightheaded.

The fire illuminated Charlotte's face. Her lashes had swooped over her eyes, casting a shadow on her cheeks. The rouge on her lips had faded. With her head tilted, her chin in the air, Andrew could see the delicate lines of her neck and shoulders. Her skin was young and plump, as were her breast. Tempted, he walked over to her wanting to glide his hands over her delicate skin. He leaned over her, bringing his mouth close to hers, but held himself back.

"If I could fall in love, it is with you my heart would be forever tied," he whispered in her ear.

Charlotte's eyes opened, but she didn't push Andrew away. She didn't want to. Instead, she brushed her hand against his cheek. He closed his eyes, and she wondered why he hid this vulnerable side of himself from her.

Urgent footsteps came down the corridor pulling them both away from each other.

The heavy footsteps came closer.

Charlotte rose, and Andrew straightened, ready to meet the intruder.

The door opened and light from the corridor shadowed a tall silhouette. It was undoubtedly, Nathanial. He paused at the sight of the two of them. Clearing his throat, he explained, "Lydia is not feeling well. She wishes to leave. She hopes you will not be disappointed to end the evening so early."

"I am sorry to hear that," Andrew said. "If you would allow, I would be happy to escort Miss Ashford home this evening, if you must leave."

"No," Charlotte interjected. "I should accompany Lydia."

"As you wish." Andrew bowed, allowing for her retreat.

Charlotte slipped past Andrew and walked to the door where Nathanial waited. His lips were flat and his eyes were dark. She looked over her shoulder to Andrew. "It has been a lovely evening. Thank you."

"Yes…" Andrew replied, meeting Nathanial's stone-cold stare. "It has been."

Nathanial noted the glasses on the table, the almost empty decanter on the sideboard, and grimaced.

Charlotte took his arm, "Come Nathanial, Lydia will be waiting for us." Turning her head, she added, "Goodnight, Mr. Knightly…"

"Goodnight, *my dearest*, Charlotte," Andrew whispered softly. His words were shared solely between him and the surrounding portraits. Charlotte had departed before his words could reach her. With the door now closed, he was alone.

OPTIONS

Charlotte slept in later than usual, the effects of the port lingering from the night before. The few extra hours still did not compensate for her pain when she finally rose, bathed, and dressed. Her head still ached; her stomach still wobbled. She lingered at the bedroom door, her hand touching the knob. The world outside was getting complicated. Her heart growing heavy.

Stepping into the hallway, *Lottington Manor* stirred. Doors opened and closed, shoes pitter-pattered against the floors, and voices bounced off the walls, through the hallways.

Her head pounded with every sound. She walked down the hall, but looked back twice, contemplating her retreat. It was too late, Hollister spotted her at the top of the stairs, luggage gripped in his hands.

"Good morning, Hollister. It is nice to see you today."

As with his usual demeanor, he nodded with little expression, heaved a bag under his arm, and passed her, stopping at the vacant bedroom, two doors down from hers.

"Morning, Miss," a servant girl said, carrying an armful of freshly ironed linens, meeting Hollister at the door of the vacant room.

Another servant, this time with towels, rushed by with a quick nod.

Charlotte watched more servants scurry past her as she made her way to the breakfast room.

Only when she came upon the drawing room did she realize the purpose.

"Charlotte," Nathanial's voice called to her. "Please come in."

Charlotte hesitated. She wasn't ready to face Nathanial, not after the previous night. After finding her with Andrew, his words were few on the ride home. Although grateful he did not come to her room that evening, she knew it was a rebuff. She tossed and turned all night, with Andrew's words repeating in her head, *"...a man who can openly express his love for you, you to him."*

She hesitantly entered the drawing room, accommodating Nathanial's request.

He did not turn when she crossed the threshold, seemingly preoccupied with a man Charlotte did not recognize. It took her footsteps pounding across the floor for the two men to turn her way.

"Why, if it is not Lottie Ashford," the stranger cried out.

"Lottie?" Charlotte placed her hand on her chest. "Oh my, I have not been referred to as *Lottie* for a very long time. Since I was a young girl," Charlotte recalled. "But no one calls me that now."

"Then I beg your forgiveness. You have obviously..." he eyed her from head to toe, "...grown up to become a woman, a beautiful one at that, who deserves a much more dignified name. What shall I call you, Miss Ashford?"

"Charlotte, will do," she said, extending her hand cautiously to the stranger.

Nathanial's brow arched. "I had not known you two were acquaintances. But if not the case entirely, Charlotte, this is my brother, David."

"Brother?" Charlotte's voice rose an octave.

"Yes. And if you do not recall, we *have* met before... at Niles Beaumont's eleventh birthday party. You wore a pink dress with white lace, and your hair was pulled away from your face, gathered in ringlets at the back, a halo of flowers crowned your head."

Charlotte touched her hair, knowing the style had not changed over the years, only her ringlets were now plaits wrapped low around her head, and the crown of flowers now replaced with a decorative comb tucked to one side. When she looked up, she found David eyeing her dress. It was pink...edged in white lace.

Charlotte blushed. "How do you remember all those details?"

"You were the prettiest girl there," he said, matter of fact. "But Niles and I were boys—mischievous boys—and would have nothing of it. We tormented you the whole afternoon trying to pull those flowers out of your hair."

Charlotte covered her mouth and giggled. "*I do* remember Niles' party. If I recall, Niles and his friends were beasts to all the young girls that day."

"That was probably true," he admitted. "I, being the one who instigated the torment."

"But you surely are not the lanky boy with the wiry hair, who had ears bigger than his head?"

He lifted his hair away from his ears. "I grew into my ears."

"I can see that you have," she laughed, remembering him more clearly.

She never would have guessed Niles Beaumont's awkward friend would grow up to be the attractive man before her. As he stood next to his brother, she could see the similarity. David was apparently younger, and slightly taller, whose tanned skin was evidence he spent more time outdoors than his brother, who was pale in comparison. His eyes were dark like Nathanial's and his face was similar in shape, with high cheekbones and a strong jawline. Although equally handsome, there was no mistaking them for brothers.

"Lydia told me Nathanial had a brother, but it never occurred to me I had already met you."

"Nor I, until I saw you."

"But surely, we should have met again after that?" Charlotte pressed.

"I went away to school and traveled when not attending classes. Nor did I attend my brother's wedding, which he has never forgiven me for," David explained, glancing at his brother. "In all honestly, he barely gave me time with the announcement of his engagement before he rushed to marry. I do not blame him. I would not have waited to seize such a beautiful woman as Lydia...too much competition!"

"Did I hear my name?" Lydia asked as she entered the room. "Oh, I see you have met Charlotte."

"I have, but once again," David corrected.

"Once again? Do you two know each other?"

"David and I met when we were younger," Charlotte explained. "He was a friend of Niles Beaumont. Do you remember him? Our fathers were acquaintances. Mr. Beaumont would call on our home with Niles in tow. You certainly would have joined us when we spent afternoons playing in the gardens while our fathers discussed business."

"It was so long ago, Charlotte. How is one supposed to remember so far back?" Lydia shrugged off the memory.

"Well," David looked at Charlotte. "We will just let it be our secret memory, then."

He smiled at her, causing her to do the same.

"How fortuitous, though," Lydia said. "You will be happy to hear David is staying with us for a few weeks, maybe longer, if we can keep him entertained. Hopefully, it will allow you two plenty of time to catch up with your childhood memories."

"I believe I would like that very much," David concurred.

"Why don't you two head to the terrace. It is such a lovely day; I would hate for it to go to waste. Especially with the joyous occasion of David's arrival." Lydia narrowed her eyes at her brother-in-law. "Even if quite a surprise."

David smirked.

Nathanial smiled. "I, for one, am happy he is here. It has been too long, brother."

David looked at Charlotte. "Too long."

No longer a stranger, Charlotte happily took David's arm and allowed him to escort her to the terrace at the back of the house.

The terrace overlooked a lawn, with stone steps that led to another lawn, which rolled to a pond, and then a forest beyond that. Clematis vines crawled up the wall and around the windows, while rose bushes mixed with lavender plants filled planters in front of the balustrade wall separating the terrace from the lawn below. It was one of her favorite spots of the house for its privacy and view–a place where she and Nathanial spent time lingering, talking, just being with each other without eyes of the servants on them, or in earshot of their conversations.

"Ahhh," Charlotte sighed, feeling the breeze against her face, "Lydia did not exaggerate. It is a beautiful morning. I am glad she suggested we talk outside and to enjoy the good weather."

"I dare say, if Lydia wanted it to be so, she would have willed it," David proclaimed.

Charlotte laughed, knowing David was right. Her will always got its way.

Charlotte spotted Nathanial now playing with Peter on the lawn. He declined to join them on the terrace, opting for time with his son who was fresh from his morning nap. He was rolling a croquet ball and Peter was diligently running after it, bringing it back to him.

"Peter has grown since I last saw him," David commented, following Charlotte's eyes on Nathanial and Peter.

"How long has it been?" Charlotte asked, turning her attention to the new guest. "Since you last were at *Lottington Manor?*"

"It was after Peter was born. Nathanial asked me to visit...Lydia was having a hard time, and he thought I would be able help. Cheer up things."

"Yes, I remember that time...by letter, of course.

Peter came soon after her parents tragically died. I cannot image the sadness intermixed with the joy of having a child. I was so far away, unaware of her hardships, and unable to help."

"Lydia isolated herself. The doctors could not explain it. They said she needed time. It was hard for Nathanial. Nanny was a godsend." He watched Peter run across the lawn, chasing after the birds. "Peter seems no worse for the wear. A stoic Hammond trait."

"Yes…I am sure," Charlotte agreed, unsure if it was admirable.

"And Lydia came back to her charming-as-ever self."

Charlotte nodded, not sure she was "back" to her charming self, knowing her discontent still existed.

"And you?" he asked. "You have settled comfortable at *Lottington Manor*?"

"But of course. Who could not be happy *here*? Nathanial and Lydia have been more than generous, making me feel like I have a home here, forever, if I choose."

"And do you…want to stay *forever*?" He cocked his head.

Charlotte ignored any thoughts of what was to come. She didn't like the fear it brought. Lost in a bubble of happiness with Nathanial, it didn't matter what her future held. It seemed she had all she needed; all she wanted, until last night when Andrew asked the questions that reached her core.

Did she deserve more? Could she stay as Nathanial's mistress? Was it enough for Lydia? Was it enough for her?

"Well?" David asked, waiting for her to answer.

She brushed off her inner thoughts and turned the question on David. "You are a curious one, David. A man who travels the world, living among strangers or flitting from place to place, only to make an appearance to your family and friends from time to time. Are you not in search of a place to call home?"

"First of all, I do not 'flit.' And I most certainly do not take advantage of the kindness of strangers. I become well acquainted to those with whom I choose to hang my hat." He stretched a smile across his face, then winked. "I enjoy traveling...is that a crime? I am doing what makes me happy until it does not."

"And then what?"

"I could ask you the same," David countered. "For a woman as lovely as you, have you confined yourself to spinsterhood?"

"No, not confined. I believe in marriage and family. But in the circumstance for many women, the opportunity may be limited, if not all together impossible. For men like you...there are no excuses."

"Excuses, no. Is there a duty to marry? Yes. We all have our burdens to overcome," he said with an exasperated sigh to follow. "If it consoles your concerns, I do recognize my responsibilities. And as far as marriage, I am a firm believer in the benefits." He eyed his brother in the distance. "My brother seems happy enough. He seems to have found the right woman."

"Yes, so it seems," Charlotte uttered. "Then it is about committing to a woman? Is it love, you question?"

"Ah, you seem to be questioning my notions about relationships. Please do not doubt my devotion to love and all its nuances. The matters of the heart do not always synchronize with the head. Love and marriage are not the same. And thus, I prefer to treat them as separate entities."

"Maybe they are," Charlotte said, releasing the words into the breeze.

David grew quiet. He searched Charlotte's face for what her words were not revealing.

"Why must you look at me so?" Charlotte turned away from his stare. "You seem to take privilege that is not yours."

He laughed, loudly.

"Are you laughing at me?" Charlotte questioned.

"You really do not remember me, do you?"

Charlotte shook her head.

David leaned over and whispered, "I kissed you."

Charlotte pulled away from him. Her eyes widened. "I think you must be mistaken. I most certainly would remember being kissed by you, or any man."

"It was at Nile's birthday party," he explained. "A game of hide-and-seek ensued, and we both hid in the armoire in the main hall. Do you remember it? It was filled with men's coats and smelled of tobacco." When she shook her head, he continued, "I was crouching inside when you crawled in. You almost screamed when you saw me. I wrapped my arms around you, pulled you against me, and covered your mouth to prevent you from making a sound. When Nile's footsteps retreated, I pulled my hand away, and you glared at me. But all I saw were your blue eyes looking at me. It was the first time a girl ever made me *stop*. My heart stopped. My mind stopped. I couldn't help myself. I kissed you."

Charlotte's eyes lit up. The memory had faded but was not forgotten.

"I should have slapped you!"

"Yes, you should have. I believe you were about to. But you did not. I have never forgotten. A boy never forgets his first kiss."

"Unfortunately for you, the kiss was not as impressionable for me," Charlotte smirked. "Nor was it my first kiss. That honor was given to Harold Pilsner. He was a chubby nine-year-old boy who was curiously kissing girls at Rita Hamlin's party. Unfortunately for Harold, his mother caught him trying to assault the poor girls with his greedy lips. His mother grabbed him by the ear and carried poor Harold away on public display, reprimanding him of his abhorrent behavior."

"Does that really count as a first kiss?"

As the memory began to resurface, Charlotte recalled her impression of the kiss in the armoire. She should have been shocked when David had placed his lips upon hers, but the soft sensation left a lingering warmth she found hard to be angry with. It was such a contrast to Harold's dry, chapped lips which scraped across her own, that Charlotte fell silent with comparison. When David pulled his lips away, even as a child she knew she should have protested, but she only looked at him through the darkness wondering if she was a bad girl for liking it. The moment was soon lost when Niles pulled the armoire door open and called out that he had cleverly discovered the two. David crawled out before Charlotte, hitting Niles in the arm, and ran off to never be seen again until that morning.

"Does any kiss that is *stolen* count?" Charlotte replied, leaving her private thoughts about his first kiss *private.*

"Fair enough. I will make an effort to make a better impression next time," David predicted.

Charlotte thought him very bold and made note. Something told her he would be true to his word.

PLAYFUL COMPETITION

*I*f the truth was known, Charlotte was growing happier at *Lottington Manor* since David's arrival. He provided a cheerful energy to the Hammond household, lifting its spirit. Everything was brighter; everyone merrier. His laughter was contagious. When he smiled, others smiled. It felt good to be surrounded by *joie de vivre*.

Charlotte had never known one person could lift the tenor of a room. His magnetism was electrifying, and each new day brought about more of the same.

"Well, you two are beaming brightly this morning," Lydia noted of David's and Charlotte's laughter as they entered the morning room. "What are you two laughing about?"

"David," Charlotte said. "He did an impression of Thomas Knightly...he is quite good at impersonations."

"Really? A hidden talent, David. Who knew?" Lydia teased. "Please sit and join us for breakfast."

David pulled out the chair for Charlotte before seating himself across from her.

Nathanial put his paper down. He said nothing.

"Good morning brother," David greeted.

Nathanial, again, said nothing.

Lydia rolled her eyes and turned to her guests. "And what is on the agenda for today, you two?"

"Shall we ride today? Or another game of croquet?" David asked Charlotte.

"You cheated at croquet." Charlotte narrowed her eyes. "And left me stranded in a mud pit."

David sliced a piece of ham and lifted it with his fork. "Then riding it shall be," he agreed, shoving the ham in his mouth.

Charlotte leaned forward with a grin. "I would like that very much."

Nathanial, noting Charlotte's bright eyes and smile just for David, took a sip of his tea, and placed the cup down on the table. "David, do you think you can pull yourself away from pre-occupying Charlotte's time, come to the office for a few days, and work with Tatum and me? There are property management affairs I would like to discuss with you before you leave."

"Are you already ridding yourself of me, dear brother? I hope I have not overstayed my welcome."

"Of course not, David," Lydia affirmed.

"Good. Because I am in no hurry to leave just yet. I

am in the company of a most charming woman, only second to your wife. I see why Charlotte adores it here."

He tipped his head to Charlotte, and she offered him a smile.

Nathanial cleared his throat, and Charlotte's smile went away.

David continued, "To Lydia's credit, it seems, my brother, you have created a piece of heaven in the middle of England. Dare you begrudge my indulgence? This is your castle, and you are king of it. But you have your queen. Before you cast me off, allow me the opportunity to find my own."

Nathanial sat higher, pulling his shoulders back. "All is good and well, brother. But I believe Charlotte should have a say in the matter. She is not one to fall for insincerity, even if charming...and from my brother."

David's voice became stern, losing its usual lightness. "Are you accusing me of something, dear brother?"

"Nothing more than you are capable of..."

Charlotte caught Nathanial's glance in her direction. His warning was not for David alone.

Their time together had been restricted since David's arrival. Days were filled with activities, like riding and croquet, and evenings were crowded with dinners that included the Kingsley brothers, Mr. Tatum occasionally, and to their surprise, even Mr. Henry, accepting a spontaneous invitation.

Lydia was at her best while entertaining, enjoying the excitement of the household preparations, the lively conversations, and the long evenings filled with company, playing cards, and mostly for the men's benefit, drinking and cigars.

Needless to say, David's visit was bringing about a whirlwind of activity, consuming Nathanial's spare time with extracurricular activities, monopolizing Lydia's attention for hosting, and engaging Charlotte to be included in it all.

Where David was, Charlotte was. Her time was taken up by him, leaving her limited opportunities to be with Nathanial. And with David two doors down from her own. Nathanial dared not risk coming or going from hers.

Nathanial and she had moments–talking in the library, a walk in the garden where they held hands, even a stolen kiss in the stables when everyone had abandoned them for the afternoon. David was at the tailor's and Lydia was visiting Mrs. Sotherby.

Besides *moments*, they had very few evenings to intimately indulge in each other.

Nathanial didn't complain. He relished the opportunity to be with his brother as much as the rest of the household. But as the days continued, his patience diminished as David's attention to Charlotte increased, and Charlotte enjoyed it more.

Lydia placed her hand on Nathanial's forearm, stopping him from speaking. "Ignore him, David. He is jealous you have captured Charlotte's undivided attention. Since her stay with us, she has been *his* sole companion."

"Except for you, of course," David interjected.

Lydia smirked, saying nothing to confirm or deny his statement.

"Lydia..." Nathanial huffed. "Careful..."

His eyes met hers, but she turned toward David.

"There is no denying Nathanial has grown fond of our Charlotte, as we all have. She has become the glue for our little family. We need her as much as she needs us."

"Then you only prove my point, dear sister. To transform a structure into a castle, a boy to a man, a scoundrel into a gentleman, it takes a good woman."

Lydia grinned at Charlotte. "Yes, I believe so."

Nathanial stood and threw down his napkin on the table. "Maybe there is hope for you yet, David." He looked at Charlotte, and then back at his brother. "But I am afraid your search may need to go elsewhere."

David stood, meeting his brother's stare. "Care to take that energy to the courts?"

Nathanial took two steps closer to his brother; his brother stepped even closer, their noses almost touching. One hand went out, and the other grabbed it. They shook on it.

"Let the best man win!" David said.

Nathanial shook his head before granting his brother a smile. "How do you get me to play into your games?"

David smirked. "I learned from the master of manipulation–you!"

"Aww, David, this is where you will never beat me. It is not about manipulation. It is about outsmarting your opponent. That way, you can live with yourself."

"Go!" Lydia pointed towards the door. "I have had enough of both of you. Leave Charlotte and me to behave like adults in this house."

"Fair enough," David bowed before her. "Queen of the castle, I dutifully obey." He turned to Charlotte. "If you will pardon my rudeness, but I will have to postpone riding with you this afternoon. I hope we can reschedule."

"Be kind, Charlotte, with any promises to my brother..." Nathanial said. "This may be his dying wish."

"Ha!" David grabbed Nathanial by the arm and pulled him out of the room. His words echoed down the hall. "Who knew you had a sense of humor?"

POSSIBILITIES

*B*lessed with another spectacular clear sky, Lydia and Charlotte walked to the court, tucked beyond the gardens, past the manicured lawns, and watched from under the protection of tall overhanging branches as the two men pounded the tennis ball over the net.

The tennis players were not as lucky. The sun beat down on them as they ran the court, aggressively trying to beat each other. All odds were against Nathanial, with the ladies cheering on the younger brother, who evidently had the advantage of youth and skill.

"Come now, brother, you can do better than that!" David poked Nathanial.

"Yes, I could, if you played with more skill," he retorted, not wanting to concede to his brother's advantages.

"Humph! Is that what you want? I was trying to be

gentle with you. But I see you have no pride. And in front of the women," David snickered. He set up his serve and slammed it down on the other side, the speed of the ball overtaking his brother.

"Now darling, you must take it easy," Lydia chided her husband. "May I remind you that you have a wife and a child to care for. I will not have you falling dead for the sake of your honor," Lydia teased.

"Be respectful, David," Charlotte added, "He is not as young as he appears."

Nathanial, wiping sweat from his face with his sleeve, bowed to Charlotte. "I will take that as a compliment."

She smiled, hoping it would help his game, but it was not likely.

"It is getting too hot, and you both need a break. Come and join us in the shade," Lydia called out to them.

The two men obeyed, dragging themselves across the lawn and plopping themselves down in front of the women, their chests heaving from exhaustion.

Charlotte wetted a napkin and handed it to Nathanial, and then did the same for David.

"I see you know where your bread is buttered," David noted. "It will be my honor if in the future I change that."

No one lost the meaning of his innuendo.

Charlotte handed Nathanial a glass of lemonade. "Have you and your brother always been so competitive?"

"It is hard not to be. He has always wanted to catch up to me. And I could not allow that to happen."

"I have done *that,* and surpassed you," David teased, throwing his now sweat drenched napkin at his brother. "There is nothing I can do that will not put you to shame."

"David, you are a grown person unto yourself. You should not have to prove yourself to Nathanial or to anyone. I, for one, am proud of the man you have become," Lydia said.

"Thank you, dear sister. It is nice to know I am appreciated in this group."

"You do not need my approval, brother. You are your own keeper, and a worthy opponent as well." Nathanial flipped onto his stomach and moaned as he tucked his arms underneath his head. He closed his eyes and tried to ignore the pain. "Maybe a little too worthy," he uttered.

"And you Charlotte, what do you think of our David?" Lydia questioned, hinting at the relationship transpiring between her and David.

David sat up.

Nathanial did not move.

Charlotte hesitated to answer, consumed with a whirlwind of feelings.

David was a tempest. He was full of life–playful, and exciting. She couldn't help to be affected by him. And with *him,* she didn't have to hide her feelings. Her emotions were unguarded. She laughed loudly, smiled freely, blushed openly. *And David made her blush!*

Nothing was a secret from anyone. Her happiness because of David was not confined to the shadows. It was a refreshing relief; a burden lifted off her shoulders, and a chance to be herself, uninhibited.

Being with Nathanial was the complete opposite. Everything was hidden. *Everything!*

Yet, her heart was filled in a way that seemed impossible to let another in. Her desire for him only multiplied with his absence. He captured her dreams and filled her prayers. Her heartbeat synchronized to his own rhythm. They were linked souls.

She loved him.

David was not Nathanial, and Nathanial was not David. Each charting a different course in life, along with different reasons to love. The relationship developing with David offered possibilities that she never imagined were hers, giving her pause to question what she wanted, and if she could actually have it.

And once again, Andrew's words came back to haunt her, or maybe remind her, "…*You deserve someone who can openly express his love to you, you to him. Do not disregard the opportunity if it should arise.*"

"If I answer, you all realize it will only encourage him…"

David stood and grabbed a racket, pushing it towards Charlotte. "Then you must play with me."

"David, I do not dare!" Charlotte put her hands up. "Do I have to remind you about our croquet game? You are too competitive for my liking…it is always about winning, with you. Besides, you were a beast on the court with Nathanial." Charlotte looked down at the half-sleeping man sprawled on the blanket. "Sorry Nathanial, but there is no denying it."

Nathanial groaned something inaudible.

David tugged at Charlotte's arm. "Come...play with me. I'll prove to you I can do better."

"David, you do not have to prove anything to me. I like you the way you are."

David beamed a smile. "Then the battle is half won."

"All right..." She took the racket from his hand. "I warn you, I have much less skill than your last competitor. Show me mercy."

"THEY SEEM HAPPY TOGETHER," Lydia commented, watching the two hit the ball back and forth over the net, David being gentle with his return swings.

Nathanial pretended to nap, his legs stretched down the blanket and arms crossed upon his chest, furtively watching the two from under his half-open lids.

"I think your brother may have reason to settle down. He seems enthralled by our Charlotte. The two have not been parted since his arrival."

"David is always charmed initially by the company of a woman. After he departs, he will change his inter-est. You should not worry."

"Do you think it is I who is worried?"

Nathanial lifted himself. Laughter wafted towards him. Charlotte's laughter, in particular, filled his ears. *He* never made her laugh like that.

He could not disagree with Lydia, Charlotte seemed happier since his brother's arrival.

"Don't brood. It does not suit you, my dear," Lydia sneered.

Nathanial turned to his wife and studied her face. He was searching for the woman he fell in love with. The woman who now sat next to him was very bitter. Her rejection of him was no longer subtle.

"If you believe my brother has good intentions, then there is nothing more than I would want for her."

"How noble of you," Lydia chided. "Is she of so little importance you can cast her aside? Had I known better, I would have guessed you were in love with her. It comforts me to know there is nothing to concern myself with. I thought I lost you forever. Charlotte has served her purpose well."

Nathanial jumped to his feet; he hovered over his wife, blocking the day's light from her face.

"I do not know what I have done to deserve your vile contempt. I never meant to hurt you, nor was my intention to ever desert your heart. I tried…Oh, God knows I have tried to be a good husband, bring you happiness. I had hoped time would heal our separation. But it was not enough for you. I was not enough for you." He straightened; his shoulders locked. "Was *he?*"

"How dare you! I am *here*, am I not? I gave you a child...your legacy will continue."

His eyes grew cold. "I only pray it is Hammond blood that runs through our son's veins." His eyes grew black, and his lips tightened.

"Ha! How little you know of me. I would never be so cruel as to deceive you as such. I know you deserve more than that. My indiscretion..."

"Oh, is that what we are calling it?" Nathanial mocked.

Lydia curled her mouth, then feigned a laugh. "Despite what you think, Nathanial, my love for you has never left me."

He snickered. "Love? I believe, darling, you and I have different notions of the meaning?"

"However you choose to define our marriage, it is what we have...what is left over. When you take a lover, it is hard to go back to any semblance of what once were our expectations."

"You mock me? I did not ask to be cast out of your bed. I was flung...into exactly the place you chose." He ran his hand through his hair, letting out a long sigh. "You do not want me, Lydia. For that, I am to be forever damaged."

Charlotte squealed, causing Nathanial to turn to the two on the courts. David stood behind her, showing her how to hold the racket for a serve, his arms wrapped around her. She stood tucked within him with her head pressed against his cheek. Had he wanted, he could have pressed his lips to hers with the turn of his head.

Nathanial physically ached, from heart to head, head to toe, as if shards of glass were running through his veins.

He wanted to be the one wrapping his arms around her!

And there was nothing he could do but stand aside, and watch his brother indulge in *his* Charlotte's company.

He turned his attention back to Lydia, who was watching him. Analyzing him.

"Charlotte does not deserve your bitterness. She has been completely loyal to you. Her heart is pure."

"Is it?" Lydia questioned. "Is stealing my husband's heart to be rewarded?"

"You cannot imagine Charlotte has betrayed your honor. Her love for you is more than you deserve."

"Do I not deserve my husband's loyalty?"

His eyes narrowed; his lips pressed flat. "If it were not for my loyalty to you and this family, I would have left long ago."

"So, my gratitude to Charlotte is ever more significant," she quipped. "I will be more careful with my treatment of our dear girl. She is far more important than I give her credit. Bravo to her."

Nathanial's jaw clenched. "Just when I think you cannot stoop lower...you astonish me, my dear."

Lydia jutted her chin in defiance. "How little you know of my heart. Do not ever forget I was the one who gave you Charlotte."

Nathanial's body pulsed with anger, his mind calculating the words for his reply.

Lydia did not allow for the chance. She rose from the blanket, and with a turn of her shoulders, walked away.

Charlotte, noting the sudden and hurried retreat of Lydia, ran towards Nathanial, David in tow. "Why did Lydia go? Is something wrong?"

"Wrong? Right? I do not understand those words any longer," Nathanial snapped. "Only you and I hold the truth to that, do we not, Charlotte?"

Charlotte stepped back, removing herself from Nathanial's direct hit of anger.

David stepped forward, shielding her. "Now hear me, brother, you are being rather boorish to Charlotte." He stepped closer, pushing back his shoulders and puffing his chest. "Apologize then, and take it out on the courts, where it belongs."

Nathanial grumbled words neither of them could decipher. He wrenched the racket from David's hands and stormed to the court.

David reached for the racket in Charlotte's grip. "I have seen him like this before." He looked over his shoulder and watched his brother's heavy footsteps hit the ground in between large, urgent strides. "I shall rather enjoy clobbering him...and there will be no mercy."

Even with David's attempt to make her smile, Charlotte's eyes were dark, the joyful light there only moments earlier, now dull.

"David, I am not going to stand here and watch you two act like vulgar animals towards each other... Foolish boys, both of you." Her head turned to the courts where Nathanial now waited for his brother to follow him. He pounded the ball between the court floor and his racket. "I do, however, feel terribly sorry for the ball."

David laughed, "There is my girl..." and rushed towards his awaiting brother. "You have been warned," he yelled to him.

Charlotte didn't wait, as promised. She turned away from the two men as Nathanial delivered the first serve. Scurrying across the lawns, she followed Lydia's lead.

RIVALRY

he times when David asked Charlotte to join him for a walk, she accepted. When he prompted her to chat, she engaged. When he looked at her from across the table, she smiled at his attention.

She recognized at first it was all a game to him. He liked to chase beautiful women. Something he openly admitted. She saw no harm in accommodating him.

Did she realize she was accepting his advances?

So, when David suggested they ride, Charlotte did not hesitate to accept. The morning's light and warm breeze promised a lovely day to take the horses through the countryside.

"You must agree, this is a much better way to spend the afternoon, "David said, slowing his horse to keep pace with Charlotte's. "I do not think I could spend one more moment in that moody house. Lydia, I can forgive. What woman would not proclaim a headache living with my brother…"

Charlotte couldn't disagree with David. The mood of the house was heavy.

After the brutal tennis match, where David won by a mere point, Nathanial only joined them for a drink before dinner, as obligation commanded him to. He did not hesitate to find an excuse when he learned Lydia made her own excuse to not attend dinner, leaving Charlotte and David to dine alone.

At breakfast, neither of them made their presence known, and no reason was sent.

"David, you are terribly beastly to Nathanial. Especially yesterday on the court."

"The man asked for it," David defended. "Did you not see his eyes squint and his nose crinkle like a young girl's? He is a sore loser. But then again, my brother should be used to it by now. That is the third time I have brutalized him."

"You mustn't rub it in his face," Charlotte scolded. "*The man*–your brother– has pride."

"Pride? Is that what you call it? Ha! Well, if you want me to go soft on him…for you I will do anything." He reached for Charlotte's rein, slowing her horse to a stop with his. "I mean it with all sincerity, Charlotte. *Anything.*"

His face grew serious, and his eyes were no longer playful.

If he was trying, David was winning over a piece of

Charlotte's heart. The same heart entangled with Nathanial's.

"David...I..."

"Tell me you cannot see a change in us?" He reached for her. "Or tell me I am a fool, and your kindness is all for naught?"

She had no answer to give him.

"If there is someone else...is there? Because if there is, I will have to hang myself with great despair!" He imitated a noose around his neck.

She rolled her eyes. "How am I to take you seriously when all you do is tease? How is any woman to trust such a rascal?"

"I may be called many things, my dear lady, but I am a Hammond. Our virtues of trust and integrity are but in our blood. My grandfather and father built their whole lives upon that reputation. I assure you my trust is something you can always count on."

He bowed to her in a grand gesture, and curls flopped over his forehead. He lifted his head brushing his hair back into place.

Charlotte caught herself staring. He was like a boy, with sparkling eyes full of anticipation, his skin radiated a youthful glow.

He was beautifully handsome.

Charlotte's heart skipped a beat in a way normally reserved for Nathanial, and she blushed at the realization of her attraction to him.

David smiled at her, not missing the rise of color to her cheeks. "Maybe my efforts are not in vain?"

Before she could confirm or deny, Andrew's steed came riding their way.

"Ah," Andrew said as he slowed his horse. "Just the person I was seeking. But I see you are not alone." Andrew tipped his hat. "Mr. Hammond, I heard of your arrival, but did not realize you planned an elongated stay. How are you?"

"Mr. Knightly," David extended his hand. "It has been a long time. Almost five years, I believe."

Andrew smirked. "I believe it was…and an eventful night."

"Was it?" David asked cautiously.

"If I recall, we started the evening at a party hosted by the Langston twins. I could never tell who was who. Was Edward the taller one, or the smarter one? Did it matter? They were both handsome and charming. The young women equally adored them. Unfortunately, they lacked in proper refreshments, served terrible champagne, and did not have a drop of whiskey. I recall it was your suggestion we leave. We moved onto the club where we paid too much for whiskey, and we both lost to billiards."

"Aww, yes. I remember. You were more than inebriated by evening's end, holding steady in a small corner of the room, sleeping it off."

A smug smile crossed Andrew's face. "Your memory serves you well. It was too bad it did not help you with your card game. I believe you left with your pockets empty."

David cleared his throat. "Well played, Mr. Knightly."

Andrew tipped his head with the win. "Let us not bore Charlotte with our less than respectful behaviors of the past. I am sure we can entertain her with more enjoyable conversations." Andrew turned to Charlotte, "It seems I have neglected you, much to mother's dismay. It is good to see you doing so well."

"I *am* well, thank you."

"And may I be so bold to say, you are lovely, as always," he added. "I have missed our afternoons together. When I noted the clear skies and temperate weather, the day begged to be enjoyed outdoors. I thought of you immediately. My quest was to entice you for a ride." He spied the golden-hair, broad-shoulder man sitting staunch on his steed next to Charlotte. "But from the looks of it, you have replaced me as your riding companion."

"And yet, I have had no word from you in weeks," She duly noted. "Have you been ill?"

Charlotte knew better.

Andrew left for Paris, without notice, the day after the party. His mother wrote to her, informing her of Andrew's sudden departure, and assured her he would return soon. In so many words, and a lot of apologies, she asked for Charlotte to be patient with him.

Charlotte granted Andrew her patience. David made it easy for her to do so.

Andrew released a slow smile cross his face, knowing his mother had contacted Charlotte. "Not ill, my dear Charlotte, only needing a change of scenery to clear my head."

"And is it cleared?"

"Is it not obvious? I am here..." he answered. "And you are the first person I wanted to see."

"I am honored," Charlotte cleverly responded, granting Andrew the absolution he was seeking. "So, please join us? We would be happy to have your company for the rest of the afternoon."

"If your companion does not mind the intrusion." Andrew tipped his head to David.

"By all means," David agreed, handing Charlotte her rein, and kicking his horse to move. "The more the merrier..."

It was the first time Charlotte saw David's jaw tighten, and his eyes grow dark.

DAVID HAD NOT ALWAYS BEEN a gentleman through his youth. Andrew Knightly knew his sordid past, for he was frequently at the same places, if not in the same company as Andrew. It was youthful exploration not uncommon among young men. Knowledge uncommonly shared with gentle women.

Andrew had no business bringing up the past to Charlotte. He had long since grown up and moved on from his irresponsible days. His parents saw to that by sending him away to travel and see the world beyond his own reality. Although he had traveled extensively, living in India cleared his mind of any privilege he was granted. Seeing people starve in the street while others merely walked over them was an awakening of his own humanity.

David was on alert to the man who had joined them. Maybe it was rivalry. Or maybe it was the way Andrew Knightly was a little too close in proximity to Charlotte; a little too comfortable in conversation, whispering in her ear.

Charlotte laughed and touched Andrew's arm, and David couldn't help but scowl. He had heard about Andrew's attentiveness towards Charlotte. Lydia spoke of it. She told him about the parties, London with Lady Knightly, Andrew and Charlotte's afternoon rides. But Charlotte gave no indication there was someone else of interest to her. Especially not Andrew Knightly.

David was not unfamiliar with the effect a woman like Charlotte could have on a man. Dare he blame Andrew Knightly for his enticement? He, too, was charmed by Charlotte's engagement, her curiosity for conversation, the way her whole face brightened when the corner of her mouth turned upward. She was affecting. *Was she not tugging away at his own heart?*

Charlotte was transforming him. He found himself wanting to stay and explore those feelings. He just hadn't calculated there would be competition for her attention, especially not from Andrew Knightly.

He was always ready for a good rivalry.

As the three riders cleared the tree line, they saw Lydia on the terrace. She waived, calling them in.

David cleared his throat, loudly, pulling the two companions apart. "We are being summoned in. Up for a race, Mr. Knightly? To the stables?"

"Against you, Mr. Hammond?" Andrew pulled his horse to David's side. "Ready when you are."

They both looked back to Charlotte to call the race to begin.

She rolled her eyes and shook her head.

"Really boys, must you?" But she did not need an answer. She untied her hat, rose it in the air. "On the count of three. One, two, three..." And her hat swung downward.

POKING THE BEAST

*D*avid, Andrew, and Charlotte dropped off their horses at the stables, and headed to the salon where Lydia awaited their return. They deposited their sweat-soaked coats, hats, and gloves with the servants at the stables, but could not cover up their dust filled attire.

Charlotte tinkered with her bun, in front of a mirror, trying to make peace with her windswept hair. But she couldn't excuse her sun-blotched cheeks, disappointed her hat's brim did not protect her from the days heat.

Andrew wiped his brow and the back of his neck with his handkerchief before securing the button at his collar, tightening the fabric around his neck. He swept his hand threw his hair, twice, to secure any loosened hairs that had fallen out of place.

David brushed down the sleeves of his jacket, swiped at his hems, and then walked to the opened windows to take advantage of the cool air, allowing it to sweep across him and dry the remnants of the wetness under his arms.

"You three must be perfectly exhausted." Lydia declared eyeing the misfits around the room. "Come and let's have some refreshments. You all look ready for afternoon tea. David, there is some whisky on the tray. Pour some for Mr. Knightly and yourself," she instructed.

"Andrew having already eyed the glass decanter on the server, commented, "How kind."

"Did you enjoy your afternoon?" Lydia bid them to sit. "It was rather a hot today to be outside, riding so long."

"It could not have been a better day," Andrew replied, opting a chair near the window. "But then, we had the company of your dear cousin. A most enjoyable companion for riding."

"Agreed," David added. "A most pleasant day for a ride. I remember riding the property when I was young–when grandfather was alive. I had forgotten how extensive it is. Before Mr. Knightly joined us, Charlotte and I covered much ground. However, we did not get as far as the trails west of the tree line. If I recall, they are very rugged, A path more suited for seasoned riders, for sure." David noted. "I do hope, Charlotte, you are careful. I would not ride them without an escort."

"Charlotte rides very well," Andrew noted. "A very capable horsewoman."

David held back any reply, satisfied with taking a sip of his drink instead.

"It is a beautiful trail," Lydia added. "Especially during the spring, when all the natural bushes bloom. The white of the meadowsweet is something worth seeing," Lydia added. "But I agree with my brother-in-law, Mr. Knightly. Charlotte should not be riding alone."

"Well, in that case, I will be sure to make myself available to your cousin more often, Mrs. Hammond, if it suits her." Andrew turned to David. "It is unfortunate your travels take you away, Mr. Hammond. Today you proved a worthy riding partner."

"Hmmm," David grunted with the loss of their race. "Do not write me off so quickly, Mr. Knightly. My brother has not kicked me out to the streets just yet."

"Nor shall he, if I have my say," Lydia interjected. "You will stay as long as you wish."

"Where *is* my illustrious older brother, anyways?" David assessed the room, empty of Nathanial's presence. "Is he too important to join us this afternoon?"

"He and Mr. Tatum have been in his study all afternoon. I asked them to tea, but they both looked at me with stern faces and proceeded back to their work," Lydia explained.

"Tatum? Here?" Andrew questioned. "How extraordinary. I saw him in London not more than a day ago."

"Yes, he just arrived early this afternoon. He will be joining us for dinner. Will you stay, Mr. Knightly? I am sure the men would benefit greatly by your company, tired of two women as their sole conversationalist. And I am sure Charlotte would agree that we also have missed your company."

"That is kind of you, Mrs. Hammond. Unfortunately, I must decline. I am far from dressed to be so elegantly entertained." He looked at Charlotte. "Besides, there seems to be enough Hammond men to keep our dear Charlotte entertained. I would only get in the way."

Charlotte's lips pursed, and her eyes glared at Andrew.

Andrew did not turn away from her, embracing the challenge of her stare down. He knew he had won when Charlotte rose, walked to the open windows, and turned her back to him.

"Ah, I have intruded enough on your afternoon, indulging in your kindness." Andrew put his glass down. "I must bid my farewells. But we will see you at my mother's dinner party in a few days. Mr. Hammond will you be joining the affair?"

"Of course," Lydia interjected, eyeing David before slipping her arm through Andrew's arm. "It is all arranged. Now, let me see you out, properly."

Charlotte only finally turned to face David when she heard Lydia' voice echo from the entry, the front door open, and finally shut.

"Is something the matter?" David asked.

Charlotte's shook her head.

David reached for her, not missing her wetted lashes, but he stopped himself. "Charlotte, are you certain there is nothing you would like to discuss?"

Her answer was curt. "No. I am just tired."

"Why did Andrew Knightly affect you?" he persisted. "Is there something more that you are not telling me?"

Without looking at him, and with no excuse, Charlotte fled the room, passing Lydia on the way, her shoes tapping hurriedly along the corridor and up the stairs.

Lydia walked to David and put her arm on his. "It is not because of you, David."

David pulled away. "I dislike *that* man."

"He is harmless. Believe me. Do not feel threatened. Charlotte is not unlike most women...we are very difficult to understand."

"It sounds as if Charlotte and Andrew spend too much time together. She needs to be otherwise occupied; find someone more...respectable."

"You are being rather protective?" Lydia questioned.

"Well, if my brother is not protecting the women of this household, someone must." He gulped down his whisky, warm in his hand.

"Your brother is doing as I wish. There is no need for concern," Lydia assured. "We will dine with Mr.

Knightly and his mother tomorrow evening. You will see, he does not have Charlotte's heart."

"If you say so…" David conceded but sensed there was something more his sister-in-law was not telling him.

SECRETS UNCOVERED

*H*aving heard about a new rival for Charlotte Ashford's attention, Lady Knightly was swift to plan another gathering–her fifth of the season, but most assuredly, not her last. A notable guest list was created, comprised of people who could, and would, gossip about her son's and Charlotte's matrimonial prospects. Rumors of their budding relationship were well-established with the knowledge of Andrew's frequent visits to *Lottington Manor*. Lady Knightly was already imagining grand-children. However, nothing had been announced, growing concerns that David Hammond's arrival was to blame. New rumors were spreading that he was stealing Charlotte's attention away from Andrew.

Andrew's mother understood a woman could not wait forever, and it seemed, once again, her son was taking his time. She had to intervene for his sake *and* hers.

Having entertained for many years, Lady Knightly embarked on cleverness to keep herself and her parties relevant. For the evening's event, she asked the women to wear dresses in shades of white, each receiving white gardenias to adorn their hair upon their arrival. The men were expected to take part equally, and to her delight, all the gentlemen came dressed in their finest white linens, handsomely complimenting the women, who were also dressed in shades of white.

The dining table was set with an assortment of white China rimmed in gold, set atop creamy lace linens layered in white rose petals. An oversized vase centered the table, filled with Madonna lilies, crunched in-between white Alstroemeria and Baby's Breath, and stems of Blush Noisette roses spilling over the rim. The assortment's fragrance permeated the room with a mixture of cloves, honey, and sweet floral aromas. Candles, some tall and tapered, others thick and round, were scattered throughout the table and around the room, their dancing flames creating an ethereal glow.

When dinner was announced, Lady Knightly sat at the helm of her long dinner table, the abundance of candlelight now illuminating her guests' faces before her. Nathanial Hammond was given the honor of being seated at the other end where her husband used to sit. She never missed an opportunity to view a handsome gentleman across from her.

The other guests were purposely positioned to relieve the married couples of their spouses, providing them with amusing companions, while ensuring the single ladies and available gentleman would be seated next to each other. That included Mr. Tatum and Mr. David Hammond, *of course,* whom she sat in between the still-single Henderson daughters. The Kingsley brothers were never left off any invitation list, for they insured even the dullest of guests to come alive. In addition to the usual suspects, like the Percles and Hendersons, the evening included Edmund and Harriet Carver, cousins of Lady Knightly, who were visiting from the North.

But the most important of her guests was Charlotte, whom she placed securely in between herself and her son, to signal to everyone with eyes, especially David Hammond, that Charlotte had a place among them.

"You are in manufacturing?" Thomas Kingsley asked Mr. Carver from across the table, tearing himself away from the uninteresting Henderson girl.

"Yes, yes...trying to build a business, but it is a difficult task," Mr. Carver replied.

"Difficult indeed!" Lady Knightly interjected, simmering the conversations around the table. "I so miss my dear cousin. It is shameful you moved her so far away...and to that dreadful place. I hear you can barely breathe because of all the manufacturing."

"Oh Martha, it is not terrible in the North," Mrs. Carver reassured her cousin. "Edmund has provided a nice house for us. And our sons are nearby. I am a fortunate woman to have them so close to me now."

"And, with a third grandchild on the way, she could not be more content," Mr. Carver announced the pending birth.

Mrs. Carver beamed a smile. "We cannot be more pleased with the news."

Congratulations went around the table as glasses raised to the happy grandparents, cheering for the child's healthy arrival.

"With a grandchild on the way, do you plan a long visit here, Mrs. Carver?" Mrs. Henderson inquired. "I can only image you will be needed in such circumstances."

"The baby is not due until October. Our plans are to stay until the end of summer…unless we have reason to extend our stay?" Mrs. Carver hinted, having heard about Andrew and his attention to the woman who sat beside him.

Lady Knightly gently squeezed Charlotte's hand underneath the table. "Wouldn't that be lovely…" she whispered.

Andrew lifted his glass, skewing a glance at Charlotte. "To happy times ahead!"

Charlotte feigned a smile but did not sip from her wine. She didn't approve of Andrew subversively feeding the rumors about them.

Nor did David, whose scowl indicated he, too, was listening to the gossip.

Lydia leaned into her husband. "They are rather comfortable together. No one could deny that they would make a handsome couple."

Nathanial stared deadpan at the couple at the other end of the table.

"It would be so convenient, would it not? Charlotte remaining so close to us." Lydia dared a smile at him. "Cheer up, Nathanial. You of all people know, not all is what it seems. Andrew Knightly is the least of your concerns." Her eyes bounced to his brother. "Be careful what you wish for. Mr. Knightly may be your best hope."

Seeing Nathanial's face tighten, Lydia had gotten the reaction she wanted.

∾

AS THE LAST of the dessert was eaten, Lady Knightly stood to indicate it was time to retreat to the salon. There, the women could drink sherry, play cards, and indulge in female-only conversation, while the men sauntered to the smoking room to indulge in cigars, liquor, and anything more she did not care to intrude upon.

As the doors closed behind the ladies, Mrs. Carver found a cozy corner of the sofa to relieve her swollen feet and aching ankles–the onslaught of over salting her meat and vegetables, her doctor warned. She turned to Charlotte who was now in proximity and where she did not have to yell across the table to speak to her. "Tell me, Miss Ashford, are you planning a long stay?"

"Why, England is home for Charlotte," Lydia answered. "She is not going anywhere."

"How fortunate for you, Miss Ashford, to have family to come back to," Mrs. Henderson added, taking a sip of sherry before puckering her lips at the sting of the alcohol. "I must ask, though, Mrs. Hammond, does your husband feel the same way? One woman can be all but enough for most men. But two women, especially as close as you two seem to be, must be demanding on Mr. Hammond."

"Your husband must be feeling a little outsmarted," Mrs. Carver quipped. "I know Mr. Carver would be intimidated."

"Quite the contrary. My husband is quite satisfied with the arrangement," Lydia remarked.

Charlotte blushed at Lydia's veiled meaning. A redness undeniable to the women in the room. She set down her little crystal glass of sherry, not wanting to exacerbate the coloring in her cheeks by the effects of alcohol.

"And you, Miss Ashford," Mrs. Henderson brow lifted. "Do you feel the same?"

Charlotte willed her voice to steady. "If it were not for the generosity of my dear cousin, I fear my life would be very altered. I am blessed she has allowed me to enjoy her hospitality...and to be among family once again."

The women all cooed their agreement to the sentiment.

"Our Andrew speaks often of visiting *Lottington Manor*," Mrs. Carver intimated.

"Yes, *Lottington* has quite a few enjoyable paths," Lydia answered. "I am sure Mr. Knightly's visits are to take advantage of them."

"I hear that your brother-in-law has been indulging in them as well since his arrival," Lady Knightly said. "How fortunate. I should not like a young woman like Miss Ashford to ride on her own."

"Why yes, it could be quite dangerous," Mrs. Henderson cut in. "Just the other day I heard of a young woman who was tossed by her horse. A broken hip the outcome. A terrible thing to happen...Indeed, Miss Ashford, you must be careful."

"Let us hope she does not have the same fate..." Lady Knightly uttered.

Suddenly the door burst open and the men converged onto the room, cigar smoke and whiskey breath permeating from their cluster.

"Gentlemen!" Lady Knightly stood. "I had not expected you so soon."

"There are too many lovely ladies this evening to not indulge," Thomas Kingsley said, the last remnants of his cigar grasped between his fingers sending a trail of smoke into the air.

"Then, by all means, please enjoy yourselves," Mrs.

Knightly ushered the men further into the room. She searched for Andrew among the crowd. "And where is my son? Did Andrew not join you after dinner?"

"He must have slipped away without notice," Thomas Kingsley replied after a quick inventory of the group of men.

"Charlotte, my dear, why don't you go and find him," Lady Knightly suggested. "He has a habit of slipping into his father's study. Shall I show you the way?"

"No," Charlotte quickly stood. "I know the way, thank you."

Relieved by the opportunity to escape, she found her way through the hallowed halls, holding her swooshing skirts, and stepping lightly against the wooden floors to quiet the clattering of her heels. The study door was slightly ajar and a sheen of light poured into the hallway. She halted just short of the door with the sound of Andrew's voice. It was ill-tempered and heated. She cautiously peered in.

Andrew was arguing with a man whose back was to her.

"Why do you concern yourself with such matters?" Andrew barked. "You have what you need."

"I have very little of what I want!" The man retorted. "You are preoccupied with *her!*"

"And I have told you, on many occasions, she is merely an amusement. I enjoy her company, that is all."

"Your mother seems to feel quite differently," the man shouted, then turned and paced the room. His footsteps pounded hard and determined against the wood.

Charlotte could now see it was Mr. Tatum with whom Andrew was arguing.

"My mother is hopeful. You know that?" Andrew walked to Mr. Tatum and placed his hand on his shoulder. "You are not jealous of a woman, are you?"

"I am concerned she is distracting you," Mr. Tatum complained.

"I cannot deny my attraction to her. She offers something I have never felt before. She is different," Andrew explained.

Mr. Tatum halted to face Andrew. "What is to become of it, and where will that leave me?"

"It leaves you where you have always been. Nothing has to change between us. You cannot expect more of the circumstances?"

"What am I to you, Andrew?" Mr. Tatum demanded.

Andrew's voice softened. "You are my pain and my pleasure. That will never change." He reached for Mr. Tatum and pulled him to his lips.

Mr. Tatum did not pull away. He opened his mouth demanding more, his tongue enticing Andrew to return with his own need for him.

Charlotte covered her mouth but not before a gasp echoed in the silence, pulling the two men apart.

Mr. Tatum's eyes met hers from across the room. He smirked, seeing the horror reflected in them.

Charlotte abruptly turned and ran down the corridor, her footsteps hurried and heavy. Andrew called her name, but she dared not turn around.

EXPOSED

$\mathcal{W}$eeks passed.

Charlotte waited for Andrew to contact her, to explain, or at least to help her understand what she had witnessed.

He never called on her, nor did he write.

She did not expect Andrew to abandon her knowing so many questions must be on her mind. Andrew had become more than an ordinary companion; he was her friend and her confident. The one person who accepted her–all of her, carrying her secrets and beholding her dreams. He was someone safe to her. He guided her in a world that was uncomfortable for her, and *that world* was growing more complicated. She felt betrayed. Angry. Lonely. Now their relationship felt like a charade, or his cruel joke on her.

With so many conflicting feelings, she tried to

write to him, but her pen faltered. Her heart ached too much. She needed time before she could express in words what she was feeling.

"Charlotte?" David called out to her, disrupting her reverie.

"I am sorry David." Charlotte offered him an apologetic smile. "Here you have brought me out for a lovely outing, and my thoughts are drifting. Please forgive me."

"All is forgiven, for I have you all to myself. It has been nice these last few weeks," David said, taking the blanket from the horse's saddle, propping it under his arm, and heading towards the shade of a tree. "With Nathanial keeping busy with his work, Lydia making calls on neighbors–remind me to thank her for that," he laughed, "And Andrew Knightly not making surprise visits, the world seems like ours alone."

Charlotte sighed, leaving her sentiments unspoken.

"Charlotte?" he questioned. "Do I need to be concerned about Mr. Knightly?"

"No," she confirmed with a shake of her head. "There is little reason to even mention his name."

"Has he..." David's brow collapsed. "Has he done anything to hurt you?"

A bird screeched across the sky and they both looked up. When Charlotte looked back at David, tears had pooled at the corner of her eyes.

"Charlotte..." David pushed for answers.

"It is nothing you may presume," she said, diverting

his stare. "We had a misunderstanding. I am sure we will settle our differences soon enough. We always do."

With a gentle nudge of her chin, he turned her face to him. "It doesn't seem like a misunderstanding. We have not had his company for weeks now. Lydia even mentioned how unusual it was. Do not misunderstand me, I am happy to have you all to myself. My fear is that it is more than you are admitting." He paused. "I want you to understand, I would do anything to protect you."

Charlotte suppressed a guttural laugh. All the men around her proclaimed they wanted to protect her when they were the ones she needed protection from.

"There is no reason to be concerned, I assure you."

"Then I will leave it at that." He finally found an acceptable spot under the tree and laid the blanket down. "Come, let us sit."

Dutifully, Charlotte obeyed. She spread the layers of skirt around her and allowed David to lay his head upon her lap, whilst the birds chirped, and a gentle breeze stirred the leaves above them.

"I could get accustomed to this," David said, closing his eyes.

Charlotte smirked. "Lounging your days away while avoiding your duties?"

"Duties?" One eye popped open. "My brother has your ear, no doubt. But no, that is not what I was referring to."

"David," Charlotte cooed. "*This* cannot last forever.

You have a life to return to. You must have plans to leave us soon?"

He raised his head. "Would it frighten you if I said I never wanted to leave?"

Charlotte studied his face. His expression was usually cheerful, but now his brow was straight and his eyes steady.

She was careful with her answer.

"It depends on so many things..." she paused seeing an eagerness in his eyes. He was looking for something to hold onto. "I do not know what it is you want from me, David. Or if I have it to give."

He sat up. "I asked you once if you did not see a change in us. You did not answer, and I assumed you did not. But do you not see a change in me? I came here a youthful man. Shamefully, I admit, eager to play with little seriousness in my life. But the time I have spent here, I see so much more to the purpose of my life. Charlotte, it is because of you I see the world not a game to play or competition to win, but an adventure to share with someone. You are *that* someone. It is you with whom I want to share it," he declared. "You spoke highly of love, and I laughed. I am not laughing anymore."

Her eyes lowered. Not that she did not expect him to declare feelings for her. His behavior had been obvious. She just did not expect him to declare his feelings so soon or with such purpose.

Love should have possibilities, and loving David

offered endless ones. She could not ignore that being with David offered her a chance at living.

He took Charlotte's hands into his. "Dear Charlotte, to receive your love would make me the happiest man in the world. There is no response I am asking for, not yet. Allow me the chance to prove my worthiness of your admiration, with the hope that one day you may rejoice in my words and share in the same sentiments."

He brought her hands to his lips and placed a kiss on them.

She turned away; afraid he might see the truth in hers—that her love was tied to someone else. Someone who was very close to him.

"You pull away?"

"Not because I do not feel happy with your sentiments," she explained. "I do not feel worthy to return them. Not yet."

"Then there is hope?"

"Yes, David. There is always hope with love."

To say David was happy was an understatement. Throughout dinner, and into the salon afterwards, he had a perpetual grin on his face. It was apparent to those around them the reason. His eyes never left Charlotte.

"Charlotte," David whispered. "You enchant me."

Charlotte peered at Lydia, hovered over needlework, then to Nathanial, who sat in a chair across the room immersed in a book. "David, it is neither the time nor the place."

"What are you two whispering about over there?" Lydia called out.

"Does my brother need a reason to be disruptive?" Nathanial chimed in.

"Care to try your hand against mine?" David taunted. "Chess? Cards? Your pick, my brother."

Nathanial rolled his eyes.

"You two tire me out," Lydia exclaimed. "I am ready for bed. Anyone care to retreat for the evening? Charlotte?"

"Not quite yet. I will stay a little longer," Charlotte made her excuse. "I will be up later."

Nathanial shook his head, seemingly immersed in a book.

David set his glass down and ran after Lydia, "Wait for me, Lydia, I will walk up with you."

"You are kind, David. Thank you." Lydia reached for David's arm to lead the way.

"These corridors are dark, and most likely, brimming with ghosts," he laughed. "I would not want anything to happen to you."

"A house this old is sure to have a few ghosts in the closets. But none that roam the hallways at night. At least, none that I have found," Lydia smiled. "Having you here has been such a pleasure to the household, David. Your brother needs you. Peter adores you. I am amused with you here."

"And Charlotte?"

"You are growing fond of our Charlotte, I see."

David nodded. "I have my hopes that she feels the same. You may know better..."

"As close as we are, she keeps her feelings of the heart to herself. However, the Hammond men are hard to resist. I am sure you will have no problem winning over her heart."

David smiled at the prospect.

"Oh my," Lydia exclaimed as they reached the top of the stair. "I seemed to have left my wrap on the sofa." Squeezing his arm, she asked, "Would you be so kind as to retrieve it for me?"

"Of course. Wait here," David ordered, and quickly descended the stairs, only to stop short at the partially opened door.

Charlotte was speaking to Nathanial. Her voice was gentle...*loving*, prompting him to lean closer and listen, his head straining to watch the two through the crack of the door.

"Come, lay your head down," she told Nathanial, patting the cushion beside her. "I will rub your head."

Nathanial obeyed, placing his head in her lap, and closed his eyes.

"I miss you," he whispered.

She offered him a smile. "Did your head truly hurt?"

"Do you blame me? It is the only way I can capture your attention these days."

"Jealous?"

"Absolutely!" he conceded.

Charlotte ran her hands through Nathanial's hair. "Your brother is very captivating. Charming as well. It must be a family trait."

"I believe he enjoys you as well," Nathanial had to admit. "I believe…he has grown more than just fond of you."

Her hands slowed around his head. Her voice lowered. "I am growing very fond of him as well."

Nathanial sat up. "So, it is mutual?"

Charlotte pulled away from him.

"Are you falling in love with him?" Nathanial questioned.

She did not answer.

Nathanial walked to the sidebar and poured himself a drink.

"You are angry…"

"I am…" He ran his hand through his hair. "…I am torn. I love my brother and want only the best for him."

"And you fear I am not the best?"

Placing his glass down, he walked to Charlotte and took her in his arms. "No, no! Never. That is far from my meaning. You are the best for any man. And if I could have you for myself…" He paused and turned away. "Who am I to deny the honor of loving you? I love my brother and if he loves you, I could not want more for you."

Charlotte hurried to him, wrapped her arms around him and buried her head in his chest.

"Nathanial…" she whispered.

He pulled her away. "If you love him, then tell me now. I will honor your choice and be happy for you. My love for you is eternally yours. You have no obligation unto me, as I have no right to ask more of you."

David backed away from the door, not wanting to hear anymore. He ran up the stairs with his heart racing.

Lydia had not waited for him to return.

He was grateful for he feared his face could not conceal the secret he had just discovered.

SHADOW OF DOUBT

*D*avid tugged at the collar of his jacket before he entered the breakfast room. He wasn't sure if he was ready to face anyone after what he happened upon last night.

Sleep had eluded him, tossing and turning with unanswered questions. He wondered if Lydia purposely sent him downstairs with suspicions of her own.

In the light of morning, he now wondered if he misconstrued the conversations between Nathanial and Charlotte. He felt disloyal to his brother, to Charlotte.

But then, he had cause.

He wanted to give all of them the benefit of his doubt before any accusations flew. Bracing himself, he slowly turned the handle of the door and entered, knowing he had no other choice but to find out the truth.

"Aww, you are up," Nathanial greeted his brother. "I wondered if anyone was going to join me for breakfast."

David nodded to his brother, avoiding eye contact, and seated himself.

Nathanial slapped his brother on the shoulder. "You look like hell! Did you have trouble sleeping?"

David pulled his shoulder away. "Yes. It was a damn, bloody, hard night!"

Nathanial backed away, and the two locked eyes.

"Good morning," Charlotte's cheery voice entered the room before she did, breaking their stare.

Her skirt rustled as she crossed the floor. She touched Nathanial's shoulder as she passed and awarded David a smile when he stood and pulled out a chair next to him, softening his hard brow and diminishing his angry scowl.

It was hard for him not to be affected by her. She was a vision of sunshine in yellow muslin. Her smile was nothing but engaging, her happy mood contagious. It was difficult to believe her capable of deception from such a woman. He wanted to erase any memory of the night before and pretend it never happened.

If only he could.

But when he looked at his brother, he saw *it*.

Nathanial's shoulders lifted. The lines around his mouth eased. His eyes sparkled. If happiness had a face, it was Nathanial's at that moment. It was obvious he felt admiration for the woman who had entered the room.

He could not fault his brother's reaction to Charlotte. Any red-blooded man would react the same.

Now David felt foolish, struggling to find his brother guilty.

"You two are quiet this morning," Charlotte said, noting a cold silence between the two brothers. "Did I disrupt something."

"David did not sleep well," Nathanial explained.

Charlotte turned to her side companion, "Oh, how terribly dreadful. I pray you are not becoming ill."

His eyes did not meet hers. "It was nothing, really. It was just a sleepless night."

Charlotte said, turning to Nathanial. "And where is Lydia this morning? I hope this is not contagious?"

Nathanial growled "Another headache…"

Charlotte reached for his hand. "Be patient with her. She has a household to run, and rambunctious child to tend to, let alone guests." She gave him a wink. "I will check on her."

"I am sure she will appreciate the attention. David and I are off today, which will help relieve her of some responsibilities, at least for today."

Charlotte set down her cup, turning to David. "I thought you were joining me on a ride this morning?" She gazed out the windows. "The day is too lovely to be indoors."

David fidgeted with this napkin, placing it upon

the table. "Oh yes, my apologies, but I must postpone our time together."

"I forced his hand..." Nathanial explained. "We have family business to attend to."

Charlotte's brow raised. "Humph! I see. So easily cast aside." Charlotte rose, setting her napkin on the table. "I suppose I will have to find my entertainment elsewhere. You have a nice day, gentlemen."

Nathanial followed her to the door. "You will forgive him?"

Charlotte looked back at David, who was standing nervously fiddling with his napkin. "Of course. Family comes first, always. I am just making him sweat a little. But I expect both of you to be extra attentive to me this evening." She winked, turned, and walked away.

Nathanial waited at the door and watched until she disappeared.

David watched Nathanial.

"She is quite a woman," David said, prying Nathanial's attention away from the door.

"Yes, she is very special, David. And deserves someone who can appreciate her."

"Are you warning me as a father figure, or as a rival?"

Nathanial's face went blank.

He cleared his throat before he spoke, careful with his reply. "I am not sure if I should be proud of you for your protectiveness of Charlotte, or angry at your accusation. Either way, you have no need to worry, dear brother. Charlotte is open to your feelings if you so choose. That much I can confirm."

David looked down, feeling like a boy compared to his brother. He knew his bother to be a good man, an honorable man. He was married to a beautiful woman and had a family to be proud of. Charlotte, as Lydia's cousin, would be treated with the utmost care, as an honored guest in his house. If there was anything illicit last evening, it was his own interpretation.

"I am sorry, brother. I am letting my feelings get the best of me. If I must confess, my affection for Charlotte has grown beyond friendship."

Nathanial's stance faltered. Even though he had expected them, David's words felt like a punch in the gut.

"You have nothing to say? Do you reason that I am unworthy of her?"

"I think..." he paused, allowing for a heavy sigh. "Charlotte deserves someone to love her. I believe you can give her everything she needs."

David nodded. "And Lydia? Do you think she will be as agreeable?"

"I am not sure of what Lydia will do." Nathanial chuckled. "She has her heart set on Charlotte living here forever. Not the best of plans for Charlotte, I admit. But it is not Lydia you should be concerned about. It is Charlotte whom you must convince." Nathanial patted his brother on the back. "I do not believe she will need much persuasion."

With the future prospect of asking Charlotte for

her hand in marriage, David pushed all his concerns aside, unable to believe his brother would be so generous about a woman he loved.

For if Charlotte was his, he would never give her up so easily to another man.

ACCIDENTS

*L*ydia heard yelling come from outside. She rushed to the window, pulling the drape aside and peered out. A man from the stables was heading towards the house, carrying Charlotte, her listless body bobbing in his arms.

Lydia dropped her book to the floor and dashed out to greet the breathless man.

"Mistress! Mistress!" he cried out.

"Dear God!" Lydia gasped, covering her mouth to squelch a shriek. Mud and blood covered the side of Charlotte's face, from an obvious wound on her head.

"Go get Dr. Baron," Lydia ordered. "Quickly!"

The stable hand carried Charlotte upstairs to her room, while a servant followed with a pot of water.

Once she was laid on the bed, Ada soaked a linen in hot water, ringing out the excess, and began wiping the blood splattered over Charlotte's face and neck, beginning with the gash across her head. When the blood finally slowed, she placed a heavy cloth on top to suppress any further bleeding.

"She'll need to be sewn," Ada informed Lydia.

"Is anything broken?" Lydia said, hovering over her.

As Ada began assessing Charlotte's battered body, she shrieked. "Dear Mistress, I am afraid something bad has happened."

A pool of blood puddled between Charlotte's legs.

Lydia came forward, seeing the amount of blood saturating the sheets.

"Oh my! Quick, help me undress her."

The two women worked in tandem, stripping Charlotte and cleaning the red stained blood covering the pale skin of her thighs. Thankfully, the bleeding stopped, and they put Charlotte in a gown, moving her carefully to rid the blood-soaked sheet from under her.

Ada made a sign of the cross.

"Try to wrap the wound on her head as best you can. I will order fresh water to be brought up. If she awakens, try to ease her pain. There is nothing we can do until the doctor comes."

"Yes, Mistress."

Lydia rushed to the kitchen and ordered additional hot water and linens to be brought to Charlotte's room. As she emerged, she ran into Nathanial and David in the foyer, returning home. Both halted at the horror of her. Lydia's white linen dress was covered in fresh blood and her sleeves, rolled to her elbows, exposed hands that were stained red. Her hair was a mess, her lips were tight, and her eyes were dimmed.

Nathanial rushed to her. "Dear God, Lydia! What has happened? Was Peter injured?"

Lydia brushed away loose strands away from her face. "No…" She shook her head, her voice breaking. "It is Charlotte."

David's eyes widened. "Charlotte?"

"She has had an accident. One of the stable hands brought her. He said her horse must have spooked. They found her tossed aside, crumpled, and unconscious."

Nathanial started up the stairs, pushing past Lydia.

"She needs a doctor," she called after him. "Not you."

Nathanial halted when the bell rang at the door.

A staff member was waiting to open the door for the doctor.

"Mrs. Hammond," he bowed. Seeing Nathanial halfway up the stairs he nodded. "Mr. Hammond. I came as quickly as I could."

"This way, Dr. Baron," Lydia said, lifting the fabric of her skirt, and hurrying up the stair with the doctor following behind. Passing Nathanial, she ordered, "You and your brother, wait. I will send Ada with news after Dr. Baron examines her."

He tugged at Lydia's arm. "Is she going to be alright?"

Lydia lowered her head. "I really do not know…"

She continued up the stairs, leaving Nathanial with nothing more to console him.

The two men found their way to the library where they waited, and paced, eventually making their way through a bottle of whiskey as the day turned to night. They were only disturbed when a servant delivered a tray of food. It was two hours later they were finally summoned to Charlotte's room.

THE MEN, faces drawn, and moods tempered from worry, entered the darked room. The windows were covered, and a lamp was lit near the bed, with another across the room. The smell of fresh blood lingered; a bowl of red water carried away by a maid as they entered confirmed their fears.

Charlotte was tightly wrapped in blankets, making her appear small. Her chest slowly lifted and fell with her weakened breath. A bandage covered the right side of her face, the other half was darkened by bruises surfacing.

The flickering fire thrust shadows along the walls, only adding to the ominous mood.

Lydia sat beside Charlotte's bed, holding Charlotte's hand in hers, her head lowered in prayer.

Nathanial halted himself from rushing to Charlotte and taking her into his arms. She looked too fragile to touch. He brought a chair to the end of the bed and sat, placing his hand on the blanket which covered her. He stared at her face, willing her eyes to open.

David stood back in the shadows.

The doctor washed his hands, rolled down his sleeves, and put on his coat. As he grabbed his bag, Nathanial stopped him.

"Will she be all right?"

Dr. Baron cleared his throat. "She needs rest. Lots of rest," he warned. "Her body has taken a huge blow, and she has lost a good deal of blood."

Nathanial tugged at his arm, wanting more.

The doctor placed his hand on Nathanial's shoulder but hesitated to speak. He eyed David in the corner and looked at Lydia.

"Feel free to speak, doctor..." she said.

"She will recover. Nothing is broken; but she will be swollen and bruised for weeks. Fortunately, the baby will survive, a mother's womb being the best protection a child has. Until then, she needs to be left alone to heal. No getting up and out of bed for a few days. She will know when she is ready. Let her rest."

Nathanial's face went white.

Lydia rose and escorted the doctor to the door, asking Ada to show him out. When the door was closed, she didn't turn around. Her shoulders stiffened and braced.

"Lydia!" Nathanial seethed through his teeth, demanding she turn around.

"I didn't know, I swear on my father's grave," she said, facing him. "She did not confide in me."

David moved from the shadows. "What in God's name is going on?"

Nathanial could not answer. The mere shock paralyzed him.

Charlotte was pregnant!

David looked to Lydia for answers, but she could only look away. His eyes turned to Nathanial.

"Nathanial! Please tell me that child in not yours?"

When he didn't answer, he lunged at his brother.

"David!" Lydia shrieked, her voice shrill and scared. "Please do not do this now. Charlotte is our concern."

Charlotte moved her hand to her head and moaned. She tried to lift herself but failed. Lydia rushed to her side, settling her back onto the pillows.

"See what you have done!" She eyed both the men who were glaring at each other, their chests heaving, their fists curled.

"What *I have* done?" David questioned. "I think it is more befitting to ask what your husband has done. Answer *that*, Nathanial!"

"You do not want to know the answer, David. Not now," Nathanial grumbled.

David lunged toward his brother, pushing hard against his chest. "Is Charlotte carrying your child? Or is she a mere whore for someone else?"

Nathanial snarled. He pushed his brother back, ripping his jacket. "How dare you!"

Charlotte's frail voice called out. "Yes…"

They all turned, and the room quieted.

Yes…" she whispered. "It is *his* child."

"You bastard!" David struck a blow across Nathanial's jaw, knocking him to the floor.

Lydia fell to Nathanial's side, but she could not keep him down. He lifted himself up, shook off the blow, and swung his fist across David's chin.

"Stop it!" Charlotte shrieked, halting the two men. She struggled to sit up. "You are brothers, and family, for God's sake." She paused and caught her breath. "This is all wrong. Everything is all wrong! I will not destroy this family or come between you. I have been on the other side of a separated family, and it is not a place I want for any of you. It is for this very reason I am laying here. So, please...go away. Take your anger, and deal with it. But do not allow it to destroy the bonds that keep this family together. Do not let my own sacrifices be in vain."

Blood trickled down Charlotte's head.

Lydia rushed back to her side, grabbed a towel, and wiped the warm path of blood.

"I am sorry! I am so very sorry, Charlotte," Lydia cried.

David looked at his brother, whose chest was puffed, chin jutted, waiting for the next hit. "I do not know what kind of sick game you all are playing, but I will have nothing to do with it!" He abruptly turned and stomped to the door.

A mirror halted him.

His face was flushed, his hair disheveled, and his coat was ripped from the shoulder. He pushed back his hair and straightened his coat. "I can mend my coat with a few stitches, brother. But you? Your damage is much more problematic."

"It is not what you think, David," Lydia whispered out, "It is more than you can imagine. Nathanial loves her. I love her..."

"Yes, we *all* do," David resigned, swinging open the door and retreating.

Nathanial watched his brother leave. He wanted to go after him and explain. But he couldn't offer anything to console him. How did one justify breaking your brother's heart and destroying his hopes?

"She is shivering," Lydia warned. "Nathanial, quickly, call back the doctor. She is slipping into a fever."

He looked at the woman whom he had loved so intimately and purely. Seeing Lydia in distress, he wanted to hold her, protect her, care for her...his love still alive for her, in spite of their failed marriage. He had not known it was possible for love to exist outside of the anger, pain, disappointment, yet it was right in front of him.

"Please Nathanial," she cried. "I am so scared."

He moved to Charlotte and placed his hand on her forehead. Her skin was hot to the touch–she was burning up. Lydia looked up at him, her eyes filled with tears. He brushed his hand across her face before he rushed out the door.

"Please hurry," Lydia called out. "I cannot lose her!"

DAVID'S GOODBYE

*D*avid planned for his immediate departure. Unfortunately, a storm suddenly arrived, postponing his arrangements. He found it befitting.

He laid his head down on the pillow, but his thoughts swirled. The conversations between him and his brother played again and again in his head. He could not fathom Nathanial capable of such deception to them all.

Having an affair under his roof was unspeakable. *But a child!*

And then there was Charlotte. The woman he had come to love. He never imagined she was capable of such betrayal, their time together a mere charade.

"Damn you all!" he shouted across the room.

His voice reverberated against the walls. He prayed no one heard it, but then when a weakened knock came to his door, he cursed himself. The knock came again. He stared at the door, unwilling to answer it. There was no one he wanted to see. A third knock was hard to ignore. He dragged himself out of bed, put on his robe, and dragged his slippered-feet across the floor. Opening the door, he found Lydia standing before him.

"May I come in?"

David moved aside.

Her bloodied clothes now gone, swapped for a royal blue dressing gown, her hair neatly pulled into a plait along her back, she stepped into his room. She circled around, taking slow, mindful steps, noting the scattered sheets on his bed and half-packed luggage splayed open.

He waited for her to speak, say what she wanted to say, and leave. When she didn't, he hesitantly moved away from the door.

"I...I am sorry for the outburst...the scene earlier," he finally said. "That was unfair to you."

Lydia laughed. "You are Nathanial's brother...your personalities are not very different."

David could not disagree.

Lydia laughed again but said no more on the topic.

She walked to the window and pulled aside the half-drawn curtains. She leaned against the frame and watched as the moon tried to escape through the heavy rain clouds, the light appearing and disappearing, but there were too many clouds drowning its efforts.

Lydia was a beautiful woman against the moonlight, David thought, which only made him angrier with his brother and resolute about leaving.

"The rain has stopped. Only momentarily, I fear," she finally spoke again. "It has hindered your escape."

She looked at him to confirm her statement.

His eyes went to his bags set by the bed.

"Shall I ring for some tea? I have a feeling you and I may not sleep tonight."

David shook his head. He did not want to encourage her company but could not bring himself to dismiss her.

She turned back to the darkness outside. "Life is like this dark night. It is all but a haze of shapes until the light appears. It is only then you can make sense of the things around you. My life was very dark, David. I felt confined by these walls, by my decisions, by Nathanial–of no fault of his own, *at the beginning*. Marriage is hard, especially for a woman. Love is even more difficult. Had I known, I would have never married your brother. But I was young, and my choices were not mine to make. Nathanial was an easy choice. But…" The words lingered. "I had this foolish notion that love could conquer anything. It cannot. We are all tied in knots in our lives. I had knots. Lots and lots of knots I could not disentangle."

"Why are you telling me this?"

She looked at him, but her stare was distant.

"I needed to catch my breath. And then, by some miracle, Charlotte came to me. I was reminded of what my life was like before I fell into darkness. She allowed me to breathe again. And for that, I will always treasure her."

David's expression turned hard. His angry eyes bore into her. "How can you say that when she has betrayed you?"

"Do not judge what you do not know of. She has been eager to please me. I do not doubt her loyalty to me. I can see that now. It is I who betrayed her. I was supposed to keep her safe and protect her. You were the one who offered her opportunity, and after what we discovered today, an answer to her prayers. I was too selfish to see what Charlotte was trying to do—keep me safe and keep my marriage together without scandal. She was so trusting, so full of love, and wanting. It was probably why Nathanial fell in love with her."

"How can you justify what my brother has done? He took Charlotte behind your back and disgraced her. Disgraced you! There is no honor in that. I used to think my brother the most noble of men. I held his relationship with you as something that I might have myself someday. I even thought...hoped...it would be with Charlotte. But he is not worthy of my respect." Bitterness rolled off his tongue. "Your marriage is a fraud."

Lydia smirked. "I suppose it is. But who are you to judge? Are you without flaws? We all have our secrets, David. Some are better at hiding them than others. Some are better at living with them."

David scoffed.

"You are so much like your brother. You are prideful. It is a quality that can destroy those you love. You expect too much from people. It is overwhelming and demanding when one cannot fulfill all those expectations. Mistakes are made. People falter. They do the best they can despite the challenges. If you are to love, you are going to have to make room for our humanness." Lydia pressed against her temples. "I was so tired of trying to pretend. I did not have the heart to disappoint Nathanial anymore. He is a good man, David. He deserves better than me. Charlotte is better. She is what he deserves."

"Stop Lydia," he demanded. "My brother was dishonorable to you."

"No, David," she continued. "If you are going to leave, you should know the truth. In spite of it all, Nathanial has always loved me. Yes, we have shown bitterness and anger towards each other. I am not sure how we could have avoided all that. But in the end, he has acted in honor because of his love for me."

David huffed. "He betrayed your marriage! How can you sit there and defend such a scoundrel of a man?"

"Because I asked him to betray those vows," she confessed.

David jolted. His eyes widened.

"Yes, David, I am just as much a scoundrel as he. I needed to be, so that I could let him go. He deserved more than I could give him. I betrayed his heart long before when I fell out of love with him," she admitted.

"Please do not look at me that way. I am my own judge. I cannot look at myself without disgust. It was only Charlotte, and the happiness she seemed to find through this all, that kept me justified in my actions. She loved and received love, even if it was from my own husband. I thought she was happy. But seeing her, all bloodied and battered...well, it was truly a metaphor for what I have done to her."

David's head fell into his hands. "Why? Why would a woman choose to be disgraced? How could Charlotte take part so freely?"

"Besides loving Nathanial, the way he needs, the way he deserves, she loves me with all her heart and soul. She holds not one ounce of deception for herself. Charlotte has sacrificed her honor for my honor. And she now sacrificed her future happiness with you. Please try to see that."

"I guess I am not the man you think I am," he warned. His jaw hardened. "Did you all laugh at me? Was I the distraction to keep your secret? I feel so used by all of you."

"That was never our intention," Lydia tried to explain, but David only snarled at her with his contempt.

"Charlotte was all I sought in a woman. I opened my heart to her, gave her my love so freely." He pinched his eyes, trying to stop the tears. "And now what is to become of it?"

"If you felt her love, then believe it. I have been the recipient of her heart. No one in this world could be so unselfish and giving as Charlotte. Trust me when I say, few of us deserve her."

"Did Nathanial deserve her?"

"He deserved more than I could give him," she confessed. "You may not be able to live with that. But I was able to."

David turned away.

"We will understand if you must leave. I hope you learn to forgive us, especially Charlotte. And in her unselfish manner, I know all she would ever ask of you is you forgive your brother. For me, I have nothing to ask of you, for I am the one to whom you should direct all your contempt, and place it upon my shoulders alone, to bear all the days of my life. Free the other two of your judgment. They love you, David. How can love be so rejected?"

Lydia's question punched his gut. He sat, no longer able to support his weary body. His head dropped into his hands.

She walked over to him and placed a kiss on his head. "Goodbye, David."

David did not look at her as she retreated. He heard the door open and shut, finally leaving him as he wished—*alone.*

THE TRUTH

*D*avid left without a word.

Lydia tried to make excuses for him, covering up for his disregard, but Charlotte understood. She hurt him. So much so, he left without a goodbye. Without a chance for her to explain.

But how did one explain deception?

Lydia saw Charlotte's wounds healing. She crawled into her bed and put her arms around her like she did when they were little girls. Face to face, where they had no secrets. She gently stroked her cheeked. "My dear, dear, Charlotte…"

"Why do you not despise me, Lydia? I have ruined everything."

"I could ask you the same," Lydia replied. She reached over and brushed away a few strands of hairs covering Charlotte's face, pushing them behind her ear. "You loved him the way I knew you would. The way he needed you to."

"I know...I needed him, too," Charlotte confessed.

"He should have been yours, Charlotte. I knew it the moment I met him. He has your heart. Maybe that is why I wanted him." She lingered. "When your father took you away, he was the nearest thing I had to you. It was not his fault I could not truly love him the way he deserved."

Charlotte sat up.

Lydia followed, propping pillows against her back.

"Why?" Charlotte let the question out.

"Why what? Why did I not love him?" She moaned. "Oh Charlotte...dear, sweet, innocent Charlotte."

"Lydia, there is nothing more left to my innocence...not anymore. Please do not treat me like a younger sister. I deserve the truth."

"Aww, the truth! It is all so convoluted now. So damaged. But if you must know, promise me your love afterwards?"

Charlotte knitted her brow. "What is it? What could change the way I feel about you, after all we have been through? We have no secrets anymore. What could you hide from me now?"

"My love. My true heart's desire. My sadness that would never leave me...until you came back to me." She grabbed Charlotte's hands and put them in hers. "Nathanial was charming, handsome, and he loved me. It was a girl's dream. But I saw it, Charlotte. I am not a fool. The look on your face the moment he touched you. The look on *his* face when he was pulled away from you. It was kismet. Was it not the way Mr. Darcy looked at Elizabeth? A hold of one's soul with one look; one touch? You did not see it, but I did. Nathanial glanced your way, many times that first evening of the party. Too many times to not notice. I thought it was the dress. I prided myself on the choice of the color for you, for you looked lovelier than anyone in the room." She squeezed Charlotte's hand. "But it happened again...and throughout the day of our wedding. He stole a glance at you here and there. I caught him. He looked at me with such embarrassment. It was not purposeful. I do not believe he was aware of what it was he was looking at. But he was drawn to *it*, like bees to a lovely flower. And I recognized it on his face. It was a spark of the heart. I was never the recipient of such longing from him. Oh, do not doubt his attraction to me. He was generous with his love, convoluting his physical attraction for love. And it was enough. I did not know better, or yearn for more...until Pietro..."

Charlotte gasped.

Lydia smirked. "I shock you."

"Lydia?" Charlotte jerked away from her cousin. "Please do not tell me you were the one to deceive Nathanial?"

"Deceive? No. Nathanial was too kind to allow me that foolery. Oh, he pretended it was nothing more than a painter and his muse. He allowed for the walks in the afternoon. The laughter on the terrace. The privacy while Pietro painted. Maybe he always knew my heart was not his. I tried to pretend for his sake. *Oh, Charlotte!* Love is so difficult to deny. It aches so deep inside, halting your breath. I wandered aimlessly throughout the day in a state of euphoria unlike anything I had ever known."

"And Pietro? Did he love you in return?"

"*Yes......*" The word lifted in the air.

The two of them fell silent, each with their memory of an illicit love.

"And where did Nathanial fit into all this?" Charlotte asked.

"We learned to pretend. I played the happily married newlywed, and he played the doting husband. We looked happy. And we were, mostly."

"And Pietro?"

"We passed him, often, in the countryside, painting. I saw him occasionally, at a party, a dance, a meeting by chance. The feeling was always there, the unspoken rope tied between his heart and mine. *Unrequited.*"

Charlotte lifted her brow.

Lydia blushed. "I will not say I am innocent when it comes to infidelity. We allowed for more than we should have. But Pietro was a gentleman. He did not want me illicitly. He wanted me as his wife. He was leaving for Italy and asked me to leave Nathanial."

Charlotte swallowed hard. Her eyes were wildly large, begging for more.

"I could not give him the answer he wanted. I was obligated to Nathanial. It was what my father wanted, and my mother dreamed for me. Nathanial was the *perfect* husband for an Ashford girl..." Lydia looked at Charlotte. "Just for the wrong Ashford girl. But you were gone, and I had no one to confide in."

"You could have written...I would have been there for you."

"Really? Do you honestly believe you would have understood my wish to leave my husband for an Italian painter?" She laughed. "It all sounds so silly now. It is not, though, is it?"

Charlotte scrunched her nose. "No. You still love him! I can see it in your eyes."

"Oh, Charlotte...I do! I always will."

"Where is Pietro now? Why have you not spoken but a few words about him?"

"Well, that is where the story ends. Pietro left. I imagine Nathanial thought it was over...a girlish, romantic infatuation with an exotic painter. But my heart was not the same. I was not the same. I could not find my love for Nathanial. I tried. I granted him that." She shook her head. "It was not enough for me. So, I wrote Pietro a letter telling him I would come to him."

"But you never sent the letter..."

Lydia was taken aback. "How do you know?"

Charlotte's head dropped. "I found it...in London."

"Oh," she said, understanding why Charlotte would be in their flat in London and find the letter. "I found out *that* afternoon I was pregnant. Before I could send the letter. I tucked it in the drawer never to pull it out again."

Charlotte covered her mouth, afraid to ask. "Pietro...*Peter?*"

Charlotte smirked. "Nathanial has his doubts, as well. I see the way he looks at Peter, questioning his son's legitimacy. Father and son are too much alike to even challenge the notion. But no. I have only granted Nathanial the privilege of my bed. Once I discovered I was pregnant, I couldn't leave Nathanial. I was now tied to him forever. Pietro wrote to me several times. Begging me to come to him. I cried each time, burning his letters. Then one day they stopped. I never received another one. Soon after, Father and Mother had their accident, and I was consumed with grief. Peter was soon born, and we moved past it all. Nathanial and I even came to an understanding. I played my role as his wife, and he as husband and father."

Charlotte sighed. "Then why, Lydia? Why are we here now?"

"Not long after I received news of your return, a letter arrived."

"From Pietro?"

"No. God was not that kind. It was from his sister, Adriana. She wanted to inform me that Pietro had passed away. He had been sick for many months but wrote me letters while he still had the strength. Adriana burned them for fear it would destroy my marriage if anyone got hold of them. "He loved you," she said. From woman to woman, she wanted me to know. His heart left this world still devoted to me, and me only."

"Oh, Lydia," Charlotte uttered. "I am so sorry."

"I am not. I found love the way it was meant to be. My heart ached at the loss of him. That is the truth and I cannot pretend it to be otherwise. It is what drove the wedge between Nathanial and me. Something broke in me. I did not want to put on an act anymore. My intentions were never to hurt Nathanial. But I no longer loved him. Not the way he needed it from me. Not the way I knew you could love him. The way it was meant to be." She exhaled. "Once I had you back in my life, I found a part of my heart again. Then I saw it happen. The recognition of love between you two. And I believed you could heal Nathanial's heart... make him come alive as you did me. Who was I to deny the love of two souls meant for each other? Maybe it was my penance."

Charlotte turned away. Her penance was yet to come.

"I do not doubt I got what I deserved–Nathanial's contempt, a failed marriage. But you, Charlotte, what is to become of you now? I want to protect you, keep you safe. And Nathanial and I can. I do not want you to worry. No shame shall come upon you. We will do whatever it takes. This child, Nathanial's child, will have the protection and love it deserves. We can be one happy family, as I always said we could be.

Charlotte shook her head. "No Lydia. I am afraid your wishes for us are merely whispers in the wind. It shan't be. I have decided to go home–return to America."

"This is your home, Charlotte." Lydia reached for Charlotte's arms and gripped them. "You always have a place here."

Charlotte knew, as did Lydia, the futility of their situation. Nathanial's commitment to their marriage would stand the test of time, even with the news of a child. Lydia gave Nathanial the one thing she valued more than her own life: Charlotte's love. For that, Nathanial would always be beholden to her. Charlotte understood the terms for which she gave herself. Was she foolish? *Yes!* Did she regret it? She loved and was loved in return by Nathanial. And now she was carrying his child. There was no room for regret. But there was no room for two women, two children, and one marriage.

She deserved more.

"If you love me, Lydia, you will let me go. I love you too much to place this burden on your family. You have much to be grateful for. I cannot help you with your feelings towards Nathanial. He is a good man. A dear man. His heart is bigger than you give him credit for. Let him love you. Let it be enough in the ways that are possible. I did."

"Oh Charlotte, what have I done?"

"Nothing that cannot be mended."

"Do you honestly believe that?" Lydia questioned.

"I must. For David's sake. Because of me, he and Nathanial now have a fracture in their relationship that may keep them separated forever. I must carry that responsibility. And it is only faith that allows me to trust they will mend."

"Do not fret. Those two are stubborn and competitive, but they are also very bonded, like you and me. It may take time, but their relationship will heal."

"Our fathers never did...and they both died without each other. It was my father's biggest regret." Charlotte lamented.

Lydia pulled Charlotte in closer and wrapped her arms around her. "I am so sorry. So, so sorry. Can you ever forgive me?"

"Always," Charlotte said. "Always and forever."

"I am going to lose you, aren't I?" Lydia cried, knowing the answer.

Charlotte pulled away. "I cannot stay," she uttered. "If I were selfish, I would choose differently. But you and I both know that could never work. Not now."

"I never meant to hurt you, Charlotte. I see now how terribly wrong I was. You deserve more...more than we could have ever offered you. I am sorry David left. I tried to talk to him, but it was more than he could bear. I do not blame him. The web we have woven is very sticky. You are right to go, I see that now. As painful as it is to me, you need to leave and quickly, so that you can get settled and prepared for the baby. I know I am losing you in body, but we have never been, nor ever will be, truly separated. We are united in love wherever you call home."

"Is there hope for you and Nathanial to find happiness?" Charlotte asked.

"Is it not you who said *if there is love, there is always hope?*" She touched Charlotte's cheek. "Nathanial and I have your love between us. We will honor that love."

GOODBYE, MY LOVE, GOODBYE

*N*athanial stood by the window, silent, with his hands folded across his chest and his stance stoic. On subsequent visits, he had resisted getting too near Charlotte for fear of disturbing her healing. Ada made sure of that. Whenever he tried to touch Charlotte, Ada shushed him away. He could only stare at her bruised and battered body from afar.

Charlotte was sitting in a chair, her wound uncovered, healing, but it was still jagged across her forehead. She claimed she looked worse than she felt. Ada had tried to make her not look less damaged by washing her hair, letting the dark tendrils fall naturally along her shoulders, and putting her in a light, summer dress. It helped. Color had returned to her cheeks, and her eyes held their brightness once again.

"Nathanial," she called to him. "Come here and sit by me."

He turned, but his eyes went to Ada, who was changing Charlotte's sheets. With a nod of permission, he did as he was asked and joined Charlotte, dragging a chair across the room to be by her side.

"Ada, would you mind leaving us alone?" Charlotte asked.

Ada nodded, and swooping the linens in her arms, she retreated, closing the door behind her.

Nathanial took Charlotte's hands in his.

His hand was warm as it enveloped hers. It had been too long since he touched her. She wanted more of him but knew that was impossible. Her body was still too fragile. Besides the wanting was futile because before her body completely healed, she would be gone.

"I have missed you," he said.

"And I you," she replied, reaching out for him. She touched his face, and he closed his eyes. It was prickly, but she didn't mind. "I need to talk to you, and I need for you to listen. Truly listen."

He furrowed his brow but nodded with his agreement.

"I…" her voice cracked. "I am leaving."

He shook his head, but she stopped him, holding his face between her hands.

"I need you to listen, not to make it harder."

He leaned to her and kissed her gently, lingering his lips on hers. He slowly pulled away and looked at her.

She was crying.

"It is best, for you, for Lydia...for the baby," she continued. "And for me."

"I do not want to lose you, Charlotte. I cannot," he pleaded. "I would lose the other half of my soul."

She smiled. "We have choices, Nathanial. We have not been very good at making the right ones in the past. We can this time," she said.

He was silent. She knew he understood.

"Why should you run away from me? Do you not believe I will take care of you?"

"I believe you would...and that is why I must leave. It would be at the sacrifice of your family. Where would that leave Peter? What purpose would it serve for your career? How many more lies would we have to tell? Is not the damage we have left behind enough? Was not David enough collateral?"

"Damn my brother!"

Charlotte put her hand on Nathanial's arm. "You do not really feel that way. I know better. And my one request of you is to heal that relationship."

His eyes darted away from her.

She demanded them back, grabbing his chin and forcing him to answer her. "Give me your word."

He closed his eyes and sighed. "You truly care about him?"

She nodded. "Yes, Nathanial. More than I should have. Maybe in another life, things would have been different. He is so much of you, what I love. Your goodness. Your heart. It was God's cruel joke on us all..."

"It is not all for naught, Charlotte. We are to have a child. A symbol of our love. I cannot regret one moment of us, of the love we shared."

"Then you will let me go?"

He hesitantly nodded. "Will my child ever know me?"

"*Our* child will know this family, and the bonds which keep us as one. I will never deny you of that. But to ask anything more of me, it cannot be. Let me go, Nathanial, heart and soul. I need that from you, or I fear I may not have the strength to do it myself."

He fell to his knees before her and pulled her hands to his lips before burying his head in her lap, his face wet with tears. Her own covered in the same sorrowful tears.

"Nathanial," she begged. "Let me go…"

He wiped his face and stood, letting her hands fall from his. He cleared his throat. "I will make plans. You will have no worries about your care. I have business affairs to tend to in the city tomorrow and all will be settled."

Charlotte smiled with the little energy she had left.

"You are tired," he said, seeing her face pale. "You will get better? Promise me. For I cannot bear to think this world can be happy without you in it…even if it must be away from me."

"You must not worry. The doctor assured me I was on the mend, our baby strong. Go now, and do what you must."

"What I must? If I were a selfish man, I would never let you go." With one last look upon Charlotte's face, he left, knowing the future outside the door would no longer include her.

PROPOSALS

 *I*t was at Charlotte's insistence that Lydia returned to her duties as mistress of the house and not continually hover over her. The doctor had declared Charlotte no longer in danger, as well as the child, and she could resume her life.

Charlotte scoffed at the notion of resuming her life. There was no going back to anything she once knew. Nor did she know what was on the horizon.

"You are looking much more yourself, Miss," Ada said. "Are you ready to leave your room?"

Charlotte looked at herself in the mirror. She slid her fingers over the slash still visible across her head. The bruising had faded to a soft yellow against her paled skin, but the wound was still raw and raised. "I think it best if I hide a little longer…"

"Very well," Ada said, but before she closed the

door, she poked her head back into the room. "Mr. Knightly is coming down the hall," she warned.

Charlotte quickly pinned the loose hairs around her face and pinched at her cheeks.

"If you are fussing over my concern, stop," Andrew's voice rang across the room as he passed Ada holding the door open. He came closer, bending over to see the reflection she was working so hard to repair. "You are quite pale, I must admit. And that cut across your head is terribly distracting."

Charlotte touched the healing wound. "I am sorry, there is not much more I can do to cover it."

"Does it hurt much?" He reached towards it but pulled away.

She shook her head.

"You will always be the vision of an angel in my eyes," he whispered in her ear.

Charlotte threw her arms around him, tears falling down her cheeks. "Oh Andrew, I have missed you so very much."

"Now, now," he pulled out a monogrammed linen from his pocket and wiped away the wetness on her cheeks. "Enough of that. I cannot forgive myself for causing such misery to your heart."

Charlotte swiped more tears away. "You do not have to pretend with me, Andrew."

"Very well," he agreed. "No more hiding from each other."

"I was not the one who was hiding," Charlotte reminded him.

He nodded. "Fair enough. But you understand? My life cannot be open. I must hide from everyone..."

"Not from me, Andrew. Never from me," Charlotte insisted.

"Does this mean you are no longer angry with me?"

"I was not angry with you. I was taken by surprise. *That is all.* Although, nothing should surprise me anymore. Not now."

It seemed like a lifetime ago when she had intruded upon Andrew and Mr. Tatum. Admittedly, she was unprepared to face what she had seen, and she did not react very well. For that, she was sorry. It was not an unfamiliar notion that there were men who preferred men, but it was not a part of her world. *Neither was becoming a mistress.* Andrew never concealed he had an alternate life, nor did he admit to it, either. It hurt that he kept his deepest and darkest secret from her. There were so many of her own secrets in his care. His abandonment of their friend-ship was harder to endure. It made her feel she was insignificant to him when she had believed she was more. He was more to *her.*

"I did not hide myself from you. I was shielding you from it," Andrew said. "Most of all, I was afraid of your disapproval."

"Of all the people in all the world, know that I will never be the one to abandon you. You have been my friend, my confidant, my shoulder of strength. I do not throw people away, Andrew. And never will it be you. It is you whom I love, not who you choose to bed."

More tears wetted her cheeks. "Let us not be deceptive to each other ever again."

Andrew took her hand and brought it to his lips. "You are truly a remarkable woman."

"There is more," she said in earnest. "I am..." she started but couldn't get the words out. She tried again. "I am going to have a baby."

For the first time she could recall, Andrew was silent.

Charlotte looked at him through wetted lashes. "Have I surprised you?"

He nodded.

"It is terribly frightening," Charlotte admitted.

"Is that what David was all about?" Andrew asked.

"Please do not taint everything," she pleaded. "I suspected, but I had no confirmation until the accident. Nor did it have anything to do with how I felt about David. He brought me laughter, companionship, comfort. They are not frivolous qualities. I was growing rather fond of him. You could say I was falling in love with him. Not like Nathanial, but love is not all the same, is it? I had hoped he felt the same about me."

"Then he found out about the baby?"

Charlotte nodded. "Unfortunately, the news was too scandalous. I do not blame him for leaving. Maybe I was wrong to imagine a conventional life was possible for me..."

"Charlotte, it is your happiness I have always wanted. If David could grant you a life imagined, then so be it. You had the best of intentions, I can see. Women have done worse. Although Lydia is not removed from her own culpability of destroying your dreams."

"Andrew," Charlotte scolded. "I will not allow you to speak about her that way."

"What is it with you, and your protection of her? I do not understand after all this time. Have you not seen yourself? You are truly a battered woman. Not just by the accident, but this whole situation has taken a great toll on you. I hardly recognize the woman I met not so long ago. It is nearly destroying me to watch you fall deeper into the pits of hell of which I am very familiar. I do not want you there."

Charlotte grew silent. Her body was not strong enough to battle Andrew's wit.

"Marry me!" he yelled out.

Charlotte's mouth fell open.

"Do not stare at me," he ordered. "I mean what I say. Marry me and let me take care of you. Do you not see? It is the perfect plan. I can offer you my name, my position, and a home for you and your child. My mother would not be more pleased. I can give you everything a woman could want."

"But Andrew..." she lingered, careful with her words. "It is not a woman you want."

He laughed. "Is not marriage about loving and caring for someone? Have you not spoken those words often to me?" Andrew walked over to Charlotte and pulled her to him. "Dearest Charlotte, you have shown me much about the human spirit and the kindness of the heart. But more importantly, you have taught me to love someone beyond myself. I care about you more than anyone I have ever known. I cherish you and want to take care of you all the days of my life. I do love you, for what it is worth."

Charlotte knew his words to be true. He loved her and she him, but not in the way a man and a woman should. His spirit could never be happy trapped in marriage.

"Despite what others say, you are truly the most unselfish man I know. To sacrifice yourself, *in that way*, would destroy you. I will not be the one to ask that of you."

"Charlotte, say yes! It would be almost ideal. You could continue your life with Nathanial, and I...well, we would have each other to keep company. We would grow old, fat, and ugly together. There is nothing I would not grant you." He added, "I know how to make you happy, Charlotte. You would be safe with me."

Charlotte didn't answer right away. She paced the room, looked out the window, sat on the sofa, and rose again.

Andrew watched her, his eyes following her everywhere, waiting.

She finally stopped and met his watching gaze. "No, Andrew." She shook her head. "The answer has to be *no*. I love you too much. It is not your job to fix my life, at the expense of your own. I learned that lesson."

"Then, what will you do?"

"I am returning to America. It was home to me once. The places and people are familiar; I will not feel so alone. I can make a new life for myself there. My father did. I am under no illusion it will be easy, but Nathanial is working on a plan for my care. I will not be forsaken."

"Really, Charlotte?" He questioned. "How can Nathanial let you go so easily?"

"He is a man who loves me enough to let me go, as I requested. As you must do. Do you not see? If I stay, I destroy all I have sacrificed, all I was trying to protect. There is no honor in that. And it is I who would only suffer more. They are my family whom I will never betray, nor destroy."

"And Lydia? What becomes of the woman whose selfish desires changed the course of your life?"

Charlotte's chest tightened. Her life had changed, but not in the way Andrew saw it.

"I made my choices. The consequences are mine, Andrew, not Lydia's. She did not use me as you propose. She asked me to help her, and in return, she helped me. I will admit, I may not have been prepared for what I entered into. But do you not see what all this has prepared me for? I was afraid and hopeless. I took from life whatever it gave me. No more. I have learned what it is to love and be loved. I know what it is I want and understand what I deserve. My child will know his worth because I am stronger and wiser for it. The power of love is most strong when it is most demanded upon. The depth of a person's character is based on those challenges. I do not regret one moment of my life here. Not one."

"Love conquers all," Andrew smirked. "Well played, my dear Charlotte. You win in the end."

"Life is not a battle all the time, with winners and losers, Andrew. Maybe I succumbed to that notion in my weakest moments. But I always have hope. No, I believe life is a balance of giving and taking, growing better, kinder, wiser for it. Life is too short; love is too powerful to waste it on bitterness and regret. Love is infinite, is it not? Experienced in many ways? You, of all people, should understand it is limiting to put conditions on the capacity to love."

"It is good you leave this place. You do not belong here, among people with small minds and trapped lives. Your spirit is too...*big*. Too beautiful to be caged. You belong in the wild to roam and explore. You will find your place, Charlotte. And you will be happy. I honor you and your journey ahead. I will miss you, but you will never be far from my heart." He placed a kiss on Charlotte's lips.

Charlotte touched her mouth, the gentle kiss causing a warm sensation across her lips.

He stepped back and smiled at her, before walking out the door.

She knew it would not be the last she heard from Andrew Knightly, but she cried all the same.

SURPRISES

*T*he hustle and bustle were familiar. Porters carrying luggage, crowds pushing against each other, loved ones hugging with their goodbyes. The train station out of London was hectic, as usual.

Hollister parked Charlotte at a bench, but she chose not to sit, eager to see Nathanial. He had sent a note to meet him at two o'clock sharp. She had not seen him since that evening in her room. He left with business to attend for her trip, and they were not granted one more night to share in their love together.

She knew it was best. The detachment of her heart from his was necessary to move on.

A whistle blew.

Charlotte looked at the clock across the tracks, lifted high above the bustling crowds, for everyone to see. Nathanial was late. She looked around, through the sea of people, in their fancy dresses and refined suits, hoping he was among them.

"Miss Ashford!" A man's voice called.

Charlotte stretched her neck, searching over the multiple of black hats in front of her.

A man pointed to her. To her surprise, it was Mr. Quigley.

"There she is…" he said. He tapped the man's shoulder next to him and he turned.

Charlotte's heart burst with joy when it was Nathanial who faced her. Her hand went to her chest, hoping to slow the quickening beats of her heart as he moved closer to her.

Mr. Quigley tipped his hat to her. "Miss Ashford."

Charlotte nodded in reply.

"Charlotte…" Nathanial greeted. He extended his hand.

She reached for it, settling her gloved hand in his.

He gently squeezed it before sliding his hand away.

"And what do I owe the pleasure of seeing you today, Mr. Quigley?" Charlotte asked, trying to ignore Nathanial's eyes on her. "Are you traveling as well?"

"No, no. I have come here with Mr. Hammond on business concerning you."

"Me?" Charlotte questioned.

"Back when Mr. Hammond came to me concerning your unfortunate situation about your father's affairs, I was more than pleased to help where I could. I was very close to your uncle's family and familiar with his own business affairs. I recalled frequently your uncle discussing the very situation concerning your father," he explained. "It took some looking into, but I knew there were documents that would uncover the truth."

Charlotte stepped closer to him. "And did you find anything?"

Nathanial and Mr. Quigley looked at each other and smiled.

Mr. Quigley pulled an envelope from his coat pocket and handed it to her.

Charlotte stared at the documents in her hands.

"Open it," Mr. Quigley ordered.

She sat down on the bench and read through the papers, slowly dragging her finger along the words as she read them. When she was done, she looked at the two men awaiting her reaction, unsure of what the documents meant to her. "My father's business is mine?"

"Yes," Mr. Quigley nodded.

"Nathanial is this true?" she questioned.

His mouth curled upward, and he nodded.

"I never imagined this could be possible." She reread the top page once again. "It says here my Uncle Edmond signed over his ownership to me. How is that possible?"

"Your father wanted more than anything to please his older brother and make him proud. When his business finally succeeded, it was with pride he placed a deed of ownership in your uncle's care, so your uncle explained. Your father wanted to prove what he valued most was not money or power, but family." Mr. Quigley continued to explain, "I found that document among your uncle's files, signed and notarized. And the courts have honored them. You are the rightful owner of Ashford Industries."

"I do not understand. If my father left his business to his brother, how is it my inheritance?" Charlotte questioned Mr. Quigley.

"Upon receipt of the inheritance from your father, your Uncle Edmond, in a reciprocal good will gesture, left documents for the ownership to return to you."

Charlotte closed her eyes and lingered on her thoughts. "My father loved his brother very much. It was his life-long sadness that they parted with few words exchanged between them. They were both stubborn. After Lydia's wedding, a strong handshake was all that transpired between them before we left. They would never see each other again," she explained. "I assumed they died never knowing how much they really meant to each other. I guess they knew."

"Family first..." Mr. Quigley said.

Charlotte rose from the bench and put her arms around Mr. Quigley's stocky body. "Thank you," she whispered in his ear, tightening her embrace around him. "Thank you, thank you, thank you."

Charlotte released him and he stepped back with a rush of color to his cheeks.

"Well, I was merely the researcher. It is *this* man who wrote a brilliant case," He referred to Nathanial, who stood quietly beside him. "Your lawyer in Boston,

Mr. Commons, is the one to whom you really should extend your gratitude. He has not stopped working on this case since you left. I dare say, that man really looked out for you. But overall, we are all pretty proud of our work," Mr. Quigley admitted. "Instructions are all written. You should contact Mr. Commons upon your return to Boston. He is working on arrangements and will have it all in order when you arrive."

"Nathanial," she turned to him, "I do not know what to say. Why did you not confide in me what you were working on? It is incredible, really."

"I did not want to encourage you. You had enough disappointment concerning your father's affairs."

She placed her hand on his arm. "This is all too much. I can never repay you for what you have given back to me. Not only my father's legacy, but faith in our family, our bonds, and our commitments to one another."

His hand covered hers. "You deserve to have the life that your father had always wanted, not only for you, but as a legacy for future generations." He glanced at her belly.

A whistle blew, and the three noticed the crowds gathering around them.

"It looks as if your train is getting ready to go," Mr. Quigley noted. "I wish you a safe journey."

Charlotte shook Mr. Quigley's hand, thanking him one more time, before he headed off.

Hollister suddenly appeared from behind Charlotte. "Miss..." he said, indicating it was time for her to leave.

Nathanial gave Hollister a nod.

"Sir," Hollister bowed and proceeded ahead of them.

He took Charlotte's arm and intertwined it with his, damning the onlookers. "You look well," he said, ignoring her concern.

"I am...we are," Charlotte said. "The doctor says I am very strong."

"I am grateful for Dr. Baron's care of you and the child," he replied, grasping her hand a little tighter underneath his arm. "But it does not take away my concern about you and your future care. I have prepared as best I can to make sure your life is comfortable. And now with your father's legacy intact..."

She smiled at him, but tears threatened at the corner of her eyes. "We are going to be well cared for," she assured. "Lydia has secured my trustworthy housekeeper, Mrs. Stratford, who was like a mother to me. She will let nothing happen to me, and will take good care of our child. I promise."

He touched her face, wiping away the first tears to fall. Drawing his hand away, his voice grew more controlled; serious. "I hope you are pleased with the outcome. I would have informed you of the circumstances sooner, but we were awaiting a decision. They came through in the last few days. There will be more to follow, but for now, you should know that your life is safe, and you will be settled," he confirmed. "I wanted to make sure that you were no longer beholden to anyone. Not to Lydia, to me…not to anyone."

Charlotte knew why she had fallen in love with him. It was his eyes. They expressed all he was feeling, even when he had no words. They were now deep and sad.

She was leaving, taking with her a piece of him, but she was leaving nothing in return. For that, she was sorry. They had waded the waters of love and became entangled in the undercurrent. They resurfaced as tattered souls. She knew time would heal them, and eventually they would be stronger from the experience.

Nathanial and she were forever bonded, but she was being ripped away from him, and she was the reason. The agony of his loss was evident in his eyes.

"Nathanial, the choice to leave was difficult," Charlotte tried to explain. "We are forever linked, and this child is a symbol of the bond between us. Our love is not broken or lost. You must know that. You are my other half. And the only choice we have to honor that sacred connection between our souls is to separate our lives. It is best for all concerned."

His eyes grew darker.

With little regard to the onlookers, she brought her cheek to his. "I love you," she whispered. "I will always love you," she added, before pulling away.

People pushed and shoved them, hurrying to board the train.

Hollister waved to Nathanial, indicating the carriage ahead.

Charlotte glanced at the clock. "I have to go," she said, stepping away from him.

"Charlotte," he grabbed for her hand pulling her back to him. "Please let me speak my heart. I am sorry for the shame I caused you, but I am not sorry that I loved you. It pains me to see you leave, and I may never know the child we have created. Maybe that is my penance for the wrongs I've done. I do not want you to leave here without you knowing. I will miss you for the rest of my life. I am granting you your wish to start anew, even against my own judgment. But you are a woman of extraordinary ability–a woman with the extraordinary ability to love. I have no doubt about your future. My only regret is I am not a part of it. At least, not in the way my heart wants it to be."

The train conductor called the time, disrupting Nathanial.

Downhearted, Nathanial nodded to Hollister standing by the door of her carriage.

"Goodbye Charlotte. I leave you in good hands." Leaning his head to hers one last time, he allowed his lips the pleasure of a kiss to her cheek before walking away.

Hollister tugged at Charlotte's arm, shuffling her away.

She glanced back at Nathanial one last time, but he had already disappeared into the crowd.

She placed a hand on Hollister's arm, momentarily stopping him. "Take care of him for me," she pleaded.

"Always," he said, rushing her to the carriage door and opening it.

Charlotte hugged Hollister and stepped inside the train. To her surprise, a gentleman sat inside her carriage, reading a paper. He rose, placing the paper down, and took off his hat.

"David?" she startled.

The door shut behind her and Hollister stepped back from the train.

She poked her head out the window and called after him, "Hollister, are you not coming with me?"

"No, Miss. Mr. Hammond will escort you the rest of the way."

"If you will allow me the honor," David interjected.

Her heart pounded.

David was the last person she had expected to see again. But there he was, his strong shoulders standing tall, his feet planted firmly, as the train rolled out of the station. Her stance wobbled, and she grabbed onto him.

"Does this remind you of the past?" David asked.

Charlotte raised a brow and shook her head.

David held onto Charlotte with one hand, and reached over to the window, closing the curtain with the other, darkening the vestibule. "I was in enclosed quarters with you once before, but from your recollection of the moment, I did not leave the most memorable impression. Maybe this time I can do better."

He pulled her close to him and placed his lips on hers. This time, he did not brush up against them, but pressed firmly, parting them open, only to press down on them again. He wanted to leave no misunderstanding. He was no longer the boy in the armoire, but a man who knew what he wanted.

When David pulled away from her, Charlotte opened her eyes slowly, lingering in the warmth of his lips, enjoying his arms around her. She wanted more... more of the sensation quickening her pulse. But it didn't come.

Her eyes narrowed when they met David's questioning look.

"Are you going to slap me?"

Charlotte slowly shook her head. "I should..." she lingered. "But I do not want to."

"Good!" A smile beamed across his face.

He encouraged her to sit, and he followed, sitting across from her, the smile only slightly receding.

Charlotte took off her gloves and hat and swooped any loose hairs to the back of her neatly pinned bun. A satin ribbon of pink, to match her dress, encircled it.

David watched her primp, noting the similarities to when they met the first time...and the second time.

When Charlotte realized the same, it caused them both to laugh.

"I am very fond of pink," Charlotte defended.

"As am I." He laughed again. "Is it serendipitous?"

"David," Charlotte's voice grew serious. "Let us be honest. Yes?" David's laughter faded. "It is wonderful to see you. There is so much I want to say to you. Sorry does not do it justice…"

He reached for her hand. "I am the one who should be apologizing. I left in anger. Disappointment," he sighed. "After Lydia came to me…"

"Lydia spoke to you?"

He nodded. "I will not lie to you. I do not pretend to understand the situation. When I left, my heart was broken in so many ways. I wanted to run to someone to confide in, to clear my head, and ease the aching in my heart. And there was no one to run to. Because the person I wanted to run to was the one I was running away from."

"Oh David…"

"And then I thought about you. Who did you have to run to, especially now?"

Charlotte pulled her hand from his. "I am in no need of a hero, David. Nor am I to become a possession of anyone ever again. I have gained a will that even I did not know existed. I do not want to live in the shadows, or behind closed doors."

"That is not why I am here," he demanded.

"Then why?"

"May I?" David indicated to the space next to Charlotte.

She nodded, and he moved next to her.

He took both her hands in his, turned them over, and stroked her palms with his thumbs. When she didn't pull away, he closed his eyes, and let his touch linger, searching for the words he had practiced more times than he could count with the prospects of seeing Charlotte again.

Charlotte didn't interrupt his reverie. She liked his touch, the warmth that seemed to flow from his hands to hers.

With his eyes closed, his head tilted, she studied his face. Closer, she could see the darkness under his eyes. He had not slept. The lines around his mouth were heavy. His hair was brushed away from his face, except for a few curls dangling over his forehead. She fingered the curls before she brushed them back, running her hand through his hair.

He sighed.

Before she could pull her hand away, he reached for it and brought it to his lips.

His eyes opened to meet hers. "I have never known feelings so fulfilling than when I am with you. You take my breath away and make my heart sing. I have traveled for so long, never finding a reason to stop, or a place I have wanted to stay. But with you, I found what I was looking for. I have found *home*. I could not walk away from that. It is love I feel, Charlotte. A kind of love I do not want to destroy because of bitterness, anger, or judgement. For if it means I cannot have you, what is the purpose of it all? I want nothing more than to prove to you I am worthy of your love in return. I want nothing you are unable to give. But permit me to love you, completely, and honorably. And if you grow to love me the way I believe you can, say you will be my wife, and allow me to be a part of your life forever."

Charlotte couldn't speak. Tears rolled down her cheeks.

"No, no, no..." David pleaded as he reached for his handkerchief and wiped away her tears. "I do not want you to cry. Not like this."

Charlotte had to pull her hand from his and attempted to wipe away the deluge of tears. "These are not tears of sadness," she assured. "They are proof of how you have moved my heart."

"What are you saying, Charlotte?"

Charlotte smiled. "I am saying, David, *this time* you have made quite an impression on me..."

The End

ACKNOWLEDGMENTS

Nathanial Hawthorne & D. H. Lawrence: For inspiring me through wonderful stories.

Lee Ann Schertz: Your dedication to my writing is astounding, no matter how many renditions I send to you. I cannot express how much your thoughts and support keep me going, but most importantly, your continual friendship means the world to me.

Therese Conte: I would be lost without your guidance on anything and everything art, *and life*. My creative endeavors have flourished under your high standards, pushing me to embrace my own artistic talents. You unwavering support humbles me, and I deeply cherish all that you do for me.

Author Billie Kelpin: Your reservoir of experience and knowledge has been instrumental in shaping me into a more adept writer. Through your guidance, my hidden writing talents emerged, transforming this book to meets its potential. Your unwavering encouragement and unshakable belief in my abilities have propelled me forward on this journey. I extend my heartfelt gratitude.

Author Janet Simcic: You personified the essence of "keep writing." Thank you for sharing Italy with me. With you, it was all I imagined it to be, and helped to ignite the spark I needed to complete this book.

Beta Readers: Thank you for all the catches and insights. I know my book is better because of your help.

Louis and Elizabeth Conte: The writer I have become is a reflection of the knowledge and wisdom you gave to me. In life and in death, your lessons, guidance, and love continue as an enduring legacy.

ABOUT THE AUTHOR

Elizabeth Conte is a novelist and a sketcher of poetry, "Creating Beauty for the mind." A native to California, she enjoys the year-round gardening weather growing roses, photographing flowers, walking her dog, Winston, or mixing up a cocktail. *She prefers whiskey!*

Visit ElizabethConte.com

Made in the USA
Columbia, SC
21 November 2023

26475696R00307